THE ANCHORMAN'S WIFE

THE ANCHORMAN'S WIFE

JOSEPH SOUZA

First published by Level Best Books 2023

Author Photo Credit: Doug Bruns

First edition

ISBN: 978-1-68512-451-9

Cover art by Level Best Designs

This book was professionally typeset on Reedsy.
Find out more at reedsy.com

To my dad.

I

Part One

SHAY

Four Months Earlier

A steady stream of people make their way inside the soup kitchen before queuing up in line. She plunges the ladle into the mashed potatoes and then the corn, serving the neediest of the needy. The food is not gourmet, but it's hot and hearty, and there's plenty of it.

A slender man wearing a wool cap approaches her station. On closer examination, she believes the person could be a woman, but she can't really tell because the person is dirty and swaddled in layers of tattered clothes. Still, she looks vaguely familiar to her. But after a while, all these homeless start to develop that same expression of hopelessness.

"This make you feel good about yourself?" Wool Cap snarls in a low, raspy voice.

"I just want to help in any way I can."

"Glad to know you're better than everyone else."

"Enjoy your meal," she says with a smile, trying not to sound too cheerful lest it come off as sarcasm.

"No, enjoy your privileged life," Wool Cap mutters before shuffling away. "While you still have one."

The words unnerve her, but she turns to the next person in line and suddenly forgets about the encounter. Occasionally, these things happen. Once dinner is finished, she goes back to the kitchen and helps with the cleanup.

She loves the camaraderie and good-natured humor that occurs among these wizened veterans of the soup kitchen. Although she hasn't gone to church in ages, she knows that this is exactly what God would want her to do.

Once everyone is served and the kitchen is clean, she makes her way out the back door. The night is cool, and she loves the city when it feels this way. A breeze blows in from the water and brings with it the briny smell of ocean.

She can't wait to get home and kiss her daughter goodnight. Nothing makes her happier than when she's with Quinn. It's why she gave up her promising career as a newscaster.

The block is teeming with loud and aggressive homeless people, much more so than usual, and the street resembles a low-grade Mardi Gras. She recognizes many of them from the soup kitchen, but they don't acknowledge her. Her husband has repeatedly warned her to never walk alone in this neighborhood after dark, but she feels safe among them.

A heavyset girl staggers past with a skinny kid by her side. She's screaming at the top of her lungs and holding a cell phone to her ear. Is she threatening the person on the other end of the line? Or is she directing her comments to the kid walking beside her? Both appear to be high, drunk, or a combination of the two. The girl's holding a lit cigarette in her free hand. Standing against the wall of the soup kitchen is a tall, unkempt man gesturing frantically with his hands and talking to himself in a rambling manner.

She makes her way to her car, which is located a few streets over because of the scarcity of parking in this neighborhood. The air feels different tonight; the molecules charged and overheated. This feeling is not something she can put her finger on. Sometimes, a certain scent or turn of phrase will remind her of the chaotic childhood she's been trying to forget.

Rounding the corner, she sees her Lexus and thrusts her key out like a swordsman challenging someone to a duel, and then clicks the button with her thumb. The lights flash. The alarm blips. She's three feet from the door when she hears something.

She turns and feels a sharp pain in her head. The blow doesn't hurt at first, but she feels herself falling to the pavement. It takes a few seconds before the full depth of the pain starts to sink in. It radiates outward from the base of her skull like waves surging toward land. The sound of piercing laughter fills her ears as she struggles to get up. It's like no other laughter she's ever heard before, yet eerily familiar at the same time. She gazes up and sees someone leaning over her. For a brief second, it's almost as if she's staring at her own blurry reflection. Before she can say anything, she feels a second blow against her cheekbone. The last thing she sees before being turned on her stomach is the moon, or two identical moons, swirling in her vision. She thinks briefly of her daughter, wondering if she'll ever see her again.

"You think you're so much better than everyone else," a voice whispers in her ear. "But you're not."

"Why are you doing this," she cries, the pain almost unbearable.

"Payback."

"For what?"

"I think you know what."

"Who are you? What do you want?"

"Don't worry about me, you uppity bitch. I'm only your worst nightmare. Make sure and keep an eye on that blind daughter of yours."

"You'd better stay away from her," she says before a blow renders her unconscious. Thankfully, she doesn't feel what comes next.

SHAY

Shay walked over to the kitchen window and stared out at the tenth hole of Woodbridge Country Club. The Realtor who had shown them this home claimed that it had the best views of the course, and that was saying something, considering that in its entirety, there were twenty-seven majestic holes surrounding Woodbridge Estates. Shay guessed the Realtor gave that same spiel to every prospective home buyer. More houses were being built along the course every month. Her house had views of a deep rolling sand trap hugging three sides of a sloped green. Tall fescue grew along the second cut. Behind the sand trap stood tall pine trees framing the course's signature hole. There was not a pasture in Ireland that could compete with the verdant lushness of Woodbridge's tenth fairway.

But the truth was, Shay hated this house. Every day she lived in, it reminded her, with increasing frequency, of the night she'd been attacked. She and Gideon had not been in it a month when it happened. She'd spent two weeks in the hospital before she was sent home to recover. And because of that, she now associated this house with that fateful night near the soup kitchen and all the terrible nights that followed.

Moving to this golf course had been Gideon's idea. He'd not necessarily convinced her that it was the right move as much as he wore her down with his subtle hints and low-pressure sales campaign. Located twenty miles outside of Boston, it sometimes took an hour for Gideon to arrive home when the traffic was bad. She'd loved living in the city and had lived there since her Harvard days and then when she worked as a newscaster. She never wanted to leave, having all the amenities at her disposal. There was never a need for a car, although Gideon had rented two expensive parking spaces for them to use. Come weekends, she and Quinn would walk to all the museums, parks, and libraries. It was a far cry from the small, grubby town she grew up in.

Their friends would be over soon, bringing desserts and wine. Before the attack, she would have been happy to host such a dinner party. But since then, she'd not been thinking clearly and didn't have the energy to entertain. Her doctor warned her that it might take months before she felt like her old self again.

She was worried more about her daughter than anything else, almost afraid to let Quinn out of her sight. Whoever attacked Shay that night had warned her to keep an eye on her blind daughter. Who could possibly want to hurt Quinn? One of the girl's teachers? Someone who might be jealous of their elevated status in life? A scorned mistress? But that affair Gideon had engaged in had occurred so long ago. And how was it that Shay could remember her attacker's words and not much else?

She had so much to do before her guests arrived. If only she could scrape the barnacles off her brain. Thankfully, the Stevenses' high-school-age daughter, Miranda, had agreed to watch Quinn this evening. She trusted the Stevenses more than anyone else in Woodbridge Estates. Their house, like all the houses in this development, was set up with a sophisticated home security system that featured all kinds of bells and whistles. And they lived only five houses down the road, on the long par four that carried over the pond. Quinn had been so excited to watch *Frozen* that she'd been humming songs from it all day. Despite the short distance to the Stevenses' home, Shay felt anxious being separated from her daughter. She only regretted that she wouldn't be able to watch her forever.

She stumbled around the house, her head in a fog, straightening things out that didn't need straightening and sweeping the immaculately clean floor. Staying busy helped keep her mind off everything.

Did she have enough food for the guests? She peeked inside the fridge and saw it brimming with pink curled shrimp, expensive European cheeses, and folded cold cuts spread out on a tray. There was more than enough food.

A brief wave of panic swept over her. Since the attack, she'd been more scatterbrained than ever. Her mind had never failed her so miserably as it did after that vicious attack. As it did *now*.

The doorbell rang, momentarily plunging her into a state of panic. Had she sufficiently cleaned the house? Would she remember everyone's name? The doorbell rang a second time, snapping her out of her stupor. She glanced down at her hand. On her palm, she'd scribbled the words "Trust Yourself, Shay!". But trust what? Her instincts? What was there to trust when her mind was failing her so miserably?

At the third ring, fear took over. Was the person who attacked her returning to finish the job?

SHAY

After a few deep breaths, she managed to calm her nerves. She reminded herself that she was expecting guests for a dinner party tonight. She moved to the door and opened it. Standing there with a bottle of Chablis was Jessica Stevens, the mother of Miranda and the wife of Stan Stevens, who was the longtime weather forecaster at Channel Four. Shay gave Jessica a big hug and took the bottle of wine out of her hand. Carrying it over to the bar, she set it down amongst the various other bottles.

Jessica was old enough to be her big sister, but at times, Shay felt as if she were the older one in the friendship. Jessica looked beautiful today. Shay thought her shock of premature gray hair made her look far prettier than if she colored it.

"You didn't have to bring wine," Shay said.

"I couldn't very well come empty-handed," Jessica replied, waving her hand in the air.

"Thanks so much for having Quinn over this evening."

"Are you kidding? Miranda loves hanging out with her."

"I wouldn't have been able to have fun knowing she was up in her room while we were all downstairs enjoying ourselves."

Jessica grabbed a baby carrot off the veggie platter and bit off the end. "How've you been feeling lately?"

"I've had better days."

"The headaches coming back?"

"Off and on. It's still been hard to show my face around this neighborhood after what I did." She'd never discussed the "incident" with anyone and, in fact, hoped it would be the one thing she could forget.

"It's not your fault that a lowlife attacked you at that soup kitchen."

"They're not all lowlifes," Shay said, setting out some dinner rolls. "Most of these homeless are really good people who are just down on their luck."

"It makes me so mad," Jessica said, shaking her head. "If only the police caught the person who attacked you."

"Glass of wine?" Shay said, hoping to change the subject.

"I thought you'd never ask."

Shay walked over and poured her friend a glass and then returned with it.

"You're not having one?" Jessica said.

"The doctor said I'm not supposed to be drinking because of all the medications I'm on."

"Come on, Shay. One small glass won't kill you," Jessica said. "You don't even have to drive home."

"Maybe just a small one, then."

Shay got up and poured herself a finger of Chablis, promising to limit herself to one drink. She watched as Jessica walked to the rear of the spacious home and stared out at the tenth hole. A frightening thought suddenly occurred to her. Could Jessica have been the one who attacked her? She quickly erased the suspicion from her mind. Jessica would never do such a thing. She was one of her best friends and would do anything for her and her family.

Jessica pointed toward the green. "Is that where it happened?"

"Yes," she replied, although she didn't want to discuss the matter any further, especially with the guests so close to arriving.

"You must have really surprised those four golfers."

"If I did, I certainly don't remember doing so."

"When Stan moved us to this neighborhood, he had high hopes that I would take up golf. He thought playing would be good for me, maybe help me lose a few pounds," Jessica said as she continued to gaze out at the lush green.

"Nonsense. You look wonderful."

"Thanks, but Stan's right: I could afford to lose a little weight."

"Couldn't we all?" Shay patted her nonexistent belly.

Jessica laughed. "Have you looked at yourself in the mirror lately, Shay? I'd die for a figure like yours."

She ignored the compliment. "So, did you enjoy playing golf with Stan?"

"Hell no! I hated it."

Shay laughed because she knew the feeling all too well.

"Don't get me wrong. It's nice living here and socializing with other couples like you and Gideon, but the golf part of it never did much for me."

"Why not?"

"Playing with Stan seemed like a battle of wills. He kept telling me how I should 'address' the ball, as if I should be calling it Mr. Callaway." She laughed, but Shay could sense the frustration in her voice. "It felt like golf became one more way he could try to mansplain things to me."

"Stan doesn't strike me as the controlling type."

"Stan's a great guy and a wonderful father, but he sometimes lacks patience when explaining things."

"I think Gideon enjoys the social aspects of golf more than the actual sport itself."

"Please don't tell anyone this, Shay, but I find a lot of the club members here to be pretentious snobs." Jessica giggled. "I'm just lucky Stan doesn't hang around at the clubhouse for long after his round."

Shay wasn't sure how to take this, seeing as how Gideon socialized quite a bit at the club and had hoped that she might do the same.

"I think it's absolutely horrible what happened to you at that soup kitchen. That's such a scary part of town to be walking around in that late at night."

"I know, but it makes me so happy to help people. Don't you like volunteering?"

"Of course I do. I volunteer at my kids' school all the time."

"I just want to give back for all the blessings I've received in my life."

"Sure, but there's plenty of other ways you can make a difference in this world without getting yourself killed. And you have your daughter to think about," Jessica said, pointing her wineglass at her.

"I'd do anything for Quinn. As would you with your two kids."

"Look, I'm not downplaying your desire to make the world a better place, hon, but let's face it, many of these homeless people have serious issues," she said, sipping her wine.

"True, but they still need to eat and have a warm place to stay at night."

"If you want to stay active, you could always volunteer at Stan's nonprofit."

"I'll consider it," she said, knowing she wouldn't. She liked working with people instead of pushing papers.

"So you don't remember anything about wandering onto that tenth hole?"

She looked away, too embarrassed to face her friend. "It's so humiliating."

"Everyone understands your situation, and no one thinks any less of you."

"Maybe so, but how would you feel if it had been you who'd run out there in your birthday suit?"

"Trust me, if it had been me running naked onto that green, those golfers would have sprinted to the next hole," Jessica said. "But you're a survivor, Shay. Everyone respects that about you."

"I'm just worried that Quinn's classmates might hear about it and tease her at school."

"Schools are kinder and gentler places than when we were growing up."

Shay laughed. "I don't for one second believe that. In many ways, they're worse with the advent of social media. Kids will always be cruel to one another, and I should know."

"Were you bullied at school?"

"Not exactly bullied. But school wasn't exactly a pleasant experience for me as a young girl. I grew up poor, and my parents could barely afford to buy us new clothes."

"That's too bad," Jessica said, shrugging. "I suppose you're right, but there's only so much you can do to protect kids these days, short of homeschooling them."

Shay hesitated before speaking. "Do you think it's strange that I have absolutely no recollection of running out onto that green?"

"Not at all. The brain is a complex organism," Jessica said. "And yours has undergone a lot of trauma as of late."

Shay was about to respond when the doorbell rang. More guests? She hoped that Gideon would arrive soon and ease the pressure on her to entertain. He was a natural host, emceeing social functions and introducing speakers. Making people feel comfortable was one of Gideon's greatest gifts, and much of that was due to his effusive charm, which he could turn on and off at will.

Gideon was the news anchor at Channel Four, currently the highest-rated station in Boston. He'd been there for over sixteen years now, well before he'd begun to woo her. She'd been twenty-one when she first saw him on TV. She remembered sitting in her college dorm at Harvard with her roommates and watching as the hunky anchor delivered the news in that deep voice, making all of her roomies swoon. Little did she know at the time that she'd one day end up marrying him.

She headed for the door, a sense of unease filling her. Ever since the attack, she found her emotions fluctuating from one extreme to the other. One minute, she was happy, the next, bitter and despondent for no apparent reason. Sometimes, this state of depression lasted for days. Other times, it would lift just as quickly as it came over her.

She opened the door and saw Fred and Gail standing there with a bouquet of flowers in hand. She could feel her face turning red with shame, having no idea they'd been invited to this dinner party. Gideon often invited people without telling her. Or maybe he did mention it, and she simply forgot.

Gail handed her the flowers as Shay stepped aside to let them in. Fred had been one of the golfers on the putting green the day she inadvertently staggered out there. They said he removed his golf shirt and covered her up before she "came to" and ran back into the house. She remembered nothing about the incident. Did it really happen? She had no doubt it did, because she discovered Fred's rumpled golf shirt on the floor of her bedroom the next morning.

They sat down in the living room while she put the flowers in a vase. After filling it with water, she returned, setting the vase down on the coffee table between them. But the sight of Fred smiling at her triggered something deep in her brain. Embarrassed, she looked up to apologize, as if running onto that green had been her fault.

"It's okay, hon," Jessica said, coming over and putting an arm around her shoulder.

"I'm so...sorry," she said, staring at Fred. Her head began to pound, and she wasn't sure now if she could make it through this dinner party.

"It's not your fault, Shay. It's the injury that's to blame," Fred said, coming over and kneeling beside her. "There's no shame in being attacked. It could have happened to anyone."

"I feel like there's two separate people living inside my head," Shay said, wiping away the tears.

Her friends surrounded her and tried to give comfort, but the attention did nothing to make her feel better. A weary exhaustion filled her. She felt unsure of herself and wanted nothing more now than to flee into the bedroom and bury herself under the covers. If only Gideon were here to calm her nerves, she might be able to go through with this. She didn't want to act all fake-happy around these people, serving up champagne and shrimp cocktails and trying to act like nothing had happened. It was difficult to accept their words of support when she had no idea who she was anymore. She felt unworthy of their friendship and their company.

Thankfully, Gideon arrived a few minutes later with Stan by his side, and the party quickly went from melancholic to joyous. It was as if her existential crisis was merely a blip in the course of the evening. But not for her. She lived with this crisis twenty-four-seven. Gideon laughed and fixed everyone drinks, and the men slapped his back and affectionately called him Gipper, his nickname back in college.

She felt bad for Gideon and for what he had to go through because of her injury. All the talk around the neighborhood was about his troubled wife and the terrible crime perpetrated against her. She thought about his golf partners and the whispers he must have been hearing down at the club. When the attack happened, she had prayed that her victimization wouldn't affect his popularity or TV ratings. Yet, surprisingly, after he'd tearfully mentioned it at the end of a broadcast one evening, his ratings soared even higher. The next day, he sat at the top of the ratings for the first time in years, slightly ahead of his bitter rival, Yolanda Brown. He admitted that it had been the greatest feeling he'd ever experienced, especially after being stuck at number two for so long.

A ringing started in her ears, and her vision began to blur. The voices of her friends became garbled and indecipherable. She thought she heard someone call out her name, so she turned and nodded in a daze. Hosting this dinner party was far more stressful than she realized, and now she wasn't sure if she could go through with it. She stood, light-headed, and checked on the rib roast in the oven. But no sooner had she taken a few steps when her knees buckled, and she collapsed to the floor. Gideon and a few of the others rushed over and helped her back onto the sofa.

"Are you okay, hon?" Gideon asked.

"Someone get her some water," Jessica said.

"No water. I'm just a little light-headed."

"Maybe you need to rest," Gideon said.

Tears filled her eyes. "But I'll ruin the party."

"That's silly," Jessica said. "All of us understand if you need to take a break. It was brave of you to hang out with us for as long as you did."

"Are you sure?"

"By all means," Gail said, sitting across from her. "Heaven knows, you made a giant step in the right direction this evening."

Shay stared at them. "No one will hate me if I go lie down for a bit?"

Voices went up in mock disapproval of even the slightest notion of hating her.

"You don't think any less of me, Fred?"

"Are you kidding? For streaking across the most exclusive golf course west of Boston?" He laughed. "To be honest, Shay, I'm actually quite jealous of you."

"Besides, it's nothing Gipper and I didn't do as idiot college freshmen," Stan said.

"Some of the club members are even calling you a legend," said Gail, and everyone laughed at this.

She tried to laugh along with them but found it impossible. She knew they were only trying to be nice and make her feel better. But the laughter only exacerbated her dread. So what if Fred and his golf partner had seen her naked on the tenth hole? She was at least thankful for the way they'd handled the situation and that nothing worse had happened.

She apologized to everyone before making her way up to the bedroom. Unsteady on her feet, she collapsed onto the bed, tearfully hugging one of the pillows to her chest. Hopefully, Quinn and Miranda were enjoying the movie.

She grabbed the water bottle off the nightstand, palmed two prescription pills, and washed them down.

Then she tried to sleep.

But everything in the bedroom began to spin, despite the room being completely dark. The party went on unabated downstairs, loud and boisterous, and she could hear the occasional peals of laughter.

And she wondered: could one of them have been the person who attacked her that night down by the soup kitchen and left her to die? Is that why they were laughing and having such a good time?

Who could she trust? Prior to the injury, she had always been an optimistic and friendly person. The attack had rewired her brain and temporarily altered her personality. She'd never experienced such crushing depression as she did now. The doctor explained that brain trauma affected everyone differently, and that sometimes it took months before a patient could return to their normal state. She'd read where some victims suffered for years before they returned to good health. Then, there were others who never fully recovered.

Despite this grim prognosis, she was determined to get better, if only for her daughter's sake. Because the truth was, she needed Quinn far more than Quinn needed her.

And the main reason to get back to good health was to make sure Quinn remained safe.

GIDEON

His wife was still asleep by the time he got dressed and ready for work. He went into Quinn's room and kissed her warm cheek. Then he tiptoed quietly out the kitchen door until he was sitting in his recently purchased Mercedes. The smell of new car leather was particularly strong, as he sat idling in the driveway, inhaling the glorious aroma.

Despite appearing on both the six and eleven o'clock broadcasts, he often went in early in order to get himself prepared for the avalanche of news pouring into the station. In addition to his duties as Boston's top news anchor, he also served as a board member on Stan's nonprofit, which was dedicated to fighting climate change. It was mostly a perfunctory position. He didn't do much other than show up at functions and spout platitudes while downing crackers and cheese and flutes of champagne.

He greatly enjoyed the perks of his position, basking in the glow of Boston's most important luminaries and politicians. It endowed him with a gravitas that on television made him appear statesmanlike and wise beyond his years, two traits he'd coveted ever since he started working in the industry. When he looked in the mirror each morning, he hoped to see traces of Walter Cronkite, Tom Brokaw, and Logan Burrows.

He had always believed his need to be loved stemmed from growing up as an only child with two emotionally spartan parents who rarely showed him affection. In fact, he couldn't ever remember his father saying he loved him. Every day, his father trudged home from the butcher shop where he worked, a white package containing a roast or pork shoulder tucked under his arm. Then he would plop down in his easy chair and start in on the Canadian Club. His mother stayed in the kitchen as his father got drunk, both of them seething with resentment. And because of that, Gideon craved the spotlight at the expense of most everything else in life. While attending the state college, he eagerly sought out attention, mostly in the form of sex, never fully understanding the wider scope that love entailed.

Gideon nodded to his underlings in the hallway before heading toward his office. Once inside, he closed the door and stood in front of the full-length mirror, admiring his stately physique. At six-two, he fit snugly into his Bruno Visconti suit. His dark hair swept back over his scalp, shimmering under the overhead lights.

Life these days was good. As terrible as that attack on his wife had been, he'd been enjoying a newly discovered freedom that he hadn't experienced in years. Shay's bouts of memory loss and forgetfulness gave him the rare opportunity to step out on his vows without consequence.

Did that make him a bad guy? That he was taking advantage of his wife's precarious mental condition to be unfaithful? He loved Shay dearly, but found that being faithful to one woman proved challenging to a man of his talents and looks, especially when he was surrounded every day by adoring, beautiful women.

How many times as a child had he heard his mother arguing with his father about his girlfriends? Gideon grew up believing that it was natural for fathers to cheat on their wives, and he justified his own occasional bouts of adultery, thinking about all he'd given Shay in their eleven years of marriage: a gorgeous home on a prestigious golf course; a precious child, whom he'd not really wanted, but whom he had grown to love; plenty of money and *things*. Yet she continually looked down at him because of that one reckless affair he'd engaged in many years ago—the one time he'd actually been caught being unfaithful. He'd not cheated much since then, but it taught him a valuable lesson about infidelity: if he was going to do it, then he needed to be careful.

There was a bit of work to get done before his secret lunch date with Mallory, the afternoon weather anchor. They'd been conducting a covert affair for the last few months now, and to her credit, Mallory didn't think any less of him because he was married and had a child. What they had was a breezy romance with no strings attached. Mallory never made any demands on him or requested that he divorce Shay to be solely with her. Instead, she showered him with affection and repeatedly told him what a great newscaster he was. Praise was something Shay had stopped giving him years ago.

He thought back to that night when he'd gotten the call from the police that his wife had been assaulted. It might have been the worst night of his life, and he knew he couldn't go on living without her, despite his cheating ways. She lay in the hospital for two long weeks before she was sent home to recuperate.

The police, he believed, didn't seriously suspect him of causing the attack. Everyone knew that he loved Shay unconditionally. She was the best thing that ever happened to him, and he always regretted being unfaithful to her, even when he was consciously committing adultery. The fact that he was between newscasts when the attack happened provided him with a rock-solid alibi for his whereabouts that night.

He rambled around the studio for a few minutes, stopping to chitchat with a few coworkers and ask about their well-being before shutting himself inside his office. He logged on to his computer and checked his emails. While doing this, his secretary walked in with his first coffee of the day and left it on his desk. Deb was in her mid-fifties and had been with him for over fifteen years. Despite the length of their working relationship and the many battles they'd fought together, he'd never completely warmed up to her. Yet he knew that without Deb, he'd never have made it this far at the station.

He returned his attention to the computer, particularly his message feed on the top left corner of the screen, where he and Mallory had been engaging in a flirtatious conversation. Although chatting with her filled him with guilt, he was too weak to stop himself from engaging in such inappropriate behavior.

"How's your wife feeling?" Deb asked.

"All in all about the same," he said, nervously eyeing the message box.

"That's too bad. We were all expecting her to be better by now."

"She's still struggling to regain her memory," he said, not wanting to mention the incident on the golf course, which had embarrassed him as much as it did his wife.

"Have you heard anything from the police?"

"Nothing yet. I seriously doubt they'll catch the scoundrel who attacked her." He sighed. "I don't know how many times I warned her about working down at that soup kitchen and how dangerous it is to walk around there that late at night. As wonderful as my wife is, she's also very stubborn."

"You did manage to convince her to move to that beautiful home."

Her snippy response angered him, and he now wished that Deb would leave his office. "Yes, I suppose I won at least one battle, although, with that amazing location, it didn't take much persuading."

"Your wife's so sweet." Deb shook her head in dismay. "And that poor daughter of yours. God help her."

"Quinn's an amazing girl. She's all the motivation Shay needs to get better."

"Such a brave child." Deb pressed her hands over her thin red lips and sniffed back a tear. "How anyone could threaten a young girl like that is beyond me."

"Let's not jump to conclusions. My wife, after all, did receive a serious head injury."

"You think she might have misheard those words?"

"Anything's possible," he said, eager for Deb to leave. "Where's Barb? She's supposed to give me a briefing on the indictments handed down at city hall this morning."

"I'll go see if I can track her down."

Once the door closed, he sent Mallory a steamy message from their last rendezvous. He knew it was foolish to be cheating on his wife during this difficult time, but he was stressed out and had no one else to confide in. He'd thought about ending it with Mallory as soon as possible, but all he had to do was lay eyes on her, and he knew he'd put it off for another day. They'd managed to keep their affair secret these last five months, and although he was twenty-plus years her senior, they got along splendidly. He had physical needs that needed looking after, which his wife, through no fault of her own as of late, had been unable to meet.

When he first heard that his wife had wandered naked onto the tenth green, he couldn't fathom how he'd explain it to the members of his club. The incident humiliated him and was an affront to his antiquated sense of civility. And knowing that Fred and his golf partners had seen his wife naked drove him crazy with shame.

The club had expressed their deepest sympathy and sent Shay a massive bouquet of flowers with a get-well card signed by all the members. The generosity of everyone touched him, despite the incident hanging over the two of them like a dark cloud over a cresting river.

Gideon scanned the message box to see if Mal had left him another message, but still nothing. He was dying to see her. A yearning stirred in his loin at the thought of her naked body sprawled over the bed, even knowing that he had to break it off with her quickly and without drama.

The more he thought about it, the more he began to believe that the attack on his wife had weakened his inhibitions, providing him with the perfect opportunity to stray. Confined to the house and with her memory in shatters, Shay was unable to scrutinize his behavior. Or keep him on the straight and narrow. And with Quinn attending school all day, he was free to play around without the fear of getting caught. Or at least until Shay fully recovered.

He sipped his coffee and perused the paper, happy to be out of that depressing house. Had it been a mistake purchasing it? Bad things seemed to have happened as soon as they moved in. Lately, the house he had chosen for his family felt cursed. And that head injury had turned his wife into someone he barely knew. Sex with Shay was out of the question for the foreseeable future, although it had been sparse even before the attack. She seemed to resent him for reasons unknown, although part of him still believed she held that one affair over his head. But that had been such a long time ago. Why couldn't she just forgive and forget?

A general feeling of unease filled him as he perused the headlines.

A sexually explicit message popped up from Mallory, and he giggled boyishly as he wrote her back. He couldn't wait to meet her for lunch in the back room of that Italian bistro and gaze upon her supple figure.

He swiveled around in his chair to gaze out at the Boston skyline. As he admired it, he heard a loud knock on the door. Believing it was Barb, the news director, he spun around, eager to hear her thoughts on the scandal brewing at city hall. Instead, he saw his wife standing in the doorway. What the hell was *she* doing here? The doctor had specifically ordered her not to drive in her condition. She closed the door behind her and sat down in the chair across from his desk. Confused, Gideon stood and walked over to her. He gave her a quick peck on the cheek and then sat down in his chair. She looked slightly different to him this morning, and he chalked it up to the aftereffects of her head injury.

"Honey, what are you doing here?" he said, glancing nervously at the message he'd forgotten to close on his screen. "You know you're not supposed to leave the house."

"I came here to see the man I love. Is there anything wrong with that?"

"Of course not," he replied. "But how did you get here? Please tell me you didn't drive."

"I took an Uber. Jessica explained to me how it worked with my phone and credit card and said that it would give me a bit more freedom."

He cursed at Jessica for suggesting his wife use an Uber to get around town, especially when Shay had introduced *him* to the service. Why couldn't people just mind their own business? The idea that Shay could move about freely now worried him. Glancing at his computer, he knew he had to put an end to this fling with Mallory—and fast. He couldn't afford to risk his marriage and bank account. When she finally agreed to marry him, Shay had called his bluff and refused to sign a prenup. He knew she could ruin him if she found out that he'd been cheating on her—again. He cursed himself for being so stupid.

"I really miss you, Gideon. You leave so early for work and then come home so late at night that Quinn and I hardly ever see you anymore."

"But we have weekends together, dear. You knew my busy schedule when we got married."

"Did I?"

"Yes, you did know because you once worked in the news industry yourself. Don't you remember?"

"Vaguely."

"Then you had Quinn and began to develop your own interests. Like volunteering at that soup kitchen, which I warned you not to do."

"Don't make me feel bad for that," she said, looking down at the floor.

He needed to change the subject. "Did you have a nice time at the dinner party the other night?"

"Remind me again who was there."

"Jessica and Stan. Fred and Gail. You really don't remember?"

"I'm sorry, Gideon. You know how forgetful I've been lately."

"You hosted the party until I came home. Then you woke from your nap and joined us, and we all had a wonderful evening."

"Was Fred the one who covered me up on the golf course?"

He nodded, trying to understand why she even showed up here today.

"Yes, and Fred was a complete gentleman the entire time," he said.

Shay frowned. "I really wish my memory would start working properly."

"It will, hon. You just need to follow the doctor's orders and rest," he said, studying her closely for any sign that she might suspect him of cheating. "Maybe I should drive you home."

"I was thinking, Gideon. I'll need more help around the house if I'm to get better."

"What kind of help?"

"With the laundry and all the chores. It's difficult to do in my condition, forgetting things all the time."

"But we already have someone that comes to the house twice a week. What else do you need?"

"I don't trust that woman."

"Since when? You've always loved Maya."

"She stole a pair of my best earrings. The ones you had engraved and gave to me on our tenth anniversary."

"That's crazy, hon." He laughed at such paranoia, realizing that her delusion could help him if he played his cards right. "Maya would never steal your earrings. She's been our maid for a long time now, and she adores both you and Quinn."

"I don't trust her, Gideon. I refuse to let that woman back into our home, especially after she stole something that means so much to me."

"You probably misplaced them."

"I keep all my jewelry in the same box. No way I would misplace something so dear to me," she said. "How can I trust her to be around our daughter when she's lifting my personal items?"

"That's ridiculous. Maya loves Quinn. She buys her Christmas and birthday gifts every year."

"I feel like you're not respecting my opinion."

"I'm totally respecting your opinion. It's just that Maya's been working for me for seventeen years now, well before we met. I can't just let her go."

"Please, Gideon. Don't force me into pressing charges against the woman."

"Pressing charges?" He felt like he didn't know his wife anymore.

"Absolutely," she said. "It sounds to me like you're choosing Maya over me."

"Of course, I'm not choosing Maya over you. It's just that this crazy brain injury of yours is causing you to behave in strange ways. You've always loved Maya. And she'll be so heartbroken to leave our household."

"I interviewed a potential housekeeper this morning whom I was very impressed with."

"You've already interviewed someone?" he said, clearly exasperated.

"Yes, and she came highly recommended."

"Who recommended her?"

"One of the girls. Oh, I can't remember which one of my friends gave me her name. All I know is that I really liked the woman. She cooks and cleans and would be perfect for Quinn."

"There's no way I can change your mind?"

"Not on this." She stood and moved around to the side of the desk, and sat on his lap. "I swear I'm going to make it up to you once I feel better."

Looking her over, he had to admit that she looked pretty this morning. Was it the makeup? She looked almost like she did before the attack. Yet something about her seemed unfamiliar. Had the brain injury altered her physical appearance in the subtlest of ways? Like a person who'd suffered a minor stroke and whose features imperceptibly shifted?

"How's this for starters?" She reached down and moved her hand over his crotch.

"Jesus, Shay! Not in my office." He stood and gently lifted her off him. This was his place of work and sacred ground. The thought of having sex with his wife in here creeped him out. She was damaged goods and fragile to the touch. Who knew how she would react from one moment to the next, especially after having sex with him?

"I'm sorry," she said, covering her mouth with her hands. "I only want to be a good wife to you."

"You're an amazing wife." He embraced her despite, to his chagrin, becoming slightly aroused. "And you're also the best mother in the world."

"Maybe we can have another child someday," she said. "Would you like that, dear?"

"Can we talk about this later?" he said, knowing that she would quickly forget such a request. The last thing he wanted was more children. Fatherhood did not come naturally to him. For five years, he'd tried to have a child with his first wife before she finally had enough—and left him. Drastically low sperm count, the doctors said. They estimated his chances of impregnating a woman to be less than five percent. Then Quinn came along and changed his life.

"I want to make love to you, Gideon. I want you to have some pleasure in life, a pleasure I haven't been able to give you since my injury."

Since your injury? Ha! How about before that homeless lowlife clubbed you over the head? "But I want you to get well first, Shay. I need you to be in the right frame of mind before we consummate our love."

"Then, at least let me hire this woman as our new maid. It will give me more time to heal. And don't worry, I'll inform Maya of our decision to let her go."

He sighed. "If it means that much to you."

"It really does." She hugged him. "The new housekeeper is so easy to talk to."

"Hispanic?"

"Russian, I think. One of those funny-sounding countries with hard consonants. I can't wait for her to start."

"Okay, how about we talk about this tonight?"

"I hope it's not a problem, but I've already hired her."

"Without consulting me?"

"Considering all that I've sacrificed by agreeing to move to Woodbridge Estates, I don't think that's asking much."

He cursed under his breath as Shay assured him that she could take an Uber home. He called down to the security booth, and the guard promised that he would watch her get into the car.

She kissed him goodbye, and the kiss lingered a few seconds longer than he would have liked. For some inexplicable reason, he tasted peach on her lips. She smelled nice, too. This sudden and involuntary attraction to his wife now worried him. Hopefully, it was only a momentary lapse, and things would return to normal. Marriage and fatherhood often drained him and took all the fun out of sex.

An uncomfortable sensation came over him as he watched Shay stroll out of his office. He didn't want to get sucked back into that asphyxiating cycle with a sick wife recovering from her head injury. Not yet, anyways, while she was still in recovery. The thought depressed him. It was almost as if he was an interloper in his marriage and in his own family. He spent most nights at work while mother and daughter deepened their bond: a bond that most definitely excluded him. Quinn was dependent on her mother for most of her needs, despite the fact that he was paying every last cent of her private school tuition. Then there was the tidy sum he'd been forced to cough up after his first divorce, which was still sending shock waves through his portfolio.

All of that seemed negligible compared to what was truly at stake: his recently anointed status as Boston's most beloved news anchor. The notion that it could all come tumbling down made him rethink his secret rendezvous with Mallory. He wouldn't end their relationship just yet, but he'd certainly need to be more discreet until the affair ran its course.

He got on the line and called the young news anchor, and canceled their lunch date. Mallory sounded mildly disappointed, but she put up no resistance after learning about the scandal at city hall. Everyone in broadcasting understood the rules of the game: work always took precedence.

The thought of firing Maya after seventeen years of service troubled him, primarily because she was efficient, honest and came cheap. But he had no intention of going against his wife's wishes. Besides, she'd already gone ahead and hired this new woman. If Shay wanted to lower the axe on the diminutive El Salvadorian housekeeper, then let *her* do it. Maybe the change would do them good, assuming this Russian woman didn't break the budget.

He left his office and searched for Barb. Everyone looked up and trembled at the sight of him. He needed to present himself as serious and somber now that high-level officials in Boston City Hall were being indicted. But this news meant nothing to him beyond how it might affect his ratings. All news was good news, but bad news paid the bills.

SHAY

Gideon had come in late last night after his broadcast and was out of bed by the time she lifted her head off the pillow. She had much to do today, including waking Quinn and making her breakfast. She stretched her arms, feeling far better this morning than she had in a long while. For once, her head felt calm and clear. The dinner party the other night seemed as if it had never happened, yet she clearly remembered how it had left her reeling for the better part of the evening.

She swallowed her assortment of pills, walked downstairs and into the kitchen, and was stunned to see a strange-looking woman standing at the table and serving pancakes to Quinn. For a brief moment, she wondered if she was seeing things. She rubbed her eyes, but the woman was still there. Before she could say anything, Gideon strutted into the room with the two ends of his tie hanging past his collar. He smiled when he saw her standing at the foot of the stairs and walked over to kiss her. She stood rigid in his arms, wondering if she was suffering from another bad dream.

"You were right, honey. Hiring Tatyana was a wonderful idea. She arrived early this morning and cooked us an amazing breakfast," he whispered in her ear.

"I'm not sure what you're talking about."

"Don't you remember telling me about her?" He waited for a response, but when it was not forthcoming, he said, "You were the one who hired her."

"I did?"

"Yes. She even has all the paperwork from the agency with your signature on it."

"But I don't need help around here. Besides, we have Maya."

"You let Maya go and hired Tatyana instead."

"I did?"

"Yes, and all of this was your idea," he said, knotting his tie.

"Oh, Gideon, what's happening to me?"

She felt like sobbing. Her mind had turned against her in the worst possible way. How could she remember some things and not others? As good as she felt this morning, she knew it could all come crashing down at any moment.

"Why did we let Maya go?"

"*You* let her go, Shay, not we." He sighed and looked away. "You claimed she stole a pair of your best earrings."

She tried to remember saying that. "But I would never accuse Maya of stealing from me."

"Good God, Shay, this is getting tiresome," he said. "You most certainly did accuse her. It's obvious that you need more help than anyone could have imagined."

"But I'm getting better, right?" She felt confused, and her vision became slightly blurred from the ocular headache now forming in her vision.

"Yes, dear, you *are* getting better. It's just taking a little longer than expected."

"Okay, Gideon. I trust you know what's best for me."

"I do know what's best for you and always have. You need to trust me from now on, dear."

"I will. I promise."

She walked toward the kitchen, studying the new maid, noticing that she walked slightly hunched and with the aid of a cane. A tangle of black hair fell in swirls around her delicate shoulders. Shay listened as Quinn discussed in dizzying detail the subjects she'd been studying in school. That her daughter had taken so quickly to the new maid somewhat lessened her anxiety. But it also made Shay slightly jealous of the woman. Quinn rarely, if ever, talked to Maya in such long outbursts. Then again, Maya was a quiet and unassuming woman, moving stealthily around each room so as not to be noticed. And her lack of fluency in English often made communicating with her difficult.

As she approached the new maid, she noticed the woman wore glasses and had a wine stain over her cheek that resembled a butterfly in flight. She was dressed in a gray plaid skirt and misshapen tan sweater. The smell of perfume hung thick in the air. Thick black mascara tailed off in a dramatic flare at the end of her eye sockets so that the line pointed toward her temples. Her eyes were dark and deep, as if trying to divert people's attention from the wine stain. Shay had seen some of the younger Russian girls at the hair parlor, and they made themselves up with that same dramatic look. If not for the wine stain and disability, Shay could see where some men might find Tatyana attractive.

Quinn suddenly, and for no apparent reason, stopped talking and remained perfectly still. She held up a syrupy wedge of pancake and sniffed the air. It took a few seconds before she realized her mother's presence in the room, and she smiled as soon as she made the connection.

"Oh, hello, Momma. How are you feeling?"

"Fine," she said, sitting down next to her daughter.

"We have a new helper today."

"I see."

"Her name is Tatyana," Quinn said.

"It's a pleasure to work for you, Mrs. Wells," the woman said in a soft voice with a thick accent. She looked up briefly before averting her eyes.

"Nice to meet you, Tatyana. Who recommended you to us?"

The woman looked puzzled. "Your friend did, Mrs. Wells. You called agency after we talked at coffee shop."

"Oh, yes," she said, having no recollection of the phone call or conversation with this woman.

"I need to go, hon," Gideon said, kissing her on the forehead. "Board meeting this morning."

She sat down at the table and allowed Tatyana to serve her a pancake with a glass of juice. She didn't have the fortitude to question Tatyana any further this morning, and since Quinn seemed to like her, maybe this whole setup was a good thing. Quinn appeared to be in high spirits, a positive sign. After the attack on Shay, Quinn had undergone a brief phase where she'd retreated into herself, afraid that whoever attacked her mother might return and come for her. After that phase had passed, she'd started to believe that she'd never have a healthy mother again.

Tatyana disappeared into another room. This might work out for the best, Shay thought, as she walked Quinn out to where her school bus picked her up. The morning was splendid, and the chill of early autumn air refreshed her. The two of them talked and laughed while waiting for the bus to arrive, taking turns telling silly jokes. Shay glanced at her watch, realizing that the driver was already ten minutes late. She tried not to be upset, despite all the money they paid to send Quinn to Hamilton Academy. The school had been good to them and had done all they could to accommodate Quinn's special needs, including sending a van every day to pick her up and then keeping Quinn until five each night while Shay recuperated from her injury. Shay was eternally grateful for the way Hamilton Academy accommodated her family after the attack.

Fifteen minutes passed before she walked Quinn back to the house. By the time she reached the front door, she found herself out of breath and light-headed. It forced her to sit down and rest. Quinn sat on the living room sofa, her backpack still on, humming a tune from *Frozen*. Tatyana came over, a look of concern on her face. Had the school forgotten to pick up her daughter? Shay pulled out her phone and dialed the school, a sense of indignation filling her. When the secretary answered, she decided that a polite tone would be the best approach.

"What do you mean I canceled the bus?" she said, not quite believing the woman's words.

"You called yesterday, Mrs. Wells. You specifically told me that you'd get Quinn to school."

"Why would I say that? I'm barely able to drive myself."

"I asked you a couple of times if you were sure about this, and you insisted that everything would be fine."

"I'm having a hard time believing you," she replied, all sense of decorum leaving her.

"I'm sorry you feel this way, Mrs. Wells, but that's the conversation we had." There was a pause. "I wouldn't lie to you about something as important as this."

"Honestly, I don't remember saying that, but if you insist that I did, then I believe you."

"Not to be disrespectful, but could the problem be related to your memory issues?"

She willed herself not to snap back at the woman.

"I apologize," the woman said. "I didn't mean to imply that—"

"Look, I'm sorry for inconveniencing you. I'll make sure Quinn gets to school this morning," she said, abruptly ending the call. "I suppose it's too late to call Daddy for a ride, since he has to be at his board meeting this morning," she said to Quinn.

"It's okay, Momma, I can stay home and read if I have to," Quinn said, a note of disappointment in her voice.

"I can drive her to school, Mrs. Wells," Tatyana offered. "I have license. I just need directions."

"You'd do that for us?"

"Of course. It is my job to help you," she said. "But might be best if I take your car. Mine's not so safe for little girl."

"Of course, you can take mine. Thank you so much, Tatyana," she said happily.

She watched as the two of them made their way to the door. Tatyana clutched her cane, held the girl's hand in her own, and exited the house. Shay shuffled over to the window and watched as the two of them made their way to the Lexus SUV Gideon had gotten her for Christmas last year, a gas guzzler she didn't really need. Once they left, she returned to her bedroom and checked inside her jewelry box. Sadly, her anniversary earrings were nowhere to be found. Why, after so many years, would Maya choose to steal from her now?

She returned to the living room and laid her head down on the sofa cushion. If only Maya had come to her with her money problems, then maybe she could have helped the woman. She dozed off while considering this.

SHAY

The days passed in a blur, and with Tatyana taking control of the household, Shay felt free from the confines of her daily life. Free to work on her health and regain the full scope of her cognitive abilities. Tatyana had proved to be a godsend in ways she'd not anticipated. She was more than a competent cook, and Quinn seemed to enjoy her simple yet hearty meals, many of which came from her country of origin. Yet Tatyana rarely spoke unless spoken to, instead choosing to listen to Quinn's rambling monologue each morning about her activities in class. And after Quinn left for school each day, Tatyana made Shay take brisk walks around the neighborhood. As much as she protested these walks, Tatyana insisted, pushing her like one of the trainers at her old gym. And she never overstepped her bounds or wore out her welcome. Aside from insisting she take her daily walks, Tatyana was compliant and evenhanded. At times, she seemed so invisible that Shay was not even sure the woman was in the house.

Shay found herself constantly reading and rereading the doctor's notes for clues about what to expect. Recovery would be slow, and sometimes, she found herself taking one step forward and two steps back. Or three steps forward and one step back. The doctor warned of the possibility of crushing depression, as well as the brief lapses of memory and debilitating exhaustion. Added to that were the bouts of anxiety and sudden, impulsive fits of anger that came out of nowhere. It was this last emotion that worried her most.

After her walks, she busied herself by reading a book or magazine article, but she often found it hard to concentrate. After fifteen minutes, she typically had to put down whatever she was reading and rest her eyes. More often than not, she'd get overcome by a terrible migraine or wave of nausea, which swept over her like a tidal surge. She slept often, but lightly, and never without experiencing strange dreams. During the daylight hours, she found it helpful to wear sunglasses in order to guard against the intrusion of light.

And not a day went by that she didn't ponder the one question that continued to haunt her: who had attacked her outside that soup kitchen?

Gideon had been nervous about changing housekeepers, but Tatyana won him over from the first day she arrived. This relieved Shay, knowing he felt better about leaving for work each morning. Still, she felt bad about having to let Maya go, even if the woman had stolen her earrings. The decision to employ Tatyana had been a sound one, she kept reminding herself, despite the fact that she had no recollection of ever interviewing her for the job. Gideon had offered to take a few afternoons off during the week and spend them with her, but Shay insisted he stay at work. She knew how much Gideon loved his job and how dedicated he was to it. Anchoring the news was his life.

She wanted badly to be healthy again, to find purpose and meaning in her life, and maybe volunteer at her daughter's school. She gave up her career in broadcasting in order to care for Quinn. She wanted to be there for her daughter, especially after the girl's illness. Now it seemed like the roles were reversed, and Quinn was the one caring for her.

At the age of three, Quinn was diagnosed with retinoblastoma in both eyes, and the ordeal required her constant presence in her daughter's life. Never had she wept so often and openly when she received the diagnosis, and she thanked God that Quinn had survived her illness and had dealt with her ordeal with such grace. In many ways, her daughter was her personal hero, and whenever she got down about her own health woes, she thought of cheery little Quinn.

SHAY

The weather this morning was mild. She peered out the window while Tatyana folded laundry in the kitchen. A week had passed since she started working here and all had been going well. The streets glistened from the hard morning's rain, and the sun's burgeoning rays caused everything around it to sparkle. She glanced over at Tatyana, feeling guilty as she watched the woman work in silence. Despite having a maid, Shay always loved the ritual of doing laundry. In fact, Jessica thought it hilarious when she admitted this to her. Jessica then informed Shay that she could come over to her house any time she wanted and fold clothes. She couldn't help but feel territorial watching Tatyana take over her chores, knowing that because of her injury, she wasn't quite up to the task.

"Go. Take walk now while sun is shining, Mrs. Wells," Tatyana said from the kitchen table. "It will do you good."

"I can't. I'm too tired today."

"You must force yourself to walk. For sake of your daughter."

Shay laughed. "You certainly know how to motivate me."

"I make hot tea for when you come back."

"Okay, you win. I will see you shortly." Shay stood.

"Take your time. I have plenty of laundry to do."

Shay put on her sunglasses and made her way out to the street. There was a touch of humidity in the air, and almost immediately, it made her feel sluggish. She walked with her head down as the road wound along the ninth and tenth tees. Dew moistened the vigorously groomed fairway, and a foursome puttered past on carts, taking their time motoring toward the green. She looked away so they wouldn't recognize her as that crazy woman from the tenth tee.

Her legs dragged, and the neighborhood appeared hazy and out of focus. Sometimes, during these walks, she had to turn around and head back home if she felt sick. Or felt a migraine coming on. Otherwise, she soldiered on. Every so often, she even stopped and chatted with one of her neighbors, although she could never remember the conversation afterwards, nor the neighbor she spoke to. She often thought it a miracle that she actually made it back home.

Being new to the neighborhood, she liked how the winding, tree-lined streets meandered through the development. Since moving out of Boston, most of her friends were the women in her husband's social circle, many of whom, like Jessica, lived on the back nine part of the course. In private, Gideon jokingly referred to that section of the development as the ghetto.

She turned the corner, and the golf course came back into view. Sweat dripped from her forehead as she slogged up the long hill leading to her house. For a brief moment, she wasn't sure she could make it. She stopped to catch her breath, spirals of light pinwheeling in her vision. Leaning against a split-rail fence for support, she debated resting for a few minutes until she was ready to move on.

A few seconds passed before she heard someone calling her name. Maybe this person would see her in distress and offer to drive her up the remainder of the hill. A shiver of nausea trembled through her body as she struggled to stand. She looked over and saw a woman running toward her. The woman appeared featureless, as if she was seeing her face through a shower glass stall. But the closer she got, the harsher the woman's voice sounded. A small dog stood by, yapping loudly near her feet.

"You crazy bitch. I can't believe you're showing your face around here after what you've done," the woman said.

"Excuse me?"

"You should be ashamed of yourself after the way you spoke to my son yesterday."

"I'm sorry, but I think you have the wrong person."

"Oh no, you're the one, all right. My sitter saw you yelling at Dylan and then kicking our dog. Thankfully, she ran out and pulled him inside before you spewed any more of your filth."

"I'm sorry, but I don't remember speaking to anyone yesterday."

"It's one thing shaking your ass out on the golf course like that, but to swear at a small boy is totally uncalled for."

"I think you're badly mistaken."

"Look, lady, you can't go around pulling that crap in *this neighborhood*. Go see a shrink, for God's sake."

"I am seeing one." Tears formed in her eyes. "It's not like I want to be this way. I was attacked and beaten to within an inch of my life."

"Then maybe you should stay inside until you stop being a threat to dogs and children. My boy doesn't deserve to be treated like that."

Had she threatened the woman's son? "No, you're right. I'm very sorry for whatever it is I've said or done."

She felt like she was going to be sick. None of this made any sense. It was not like her to behave erratically and cuss at young children. She staggered up the street toward her house, but to her dismay, the woman followed on her heels, continuing to berate her for something she couldn't recall doing.

"If you ever talk to my son like that again, you'll regret it," the woman shouted, bellowing in her ear. "Do you understand me?"

"Please leave me alone."

She staggered up the street, her cement-like feet dropping one in front of the other until she arrived home. She opened the door and flung herself inside, not resting until she lay prostrate over the sofa. Her head pounded, and the ringing in her ears was so pronounced that she could barely hear the sound of Tatyana's voice croaking above her. Was she losing her mind?

"Tatyana, what's happening to me?"

"Take it easy, Mrs. Wells. You had bad injury."

"I can't remember anything lately."

"Rest up. You'll feel better."

"For God's sake, I can't even remember meeting you in that coffee shop or striking up a conversation with you."

"I remember," Tatyana said, looking hurt. "But you're glad we met, *da*?"

"Of course I am. You've been a blessing to this family."

"Don't worry, Mrs. Wells. I will look after you. Everything will be okay."

"Something happened to me on that walk."

"What happened that upset you?"

Shay covered her eyes with the back of her hand. "One of the neighbors started to yell at me. She said I cussed at her son and kicked her dog."

"Is true?"

She burst out laughing through the tears. "If it is, I don't remember doing so. Swearing at young children is not something I've ever done before."

"I wonder why she would say such a thing."

"I'm going to pass on the tea, Tatyana. I think it's best I lie down for a while."

"Yes, good idea. Would you like to go into bedroom?"

"No, I'll lie on the couch if it's okay with you."

"Is your house, Mrs. Wells. You do whatever you like."

"I won't bother you?"

"No. I try not to wake you while I do the dishes."

"I'm so tired I'll not hear a thing," she said as the woman stood to leave. "And, Tatyana, thank you so much for everything you've done for us. And for me."

Tatyana nodded. "I wake you before Quinn gets home. Hopefully, you'll be rested up by then."

"I don't remember speaking to you at that coffee shop, but I'm very glad I did."

Shay closed her eyes, hoping that when she woke up, she'd forget everything about that dreadful experience with that dreadful neighbor. Despite all that had happened, and her recent memory lapse, she knew in her heart that she would never treat another person in such a disrespectful way, especially a child.

Then again, the woman she was right now was not the real Shay Wells. She was someone else: an imposter who had her mind stolen from her.

The woman who had accused her of cussing at her boy had obviously been mistaken. Or else, Shay realized, she was a lot sicker than she initially believed. The truth might be more painful than she cared to admit.

GIDEON

Gideon entered Mallory's luxury condo and sighed with envy. As much as he'd once looked forward to returning to his new house situated on the tenth hole, there was something satisfying about living so close to downtown. He didn't think he'd miss the city as much as he did. Walking over to the window, he pushed the curtain aside and took in the bustling Seaport District, with its gorgeous view of the bustling harbor. A succession of planes lined up in the sky to land on Logan's runway. In thirty short years, this area had gone from a sleepy fishing port to being one of the trendiest neighborhoods in Boston.

He went back inside and studied the assortment of liquors along the bar as he waited for Mallory to come out. The desire to pour himself a drink was strong, especially since he felt terrible about being here in the first place. It had been a rough day thus far, and he longed for two inches of good bourbon to ease his guilt. He remembered a newscast ten years ago when he'd gone out between broadcasts with some of the crew to celebrate their recent ratings spike. Two margaritas was all it took to throw off his delivery. When he went on the air that evening, he knew instantly it had been a mistake. He garbled his words and slurred his way through the broadcast. The next day, the *Boston Herald* plastered his photo on the front page with the words, "Boozecast At 11!" He had to go on air the following night and apologize to his audience, claiming that a newly prescribed medication had caused him to slur his speech. From then on, he swore never to drink until *after* he'd signed off for the night.

He returned his attention to a tugboat puttering out in the harbor, recalling the visit paid to him this afternoon by that Boston police detective. The cops had interviewed everyone down at the soup kitchen and still had not located any witnesses to the crime perpetrated against his wife. The detective, a wily old veteran with but a few years left on the force, had eyed him warily. Did they suspect him of trying to kill his wife? He knew the husband was always the first suspect in the attempted murder of his own wife.

He had a slight problem in regard to his alibi. It was the reason why he hadn't told the cops the truth about his whereabouts that evening. Because he was here in this condo at the time of his wife's attack, having just finished a glorious session with Boston's most voluptuous weather girl. Detective Carr didn't look fully convinced when he informed him that he'd gone out for his evening walk, which he usually did between the six and eleven o'clock newscasts. Fortunately, he'd made a habit of these walks, and his staff and producers could back him on this. And the station's security camera verified that his car had never left the lot. The walks had merely been a convenient alibi for when his wife called the station asking for him.

Thank God Mallory had picked him up and returned him to the station in a timely manner.

The time to cut Mallory loose had come, despite how painful it would be to break the bad news to her. He'd greatly miss all the fun they had together. For the time being, he needed to make sure that Detective Carr didn't learn the truth about that night. Or about the affair. Of course, if he did find out, it would provide the police with a rock-solid alibi for his whereabouts, thus clearing his name. But there was a danger in that information going public. If his audience found out that he'd been cheating on his wife the night she'd been savagely attacked, his career might be finished.

He returned to the window and watched as the tugboat chugged out of the harbor. As soon as Mallory emerged from the bathroom, he turned and saw her dressed in the skimpy lingerie he'd purchased at Victoria's Secret. They'd wandered inside the mall store one day at her insistence, and after a playful remark he'd made, telling her how sexy she'd look in one of those flossy undergarments, she'd surprised him by picking out something expensive and making him pay for it.

As soon as he saw her in it, he almost forgot about the pledge he'd made to break up with her. At five feet eleven and twenty-five years of age, Mallory was almost as tall as he was. She had shapely legs and the toned body of one of those female beach volleyball players. Her black hair shimmered in waves over her delicate shoulders, and her skin had that pale color he so loved. He ran his fingers over her smooth waist, admiring how it tapered down before flaring out at her hips. He could feel himself becoming aroused, and this worried him, because he knew their time together was coming to an end.

Just recently, he'd called his friend at the Your Weather Channel to see if they'd be interested in hiring Mallory away from the station. She was ambitious and talented, and convincing her to move away from Boston would be the perfect solution to his problem. He could say goodbye without angst or drama, wish her well on the national stage, and then try once again to be the dedicated and loyal husband he kept promising himself to be.

"This is the lingerie I picked out for you. Do you like it?"

"Very much so."

"I knew you would."

"Say it for me, hon."

"Don't be silly, Gideon."

"Just one time. I'm begging you."

"You're such a nerd." She hesitated for a moment before assuming an exaggerated weather-girl pose. "There's a storm warning being issued for this evening, with sustained winds up to fifty miles per hour and gusts up to seventy."

"You make the simplest of storms sound so sexy."

"Come on in the bedroom, and I'll show you a good blow," she said, leading him by the necktie.

As Mallory fell back on the bed, biting her long polished nail in anticipation, Gideon took off his clothes until he stood in his golf-themed boxers. A terrible sense of guilt swept over him.

He was about to strip naked when his cell phone rang. Now, who could that be? He debated whether or not to answer it, but then maybe some big news had broken down at the station, requiring his presence. The last time he skipped a call, a disgruntled government employee had gunned down three people in the Boston Commons, and he missed out on reporting on a huge breaking story.

"Do you have to answer that?" Mallory sulked.

"You know I do."

"How about ignoring it this once," she said, flinging a long porcelain arm over her head.

"You, of anyone, know that breaking news waits for no reporter," he said, fishing for his phone on the floor.

He answered without looking at the caller ID and was horrified to hear the sound of his wife. She was sobbing and trying to tell him something, but he had no idea what she was saying. He told her to calm down, but her hysterical sobs made it impossible for him to speak. Was it Quinn? Had something tragic happened to his daughter? The only thing he could make out was her muted gasps, begging him to come home right away. He beseeched her to take a deep breath before instructing her to hand the phone over to Tatyana, assuming the maid hadn't already fled the house in horror.

"I'm here, Mr. Wells," Tatyana said in her thick accent.

"What's wrong with my wife?"

"I think you should come home right away. Police are here."

"The police?" He wondered if they'd found the person who attacked her. "Why are they at my house?"

"Something to do with neighbor's dog."

"The neighbor's dog?"

"Yes. Please come home right away."

"Will you do me a favor and keep her calm until I get there," he said, hanging up the phone before she could reply.

He grabbed his shirt and flung it back on, not concerned which button went where or if his shirt was properly tucked in.

"Where do you think you're going?" Mallory asked, sitting up.

"Emergency at home." He averted his eyes so as not to be tempted. "I have to go."

"She forget how to wipe her ass now?"

"Be nice, Mal."

"And I was so looking forward to being with you."

"How do you think I feel?"

"It must be hard being married to someone with CRS." She coolly studied her long nails.

"CRS?" He put on his jacket.

"Can't remember shit," she said, falling back down on the bed so that she was lying on her stomach and giving him a full view of her backside.

He cinched his belt and passed it neatly through the loop, letting her snarky comment pass.

"By the way, did you mention me to your friend at the Your Weather Channel?"

"I did, and with my referral, you're sure to land on his Doppler," he said as he straightened his tie in the mirror. "Now, if you'll excuse me, Mal, I have to go."

He got into his car, forty-five minutes still left on the parking meter, and merged into rush hour traffic. The gridlock persisted deep into the city, circling around the green belt that separated the wharf from the downtown district.

While waiting in the logjam, he rang the office and called out sick for the six o'clock broadcast. Normally, he felt derelict when skipping out on his duties. As popular as he was in Boston, he was insanely insecure about his brief reign as the city's top news anchor.

Whenever he was at home or on vacation, he found it almost impossible to relax. He'd watch Lancaster Rand—his replacement—sitting in *his* news chair, peddling his youthful good looks and journalism degree from Columbia. With a stiff drink in hand, Gideon would then spend the next thirty minutes cursing Rand out as he delivered the news in his best Boston Brahmin accent.

He despised Rand because he believed the younger man coveted his job. He'd hoped to find a way to get him fired, but so far, his plan hadn't succeeded. Rand was competent, hailed from Beacon Hill, was an Ivy League grad like Shay, and well-liked by everyone in the newsroom. Even worse, Rand was gay, which gave him wide latitude in the office and beyond. Gideon avoided him like the plague, both socially and professionally. He hated Rand almost as much as he hated Yolanda Brown, his number one competitor. He hated her even more now, as she smiled down at him from Boston's largest billboard.

An hour and fifteen minutes later, he turned into his leafy neighborhood. He sped through the tree-lined streets until he arrived home. Two police cars sat parked along the curb. Fortunately, they were far enough away from the fairway so as not to be seen by any passing golfers. What would the members at the club say if they heard that two police cars were parked in front of Gideon Wells's home? It was how vicious rumors spread, and reputations got ruined.

He pulled into the driveway and saw something that horrified him: two members of the club walking lazily toward the tenth hole. They waved genially upon seeing him, and he waved back before quickly disappearing inside his home.

The first thing he saw were two police officers, a man and a short woman with her red hair tied into a crisp ponytail. He saw his wife lying on the couch, her eyes red as if she'd been crying. Despite the mild autumn day, she had an ugly olive blanket pulled up to her chin. Tatyana limped into the room with a glass of water and two horse pills sitting in the palm of her hand. She turned to him, her face expressionless, and gave him the slightest of shrugs. Gideon cringed at the butterfly-shaped wine spot splayed across her cheek, partially hidden by her black hair. Every time Tatyana talked, it appeared to him as if that butterfly was flapping its wings.

The officers turned and looked at him, whispering conspiratorially to one another. Everything seemed so surreal that he felt like a stranger in his own home. And to think that a few hours ago, he was preparing to bed the hottest weather girl in Boston. The thought filled him with guilt, and he swore to break it off with Mal tomorrow, before she could cause him any more trouble. Why, he wondered, did he continually keep flirting with disaster?

Tatyana grabbed her cane and hobbled over to him. The scent of her caustic perfume filled his nostrils with decay. He glanced at her briefly, trying not to stare at her birthmark, its bright merlot color nearly hypnotizing him. His wife lay on the couch, mumbling incoherently into her clenched fists, her body trembling in a way he'd never seen before. Something terrible must have happened. The female officer crouched down next to his wife and whispered something he couldn't make out. His wife nodded and then began to weep into her hands.

"What seems to be the problem?" he said, watching as Tatyana nibbled on her fingernails.

"You're Gideon Wells," the male cop said. "My wife loves you. She watches your newscast every night."

"Please thank your wife for being a fan of mine," Gideon said, forcing a smile. "Now, what seems to be the issue with my wife?"

The female officer stood. "One of your neighbor's dogs was attacked and discovered wandering around in the woods. Someone hit it over the head with a large rock. Luckily, the dog is going to be okay."

"That's horrible," he said. "But how does that concern us?"

The two officers glanced uneasily at each other.

"Please, Officers, my wife is upset and can barely speak. The news of this will only make her symptoms worse."

"Your wife recently had a confrontation with the dog's owner. It happened while she was out walking through the neighborhood."

Gideon laughed. "Surely, you don't think my wife had anything to do with this?"

The two cops stared at him.

"She would never harm a hair on any creature's head. Shay is a warm and loving person."

"The dog ran out of its owner's yard and approached your wife as she was walking past the property. She kicked it, and the sitter recorded it on her phone."

"Maybe my wife felt like the dog was attacking her," he said.

"It's a small dog, sir. It can't weigh more than ten pounds," the woman officer said.

"The woman discovered it this morning in the woods behind her house, bloodied and confused," the male officer said.

"And a few days before that, the woman claims your wife berated her young son as she walked past their property," the woman cop added.

"This is ludicrous," he said. "My wife has suffered a serious brain injury. She was assaulted and left to die near the soup kitchen where she volunteered. The last thing Shay would ever do is threaten a child or hurt a small dog."

"I'm sorry for not keeping eye on her," Tatyana said.

"It's not your fault, Tatyana. I appreciate all you've done for this family," he said, placing a hand on her shoulder. She shot him a look that nearly chilled his soul, and he quickly removed his hand. He turned to the officers, wholly mindful of the strong image he hoped to project. "Tell me you won't be pressing charges. Do you have any idea how this could hurt my reputation if word of this got out?"

"We won't be pressing charges at this time, Mr. Wells, seeing as how we don't have all the information yet," the male officer said. "I'm sure we can handle this in a confidential manner. Of course, we can't prevent your neighbor from talking to the press, or pressing charges."

"I'll sue that woman if she breathes a word of this to anyone. For God's sake, she should have kept that mutt on a leash."

The officers spent a few minutes speaking to his wife before thanking her for their time. When they had all the information at hand, Gideon walked them to the door, looking nervously back toward the golf course, eager to shield them from the view of any passing club members. Luckily, the tenth fairway was empty at the moment. As soon as he returned inside, Tatyana offered to make him a cup of coffee. He walked into the living room and sat down on the sofa next to his wife. Seeing as how he'd called in sick for the night, a double olive martini sounded nice right now, but he knew this was not the time for a drink. He caressed his wife's cheek as he tried to reassure her that everything would be all right.

Tatyana returned with his coffee, prepared just the way he liked it. She stood above him, her eyelids heavily rouged, and stared down at his wife. She smelled as if she'd splashed on half a bottle of perfume. But considering all that she'd done for his family, he thought it best not to say anything.

His wife had stopped crying and stared ahead in a mindless daze. It almost seemed as if she'd slipped into a catatonic state. Her eyes appeared glassy and unmoving. He removed his hand from her mess of blond hair. None of this made any sense. Then again, the doctor did say that his wife might experience a wide range of emotions during her recovery. But it had been four months since the attack. He would have thought her symptoms might have receded by now. Only the opposite seemed to be happening; she appeared to be getting worse.

As Shay closed her eyes, Gideon had the sudden urge to turn on the television and check out how Lancaster was faring in his place. When he watched Rand, he secretly hoped for a major screw-up of some kind: a wardrobe malfunction, coughing fit, or embarrassing mispronunciation. And on the rare occasion that Lancaster did falter, his heart skipped with joy.

"What happened with this dog?" he whispered to Tatyana.

"It is true. Your wife kicked it. I saw it on policeman's computer."

"Did you ask Shay about the encounter?" Her scent was making him nauseous.

"Says she does not remember kicking it. Or swearing at young boy."

"This is not good."

"It is my fault, Mr. Wells. I forced her to take these walks. I thought exercise and fresh air might help her feel better."

"You can't blame yourself, Tatyana."

"She was doing so good. Then this happened."

He asked Tatyana to keep an eye on her while she slept. An aching throb of uncertainty fell over him as he made his way to the easy chair. Clicking on the seventy-inch flat screen, he switched the channel until he stopped on the familiar face of Lancaster Rand. With his perfect elocution and chiseled good looks, Rand could have had any woman in town had he not been….

His fists tensed. The mere sight of Rand sitting in his chair pissed him off. He thumbed the remote as if gunning down his rival. Like a roulette wheel, the channel stopped on Yolanda Brown. After many years on top, Brown was now the number-two-rated anchor in Boston, and he hoped to keep it that way. He watched Brown for fifteen arduous minutes and found her entertaining in the worst possible way.

The next thing he saw caused him to jerk forward in his seat. A reporter stood on a tree-lined street, interviewing a vaguely familiar woman in an even more familiar location. The interview was followed by a clip of an even more familiar man. The man was ridiculously handsome with feather-blown hair and a square jaw, and he was sitting behind a news desk with the backdrop of the Boston skyline behind him. Then came a grainy video of a yapping dog being kicked by an angry woman.

He couldn't believe his eyes because *he* was the man sitting behind that desk. And the woman kicking that little dog *was* Shay. That goddamn Brown was trying to capitalize on his woes and regain her lead in the ratings. How dare she use his wife's misfortune as the lead story for her newscast.

It was a low blow and totally uncalled for. But at least she hadn't reported about the dead dog. That could never be revealed to the public. He realized he had to make sure that story never came to light.

SHAY

Shay couldn't remember getting up off the couch last night. So when she woke up in her own bed, she felt a pang of hopelessness. *What's wrong with me?* She lifted the satin sheet off her damp body and sat up on the edge of the mattress, trying to keep her head from spinning. On the nightstand sat her water bottle and two prescription pills laid out in a perpendicular fashion and resembling an equal sign. She popped them in her mouth, took a swallow of water, and sat back on propped arms. Her clothes for the day sat folded neatly on the dresser, but she didn't feel like peeling off her pajamas just yet.

An ominous feeling swept over her as she shuffled out to the living room. Was it dread? A sense of futility? She didn't even know what day it was. Suddenly, her surroundings seemed unfamiliar and cold. It took a few seconds of wakeful mindedness before she reoriented herself to her environment. Yes, this was her home. But who was that dark-haired woman sitting on the sofa next to the blind girl? Such an odd pair the two of them made. Something reptilian inside her brain kicked in, causing her to weep inconsolably. The little girl was her daughter, and the woman sitting across from her was their new housekeeper. How could she not recognize her own daughter?

Upon sensing her mother's presence, Quinn got off the sofa and navigated over to where she stood. Quinn wrapped her arms around her and squeezed. How she loved this little girl. And what about the woman on the sofa, dressed conservatively in a linty Mohair sweater and drab black dress and with that wine spot splashed over her face? She couldn't begin to express her gratitude to the housekeeper for keeping an eye on her daughter in their time of need. If only she could remember the woman's name.

"It's okay, Momma. Please don't cry," Quinn said, squeezing her so tightly that Shay felt her diaphragm getting compressed.

"I'm sorry for the way I've been acting as of late."

"You don't need to apologize. It's your injury that caused you to do it."

"Do what?" She lifted Quinn's head so that her useless eyes stared up at her.

Quinn turned to Tatyana as if asking for the woman's permission, but the dour maid averted her eyes.

"I couldn't have done anything *that* bad," Shay said, wiping strands of hair off her daughter's ear.

"The police said you kicked the neighbor's dog," Quinn said.

Shay burst out laughing. What kind of sick joke were these two pranksters playing? Never in her life would she hurt another living thing. A good deal of her life had been dedicated to helping people, whether volunteering at that soup kitchen or reporting the news. She'd always operated under the belief that improving people's lives was a worthy goal. For her daughter to say such a thing was laughable.

She guided Quinn back to the sofa and then sat in the easy chair, staring at the sad-looking woman who refused to make eye contact with her.

"Why are you saying this, Quinn? Are you trying to hurt my feelings?"

"No, Momma. That's what they said on the news."

"I would never do anything like that. You believe me, right?" She knelt down so that she was face-to-face with her daughter. "Whoever is saying this about me is lying."

"But they have a video of you doing it," the girl said.

"Who's 'they'?"

"The police," Tatyana interrupted. "Your husband went over and threatened to sue neighbors if they lied to reporters about you."

"But I would never kick a dog."

"Is okay, Mrs. Wells. It is injury that caused you to do it," Tatyana said.

"Let me see that video." She held her hand out for the woman's cell phone.

Tatyana picked up her phone and fiddled with it for a spell before handing it to her. Shay saw a video at the bottom of the screen. She pressed play and watched as a pretty woman in an ugly tracksuit, wearing her blond hair tied up into a neat ponytail, shuffled down the street. A dog barked in the background, followed by the dog running out and nipping at her heels. The woman turned and delivered a series of swift kicks into the dog's ribs, causing it to whimper before scampering off.

"Is that really me?" she uttered under her breath, staring down at her daughter in disbelief.

"That dog was trying to bite you, Momma. You were just defending yourself."

She pressed play again and watched the video for the second time. The dog ran over to the woman and started to nip at her heels. The woman stopped abruptly, turned toward the dog, and then delivered a few fierce kicks to its midsection. She played it again and again, unable to believe that she was the woman in the video. But it was definitely her; there was no disputing it. And the video must have been taken by the dog's owner. She had absolutely no recollection of having done such a despicable thing. But after watching it three more times, there could be no doubt. She was wearing her newly purchased tracksuit, as well as the same perforated seaside sneakers that she'd purchased last summer while vacationing with her family on Martha's Vineyard.

Nothing in her personal history would have ever predicted such violent behavior. Yet there she was in the video—kicking it. She closed her eyes and tried to remember anything about the past few days, but nothing came to her. Maybe this brain injury really had changed her personality for the worse—a frightening thought.

The idea of going for a walk this morning now lost its allure. Besides, how would the neighbors react after what she'd done?

How could she live with herself knowing she'd committed such a vile act? Of course, she didn't really believe she kicked that dog, no matter how many times she'd watched the video. With this faulty brain of hers, which seemed to be getting worse with each passing day, how could she know anything about herself?

"Are you okay, Momma?"

"I'm sorry, honey. You know the real me would never hurt an animal like that."

"That's what we've been trying to tell you, Momma. It's not your fault."

"You have meeting with detective this morning, Mrs. Wells," Tatyana said. "I told you about it yesterday, remember?"

"No, I don't recall you telling me that," she replied, realizing how foolish she sounded. "I'm afraid I'm beginning to sound like a broken record."

"Detective says he'll be here in one hour to speak with you."

"About the dog, I assume?"

Tatyana shrugged and looked down at Quinn. Shay hadn't realized that her daughter was playing Braille Scrabble with Tatyana when she'd interrupted them. The sight of the two of them hunched over the board suddenly made her envious. Why wasn't Quinn playing the game with her instead of the housekeeper? As grateful as she was to Tatyana for helping her family, she felt the need to resume her role as caretaker and mother. If only her mind would cooperate.

"Tatyana, would you mind making me some tea and something to eat?"

"But I'm in the middle of game with Quinn."

"It's okay. I'll take over for you while you prepare it."

"Awww," Quinn complained.

This hurt her feelings more than she cared to admit. "Don't you like playing with me?"

"Sure, but you always let me win."

"That's not true," she lied. "I always try my hardest."

"I've yet to beat Tatyana, and English is her second language."

"Well, I'm going to beat you this time."

Quinn laughed. "You know you won't, Momma," Quinn said. "You're too nice."

Yes, I am too nice, which is why I would never have hurt that dog. And why I'll never beat you at Scrabble.

Tatyana got up and headed toward the kitchen. Shay eyed the woman carefully as she prepared the tea and snacks. Her shoulders slouched, ruining her posture, and her clothes seemed a half size too big. And that tangle of black hair begged for a hairdresser's gentle touch. But other than that, she seemed like a very nice woman. Maybe, when she recovered, she'd pay for Tatyana to get a cut and color. Everything about the woman shouted makeover, including her choice of perfume. Yet despite it all, there was a part of her that was envious of the housekeeper. Maybe because she had somehow managed to win the approval of her daughter, a cautious girl when it came to choosing friends.

Shay glanced at the clock. The detective would be here in less than forty-five minutes. What would she say to him? Her mind raced, and she felt helpless to control it. She waited impatiently for Quinn to form a word, remembering why she never enjoyed playing Scrabble with her. Shay lacked patience, and it continually unnerved her when playing board games with her daughter. Quinn would often sit in deep thought for minutes on end, staring straight ahead, before forming her squares into a word.

A familiar song from her youth started to play over the speakers. It brought back a whole host of emotions about her childhood. A wave of anxiety swept over her after remembering the dysfunctional home she'd been raised in. When she looked down, she realized her hands were trembling, so she asked Tatyana if she wouldn't mind playing a different song.

She waited impatiently for her daughter to make a move. The kettle on the stove whistled. Somewhere in the room, a clock ticked a bit too loudly. Shay grabbed the remote and clicked on the television, hoping to drown out the music. What was taking her daughter so long? She glanced down at her squares, a big-score word already in her head.

The voice of a newscaster bellowed out of the screen's speakers. As soon as she heard it, Tatyana walked over and shut off both the music and the TV.

"What are you doing?" Shay protested. "I was watching that."

"Your daughter hates when television is on during games. Don't worry, Mrs. Wells, the peace and quiet will do you good."

"Tatyana's right, Momma. I can't concentrate with the TV on."

"Okay," she said, eyeing Tatyana suspiciously.

After what seemed like forever, Quinn moved her squares until she'd spelled "drug" vertically. The word caused Shay to reevaluate her own decision now that she'd been given license to win. She quickly picked up her squares and spelled "quitch" using her daughter's *U*. Triple letter on Q plus ten points for the remaining letters. Forty points. As soon as she finished placing her tiles down, she felt a sense of regret.

"Quitch?" Quinn said, running her fingers over the tiles. "Is that even a word?"

"Of course it is."

"What does it mean, then, smarty pants?" Quinn asked.

"Quitch is a stubborn weed that spreads quickly," Tatyana said, placing cup, saucer, and plate down on the table. On it sat triangles of crustless sandwiches filled with avocado and egg salad.

Shay picked up a triangle and took a bite. "This is delicious, Tatyana. Where did you learn to make this?"

"I used to work as cook," Tatyana said. "I could give you recipe if you like."

"Forget the sandwiches. How did you know the meaning of that word?"

Tatyana shrugged and leaned over to study the board. "I read many books when I first come to America. It helped with my English."

It felt as if the woman was showing her up, but that seemed impossible given the mild nature of her personality. Shay picked up another wedge and bit into it. The sandwiches made her realize how ravenous she'd been. It had been over twelve hours since her last meal. The herbal tea had a calming effect on her and was much needed at the moment.

Quinn rocked in her chair, contemplating the next word she might form. Although Shay hated to do it, she excused herself from the game. Surprisingly, Quinn didn't mind. She actually seemed happy that Tatyana was resuming her place.

Shay felt dizzy now and sat back in the chair, watching the two of them compete. The up-and-down nature of her moods was the most frustrating aspect of her recovery. Just when she thought she was doing better, she seemed to suffer another setback. This caused her to doubt herself and her judgment. She often felt like a ghost inhabiting this house, with no purpose or reason for living except to eat, sleep, and recover from her injury. At times, she found it difficult to love her own daughter.

A sense of resignation spread through her. She closed her eyes and listened to the sound of Quinn and Tatyana debating the merits of a word. It almost felt as if the two were aligned in some quixotic scheme to overthrow her maternal reign. She opened one eye and studied Tatyana, whose wry, choppy commentary throughout the game caused Quinn to giggle. Yet the woman barely smiled as she stared single-mindedly down at the board, one hand supporting her chin. The wine stain, Shay noticed, darkened when exposed to the light. And her eyes were as dark as coals. She couldn't help thinking that there was something tragic about this housekeeper.

"Is that a Russian accent, Tatyana?"

The woman glanced up at her. "Yes."

"What part of Russia did you come from?"

"I'm Chechen." She returned her gaze to the board, seemingly not eager to discuss the matter any further.

The name of that region sent a tremor through her system. No wonder Tatyana didn't care to discuss her past. Shay remembered being a teenager and watching reports of the Chechen War. Bloodshed and tragedy had forever haunted that backwater region. Thousands of Chechens had died in the conflict or fled to other countries. She imagined a terrified young orphan sporting a butterfly wine stain, escaping her homeland, and then arriving on these shores, scared, lonely, and with the emotional scar of war etched deep on her soul. Thinking about Tatyana's past caused her to have pity on the woman. She admonished herself for feeling jealous and promised to never bring up the woman's history again.

The doorbell rang, the effect similar to an air horn going off in her head. She sat up and tried to collect her thoughts as Tatyana stood. How would she answer all the detective's questions?

"Is detective, Mrs. Wells," Tatyana called out to her.

"Please let him in."

The door closed, and Tatyana led the man over to the board game.

"Hello, Mrs. Wells. I'm Detective Carr from the Boston PD."

"Nice to meet you," she said, shaking his hand. "You've met Tatyana, our housekeeper. And this is my daughter, Quinn."

"I'll have you know, Quinn, that I'm the reigning Scrabble champ in the family. You any good?"

"Yup, but not good enough yet to beat Tatyana. But I will one of these days," Quinn said, looking up and smiling.

"Would you like us to take our game in the other room, Mrs. Wells?" Tatyana asked.

"That's all right. The detective and I can talk in the rotunda." She turned toward the man. "We shouldn't be very long, right?"

"I wouldn't think so."

"Good, because I'm starting to get tired."

He followed her to the very end of the house, where they sat on matching leather sofas. She couldn't wait to be done with this cop.

QUINN

After her mother and the detective left the room, Quinn turned her focus back on the game.

"Whose turn is it?" Quinn asked.

"Yours," Tatyana said.

She felt her tiles again to see what letters she had.

"You were right about your mother," Tatyana said.

"What was I right about?" She continued to feel her tiles.

"She's too nice to beat you at Scrabble. Is why she will never be able to keep you safe."

"Because she's too nice?"

"No, because she's has bad side to her."

Quinn lifted her head, surprised to hear this. "You're wrong about my mother. She's an amazing person."

"I wish that were true, Quinn, but I know things about people, and your mother has bad side to her. Of course I never knew her before her injury."

"Stop saying that, Tatyana. You're making things up."

"No, I'm right about this. Your mother is very sick lady."

"You watch. She'll get better and be herself again."

"I don't think so. Someone with her type of brain injury only gets worse with time. You watch and see how badly she starts to treat you."

Quinn removed her hand from the tiles. "You're wrong about that. Maybe you shouldn't be working here if you feel that way about my mother."

"Can you keep a secret?"

Quinn nodded, nervous about what this woman might say next.

"I followed your mother when she took her walks. Make sure she was alright."

"Okay."

"I saw her kick that dog and swear at that little boy. I also saw her hit dog over the head with rock. I rushed over to her before she killed it."

Quinn felt tears forming in her eyes.

"Then I took your mother home and cleaned her up."

She knew this woman was lying. Or was she? They did have her mother on video kicking that dog. And yet there was no way she'd ever believe that her mother was an evil person, head injury or no head injury.

"I don't believe you," Quinn said.

"It doesn't matter if you believe me. Is the truth. Your mother hurt that dog, and I'm afraid she might hurt you, too."

Quinn lifted her arm and swiped the Scrabble pieces off the board. They crashed against the floor. She ran up to her room, tears spilling down her cheeks, and fell into the mattress. No way that awful maid was right about her mother. Once she got her health back, she would return to being her old, loving self. Maya never would have spoken to her like that. Quinn told herself to never let her guard down around Tatyana, even though a small part of her was worried that the housekeeper was right.

SHAY

The oval room had large windows that overlooked the tenth hole and let in plenty of sunlight. Shay switched on the gas fireplace, feeling perpetually cold since the attack.

Detective Carr glanced around at his surroundings, obviously impressed with what he saw. The shelves were filled with hardcovers, and they lined the surrounding walls. From their vantage, they were afforded a full and unobstructed view of the tenth green. No golfers were on it right now, and she was thankful for that. Then again, she could always close the shutters, but that would block out the natural sunlight. Sometimes at dusk or dawn, while enjoying a cup of coffee, she'd gaze out over the course and see a deer traipsing across the fairway or scuttling past the flagstick before disappearing into the woods.

"Arc you here about the attack, Detective, or about my neighbor's allegations?" She sat down across from him.

"I suppose you could say this is an all-encompassing visit."

"Forgive me, but I neglected to ask if you'd like some coffee."

"Thanks, but I'm afraid I've had too much coffee already," he said, taking out his notebook and pen the old-fashioned way. "It's been four months since the attack, Mrs. Wells. Has anything come back to you about the events of that night?"

"Unfortunately, my recovery has not been going as smoothly as I'd hoped, which means that I still have no recollection of what happened, other than what I've already told the police."

"According to my notes, the last thing you remember that night is walking back to your car."

"Yes. I remember it was warm that evening and that there were lots of street people roaming around."

"And you weren't afraid to be walking around in that area that late at night?"

"I'd been volunteering at that soup kitchen for three years, and nothing remotely like that had ever happened to me. The one time someone ever gave me a problem, a group of them cornered the guy and told him to leave me alone."

"They must have liked you."

"Maybe *respect* is the right word. I'd been serving that population long enough that many of them had become accustomed to my presence there."

"Maybe your attacker didn't know you as well as you thought."

"It's possible, but I highly doubt it."

"Why?"

"You must have read my statements, Detective. My attacker called me an uppity bitch. Then she mentioned my daughter. . It's the one thing I remember about my attack.""

"Maybe someone was using you to get back at your husband."

"Get back at him for what?"

He shrugged. "I have no idea."

"I'm so confused right now because of this head injury. But one thing I'll never forget and that's what my attacker said to me that night."

"I've been over to the shelter a number of times and questioned many of the people there. No one claimed to have witnessed your attack."

"Lucky me."

"And like you said, most of them seemed to genuinely like you as a person. A few even said they would have stepped in if they saw someone trying to hurt you."

Shay smiled. "That makes me feel a little better."

"It should," he said, staring at his notebook. "Have you any enemies that you know of?"

"None that I can think of—until that attack."

"How about your husband? Does he have any enemies?"

"Everyone loves Gideon. Look at his ratings. Number one newscaster in the Boston market."

"Maybe someone's jealous of his newfound success. After all, he's played second fiddle to Yolanda Brown for many years before his recent ratings spike."

"You believe that someone close to Yolanda Brown may have attacked me in order to pay back my husband?"

"We have to keep an open mind," he said. "Not that it's in my jurisdiction, but would you care to elaborate about those incidents with your neighbor?"

"I honestly can't remember doing any of that, but I don't deny that it was me in that video."

"I take it you have no recollection of kicking your neighbor's dog."

"Good God, no," she said, already exhausted from this conversation. "I've never in my life hurt another living thing. I even trap spiders and houseflies and send them on their way."

"From what I know about brain injuries, which isn't a whole lot, I'd say having memory lapses is a pretty common occurrence."

"Yes. Headaches and light sensitivity, too. And lots of ear ringing." She studied his expression for a clue as to what he was thinking. "Does this mean I'm under arrest?"

"No, but I should inform you that your neighbor is considering pressing charges. We have no proof that you bloodied her dog with a rock, and even if you did, I'm sure there's extenuating circumstances on account of your injury," he said.

"I'm telling you, it wasn't me," she said, remembering that video. "Or at least the real me didn't do it."

"As for kicking the dog, there's reason to believe that you felt under attack. Technically, her dog should have been on a leash."

"This is completely out of character for me," she said. "Do you realize what might happen to my husband if people found out about this?"

He paused to let the moment pass. "You mean you haven't seen the news?"

"No." Then she remembered the video of her kicking that dog, and she winced.

"I'm afraid it's too late for that, Mrs. Wells. That video of you has been shown on all the news stations."

"Did they speculate on who injured the poor thing?"

"No. Your husband threatened your neighbor with a lawsuit if she claimed you were involved in the dog's injury. So they decided not to say anything to the press, seeing as how it would be pure speculation."

"I can't believe this is happening."

The weight of his words came crashing down on her. She now understood why Tatyana hid the newspaper from her and had shut off the television before she had a chance to watch it. The video of her kicking that dog must have surfaced and made the rounds all over town. She pictured herself gracing the front page of the *Boston Globe*, foot frozen in the air like a field goal kicker booting the ball through the uprights. At least they hadn't reported that she bashed it over the head with a rock. Just the thought of doing that made her squeamish, and she couldn't imagine how badly that would hurt Gideon's reputation. Or how it would play out with the members of his golf club, never mind her own fragile psyche.

"Did you have any problems with this neighbor prior to the incident?"

"No. I barely know the woman except to say hello at the club."

"The club being Woodbridge Golf and Tennis?" he asked, nodding toward the tenth green.

"Yes. Moving here was my husband's idea. Personally, I have no interest in golf or tennis."

"How have you and your husband been getting along?"

She thought of the many months they'd gone without sex, even before that violent assault. "As well as can be expected, considering all that's happened in the last few months. And he spends a lot of time at work, but who doesn't work long hours these days in order to make ends meet?"

"Tell me about it." He tapped his pen against his notebook.

"I won't lie to you, Detective. This injury has put a strain on our marriage, but we're working through it."

"I take it you don't—" He stopped in his tracks. "Except for the volunteering, you don't work outside the home?"

"Our daughter is blind, as you probably noticed. Gideon and I agreed early on in our marriage that it would be best if I stayed home and took care of Quinn."

"I've never seen Braille Scrabble before."

"She has dozens of Braille board games to play. And many books as well. Her life is vibrant and intellectually challenging, and we try to enrich it as often as we can. That's why I chose to stay home when she got diagnosed."

"Seems like a great kid."

"Quinn means the world to us."

To her relief, Detective Carr stood and thanked her for her time. She walked him out through the living room, where he said goodbye to Tatyana. Quinn must have quit the game and gone up to her room. Tatyana barely looked up as he left, peering into her phone, the tips of her chewed fingernails pressed against her stained cheek. Shay opened the door and watched as the detective walked down to his car. A sense of relief came over her once he drove away.

She couldn't believe she'd made it through the entire interview without crying. It gave her a small ray of hope that she might be on the road to recovery. But it had also taken a lot out of her. She excused herself from their company and dragged herself up to her room. It was all she could do to keep her eyes open. She fell onto the bed, hoping that a brief nap might refresh her.

GIDEON

The news spread quickly through the newsrooms and households of Boston and its metropolitan areas. Despite everyone in the building treating him as if nothing had happened, Gideon couldn't wait to hole up in his office and hide out from the world. He had a special button attached to his desk that allowed him to lock and unlock the door from his seat. It afforded him much-needed privacy when the stress of the job got too much. All his calls were put on hold unless urgent. Mallory had left him a few messages, but he'd been avoiding her at all costs. He desperately needed to speak again to his contact at the Your Weather Channel and see if they'd take Mallory off his hands. He could feel her growing closer to him with each passing day, which meant he needed to end this affair before it swallowed him whole. What a fool he'd been.

He blamed that Russian housekeeper for their current woes. What was she thinking by encouraging his wife to take long walks around the neighborhood? It sounded fine in theory, but the reality had proved disastrous—for both him and Shay. His wife was obviously in no shape, mentally or physically, to go anywhere by herself. The news of the dog's injury had compounded the matter, and now he worried that this fiasco might go public and reflect badly on him.

What if Shay had somehow discovered that he'd been sleeping with Mallory? Would she try to kill him like she tried to do to that dog? Or divorce him and take him to the cleaners? He didn't know his wife anymore, or understand what she was capable of doing. Yet at the same time, he felt protective of Shay, wanting to shelter her from the cruelness of the world, which, to his chagrin, he had a major part in making. The Shay from before the attack would never have done such terrible things.

Despite everything that had happened, the ratings had come out this morning, and he'd been surprised to learn that they'd climbed a notch higher. Maybe his audience had tuned in to see if he might have an on-air meltdown. Or maybe they genuinely felt sorry for him and his family. In any case, this surprising development lifted his spirits. How many years had it been since he'd beaten Yolanda Brown two weeks in a row?

He opened his laptop and saw that he had a dozen new emails. The majority of them were spam, which he quickly erased. There were three from Mallory. Nervous, he opened the first one, immediately regretting his decision. The email opened to a photograph of her lying half-naked on the bed, wearing only the silky lingerie he'd purchased for her at that suburban mall. Why was she sending him this? He deleted the email and up popped the next image: a photo of the injured, bloody dog in the woods. He thought briefly that she might be blackmailing him, and it made him furious.

His phone rang, and he picked up.

"How dare you send me those pictures, Mal," he whispered into the receiver. "What is it you want from me?"

"What the hell are you talking about?"

"That racy photograph of you lying on the bed. And how in the world did you get your hands on a photo of that bloody dog?"

"Stop it, Gideon. You're upsetting me."

"Are you trying to get back at me because I haven't answered your calls?"

"You bastard!"

"And after everything I've done by referring you to the Your Weather Channel."

"Hey, jerk, I only called to check on you and see how you're doing. I can call the cops if you want and provide them with a rock-solid alibi for the night your wife was attacked."

"You wouldn't."

"Remember that selfie we took that evening? I can send it to the cops if you'd like. That way, you can explain to them how we were screwing our brains out the night your wife was beaten. Maybe your audience might like to know about that story."

"I'm sorry, Mallory," he said, panic filling him. "I've been under so much stress lately."

"I'm well aware of that."

"I don't understand what's happening to me. These pictures were sent from your email." He tapped his finger nervously on the desk.

"I can assure you that it wasn't me who sent them," Mallory said. "I only called to thank you for what you'd done."

"Thank me for what?"

"The Your Weather Channel just offered me their weekend anchor slot."

"That's wonderful," he said, his spirits suddenly buoyed by this good news. "I assume you'll be taking the job?"

"I haven't made up my mind yet. But no matter what decision I end up making, it's imperative that we don't see each other anymore."

"Although it breaks my heart, I know you're right."

"When I told our general manager the news, he immediately offered me the evening weather desk. It's a very enticing offer."

"But you can't replace Stan. He's been reporting the weather at Channel Four for over fifteen years and is a fixture at the station."

"All good things must come to an end." She laughed. "Besides, Stan's had a long and successful run. This way, he'll have more time to brew his beer and save the planet from burning up."

"But Stan's practically a legend in weather forecasting circles."

"Fortunately for Stan, I haven't made up my mind yet."

He sat back in his chair, clearly exasperated, but unable to fully express his opinion that she'd be making a big mistake by not taking the job at the Your Weather Channel. There was no way he wanted Stan to lose his job because of his irresponsible and cheating ways. He'd feel terrible if that happened, betraying an old friend like that. But the more he pressed Mal on the issue, the more likely she'd push back. And no matter her denial, he was convinced that she'd sent him those photos. Who else could have done it?

"I've got to go now. I need to prepare for my newscast."

"Do you really believe your wife tried to kill that dog?" There was a titillation in her voice.

"Of course not. My wife's incapable of doing such a terrible thing."

"But I saw her on the news kicking that poor thing."

"That dog was attacking her. That's the only reason I can think why she kicked it."

"How's your daughter handling all this?"

The mention of his daughter irritated him. They'd agreed to never bring Quinn up in conversation. "She'll be fine. She's a resilient child."

"She must be resilient if she's seen that video." Silence at the end of the line. "I'm sorry, Gideon. I didn't mean it that way."

"I'm quite sure you didn't, Mal, but her making fun of her disability is nothing to joke about," he said, barely able to contain his anger. "Just make sure to think long and hard before you turn down that gig at Your Weather Channel. An opportunity like that may never come your way again."

"Believe me, I know."

After hanging up the phone, he turned and stared out the window, thinking about his life. Growing up as a child without good role models, he idolized anchors such as Brokaw and Rather, spending many hours studying tapes of them. He'd always wanted to be respected and thought of with the same reverence as the legends from years ago. He wanted to be loved by people, two things he didn't get at home. Much of his college years were spent shedding the vestiges of his lower-class roots, as well as that thick, career-hindering Boston accent that made him sound like a hood.

During his early years, he'd hoped to one day be culled for greatness by one of the major networks. But now, at the age of forty-five, he'd given up on his dream of achieving national prominence and had come to a begrudging acceptance of his status as a big fish in a small pond.

Gideon reflected on how he'd gotten into this terrible mess. After one failed marriage that produced no children, he'd been fully prepared to take advantage of his bachelor status and date Boston's most eligible women.

At thirty-three, he'd been at the top of his game, both professionally and sexually. He'd suffered a messy, public divorce, which put a major squeeze on his bank account. After three miserable years of married life, he'd finally been set free—and he wasn't going to waste the opportunity.

But shortly after his divorce, he'd met Shay and fell crazily, madly in love. She was the most beautiful creature he'd ever laid eyes on. What was it about love that caused temporary insanity in men like him? A kind of love that turned testosterone-addled brains into corn mush. He'd been warned by all his friends not to fall for anyone while on the rebound. But he had, catching the love bug before he even knew what had hit him.

Shay had been a midday anchor at the station and had rebuffed all his advances, until finally relenting over a glass of wine at a party held after the Emmy Awards. He thought back to those heady days and the sheer exhilaration of the chase, and then falling in love. It was like being high on a two-cocktail buzz, twenty-four-seven. She'd been a stunning visage when the two made their rounds about town. Arm candy, his closest friends teased him. But Shay was anything but arm candy. She had a fierce intellect, which was evident by her Harvard degree and one Emmy Award. And like him, she was the child of a dysfunctional upbringing, the extent of which she never fully explained.

Six months into their relationship everything seemed wonderful. Coffee and bagels on Sunday morning while she read the *New York Times*. There were no random trips to the jeweler's to pick out wedding rings. No subtle hints that she was eager to tie the knot. For someone who was so strikingly beautiful and smart, she was surprisingly *nice*. She never forced him into a committed relationship, even when he asked her twice to marry him.

But then everything changed when she announced her pregnancy. Three years of trying with his ex had left a trail of bitterness and acrimony, much of it centered around his refusal to spend vast sums of money at an IVF clinic. His ex had pleaded with him to no avail. Truthfully, he had no burning desire to be a father and take time away from his busy career. So, he agreed to a quick divorce.

He hadn't been overly worried when Shay told him the news about her pregnancy. She was twenty-four at the time and seemed as ambitious as any of the other cub reporters eager to climb the ladder. And she had that one Emmy to her name, the one hole in his otherwise stellar resume. He knew he could help advance her career. And then, as her belly grew, he had asked her to marry him again, and, surprisingly, she said yes. They sealed the deal in a quickie ceremony at city hall. That was followed by five days in the Bahamas. And because she was pregnant and couldn't drink, Gideon found himself sitting alone at the bar, horny and ready for action, but unable to hit on all the gorgeous babes in string bikinis knocking back the Bahama Mamas.

He supposed he didn't have to marry Shay, but by that time, he'd been so in love that he couldn't *not* marry her. Not to mention, she was pregnant with his first and only child.

He'd become maniacal about his ratings. Even the slightest threat to his second-tier status caused him to worry about his future. What would happen if he failed to marry Shay, and she made a big stink about it? What if she complained to the media and said that he'd not been a good father and partner? How would that play out with his audience? Would he fall to third place and cease being Yolanda Brown's biggest competitor?

And then Quinn was born, and everything changed. There was no doubt that he grew to love his daughter and was thankful for her presence in his life. She grounded him. She added depth and richness to his life where it had not previously existed. There was an added benefit as well; it made it easier for him to fit in socially at work. At various functions, he'd take out his cell phone and proudly show everyone his hundreds of baby photos.

Everyone said how much having a child humbled him and made him more relatable. Surprisingly, and completely unexpectedly, the arrival of his daughter altered his public image, transforming him from an eligible bachelor into Boston's most consummate family man. The new image of Gideon Wells pleased him immensely, and he stepped right into the role with frequent television and billboard ads. The *Boston Globe* even did a flattering piece on him, with a splashy photo of him cradling Quinn in his arms. It opened him up to endless marketing campaigns, and after the story appeared in print, he used every opportunity he could to promote his deep ties to family.

Was doing this exploitative? Most certainly. But why let a good story go to waste? His family had become a valuable asset, one he couldn't deny or ignore. And he did really love them, even if that love was entirely in the abstract. The situation benefitted everyone involved as long as he kept his libido in check—his one major flaw in life. The only troubling aspect of his new status as a family man was that the women around town now found him even *more* attractive. For that reason, he rarely took off his wedding ring, which only made the problem worse.

His life became further complicated when a tumor was discovered along Quinn's optic nerves. The diagnosis jarred him, and Shay nearly lost it when the doctors informed her that Quinn would most likely lose her sight. It was a devastating blow to a couple who, on first appearances, seemed to have everything. He needed to take time away from his broadcasts, which secretly pained him. The story of his family's struggles played out in all the Boston newspapers and local television shows, burnishing his image in ways he'd never expected. The nights he took off made his audience miss him even more. Fortunately for him, this was before Rand Lancaster got hired. There were no superstars waiting in the wings, eager to steal his job. Even if there had been, none could have matched his combination of trustworthiness and charm. The confluence of family, celebrity, and personal tragedy had turned him into one of Boston's favorite sons. An icon of sorts. Well-respected and trusted by the millions of viewers who hung on his every word. He even beat Yolanda for three consecutive weeks during that ratings period. Only those closest to him knew how much his daughter's diagnosis pained him.

A loud knock on the door shook him out of his thoughts. The interruption irritated him, especially after he'd given his underlings specific instructions that he not be disturbed. He directed the person to go away, but the door opened. The head of a husky gray-haired man poked through the opening. The man looked familiar in the way one of those old movie stars from the fifties did. Square jaw and the wide, flat nose of a boxer. Obviously, a cop nearing retirement.

"Sorry to bother you, Mr. Wells," the man said, not pronouncing his *Rs* in true Boston fashion, sounding like his father did those many years ago. In his left hand was an oversized cup of Dunkin' Donuts coffee.

"Can I help you?"

"Detective Carr of the Boston PD. I spoke to your wife the other day."

"Yes, come in." The detective moved nimbly, and he could tell that the man had been an athlete in a previous life, something he'd never been. "How can I help you, Detective?"

A smile spread over his blocky face.

"Something amuse you?"

"No, it's just that my wife would go bananas if she knew I was in Gideon Wells's office. She watches you religiously every night."

"She does, does she?" Flattery never failed to charm him, and the fact that he was aware of this insecurity made him feel better.

"You're practically like a member of our family. I often think she'd throw me to the curb if you came knocking."

He laughed. "Since we're practically like family, then, why don't you call me Gideon?"

"No, sir, I don't want to get too cozy. I'd hate to start watching Yolanda Brown because of the conflict of interest."

"Don't even go there," he said, pointing at the cop. "So, what brings you here?"

"I'm afraid we've made little progress in finding the person, or persons, who attacked your wife. We questioned every staff member and client at that soup kitchen and have thus far come up empty-handed."

"I imagine that someone must have seen something," he said, staring anxiously at the coffee ring on the edge of his desk. "I want the person who did this to be held accountable and thrown in jail."

"I couldn't agree more." The detective's expression changed, and now he appeared uncomfortable with what he was about to say. "Can you tell me again where you were that night?"

The question penetrated him like a hollow bullet, and he knew that any delay in answering would reflect badly on him. "I told everything to that other detective."

"Yes, but we need to double-check our information in case we missed something."

"Are you implying that I attacked my wife?"

The detective stared at him as if offended. "I would never accuse you of that, sir. We're simply covering all our bases in order to be thorough."

"I'll tell you what I told the other cop. I often take long walks between the evening broadcasts. It helps clear my mind before delivering the news."

"And that night you took a walk?"

"Yes, and you can see me on that video walking through the gate just like I did every other evening. When I got the call that my wife had been attacked, I immediately called the station and told them I wouldn't be returning. Then I went straight back to the station, got in my car, and drove to the hospital to be with her."

"Why would you allow your wife to be in that neighborhood so late at night? It's not the safest place after dark."

"Allow?" He laughed. "You obviously don't know my wife, Detective. She's a headstrong woman who was hell-bent on volunteering at that stupid place. Nothing I said or did could persuade her to give it up. Not even the arrival of Quinn."

"I met your daughter the other day, and she seems like a remarkable girl."

"She is." He felt horrible about his adulterous behavior when he considered all that Quinn had gone through with the chemo, radiation, and losing her eyesight.

"I don't mean to delve into your personal life, but was your daughter born blind?"

"No," he said, always happy to show off his paternal side. "She was diagnosed with retinoblastoma at a young age. Surprisingly, it wasn't the cancer that cost her her eyesight. It was the toxicity from the treatments, which included two years of radiation and cryotherapy."

"That's a shame," the detective said, shaking his head.

"We're just happy she survived the ordeal. We see Quinn as a fully functional girl with a bright future ahead of her."

"That's wonderful," he said, pronouncing it "wunnaful." "Can you think of anyone who might want to hurt you?"

"By attacking my wife? No." He laughed at the absurdity of such a question, knowing it wasn't absurd at all. "Sure, we newscasters engage in friendly rivalries from time to time. We're all jockeying for the top position, but not to the extent that we would hurt our loved ones. At the end of the day, Detective, we're all friends," he said, knowing that he'd *never* be friends with Rand Lancaster or Yolanda Brown.

"Have you had any problems with fans?"

"Back in my early days when I was single and far better looking than I am now," he said, laughing. "I remember a few crazy stalkers, but it's been many years since anyone has become obsessed with me in that way."

"Do you remember their names?

"No, it happened too long ago for that."

"I guess that's all the questions I have for now," the detective said, standing. "Thank you for your time, sir."

"No, thank you. If I can be of any help, Detective, please let me know."

"I most certainly will," he said, his face breaking out into a smile. He stood unmoving as if expecting more.

"Is there something else I can help you with?"

"This is kind of an awkward request, but would you mind taking a selfie with me? I want to show the wife. Make her a little jealous."

"My pleasure."

Gideon slid out from his desk and wrapped his arm around the detective's thick shoulder. The detective stuck his phone out as far as he could as Gideon leaned in for the kill. He flashed one of his most charismatic smiles as the two of them posed for the shot. Once the detective snapped a photograph and appeared happy with the result, he shook his hand and thanked him for his time.

Alone in his office, Gideon sat at his desk, resting his forehead in his hands. Now more than ever, he needed to message Mal and convince her to keep quiet about his whereabouts that night. Not only had he lied to the police, but if they found out he'd been cheating on his wife and had lied about it, it would look very bad for him. It wasn't out of the realm of possibility that they already considered him a suspect. If the truth came out, he would be branded as the cheating news anchor who schemed to dump his wife for the gorgeous young weather girl.

The wife who seemed to want little to do with him even *before* the attack.

He called Tatyana's cell phone and waited for her to pick up. No way he could afford his wife sneaking around in Uber cars with half a brain in her skull. Too much damage had already been done, and he couldn't afford yet another disaster. He had to clean things up.

"Yes, Mr. Wells."

"How's my wife doing?"

"About same. Very sleepy."

"Remember what we agreed upon."

"Yes."

"Whatever you do, do not let her out of your sight."

"I understand."

"Do not let her walk in the neighborhood or get out of your sight."

"I will stay with her at all times."

"And, Tatyana?"

"Yes."

"Thank you so much for helping us. You don't know how much I appreciate all that you've done for this family."

Silence.

"There might even be a nice bonus for you come Christmas."

He hung up and sat back in his chair. Thank God for Tatyana's calming presence. Despite Shay's physical confrontation with the neighbor's dog, which had been partly due to Tatyana's insistence that she go out for walks, he'd have been lost without the Russian maid.

He heard a hard rap on the door and looked at his clock. Somehow, he'd forgotten about the meeting scheduled with Barb, the station's news director. It would be a welcome distraction to everything that had happened. He stood and examined himself in the full-length mirror. Straightened his tie. Cleared his throat. Tightened his cuff links. And put on his suit jacket. Then he walked over and opened the door, smiling at his staff as if everything were all right with the world.

SHAY

Three frustrating days had passed, and Shay felt as if little to no progress was being made in regards to her health. She felt tired and disoriented all the time. Why was she not getting better? She *needed* to get better before she did something else that might get her in trouble. Despite the doctor explaining that it could take months for her brain to return to normal, she wanted to hear that a full recovery would be sooner rather than later. This continuous state of not knowing left her exhausted, as did the lapses of memory and muddled thinking.

She shuffled out to the living room and saw Tatyana taking utensils out of the dishwasher and stacking them in the cabinet. The loud, tinny racket made by the Chechen housekeeper caused her anxiety to spike. It felt like symbols being clapped in her ears. She sat down on the sofa, hands stuffed in the pockets of her robe, and looked around for Quinn, but her daughter was nowhere to be seen. It made sense when she saw the time. Quinn had long ago left for school. She wished Tatyana had woken her to see Quinn get on the bus, but in her current mental state, she'd completely lost track of the time. She didn't even know what day it was.

After stacking the dishes, Tatyana walked over and greeted her with a barely suppressed smile. She handed Shay a Dixie cup brimming with the prescription medicines, krill and CBD oils, and vitamins the doctors had prescribed for her. Three times a day since the attack, she followed this regimen. Shay held the cup in her hand, debating whether or not she wanted to swallow the contents. Instead, she placed it back down on the coffee table.

"You have doctor's appointment today, Mrs. Wells."

"Do I really have to go?"

"Seeing doctor will help you get better."

"Will you be taking me?"

"Yes. Doctor wants you to stop at lab first and get your blood drawn."

"I hate it when they draw blood. They usually have to poke me like a pincushion before they find a vein."

"If you like, I can draw your blood here before we go. I'm very good at it."

"You?" She laughed. "What do you know about that?"

"I trained to be nurse back in my country. Drawing blood is easy."

Shay stared at the housekeeper. "I'm amazed at you, Tatyana. What *can't* you do?"

Tatyana grabbed her forearm and tapped it for a plump vein. "What you need is lots of rest, Mrs. Wells."

"But I'm getting plenty of rest right now—maybe too much."

"No, this is not the kind of rest I'm talking about. Too much stress and worry in this house."

"What are you suggesting?"

"You and your family need time away. I can talk to your husband about vacation if you like."

"Vacation?"

"Help clear your mind and spend time with the ones you love."

"We haven't had much family time as of late."

"Stay here, and I will get medical kit."

Shay sat back in the chair and closed her eyes, thinking about somewhere warm and sunny, with a nice beach where Quinn could sit in the sand and make castles. Tatyana returned with her kit. She pulled the robe up over Shay's elbow and tapped the delicate veins along the underside of her forearm. The woman seemed to know exactly what she was doing, so she didn't complain, especially if it would speed things up at the doctor's office. She closed her eyes, held her breath, and felt the quick pinch. Once the needle penetrated the vein, she turned her head away so as not to see the vial filling with blood. In less than a minute, the entire ordeal was over.

"Sorry, Mrs. Wells, but I missed finding a good vein."

"It's okay, Tatyana. You tried your best."

"My best wasn't good enough to help you."

"That's okay. The nurse at my doctor's office will take my blood," she said, trying to cheer the housekeeper up. "I've been thinking about that vacation you mentioned. It does sound rather nice."

"It would be, trust me."

"But where would we go?"

"I know perfect place."

"Somewhere warm and secluded with sandy beaches and blue lagoons?" She smiled at the thought.

"No beach."

"Where, then?"

"An hour and a half from here. Western Massachusetts."

"Western Massachusetts? Why in the world would we go there?" She laughed, although she wasn't sure why. For the life of her, she couldn't think of anything for a family to do there—and she'd grown up in that neck of the woods.

"I know this farm where your daughter can work with animals and pick apples. Maybe you and your husband can have some time alone."

"Alone time? That's just what Gideon and I need."

Tatyana glanced up at her. "You like idea?"

"Yes, I do," she said. "What were you doing in Western Massachusetts?"

"I worked there years ago. That's where I learned to cook."

"You've done quite a lot of things in your life."

"No, not too much." The woman shook her head sheepishly. "I'm not important person like you and your husband."

"Don't be silly. You're extremely important to us," she said, patting Tatyana's hand. "Without you here, I'd have been lost."

"Thank you," the woman said, staring up at Shay's Emmy trophy on the shelf. "Can you tell me how one becomes news reporter like you, Mrs. Wells?"

Shay felt slightly embarrassed by the question and tried to formulate a response that would not hurt Tatyana's feelings. It would be wrong to lead her on and make her think she had a chance of getting hired on as a TV reporter. With that thick accent, nervous demeanor, and noticeable wine stain on her face, Tatyana stood little chance of ever becoming an on-air talent.

"I studied journalism in college," she said. "After that, I worked as a reporter for a few years before they offered me a desk job."

"You are very beautiful woman. That must have made getting job easy."

Shay blushed. "Thank you for that compliment, but I'd like to think that my intelligence and work ethic had something to do with it."

"I'm sorry, I didn't mean to imply..."

"It's okay. I know what you meant."

"Why quit such important job that made you so rich and famous?"

"I was never rich or famous," she said, laughing. "After becoming pregnant with Quinn, my priorities changed. Having a child with a disability does that to a person."

"But your husband didn't quit his job."

"We both agreed that I'd be the one to stay home and care for her."

"Why you? You were the one who won Emmy."

"Winning awards is not everything."

"You could still be reporter if you wanted. Many women return to work after having children."

"I was planning to return to work," she said, lying back and resting her head. "But then Quinn's cancer was discovered, and everything changed."

Tatyana averted her eyes and stared down at the table. "I would love to be a TV reporter someday and become famous like you and Mr. Wells."

"Then you should go back to college and earn your degree," she said, trying not to sound too disingenuous.

"You should think about going back to news station and becoming big star again like your husband."

She laughed. "I'm not sure I want to return to that hectic lifestyle again."

"You mean you don't want to be famous and make lots of money? And win more Emmys?"

Shay didn't know how to respond to this. Maybe the housekeeper was right. Why didn't she want to be a star like she once had been? Was it because she was too old and out of practice? She couldn't even remember if she'd garnered decent ratings or not. Or what it had been like to be on TV and earn a nice paycheck. But she did win that Emmy, and that meant something. How could she ever go back to being a reporter when she couldn't even remember what she had for breakfast?

"Your husband is very good on TV. But why should he get all the attention and not you?"

"I don't know, Tatyana. It just happened that way, and I'm okay with it."

"You should really think about it, Mrs. Wells. But first, you have to make your mind and body strong again."

Shay looked away, not wanting to talk about this subject anymore.

"You need to get dressed now so I can take you to doctor."

"I'm so tired. Can I rest for a few more minutes before we go?"

"No, or we will be late. I will get shower ready for you."

Tatyana walked toward the bathroom and disappeared. The last thing Shay wanted to do right now was leave the house, especially after that disastrous confrontation with her neighbor down the street.

Her phone buzzed. It was a text message from Jessica saying she wanted to swing by later in the day with some baked goods and coffee. It had been some time since Shay had interacted with anyone outside the house apart from her family and Tatyana. She texted Jessica back and asked if she could come by this afternoon. Jessica replied almost immediately to say that she could. The last time they'd gotten together was the dinner party she and Gideon had hosted. At the time, she had thought she might be coming out of the hazy fog she'd been mired in. But the setback had informed her otherwise, and now she felt as if she was back to square one.

Tatyana helped her into the bathroom. Although a private person, Shay didn't feel the least bit self-conscious undressing in front of the woman. It was almost as if this housekeeper was born to care for the needs of others. She reminded her of one of those humble servants in *Downton Abbey,* happily resigned to their fate.

The hot water streamed behind the glass shower door. Clouds of steam filled the room and swept up into the clattering exhaust fan. She stood for a few seconds, staring at herself in the mirror over the sink. She'd lost ten pounds—ten pounds she thought she needed to lose. But in reality, she looked pale and gaunt at this weight. Even her blue eyes lacked their usual vibrant color. If only her mind would begin to start healing, then maybe she'd look pretty again.

She opened the door and stepped into the shower stall, letting the hot water work its way into her skin and scalp. It felt so relaxing that she swore to shower every morning instead of lying in bed and staring groggily up at the ceiling. Ten minutes later, she turned off the water. Tatyana entered the room and tried to towel her off, but she shooed the woman away. Good God, she'd suffered a terrible head injury, but she wasn't helpless.

For some reason, the conversation with Tatyana kept replaying in her head. Why wasn't she back working in journalism? She'd won a coveted Emmy, something her husband had never done. She'd enjoyed a good run as a news anchor, but now she was a stay-at-home mom and seemingly content to be one, especially with Quinn's disability. Tatyana had planted the seed of doubt in her head, and now she couldn't quite remember if she'd ever *wanted* to return to her chosen field of study.

Tatyana had spread her clothes out over the bed. Although she knew Tatyana was only trying to help, the housekeeper's assertiveness seemed intrusive and unwanted. Ignoring the wardrobe picked out for her, she went into her closet and picked out something completely different. But the wardrobe on the bed was exactly what she would have chosen if given the chance. It was almost as if the woman could read her mind, which was not exactly a difficult thing to do in her feeble state.

Tatyana spoke on the phone as she made her way into the kitchen. She sat down at the breakfast bar and listened to the conversation. It didn't take long for Shay to realize that Tatyana was speaking to someone at Quinn's school. This infuriated her, but as she listened to the housekeeper, the words started to blur, and she lost track of the conversation. She badly wanted to grab the phone and handle this matter herself. Tatyana reached over and placed the Dixie cup filled with meds in front of her. Dutifully, she swallowed them with a glass of juice.

While riding to the doctor's office, she had half a mind to tell Tatyana what she thought of her meddling behavior. Explain to her that she'd been inserting herself a bit too forcefully into her family's life. Shay wondered if she was being petty. But the truth was, she would have been lost without Tatyana's help.

The landscape flew past as they drove through the quiet streets. The more Shay thought about it, the more she thought it better to hold her tongue about Tatyana's assertive nature—for now. Maybe after she recovered, she could talk to Gideon about cutting the housekeeper's hours and allowing Shay to resume her normal household duties.

Tatyana sat reading *People* magazine outside the medical office while her doctor conducted a series of tests. All her vitals seemed normal. The results of the blood tests might reveal abnormalities, but the results wouldn't come back until later. The doctor ruled out the possibility of a stroke or blood clot. Reviewing the MRI of her brain, the doctor saw nothing that caused her any concern, explaining that brain injuries were often hard to detect and that sometimes victims suffered temporary setbacks before they could begin working their way back to good health. Shay nodded, frustrated at the lack of answers, and agreed to return after the results of the blood test came back.

She felt exhausted by the time she returned home and glad when Tatyana said she needed to go out and run a few errands. The time alone would do her good. She needed some peace and quiet, and time to reflect on all that had happened. But a quick glance at her cell phone revealed that Jessica would be over in less than an hour. Hopefully, that would give her enough time to build up her strength. Maybe Tatyana wouldn't even be home by the time Jessica arrived. She wanted to speak to her friend in private and without Tatyana in the room.

"I must go now, Mrs. Wells," Tatyana said. "I need to buy groceries and then go to your daughter's school."

"Quinn's school? For what?"

"Permission slip for outing. She forgot to bring it this morning."

Shay hadn't remembered seeing a permission slip or hearing about a field trip.

"Please think about vacation idea in Western Massachusetts. Getting away from here will do you wonders. Clean air, hikes on trail, and delicious food," Tatyana said.

"The more I think about it, the better it sounds. I'll certainly give it some thought."

"Goodbye, Mrs. Wells."

Shay's eyelids began to close.

"Get some sleep, and I will see you later."

"Yes, a bit of shut-eye is just what I need right now."

SHAY

Shay was startled out of her sleep by the sound of the doorbell ringing. Glancing around, she wondered about her whereabouts. Was she at home or on vacation? In the dream she'd just woken from, she'd been hiking in the country with Quinn, who used her walking stick as if it was another set of eyes. Gideon lagged happily behind, observing the various flora and fauna. The air felt dry and inviting, and Quinn held her hand while leading her along a narrow path. The last thing she remembered in the dream was Quinn stopping and leaning over as if she could see something. Then, as if in slow motion, she reached down and allowed something to crawl into her hand. When Shay looked over her shoulder, she saw a scorpion sitting in her daughter's palm. Its two claws opened and its tail curled up over its backside so that it sat coiled above its head. Quinn turned and smiled at her. Did she know that a poisonous creature lay waiting in her hand, poised to strike?

The doorbell rang again. Shay realized she could have easily slept a few more hours. She shuffled mindlessly to the door, not caring that her hair lay in a tangled mess, or that she looked like hell. Through the peephole, she saw Jessica standing on the stoop, a white box of pastries in hand. The doorbell rang again, and she quickly opened it, cursing herself for having forgotten about their planned get-together.

"Goodness, Shay, I was getting worried about you."

"I'm so sorry, Jessica. I was taking a nap when you rang." She motioned for her to come inside. "It's why I look so awful."

"Girl, you never look awful," Jessica said, placing the white box down on the counter. "I picked up some pastries from Levain. It's only the best bakery in Boston."

"Gideon and I used to go there every weekend when we lived in town."

"Do you know how hard it was to get my hands on these? I had to find a parking spot and then wait an hour in line for these delicious confections."

"Can I make us some coffee?"

"Are you able?"

Shay laughed. "I may be brain-dead, Jessica, but I can still brew a mean cup of coffee."

"Good. You make the coffee, and I'll plate the goodies."

Shay poured water into the reservoir and loaded grounds into the filter. She pressed power, and the water began to gurgle. Once the coffee finished brewing, she carried two cups over to the living room and placed them down on the table. She sat across from her friend, suddenly ravenous for the crusty *pain au chocolat* waiting for her. Her empty stomach rumbled, and she realized that all she had to eat this morning was a piece of stale toast and a glass of orange juice. She forked off a section, watching as the crumbs sprinkled onto the plate, and placed it in her mouth. The buttery layers of pastry crust and chocolate dissolved over her tongue.

"This is lovely, Jessica. Thank you."

"Bet your ass it's lovely," she replied. "I was getting a little worried that our get-together might not happen."

"Sorry. I know I haven't been myself as of late."

"Is that why you haven't been returning my calls?"

Shay looked over at Jessica. "I had no idea you've been calling."

"God, you really have slipped. I left three messages with your maid."

"She probably told me, and I forgot." Shay laughed. "And she's a housekeeper and not a maid."

"In my household, the maids are named Miranda and Jeff."

Shay laughed. "Don't be mean to your kids. They might have to change your diapers someday."

"Good point," she said.

"And don't knock Tatyana. She's been a godsend to us."

"Maybe, but that woman's accent is enough to make my skin crawl. She sounds like one of those Russian villains in a James Bond movie."

"Come on, Jessica, she's not that bad. And the way I've been behaving lately, I'm no prize to be around, either."

"Maybe I'm making too much of everything. Stan accuses me all the time of being a drama queen."

Shay took another bite of her pastry.

"How have you been feeling lately?"

"I went to the doctor today, and she said that with these kinds of injuries, it's often two steps forward and one step back. But otherwise, I'm in good health."

"Hurry up and wait, right?"

"Exactly."

"Four months have gone by since that attack. I would think you'd be feeling better by now."

"Everyone reacts differently to brain trauma. But this ordeal with my symptoms has certainly been puzzling. My doctor said the results of the blood tests might reveal more."

"The police still have no idea who did this to you?"

She shook her head.

"Have they resolved the case with your neighbor's dog?"

"The police are not pressing charges. They're saying I was defending myself, and the dog should have been on a leash."

"That woman's a witch. None of her neighbors like her, although her husband seems to be a decent guy. Stan plays in a foursome with him from time to time."

"I just wish all this would go away."

"You still don't remember any of it?"

She shook her head.

"There's no way I'd ever believe you purposefully harmed that mutt."

"I agree, but who else could have done it? It was definitely me kicking it in that video."

"Not to be gross, but wouldn't you have had blood on your clothes? I mean, the poor dog was bashed over the head with a rock."

"Please, Jessica, it's too much for me to even think about right now."

"I'm sorry," Jessica said, lifting her shortcake and taking a bite out of it. "Why were you out walking? You're not ready to be by yourself just yet."

"I thought exercising might do me good. Besides, this is a safe neighborhood. It's one of the reasons we moved here."

"I still miss our home near Boston," Jessica said. "It was so close to the city and the T station."

"I also miss living in the city."

"I often think of all the pretentious women who live here in Woodbridge Estates. They're more venomous than the hardened criminals waiting to kill us in the city." She broke out into a peal of laughter.

Shay covered her mouth and laughed.

"Seriously, though, why would you go out walking by yourself if you weren't feeling well? Especially when you have a treadmill in the spare room."

"Tatyana said the fresh air would be good for me."

"So now this Russian housekeeper is your personal trainer?"

"Be nice, Jessica," Shay said. "She's helped us in so many ways. And she's Chechen, not Russian."

Jessica rolled her eyes.

"I'm being serious. She's done a lot for us since arriving here."

"How many days a week did Maya work?"

"Tuesdays and Thursdays."

"Everyone was shocked when you guys let her go. The Bordens snatched her up right away, and now everyone in the neighborhood is jealous of them."

"It was a mutual parting," she said, not wanting to tell her about the stolen earrings. "We both thought a change might be good."

"You can always call me if you need a hand with anything," Jessica said, reaching over and touching her arm. "I'm only a fairways away."

"Thanks, Jessica. You're a good friend."

"How did you meet this Russian woman, anyway?"

"At the coffee shop. Someone arranged the meeting." She actually couldn't remember anything about it.

"Maybe you should do a background check on her."

"No need to. She's an agency girl, and they do thorough background checks on all their hires."

"So what will you do now? You can't go back to volunteering at that soup kitchen."

"I suppose I'll need to find something else to keep me busy, especially now that Quinn is getting older and becoming more independent."

"You're so lucky to have her."

"Your kids are pretty amazing too."

"They drive me crazy at times with their constant bickering and fighting. Two teenagers is enough to send me to the funny farm."

"I couldn't even begin to imagine."

"Have you ever thought about going back to work?"

"You mean working at the station again?"

"What else could I mean?" Jessica said. "You haven't forgotten about that illustrious career you once had?"

"Of course not." But she had forgotten much of it.

"I remember watching you on TV back in the day. You were a rising star before you got pregnant with Quinn. Stan used to say that you'd one day be working at one of the big cable networks."

"That was a long time ago when I was younger and much prettier than I am now."

"Oh my God, Shay, you're even more beautiful today than when you were a young buck and all legs."

"I've forgotten everything I've ever learned about news broadcasting. And do you know how hard it would be to get back to where I once was? No, I'm happy being a wife and mother for now."

"Gideon has a lot of pull in the industry. And you did win that coveted Emmy, something he's never done in all his years on the desk."

"I'm only focused on getting healthy, not resuming any career I once had."

"It seems like you've been getting worse after you hired that maid."

"You're sounding paranoid, Jessica."

"Yeah, it's a bad habit of mine."

"You're certifiable, but that's what I love about you."

"Coming from someone who can't remember shit, that's quite a compliment."

Shay bit off some of her pastry. "We're actually considering taking a vacation. I think it'd be good for us to get out of town for a week. Then, when I get back, I'll be able to make some important decisions about where my life is headed."

"A vacation sounds nice."

"It does, doesn't it? That way, I can get some rest, and maybe we can spend some quality time together as a family."

"When did you all agree to that?"

"Actually, Tatyana suggested it just before you arrived. The more I think about it, the more I'm starting to believe it would be nice to spend time with Gideon and Quinn."

"Would you mind if Stan and I tagged along? I might be able to get my mother to stay with my two hellions."

"Honestly, I haven't even broached the subject with Gideon yet. Do you know how hard it's going to be to pry him away from that news desk?"

"Stan's the complete opposite. He can't wait to use all his vacation time to go on a cruise or hang out in the Bahamas drinking rum swizzles."

"I wish Gideon was more like Stan in that regard."

"Where are you guys thinking of going?"

"Tatyana suggested we go to a ranch in Western Massachusetts. It's a place we can hike and be in nature. A place where Quinn can ride horses and work with animals. And if we want, Gideon and I can spend some time to ourselves."

"Your Russian maid suggested all that?"

"Chechen housekeeper."

"Why go to Western Massachusetts when there are so many other great places to go?"

Shay shrugged. "Tatyana said she once worked there as a cook and claimed it's a wonderful vacation spot. Besides, it was just a suggestion. But the more I think about it, the more appealing it sounds."

"Your housekeeper seems too good to be true."

"I get the impression she's had a difficult life."

"Why do you think that?"

"There's something tragic about her. It can't be easy to live with that birthmark over her face, as well as finding a suitable mate."

"Yeah, must be tough."

"Poor thing asked me this morning how she could become a news anchor. I didn't have the heart to tell her the truth."

"That with that birthmark on her face, she's better off pursuing a career in radio?"

"Not to mention that thick accent and bum leg." She broke off another piece of pastry. "It broke my heart when she asked me about it."

"What did you tell her?"

"I said that she should earn a degree in journalism like everyone else. By that time, even if she did decide on such a career, she'd realize her limitations."

"She'd realize that the news industry is a highly competitive field even if you're Miss Universe blessed with a Mensa IQ."

"Now you're getting it."

"Stan's always worried that he'll lose his job to one of those daffy bimbos who can point at a weather map and show off her big boobs. He's fortunate to have a loyal following and a GM who loves him."

"I'm so glad you came over today, Jess. You've made me feel so much better."

"We need to do this more often. I may not be able to heal you, Shay, but I can sure make you laugh."

"That you can do."

"Just do me a favor and keep your eye on Natalia."

Shay laughed. "You know very well her name is Tatyana."

Jessica stood to leave. "Take care of yourself, girl."

"Aye, aye, Captain."

"And good luck with those vacation plans. Nothing better than getting your hands dirty and shoveling cow shit."

"Please don't say anything to Stan. I have to ease into this gently with Gideon."

Jessica zipped her lips shut and walked toward the door. Shay followed, giving her friend a big hug before she left. On the counter sat the box of delicious pastries Jessica had left behind. She could barely finish her *pain au chocolat* she was so full. What would she do with the leftovers? Gideon had become fanatical about his carb intake the older he got, and Quinn ate the same bland cereal every morning. She figured she'd give the box to Tatyana to take home.

By the time she reached her easy chair, she felt exhausted. How could that be? She'd consumed an entire cup of coffee. If caffeine couldn't keep her awake, then nothing would. No need to fight it. She reclined in the chair and closed her eyes. Hopefully, she wouldn't return to that dream where Quinn held that scorpion in her palm. If every dream could be interpreted, what did that one mean? Before she could come up with an answer, she drifted off.

GIDEON

Two days passed without incident. Gideon felt deathly afraid to move lest he rouse the gods and incur their wrath. The only good news as of late, other than besting Yolanda in the ratings three weeks in a row, was that he'd been nominated for another Emmy. But the Emmy Awards were a sore topic for him. In polite company, it was the one subject everyone knew not to bring up in his presence. Not winning an Emmy in the last sixteen years had been the only stain on his otherwise unblemished résumé.

Gideon knew that the odds of him winning this year were low. He believed that insiders within the industry knew his reputation as a narcissist and insecure cad. Hell, he even knew this about himself. The family man image he projected was mainly for the public, and they ate it up. Nevertheless, sixteen years of solid ratings spoke volumes about his influence in the Boston news market. He could be effusive in his praise for staffers who served him well, helping them advance their careers. But he could also dispatch misfits and potential rivals with little to no remorse. For this reason, staffers kept their mouths shut about his sometimes unprofessional and inappropriate behavior. Everyone knew that a bad word from Gideon Wells could torpedo a young reporter's career. Even those who left for greener pastures spoke highly of him, knowing that his reach in the world of broadcasting was long.

His phone rang. This was his private number, and he'd given it to only a few trusted people. Like most days, he had little work to perform other than deliver the news. Sitting unfinished on his desk was the daily crossword puzzle.

"Hello," he answered.

"Listen to me, Gideon, and don't say a word until I'm finished," an unfamiliar woman's voice said in a posh British accent.

"Who is this?"

"We both know that Logan Burrows is getting on in age and past his prime."

"Who is this? And why have you called my private cell number?"

"Forget who I am," the woman said. "The question is: Do you know who Logan Burrows is?"

He laughed at such inanity. "Of course I do. He's a legend in the industry. Without question, the finest news anchor of his era."

"Too bad he's old news."

"Now you listen here—"

"No, you listen, Gideon. I can't give you my name right now, because it's all hush-hush here at the network, but upper management is looking to force Burrows into retirement. That means he'll need to be replaced."

"Replaced?" The remark intrigued him. "I'm sorry to hear this about Logan, but how in the world does that affect me?"

"Your name came up as his possible replacement. It's the reason why we need to keep this conversation close-lipped."

He couldn't have been more shocked if someone told him he'd won the lottery. Or his first Emmy. He'd always believed his time had come and gone at one of the major networks. "But what about Alyssa Gomez at the White House Bureau? I hear they're very high on her."

"Her test screenings were abominable. The future does not look promising for Ms. Gomez at the moment."

"How about Dalton Ruggles, your weekend anchor?"

"We considered Dalton until we discovered a few skeletons in his closet involving a brown-face Halloween party he's alleged to have attended at Dartmouth."

"Yes, brown-face is definitely a no-no these days," he said. "Could you at least tell me your identity and who you work for?"

"I'm not at liberty to do that right now, but suffice to say, if you breathe a word of this to anyone, the network will vehemently deny it, and you'll end up out of the running. And if that happens, Gipper, you'll be history in this industry."

How did she know his nickname? "I swear I'll keep my mouth shut."

"So, are you interested if the position opens up?"

Am I interested? "It's so sudden, but I'd be lying if I said no."

"Good, because there are people here at the network who are quite impressed with your résumé and long track record of stellar ratings."

"Thank you."

"No need to thank me. You're the one who's putting in all the hard work."

"I'm just happy to hear that someone appreciates my talents." He didn't know what else to say, he was so flabbergasted.

"We'll be in contact, Gideon. Make sure you don't utter a word of this to anyone."

"Trust me, I'll not."

The line went dead. Was he imagining this conversation, or had that call been real? He pinched himself and sat back in his chair in shock. The notion of replacing Logan Burrows seemed both daunting and exciting beyond his wildest dreams—and he couldn't think of anything he coveted more. He envisioned himself reporting to a huge audience: an audience that dwarfed the one he currently broadcast to every night. And what about the salary? It had to be in the eight figures. He rubbed his hands together and thought about the possibilities. If it happened, and there was no guarantee he'd get the job, he could see himself being talked about in the same breath as Cronkite, Huntley, Brokaw—and Logan Burrows himself.

The crossword puzzle lost its allure due to his excitement. Keeping this secret was killing him, but he knew enough to keep his big mouth shut. Or get his hopes up. This job offer could blow over in seconds. But what an honor to even be considered for that prestigious desk assignment. And what if, by some miracle, they did offer it to him? He'd need to convince Quinn and Shay to leave their comfortable surroundings and move to Manhattan.

He wanted to run out into the hallway and shout to the heavens, announce to the world that he was being considered for one of the top anchor jobs in the country. Heir to the throne of legendary newscaster Logan Burrows, whom he'd briefly met at a broadcasting convention in San Diego. He recalled how he could barely talk to the great man he was so enthralled to be in his presence.

Fifteen minutes passed before there was a knock on the door. Happy for the distraction, he watched in horror as the family's housekeeper hobbled into his office with the help of her cane. She averted her dark eyes as she approached. Then she sat uninvited in the chair next to his desk. He felt embarrassed by her presence. And the wine stain made it even more difficult for him not to stare. She had such a deflating effect on his otherwise buoyant mood that he wished she'd stayed home and watched Shay like she was paid to do.

"What are you doing here, Tatyana? I thought I asked you to keep an eye on my wife."

"Mrs. Wells is with her friend. She went to see the doctor today because she is still very sick."

"Thank you for taking her to that appointment."

She looked up briefly and took in her surroundings. "Is very nice office, Mr. Wells."

"Yes, I rather like it," he said, settling uncomfortably in his leather seat. "Is this about money? Because I know you've been going above and beyond lately."

"No, this is not about money."

"Then what can I do for you?"

"Not for me. What you can do for your family."

"Everything I do is for them," he said, gesturing with his outspread arm, trying to hide his irritation.

"Your wife needs a vacation, Mr. Wells. To go away and breathe in fresh air and clear her mind. I think a vacation would do wonders for her."

"Did she put you up to this?"

"No, but she also thinks a vacation is good idea. I can come with you if you like and keep eye on Quinn. Give you and your wife alone time together."

He laughed. "You want to go on a vacation with us?"

"Yes, as your nanny."

"So, where do you suggest we go?"

"Western Massachusetts."

"Western Mass?" He laughed at the suggestion. "I thought you were going to say somewhere more exotic."

"It's quite beautiful this time of year when all the leaves turn color." She stared down at the desk as if embarrassed. "And it's not far from home if your wife starts to feel sick."

"I have to admit a vacation does sound rather nice." The idea of getting out of town for a week intrigued him, especially now that he had to keep the news of his potential job offer quiet.

"You have big smile on your face, Mr. Wells," Tatyana said, looking up. "Something on your mind?"

"No, I was just thinking about your idea of a family vacation. It sounds quite lovely, actually. The sounds of crickets, picking apples, and hiking along winding trails. What could be better?"

Tatyana stared blankly at him.

"Shay and I could even take a day trip. And you could stay and watch Quinn. She really likes you, you know."

"I like her, too." Tatyana stood, doddered over to his showcase, and admired his meager awards in the glass cabinet. "You are a famous man, Mr. Wells. I watch you on TV almost every night."

Gideon blushed. "Thank you, but I wouldn't exactly say I'm famous."

"Oh yes, you are very famous. I watch you ever since I moved to Boston."

"I appreciate that."

"I don't know why anyone watches Yolanda Brown. She's terrible."

The maid's words warmed his heart. "Not everyone watches her, if you've happened to notice. I've been whipping her in the ratings as of late."

"Yes, I've heard," Tatyana said. "Sometimes I think I would like to be on TV, traveling to interesting places and reporting on news. Maybe become rich and famous like you."

He looked away, trying not to dash the poor woman's hopes.

"Is there any advice you can give me?"

"You must have a college degree for starters," he said, watching as she stared at his awards, minus the Emmy. "Then you have to make your bones with a network willing to take you on."

"Make my bones?" She turned to him, her unsightly face scrunched up in confusion. "What does 'make my bones' mean?"

"It's an expression us Americans have. It means you have to put in many hours of hard work for very little money. Become a field reporter and climb the ladder of success. Mind you, it could take years to accomplish your goal."

"Not a problem. I'm very hard worker." She patted her chest.

"That's the spirit. It's a great starting point for you to begin your journey."

She turned and stared at him. "Do you think I'm pretty, Mr. Wells?"

"Pretty?" He struggled for the right words.

"Yes, pretty like your wife." She stood and walked over to his desk.

He gulped. "Of course, you're pretty, Tatyana, but it's your competence that matters most in journalism," he said, knowing that to be a half-truth.

"Your wife is very beautiful. I heard she was great reporter in her day."

"Yes, she certainly was."

"And you are very attractive man, Mr. Wells."

He laughed nervously, trying not to stare at the butterfly stain on her cheek. His nose suddenly detected the smell of her cheap perfume. He sat back in order to keep some distance between them. But then she leaned over and shocked him with a kiss. For a brief second, he couldn't move. He closed his eyes and froze. What balls this Russian broad had to kiss him in his own office. To his surprise, he found the kiss to be quite sensual. As long as he kept his eyes closed and didn't breathe in through his nostrils, the kiss didn't repulse him. But when he opened his eyes, he noticed the whorls of black hair covering his face. He pulled away, aghast, trying not to offend her.

"What the hell do you think you're doing?"

"I'm so sorry." She collapsed in the guest chair and began to sob. "I've never been around such powerful and handsome man before. I'm so ashamed."

Her glowing praise took the sting off that offensive kiss. "There, there, Tatyana. What you did is in no way appropriate, but under the circumstances, I'm willing to forgive and forget if you are."

"I'm not beautiful woman, am I?"

"Don't be so hard on yourself. You're an absolutely lovely girl." He needed to dispatch her fast.

"You really think?" She looked up at him between sobs.

"Absolutely. Not only are you attractive and kind, but you've done wonders for my family. One word from me, Tatyana, and you'll have your choice of housekeeping jobs in Woodbridge Estates."

"But I don't want to be housekeeper anymore. I want to be reporter like you."

"Okay, so get to work at being a reporter. Enroll in college. Work on perfecting your English."

"Yes, you are right. I'm going to be reporter." She wiped her eyes. "Will you put in good word for me when time comes?"

He sighed, not wanting to crush her dreams. "First, you must dedicate yourself to the craft. Finish college and earn your degree. At that point, I'll be happy to put in a good word for you."

"Thank you for advice, Mr. Wells. I am going to try to be the best news reporter I can be. After vacation, I will quit being your housekeeper."

"Are you sure about this?" Now he was not so sure he wanted to lose her.

"Yes. I'm so ashamed about kissing you in your office."

"It's perfectly all right. No harm done." He felt bad for the poor girl. And at the same time flattered by her words. "There's nothing I can say or do that might change your mind?"

"No." She stood from the chair and turned to leave. "I will go with you on vacation. After that, I will start my training as reporter."

"I can't thank you enough for all you've done for my family. You'll be sorely missed."

"I will make all the arrangements for trip. I know of wonderful place that has horses and trails and apple orchards. Your daughter will love it."

"Then, by all means, make the arrangements. And the sooner, the better, as far as I'm concerned."

She hobbled out of his office. Frankly, he was just happy to see her leave. No sooner had he returned to his crossword puzzle than she popped her head back into his office.

"Did you forget something?"

She paused for a few seconds. "I forgot to tell you this, Mr. Wells."

"Tell me what?"

"Is about your wife."

"She's okay, isn't she?"

"Yes, other than head injury, she's fine," Tatyana said, staring down at the floor. "Mrs. Wells was one who hit that dog with rock."

"Excuse me?" He couldn't believe his ears.

"I didn't want to say anything with police around, but I followed her that day like I did most days. I saw her pick dog up by collar and then walk away with it. I tried to catch up to her, but it was too late."

A sinking feeling came over him.

"She picked up big rock and smashed it over dog's head."

He moved over to the door and whispered, "You can't mention this to anyone, Tatyana. Do you understand me? We need to keep this between the two of us."

"It's brain injury to blame," she muttered before disappearing out the door and down the hallway.

Stunned, Gideon closed the door. He tried to make sense out of everything. Even if his wife had done such a horrible thing, it really wasn't her who hurt that dog. Like Tatyana had said, her brain had been compromised. The Shay he knew would never hurt an animal or cuss out a child. She'd been one of the most caring and sympathetic reporters he'd ever met, doing feel-good stories that celebrated the human spirit. But she had another side as well: a dogged personality that made her do whatever was necessary to run down a story. Not many people knew she hid a fierce competitive streak. But attacking a helpless dog was certainly not the actions of the woman he married—and loved.

He returned to his desk and started back on the crossword puzzle, unable to concentrate or get that perfume scent out of his nose. It took him a few seconds to realize that everything might work out in his favor if he played his cards right. This pathetic Russian maid would be out of their life forever once they returned home from vacation, and the prospect of a new job on Fifth Avenue awaited him.

He'd always dreamed about living in a Soho penthouse and being chauffeured to work every day in a stretch limo. After Mallory accepted Your Weather Channel's offer, she too would be out of his life. Shay would eventually recover from her injury and return to good health. Quinn would attend the finest school in Manhattan, receiving the best of everything the city had to offer. It would all work out splendidly once they returned from vacation. He even promised himself to cease his reckless philandering, although he'd made that vow time and time again. This time, he truly meant it.

He smiled at his good fortune. Lady Luck seemed to be smiling down on him for whatever reason.

GIDEON

He decided to take the next day off to celebrate the news of his potential promotion. Of course, he knew he couldn't tell anyone, least of all his family. If indeed he got offered the job, and he felt confident he would, Shay and Quinn would need to be persuaded to move to New York City. He'd researched some schools and found a very good one for Quinn located in lower Manhattan. It would be an expensive place to live, but with his new salary, they wouldn't want for anything.

Confidence had never been one of his problems, even if his deep insecurities often got the best of him. Thus, it never occurred to him that he would *not* get the job. Success had been his birthright, and everything he'd done in life seemed to lead him to the pinnacle of his chosen field. His success in Boston had always seemed a fait accompli. Now, all he had to do was wait for the word to come down from the network executive—his mysterious British contact—announcing that he would be Burrows's handpicked successor.

His family seemed to know something was up as he scrambled around the kitchen, preparing one of his rare homemade dinners. He'd splurged for a thick rib roast, prehistoric in its girth, and now it roasted away in the oven, covered with a mosslike web of herbs and spices and stuffed with teardrops of garlic cloves. Along with that, he'd smashed potatoes and creamed spinach. The day before, he'd watched one of those fancy cooking shows and learned how to prepare it all.

He sipped his Merlot as he scuttled about, and when everything was done, he set the table and called his wife and daughter over to eat.

"You seem unusually happy today," Shay said.

"I'm beyond happy. What could be better than spending quality time with my family?"

"But you hardly ever take time off from your job, Daddy," Quinn said, sitting perfectly still next to him.

"Well, buttercup, I did tonight. And next week, we'll be spending the entire week vacationing together as a family." He reached out to hold Shay's hand, but she quickly retracted it so she could spread a napkin over her lap.

"No one told me about a vacation. I have lots of schoolwork and an important chorus recital next week," Quinn complained.

"I admit it's a bit of a surprise, dear," Shay said to her daughter. "But a good one, right?"

"Your mother and I thought it might be nice to get away for a spell. That way she can get some peace and quiet and finally recover from that nagging head injury of hers."

"Whose idea was that?" Quinn said, crossing her arms in protest.

"Actually, Tatyana suggested it," Shay said, glancing over at him. "Your father and I agreed that we would all benefit from some time away."

"What does Tatyana know, anyway." She crossed her arms and pouted.

"I thought you loved Tatyana," Shay said.

"What made you think that?"

"You two are always playing board games together," Shay said.

"I miss Maya. She was the best housekeeper ever."

"Did Tatyana say something inappropriate to you?"

"No. She's just strange. I don't know how to explain it," Quinn said.

"Tatyana comes from a war-torn country and has had a difficult life. She's been very good to us since she started working here," Shay said.

"She uses way too much perfume," Quinn said, wrinkling her nose.

"Not everyone in this world is as fortunate as we are."

"I understand, Momma. It's just that she makes me feel weird at times."

"Don't you even want to know where we're going?" Gideon said.

"But I don't want to go on vacation."

"The three of us are going to a ranch in Western Massachusetts."

"Western Massachusetts," Quinn said as if it were halfway across the world. "Why are we going there?"

"You'll love everything about it. Your mother and I might even make a day trip if the mood strikes us."

"Then who will watch me?"

"Tatyana's coming along with us, dear," Shay said.

The frown on Quinn's face told him that this might take some additional convincing.

"Why does *she* have to come?" Quinn said.

"So your mother and I can get some peace and quiet. This trip is primarily to help your mother heal from her injury. But it will be good for you, too."

"Why can't I go on a day trip with you guys?"

"Because you'll be too busy riding horses, taking hayrides around the mountain, and grooming sheep and alpacas. They have all kinds of animals at the ranch we're staying and lots of apple trees. Oh, and a wonderful indoor pool with slides and a sauna," he said.

"You mean I'd get to ride horses?"

"And groom sheep and hold cute little bunnies to your heart's content."

"But we can still go without Tatyana, right?"

"With her there, your father and I can have some alone time together."

"But I want it to be just the three of us."

"Quinn, dear, after this vacation, Tatyana will no longer be working for us."

"She's leaving?"

"Yup. Right after our vacation," Shay said. "Which is why you need to be extra nice to her. She's done a lot for this family."

"I'll really get to ride horses and play with animals?"

"And shear sheep, feed the hens, and collect their eggs each morning."

"Okay, I guess I can go if there's horses there."

"Then it's settled," Gideon said, carving knife poised to slice off a thick slab of beef. "We're going to Western Massachusetts."

He cut happily through the tender roast, juices running down the pink grains of filet. That Barefoot TV lady would be proud of the meal he had prepared for his family. A vacation was just what he needed now, lest he open his big mouth and accidentally spill the beans. He spooned dollops of smashed potatoes on their plates alongside the creamed spinach.

Woodbridge Estates and Boston felt like part of his past now, small and provincial. First, they would go to that vacation ranch. Then, New York City awaited their arrival. It would be the final feather in his illustrious career as a Boston news anchor. *That* would show Yolanda Brown: him leaving this market at the top of his game.

Once everyone was served, he lifted his glass. Merlot for him. Juice for Quinn and Shay.

"A toast to our upcoming vacation," he said. They clinked their glasses together and sipped from their drinks. Then, the three of them ate in silence.

SHAY

She lifted her glass and toasted along with her husband and daughter. She'd never seen Gideon so happy. Was it their vacation plans that made him this giddy? She couldn't see how knowing how much he hated being away from the news desk. Or had he started another affair? She found it insulting that he thought her so stupid, and suddenly, she was glad she remembered this ugly secret about him.

All the blood tests had come back normal. So why should she keep taking the assortment of meds the doctor had prescribed? She'd called back and left a message asking the doctor about this, and he had messaged her back, saying that to go off her meds now could have a detrimental effect on her brain chemistry, regardless of how she felt at the moment. The time to taper off would be when the symptoms had begun to fade.

She sawed off a tiny sliver of prime rib and plunged her fork into the beef. Usually, she couldn't bear the sight of rare meat. But today, she found herself ravenous with hunger. And she knew why; she'd not taken her meds this morning. If Tatyana found out about it, she'd be furious and insist that she follow the doctor's orders. Maybe even call the doctor and have him lecture her over the phone. If she felt great without them, then why take her meds? She'd hidden the pills in a plastic baggie when Tatyana wasn't looking, and then stashed them in the heel of one of her boots. After their vacation—a vacation she hoped to enjoy now that she felt healthy and clearheaded—the housekeeper would be out of their lives forever.

Everything tasted so wonderful that she had a second helping, to Gideon's delight. Something seemed out of sorts with her husband this evening, and she couldn't understand why. Or what had caused his unusually good mood. Why had he taken a night off from his precious news desk? He never did that unless there was an emergency of some sort, or he was sick with a debilitating fever and sore throat. His unusual exuberance kept her vigilant as she watched him for a clue as to why.

She knew he'd been nominated for another Emmy. Would he lose yet again to Yolanda Brown? Or had he insider information that this year might be different? Maybe he found another hussy in the office to screw? She'd heard a vague rumor about him and the weather girl, Mallory, but thought it just a rumor. Had it not been for Quinn and her myriad of health problems, as well as all the expensive medical bills that came with Quinn's disability, she might have left him years ago on account of that devastating affair he'd engaged in. But deep in her heart, she still loved him and wanted to make this marriage work. And she knew he loved her too, despite all the whispers about his infidelity.

They'd talked abstractly about having children those first six months they were together, and he seemed quite receptive to the idea. She'd envisioned a perfect life being married to the famous Gideon Wells and staying home to raise their two or three small children. A month later, he had gotten her pregnant, and she was beside herself with joy, knowing that their marriage was meant to be. Upon hearing that she was pregnant with his child, a surprised and happy Gideon proposed to her on the spot. After the third time, she finally relented and said yes.

But then he engaged in that affair, and it nearly destroyed her, making her wonder if marrying Gideon had been a mistake.

Still, all she had to do was look at her beautiful daughter to realize that it had all been worth it. Maybe Quinn's illness was the price God had exacted on Gideon for committing adultery. But what about her? Why should she and her daughter be punished for his mistake? She stayed with him out of love, praying that his philandering was a thing of the past and that the rumors of his infidelity were untrue.

She gazed across the table at her husband. His relationship with Quinn was often distant and aloof, although she had no doubt he loved her. His primary concern in life was his job and his TV ratings. Maybe she could love Gideon once again like she had when she was young and naive and believed in true love. If only he could control his libido and stay away from all those pretty young staffers willing to do anything to get ahead in the industry. She once confronted him about these rumors, but he always vehemently denied it.

She prayed that this vacation might rekindle their romance and be the means to a fresh start. But whatever happened, she always had Quinn. Quinn was her flesh and blood, and she'd sacrifice her life for this girl if it came to it.

And if Gideon failed to change his ways after they returned from that ranch, she'd make plans to leave him once she'd made a full recovery.

SHAY

With one day of vacation left, Shay couldn't believe how much fun they all had. Why hadn't they done this sooner? Part of her didn't want to leave. Quinn loved everything about the ranch, especially riding horses along the trails and helping corral and feed them. They'd picked apples and bushels of blueberries, and she watched her daughter feed and milk cows and shear sheep. They made freshly squeezed cider, baked apple pies, and fried cinnamon donuts. And when the sun set behind the nearby hills, Shay thought it might have been the most beautiful thing she'd ever seen. If only Quinn could have witnessed such a spectacle. But then the stars came out at night while they sat around the bonfire, drinking wine and hot chocolate and roasting marshmallows while singing camp songs. Shay had never seen so many stars in her life. There were so many of them that they seemed to meld one into another. She thought the universe was so vast and incomprehensible that she experienced a joy she'd never quite felt before.

Tatyana barely left her cabin the entire time, and that surprised her. Shay saw her only at breakfast, Tatyana choosing to eat most of her meals alone in her room. If Tatyana had found this area to her liking, she hadn't shown it. Not that Shay was complaining. They certainly benefited from having more time together as a family, and Shay could see how Tatyana's dour disposition might have spoiled the mood.

She was careful to play the role of dutiful patient with Tatyana by pretending to swallow her meds each morning. Then she'd spit them out in a plastic baggie, which she stuffed into her zippered belt bag. Flushing them down the toilet polluted the wells and aquifers, so that was out of the question. She was afraid to leave them behind and have someone find the meds and possibly overdose. Or maybe the ranch owners would call her at home and question her about the leftover pills. No, she'd safely dispose of them once she was back in Woodbridge Estates.

The upshot was that she felt much better than she had in weeks, despite at times thinking about the confrontation she had with that poor dog. Her mind and body seemed to operate as one. She took pains not to overdo any physical activity, napping in the afternoon and taking frequent water breaks throughout the day. And because Tatyana was not there to monitor her during their daily hikes, she carried on until she felt exhausted. By the end of the day, she could barely move. Every fiber in her body ached, but in a good way. She'd experienced a few moments of dizziness and headaches, but for the most part, she felt wonderful. More amazing than she had in some time. One night at dinner, when Tatyana once again failed to appear, she even had a small glass of wine. And every night, she made sure she was in bed before ten, sleeping soundly through the night.

She'd never seen Quinn so happy. Or Gideon. Typically, when vacationing, he was constantly checking his phone for messages about how his replacement was doing. Or any news regarding Yolanda Brown. He'd not exactly wanted his replacements to fail, but he didn't want them to be wildly successful either. His insecurities ruined most vacations they took, and he ignored her at dinners with his constant worrying and staring down at his phone. But this trip was different. Not once did he check on his replacement back in Boston. He seemed joyous, almost liberated from the confines of his suffocating celebrity.

Did he know something she didn't? Or had he finally come around to smelling the roses and enjoying life and his marriage to her? On one hand, it unnerved her. Yet she found that she liked this new version of Gideon Wells far better than the previous version. If only it could stay this way once they returned home. That way, she could learn to love and trust him once again. So that he wouldn't feel the need to cheat on her with those ambitious young bimbos constantly cozying up to him.

But the effect on Quinn was the most dramatic, leading her to believe that they needed to return here every year. The girl's confidence soared, and she seemed a natural caretaker around the animals, especially the horses, who seemed to gravitate toward her whenever she approached. Her energy appeared boundless during the mountain hikes they took, and she often stopped to smell the plants and flowers that attracted her. Shay wondered why she hadn't exposed Quinn to nature earlier in life. Still, better late than never. Boston was a beautiful city and an integral part of her identity, but it couldn't compare to the grandiosity of this rural landscape.

The three of them had such a wonderful time that she and Gideon had completely forgotten about getting away for a day trip, and they were none the worse for it. Leaving the ranch would have only depressed her after witnessing this stunning landscape. Not only that, but she didn't want to leave Quinn behind.

Nearing the end of this vacation made her sad. She didn't want their newfound family unity to end. She feared it might dissipate once they fell back into their everyday routines. For this reason, she felt eternally grateful to Tatyana for setting this all up. After what she'd done for Shay and her family, the woman deserved a better send-off than a mere handshake and promise of a good reference. Shay figured she might throw a little going-away party for Tatyana with a cake and a bonus check. Something to show her appreciation for all that she'd done for them.

Gideon walked over and hugged her after dinner. In his hands sat a box wrapped in floral paper. She ripped it open and pulled out a beautiful set of turquoise earrings.

"Oh my God, Gideon. They're stunning."

"The man at the store claimed that they were mined nearby."

"But why did you get them for me?"

"Because your other ones were stolen. And because I love you and want to be a better husband in the future and a better father to Quinn."

She put them on. "They must have cost a small fortune."

"Whatever they cost, you're certainly worth it," he said. "It's obvious that this vacation has done wonders for you."

"It has, and we have Tatyana to thank for it."

"All the same, I'll be happy when she's moved on to greener pastures."

She laughed. "Be nice. She means well."

"Things are going to change when we get home, dear. We're going to be so much happier; you wait and see. And Quinn, too."

"But I don't want our stay here to end."

"Nor do I, but we can always come back next year."

"Yes, I'd like that," Shay said. "Did you notice how Quinn has thrived out here?"

"She certainly has."

"You could see her confidence soar when she was around the horses or caring for those rabbits."

He laughed while clutching her in his arms. "That girl left me breathless on those hiking trails. I could hardly keep up with her."

"It's almost as if she could see where the trails were and anticipate the twists and turns in the landscape."

"I love you so much, Shay."

"I love you too." She kissed him and then pulled away. "Are you hiding something from me, Gideon Wells?"

"I gave you your present. Unless you're hinting at something else?"

"You seem happier than I've seen in some time, and you're rarely this happy or attentive while on vacation." Despite growing closer to him on this trip, she was still not ready to make love to Gideon.

"Maybe I'm getting mellower in my old age."

"Oh, I doubt it. It's something else. I know you all too well."

"Maybe I'm just in love with my wife. Can't it be that simple?"

"Nothing is that simple with you." She laughed happily. "Now tell me what's really going on."

"I've already told you."

"Okay, be that way, then."

"Let's take a walk and catch the sunset. Quinn is busy feeding the chickens or baling hay or whatever it is they do on this ranch."

He grabbed her hand as they walked under the fading blue sky. Nestled in the mountains and with Gideon by her side, she experienced love like she hadn't in years. Something within her finally felt ready to forgive him and move on. She felt like she did when they first started dating.

They turned past the horse corral and headed back toward the main house. The hills seemed aglow from the setting sun. A few wispy clouds radiated above the mountaintops. As they approached the house, she saw a lone figure standing against one of the fence posts. This person had been staring at them the entire time. It took a few seconds for her to see that it was Tatyana. She considered waving to the housekeeper, but the strange look on Tatyana's face gave her second thoughts. Shay pulled her husband along and headed nervously toward the front door, doing her best to ignore the woman.

Was Tatyana jealous of her relationship with Gideon? It didn't much matter, she thought as she made her way into the kitchen. Once through the door, she saw Quinn lift a scoop of cookie mix and form it into a ball. Then she set it down on the baking sheet next to the others. Shay watched on happily, unable to erase the memory of Tatyana's odd expression.

II

Part Two

SHANNON

Gideon loads the suitcases into the SUV, and away we go. To Western Massachusetts for the start of our family vacation.

I gaze out the window as the SUV passes the iron-rod gates and pulls into the ranch's driveway. After parking in front of the main house, Gideon jumps out and opens the doors for Shay and Quinn. They have to wait for me because of my "disability", although the last thing the Wells family wants is to be seen with their crippled Chechen maid. I know they'd be happy to stick me in one of the cabins on the far end of the ranch and dump me there for the week. And it's hilarious that they think I'm quitting after their vacation is over and that they'll never see me again. They're under the impression that I'm heading off to college to become a "journalist." What a hoot. Then they can return to their McMansion on the tenth hole of Woodbridge Estates and forget I ever existed.

* * *

It must be told that I bashed that dog over the head while I was out walking, pretending to be Shay. I didn't want to kill it, just create enough of a spectacle. The real Shay Wells was passed out in her room when it happened, zonked out on the Ambien I gave her. Yes, the mutt had it coming to him for the way he ran out and tried to viciously attack my ankle. It must have weighed all of ten pounds, soaking wet, and I had to keep from laughing as it nipped at my heels. The two dumb cops believed that I had kicked it out of self-defense. Even better, they believed it was Shay doing it on the video. And Shay, who cussed out the kid. And Shay, who picked up that rock and....

To be honest, I didn't enjoy hurting that dog, but it had to be done. And he'll one day make a full recovery. That'll teach him to come running after me when I'm walking.

Prior to tracking down my twin, we hadn't seen each other in over twenty years. We were fifteen going on twenty, and I'd been making life miserable for her ever since we'd shared real estate in our mother's womb, competing to see who would be the first one to make a grand entrance. Knowing me, I probably punched her numerous times while we floated in that amniotic fluid. And yanked on her flailing limbs. Then mule kicked her one last time before sliding headfirst out of the birth canal.

It made me happy to torture my sister while growing up. It was better than taking it out on myself, like a lot of those self-loathing girls at school used to do. No sense cutting my own wrists when I had a perfectly good sister to cut. A goody-two-shoes bitch who was the spitting image of me.

But then she had the nerve to burn down our fosters parents' home one night. And then plunge a penknife into her thigh when no one was looking—and blame it all on me. I couldn't believe she had the balls to do it. I still remember the bloody handle sticking out of her thigh. It was one of the coolest things I'd ever seen, and if she hadn't thought of it first, I might have beaten her to the punch.

I remember running back inside the house and seeing Cherish engulfed in flames, a needle sticking out of her arm. The smell of gasoline was strong, and the intense heat nearly melted me into a puddle like it did the Wicked Witch of the East. Seeing I'd been too late to save my friend, I took off running before anyone discovered the truth. Before the police arrested me for arson and assault with a deadly weapon.

I took off in Cherish's car that night and drove out west, assuming her identity, knowing that everyone would think that I had died in that fire. A week later, I ended up on the streets of Las Vegas selling drugs in order to make ends meet. The week after that, I got busted by the cops and sentenced to six months in juvenile detection.

Sure, I had a long record of juvenile offenses: running away from foster homes, stealing, smoking, skipping school, fighting, drugs. By the time I reached my teens, I possessed the body of a Victoria's Secret model and began to grasp the power I had over men. Without limitations, such attributes can end up being a bad combination for a girl like me, growing up poor and neglected. Revenge was my currency and a way to make me happy, and that was all that mattered at the time. Making Shannon happy.

I had lots of time to reflect on my life while serving time in that juvie hall. Like how to commit crime more intelligently in order to have the kind of life I believed I deserved. And how to pay back my sister for the way she tried to set me up, which I wanted more than anything else. I also wanted money and fame and to be like those talentless idiots on TV.

Our biological father died in a car crash when we were thirteen. I'm glad he never had the opportunity to see me become a criminal. Or learn that I was the one who caused his untimely death. My mother went out for a smoke one day and never returned home. In some ways, it makes me happy knowing they hadn't seen me in such a negative light.

Then being shuttled from one foster home to the next, along with my twin bitch, fending off those sick pervs trying to cop a feel.

Twenty years later and I'd found her. I would have killed Shay that night if it wasn't for all those homeless deadbeats loitering about. Now I'm glad she didn't die. It would have ruined my Plan B, which is far more ambitious than my original plan.

At first, I thought it would be difficult to make myself up as this Chechen housekeeper day after day, night after night. But after a while, it became kind of fun. I felt like one of those actresses on TV playing a role. Even speaking in that Russian accent became a challenge, as did drawing the same butterfly stain on my face day after day. I took continual selfies to make sure I followed the same lines. When it rained, I feared it might streak over my cheeks, but thankfully it never did. The black wig and noticeable limp did the trick as well. I bought a cheap bottle of perfume and doused myself in it every morning. That was for the blind kid's sake, but they all noticed.

Little did my sister know I'd been drugging her the entire time with Ambien and watching her every move. I broke into Gideon's phone one night and downloaded all his computer passwords, photos, and emails. Before I got hired on as their maid, I even snuck into the Wells's house, switched out her medications, and copied her house keys, using the spare she kept hidden under a rock off the front steps. She thought it was the brain injury causing her memory loss and fatigue.

It was why she couldn't recall running naked onto that tenth green as her husband's golf partners measured their putts. With Shay passed out in the bedroom, I shed all my clothes and jogged onto that golf course, pretending to be her. I remember the stunned looks on those men's faces when they saw me walking butt-naked toward them. I let the dumb one named Fred cover me up with his golf shirt before I ran back inside, knowing the hubbub it would cause in the neighborhood.

Drawing her blood had been easy, as I'd mainlined thousands of addicts while living on the Strip. I kept the vial of her blood for when I would need it, knowing the doctor would never test for Ambien in her system. Everything else about my sister I learned on the job.

* * *

I discovered in juvenile detention that I had certain leadership qualities that other girls lacked. To my surprise, all those tough-talking hoes would jump when I barked. The social workers wrote as much in my file, marveling at my intelligence and ability to persuade other bitches to do my bidding. But being a charismatic leader in juvenile detention had its limits. I needed those skills to translate to the real world. I needed to make *money*.

A fellow inmate convinced me to start turning tricks on the Strip once I was released. She claimed that with my body and looks, I could make bank as a high-paid escort. With nowhere else to go and no money to my name, I agreed to join up with her as soon as I got sprung from juvie. Paying my sister back would have to wait.

I began hustling, moving drugs, and running cons, only to end up behind bars yet again. This time, it was for drug possession with intent to distribute. Who knew that muling a quarter mil worth of coke was a federal crime?

For that, I received a nine-year sentence. My life in prison was one of the few times I followed the rules. Five years later I got released early for good behavior, promising to be a better person, when what I really wanted to be was a more efficient and enterprising criminal.

I returned to the streets, hustling and grinding, hoping each time to be more productive than the next—and more profitable. I believed in myself and my God-given talents. I believed I was cut out for greater things in life than merely having sex with sleazy businessmen and selling drugs. Money, fame, and celebrity would one day be mine, I kept telling myself. After all, it's the American Way.

Despite my ambitious plans, I'd never forgotten about my plan to pay back Shay. But first, I had to find her.

I was earning a thousand bucks a night when I woke up one afternoon and saw a strange man reclining in an armchair in front of me. He claimed he could change my life for the better and get me out of whoring and selling drugs. Just hours earlier, I'd laid my head down in a Bellagio penthouse with a miserable old folksinger who used to be semi-famous in the sixties. And for two thousand bucks, all he wanted me to do was spread Skippy peanut butter over my feet.

George said he'd been watching me work the last few nights and that he admired my skills. He was tall, lean, and good-looking, with one of those droopy mustaches that looked super cool when he smiled. I sat up in bed and studied him as he puffed on a Marlboro. My head felt blurry and unfocused: George had to drug me in order to get me up to his room. The stench of peanut butter still clung to my skin, and I realized I wanted out of this life. That's when he presented me with his business proposition. I was furious and stood up to leave, but not before he explained how I could make a small fortune working with him. Way more than a grand a night—and I would never have to spread peanut butter over myself again. He claimed that it would be easy money setting these men up and that we would never get in trouble with the law.

By that point, I'd been so tired of hooking and muling drugs for the syndicate that I sat back down on the mattress, bummed a smoke from him, and listened to what he had to say. It was the start of a beautiful relationship.

* * *

Gideon hits the horn, bringing me back to the present. Then, the four of us wait patiently for the Hispanic farmhands to retrieve our luggage. Once they take it out of the vehicle, we walk—I hobble—toward the ranch house.

Poor Gideon. Prior to working for his family, I had been following him everywhere. I knew where he dined for lunch and dinner and with whom. I knew who he played golf with and what time he teed off. I walked into his office that day disguised as Shay and tried to seduce him. When he refused, I told him about the Chechen maid—me!—I had hired to replace the old one. I pocketed Shay's expensive earrings and told everyone that the Salvadoran housekeeper had purloined them. Then, once I started working as their housekeeper, I broke into his phone and read all his text messages. It's how I found out he was cheating on my sister with Mallory, the gorgeous weather girl.

Gideon and Shay stop to admire the compound. Quinn makes them describe everything to her in exquisite detail. It pleases me to see the three of them so happy, knowing that everything in their life is about to change. I let a smile form over my wine-stained face, listening as my sister describes the ranch.

A tall cowboy straight out of casting walks over and greets us with a weathered smile. He resembles a younger Tom Selleck on steroids. On one side of the field, cows graze as if chewing Prozac. On the other side, horses strut around in their fenced-in pasture. Quinn peals with delight when Magnum PI mentions the horses, lifting her head to catch a whiff of their scent. By the time I get settled into my closet-sized room, I'm beside myself with excitement. This is certainly going to be a fun week.

I lie back on the bed, wishing I had a joint to smoke or a shot of Jack Daniel's to knock back. Wouldn't hurt to let my hair out of this two-bit wig, either, although I don't want to get too far out of character and ruin all my hard work. There's too much at stake.

Before I started working on my plan to pay back my sister, I asked George if he wanted to join me, knowing that he had stage four testicular cancer and had nothing to lose. He said he'd think about it. When I told him that his kids would be set for life after we pulled off this job, he shook my hand and agreed to work with me one last time.

I think of how thrilling it will be when I eventually call Gideon and tell him that he won't be getting Logan Burrows's job after all. When you feed into a person's deepest, darkest desires, the con practically runs itself. There's no sense rushing things along. I want to enjoy every last second of my time with Shay before she goes down. I want to prolong her torture and watch as that phony husband of hers suffers from the pitfalls of his own vanity. Just the thought of shattering Gideon's dreams nearly makes me wet my panties. But it's Shay I'm gunning for. Her downfall will one day be my gain.

SHAY

Everything felt different when Shay woke up. Her head pounded as if she were suffering from a bad hangover, and she couldn't remember anything about the last day at that ranch. These setbacks in her health were so unsettling that it left her feeling hopeless. Why couldn't she just recover at a normal rate?

She lifted her head off the rock-hard pillow and sat up. This wasn't the room she and Gideon had been vacationing in for the last week. She gazed around at her unfamiliar surroundings. Flakes of concrete peeled off the wall, and a tiny window high above let in the barest hint of light. She stood, her back aching from sleeping on the flimsy mattress. Was she dreaming? Like that recurrent dream she'd been having where Quinn held that scorpion in hand? She took a few steps before her knees gave out, and she collapsed to the dusty floor. This was real and no dream.

An incessant ringing plagued her ears. She crawled over to the door and pulled herself up. The ceiling looked to be ten feet high. She walked over to the door and began to bang on it and cry out for help. Certainly, one of the ranch handlers would hear her making a racket and come downstairs and unlock the door. She must have sleepwalked last night and unknowingly trapped herself in this basement room. But after thirty minutes of banging and shouting, no one came to let her out. Fatigued, she returned to the mattress and tried to think of a way out.

She did a quick inventory. The zip bag around her waist was still there. She opened it and saw the plastic baggie filled with her unused meds. Reaching up to her ears, she realized that the turquoise earrings Gideon gave her were gone.

This had to be a mistake, but the fact that her earrings were missing troubled her. Why would someone steal her earrings and kidnap her? If someone did manage to snatch her up, surely her husband and daughter would have noticed by now and called the police.

Her head started to pound, and she felt nauseous. She fell back against the pillow, but it felt like a cement bag against her scalp. When she couldn't take it anymore, she slipped it out from under her head and threw it toward her feet, where she used it as a footrest. Then she fell into a dark, stormy sleep.

Sometime later, she was awoken by a man's deep, growly voice. Pain thundered in her head when she opened her eyes and peered into the darkness. She arched her neck and noticed that the window above had gone black. It must be nighttime, she guessed, but she couldn't be sure.

"Gideon? Is that you?"

"Damn," a man said in a low voice, sitting on a stool in front of her. In his hand, she could make out a glass filled with amber liquid. In the other, he held a cigarette between his long fingers. His gaunt face flickered in the smoldering light.

"Who are you?"

The man let out a bellowing laugh that echoed throughout the room.

"I think you've made a terrible mistake, mister. I was vacationing with my family, and we were staying at one of the nearby ranches."

"I don't care how you ended up here. I only care that you stay put and don't give me no trouble."

"And who might you be?" She tried to focus on the man's ruddy face.

"The only person who can save your sorry ass."

"You'd better watch yourself. I have a powerful and well-known husband who's probably looking for me as we speak."

"Oooooh, so scary," he said.

"You won't be saying that when he finds me here."

"Don't worry, lady, your husband won't be looking for you."

"What have you done to him and my daughter? Are they okay?"

"They're fine."

What did he mean by that? A few uncomfortable seconds passed. Was he holding her hostage? Would he kill or torture her? Just when she thought she couldn't take this silence any longer, a light came on overhead. The suddenness of it caused her to fall back on the mattress in shock. She closed her eyes and felt the light penetrate deep into the recesses of her brain. She squinted, allowing her eyes to slowly adjust to the room's dimness. Finally, she saw a bulb dangling from a gnarly black cord hanging from the ceiling. The man stepped in front of her, blocking the light. He dropped his cigarette butt to the ground and stomped it out with his heel.

"You're a bit thinner than her, but just as pretty."

"Look, mister, I've never seen you before, so you'd better…." His long hand reached down and squeezed her wrist.

She tried to take it back, but his grip was too strong. He was good-looking in a very down-to-earth way, with salt-and-pepper hair and a thick, droopy mustache. His hypnotizing blue eyes seemed to draw her in.

"You really have no idea who I am?"

"Honestly, I don't," she said.

The man shook his head and coughed.

"How would I know who you are?" She started to tremble.

"Take it easy, lady. I'm not going to hurt you—not yet, anyway."

"Maybe you're the one who needs to take it easy," she said. "Why are you squeezing my wrist so hard?"

"Because you need to know that this is for real and that I'm not playing games."

She concentrated on his squinty eyes. There were lines around the edges and a tiny scar over his left eyebrow. Despite this ominous warning, his eyes had a glimmer of warmth to them.

"Better get used to seeing me for a while. You and I are going to be best buds."

"You don't understand. I need to get out of here so I can be with my family."

"You ain't going nowhere." He leaned over and caressed her cheek. "I still can't believe the resemblance."

"Resemblance to what?"

"Never mind. You just get some rest, okay," he said. "I'll be down later with some grub."

"No, please don't go!" She grabbed his arm and held onto it. "Don't leave me alone in this basement."

"You'll survive."

"My daughter is blind and badly needs me."

"I already told you that she's okay," he said, taking back his arm. "Now, do as you're told if you want to see her again."

"Why are you doing this?"

"Because I can," he said, standing with an irritated look on his face. "Rest up. Tomorrow will be another day."

"What do I do if I need to go the bathroom?"

"I'll blindfold you and take you upstairs," he said. "Do you need to go now?"

"No."

"Good. I'll come down later and check in on you."

He shut off the light and headed toward the door, and she was once again thrust into darkness. She had no idea where she was, but she knew that she had to formulate a plan if she wanted to get out of there.

She tried to think of her last moments before ending up in this cell. They ate breakfast as a family, the last one they enjoyed at the ranch. Everyone sat family-style around the large table, which was carved out of a twenty-foot oak log, with the bark still attached to the underside. Platters of bacon, eggs, and pancakes got passed around. Coffee and juice flowed freely, as did the laughs.

After breakfast, she remembered Tatyana asking her if she wanted to go for a hike along the northern trail. Quinn was scheduled to go horseback riding, and Gideon had a fly-fishing lesson with one of the ranch hands, so she agreed to go with her. Tatyana had even prepared a lunch basket with bottles of lemonade.

She recalled hiking in silence for quite some time, slowing her pace because of Tatyana's disability. At the top of the hill, she remembered seeing the amazing vista from both sides. A beautiful blue lake sparkled below. Tatyana pulled bags out of the pack, and the two of them enjoyed a lovely lunch of crustless cheese sandwiches with fruit and homemade cookies. Then they washed it down with the cold, sweet lemonade.

By the time they started down the hill, she remembered feeling dizzy and light-headed. She chalked it up to a minor case of altitude sickness. The last thing she remembered was wobbling down the steep hill, holding Tatyana's arm for support. But how could that be? The woman was crippled and required a cane to keep herself upright.

Tatyana! Had she been the one responsible for her being here? She should never have trusted that woman. But why would the Chechen housekeeper turn against her? All that time she'd been feeling unwell, it had been Tatyana drugging her and causing the fatigue and memory loss. Had she also killed the dog? But Shay had watched that video over and over and knew that she'd been the one who'd kicked it.

Nothing seemed to make sense. There'd be time to figure everything out later. First, she needed to acclimate herself to her new surroundings and then decide how best to deal with this situation. Escaping from this hellhole was her only option. It sounded crazy, but she felt as if she'd been brought here for a specific reason.

Now, she had to figure out why.

GIDEON

Two Weeks Later

Gideon couldn't understand how he could be so lucky. He'd never been happier at work and in his life, knowing full well he could see the light at the end of the tunnel. The last phone call he'd had with his contact at the network sounded cautiously optimistic, which, in his view, meant that it was all but a foregone conclusion that he'd get the job. The mere mention of his name for such a prestigious position would generate significant interest in his stock, providing him with ample leverage to bargain with the higher-ups at his station. But he had absolutely no desire to return to local TV now.

Because of this, his broadcasts had been more superlative as of late, sharp and heartfelt without the overarching narcissism that often crept into his reporting. It helped him achieve the highest ratings of his career. Commentators and fans alike remarked on his joviality and breezy confidence. The gravitas with which he delivered national and international events didn't go unnoticed, either. He projected a statesmanlike image that transcended provincial Boston interests and made him almost larger than life. Gone were the insecurity and petty jealousies against his cohorts and underlings. Even his overworked staff remarked on his uncharacteristically cheerful demeanor. At the water bubbler one morning, he even managed to exchange a few heartfelt words with Lancaster Rand.

Rumors spread around the office that his wife had been behind this remarkable transformation, and on the whole, he couldn't argue. Not a one of them knew about the prospects of his new employment, and there was no way he could breathe a word of this to anyone lest he blow the deal. He'd heard of this happening before. In fact, he'd been so tight-lipped about it that he hadn't even mentioned it to Shay.

Life couldn't be more wonderful, he thought as he sat staring at his half-finished crossword puzzle. He was supposed to meet Shay at Luca this afternoon, the Italian bistro along the waterfront. It had been many years since he'd been excited about the prospect of meeting his wife for lunch. Not only had Shay been feeling better, but she seemed to emerge from their trip a completely different person, a woman who adored her famous husband and had completely forgiven him for his past indiscretions—at least the one she knew about. And at this rate, it would be his last.

That vacation in Western Massachusetts had changed her whole outlook on life. No, it had changed all of them. Even Quinn returned home with a renewed vigor for nature. Now all she talked about was horse riding and shearing sheep. It would have been a distraction had she not been so happy. Come spring, they'd agreed to sign her up for extensive riding lessons, assuming they still lived at Woodbridge Estates. With her disability, he thought it prudent to take the time to find a stable that could accommodate her special needs, as well as teach her everything there was related to horse care and maintenance.

He stared at his crossword puzzle, unable to concentrate or think clearly. Sugarplums of stardom danced in his head. He recalled his last sexual liaison with Shay. In that regard, she'd come back from that trip a *totally* different woman, clearly proving the principle that "behind every great man…." After many months of denying him the fruits of their union, she'd had a change of heart. And the sex was fantastic. No, better than fantastic. Spectacular. All the cute interns and sexy cub reporters were mere afterthoughts after a romp in the hay with her. It had been so long since she'd performed with unbridled enthusiasm that he'd forgotten her considerable talents in the bedroom. She'd been by far the classiest, most beautiful woman he'd ever been with, and now she outshone her competition in the most important way. He'd briefly considered that her head injury had shaken things up in that department, but she'd insisted that she was the same woman she'd always been, only happier. He vowed to book a week at that dude ranch every year.

Things had fallen neatly into place. Mallory had accepted the weekend anchor job at the Your Weather Channel, thereby eliminating any possible threat to his continued happiness while at the same time keeping his best friend, Stan, gainfully employed at the station. With Mal now out of his hair, he swore to never again stray from his vows. He had everything he needed right at home: a loving wife, an amazing daughter, and a great job with the prospect of an even greater one on the horizon. He had his sights focused on his legacy.

His cell phone exploded: *Journey's* "Don't Stop Believing." He glanced down at the text message and saw that his wife was waiting for him in the bistro. His stomach growled as he balled up the newspaper and tossed it into the trash. Visions of handmade pappardelle noodles swimming in Bolognese sauce danced in his head. He strutted through his office, waving happily to his surprised underlings, and drove over to the waterfront.

He saw Shay seated at one of the back tables when he arrived. As soon as he saw her, he did a double take. She looked more beautiful than ever. Her teased blond hair cascaded around her delicately exposed shoulders, and it was feathered back in a pseudo ponytail, almost as if she'd set it haphazardly that way. Her blue eyes appeared like dialing harvest moons, grand and voluminous under the etched lines of carefully drawn charcoal. And the brushstroke of ruby over her tumescent lips set just the right touch. She would have stood out even at the Playboy Mansion.

He sat down in the faux Thomas Moser chair and reached for her hand beneath the flickering candle. Her eyes seemed to want him, and him only. It pained Gideon to keep his secret to himself. If only she knew about his new job offer, it might bring years of hard work, dedication, and marital struggle into harmonious union. For the first time in his life, he felt as if he could do no wrong.

"It's so wonderful to see you, dear," he said, hunger tickling his belly.

"Did you notice? I'm wearing the turquoise earrings you gave me while on vacation." She moved her hair away and showed him.

"They look absolutely gorgeous on you."

"I know," she said, letting her hair back down. "I even found the earrings Maya supposedly stole from me."

"So she didn't steal them?"

"No, I obviously misplaced them. But hiring Tatyana proved to be a blessing in disguise."

"I'll say. That was one of the best things you ever did for our family."

"Oh, Gideon, I'm so close to being completely happy."

So close? What did she mean by that? "But you look ravishing. That vacation obviously did wonders for you."

"It did wonders for all of us."

"I've never been more in love with you."

His wife let go of his hand. "If only I could contact Tatyana and thank her for changing our lives."

"It's probably best we let her get on with her life."

"A quick note of thanks might be in order, don't you think?"

"Did you call the agency? I'm sure they could track her down if you really need to find her." He recalled that odd kiss in his office and the blistering smell of Tatyana's cheap perfume, and he realized he had no desire to ever see that woman again.

"You don't know how hard I tried, but they kept refusing to put me in touch with her. Something about company policy. It was only when I stormed in there and made a scene that they finally admitted that she no longer works for the agency."

"Did they give you a reason?" He knew the reason why she quit.

"They didn't say. But I told them that if she ever returns, I'll give her the highest recommendation possible. Then I rated the company five stars for hiring her."

"You're such a wonderful person."

"Thanks, but not as wonderful as you," she said, grabbing a breadstick out of the mug and nibbling off the top. Had she gotten her teeth whitened? She looked slightly different to him for some reason. The hint of a tan? The glow of renewed health? Or maybe he was finally paying attention to her and only now noticed this.

"Everything's going splendidly, Shay, and I've been so happy. I just need to ask you about something you said a few seconds ago."

"What is it, hon?"

"What did you mean when you said you were so close to being completely happy?"

"I have a loving husband and a wonderful child. Quinn is growing up so fast that she doesn't need her mother hanging around her like she once did. All I need now is something to fulfill me."

"Fulfill you?"

"Yes," she said, resting her chin on her interlocked fingers. "Look at you. You've reached the pinnacle of success in your chosen field."

Not just yet, Shay, but very soon.

"Where does that leave me?"

"You still have your volunteering and charitable work, although I fully expect that you'll not be returning to that soup kitchen."

"Oh no. That assault made me rethink everything in my life. For all the hours I put in at that place, trying to make the world a better place, getting mugged is the thanks I get?"

"I couldn't agree more. And these useless police still have no idea who hurt you."

"Maybe it'll come back to me someday, when my memory fully returns. But what I need right now is something that will give my life purpose and meaning."

He cringed at the notion that he'd be moving her away from Boston just as she started on some silly new venture. Maybe he should tell her his exciting news, but then he realized the stakes involved and decided against it.

"I need a career like you have, Gideon."

"What have you in mind?"

"I want back in the game."

He laughed. "You want to go back to being a news reporter?"

"Yes, but not reporting about cats stuck in trees and kids helping grannies cross the street. I want a prime-time desk job like you have."

He giggled. "That's quite a leap, wouldn't you say?"

"Yes, but it's what I want."

"But, dear, you've been out of the business for quite some time now," he said, knowing full well that this voluptuous creature sitting in front of him could get hired on the spot and by any station in the market. But as a prime-time anchor? "And what about the video they have of you kicking that dog? Won't that hurt your chances?"

"I doubt it. Look at how it benefitted you. Your ratings spiked up after that incident."

"Yes, but—"

"I'm still attractive for my age. And for God's sake, Gideon, it's not rocket science."

"Delivering the news each night is harder than you think, dear."

"If it's so hard, dear, then why am I the one with the Emmy."

He swallowed his tongue and let this personal slight pass. "The job is so much more than merely reading off a teleprompter." He thought of all the hours he spent in his office working on crossword puzzles, studying himself in the full-length mirror, and watching tapes of his newscasts. "And the hours can be grueling. Then there's our darling Quinn to consider."

"That's another thing I wanted to talk to you about. I think we've been doing a major disservice to our daughter."

He leaned over and rested his chin on his palm. "You're so cute when you're thinking."

"Don't joke about this, Gideon, especially when I'm trying to talk to you about something this serious."

"I'm sorry. Please go on." His belly rumbled, and he thought of the pappardelle Bolognese he would soon be dining on.

"Quinn's growing up and becoming quite the confident young lady. You saw how she behaved on that vacation."

"It's true. She loved it."

"She sprouted wings for the first time in her life and seemed to fly."

"Hard to believe she'll be twelve this summer and almost a teenager."

"What better reason to enroll her in boarding school. She'll make lots of friends there and learn far more being away at school rather than stuck at home with her fuddy-duddy parents."

"Boarding school?" he muttered, clearly taken aback by this request. Before the accident, she never would have suggested such a drastic move. Had her mental state swung too far in the opposite direction?

"We don't have to enroll her right away, but do you really think we're doing her any favors by being helicopter parents? She needs independence and freedom, without her parents there to supervise her every move."

He scratched his chin as if in deep thought. Two cocktails arrived, courtesy of his wife, who had arrived before him. He always ordered a nonalcoholic drink, on account that he needed to keep a clear head for his newscasts.

The pretty waitress stood tableside with pen poised, waiting for them to order. It occurred to him that he hadn't looked at the menu or perused the daily specials. It didn't matter; he knew Luca's menu by heart and for years had always ordered the same thing. Before he could speak, Shay ordered the pappardelle Bolognese out from under him. He privately fumed at her selection, but thought it best not to say anything. Besides, he needed to eat light today, considering he had to go on-air this evening. For all he knew, the network people were keeping tabs on his every performance.

"I thought you despised pappardelle Bolognese?" he said after the waitress left.

"People change, Gideon."

"It's just that in all our years together, I'm the one who always ordered that dish."

"I've been reading about the symptoms of head trauma," she said, pointing the sharp breadstick at him as if it were a jagged piece of glass. "Did you know that some people wake from comas able to speak foreign languages or play the piano?"

"But you weren't in a coma."

"They're not much different when you really think about it. Both are severe brain injuries." Her blue eyes threw off an incandescent beam in his direction. "Do you remember what happened when I was pregnant with Quinn?"

Gideon laughed. "All you wanted to eat was nacho dip and Tootsie Rolls."

"Exactly. That's brain chemistry for you."

"Are you saying that your taste buds are different now?"

"Yes, and not just for food," she said, winking. "Remember our little rendezvous last night?"

"How could I forget?" Those blue eyes kept him enraptured. If she were a cobra, his poison-infested body would be working its way through her gaping jaws.

"Could you talk to someone at the station and maybe get me an interview?"

Talk to someone? "You don't just 'talk' to management about something as important as this."

"But you're a star, Gideon. Aside from Yolanda Brown, you're the biggest news celebrity in town and practically a legend," she said, sipping her chocolate martini. "With one snap of a finger, you can make things happen—and I really want this."

"Becoming a news anchor doesn't happen overnight. They might want you to start at the bottom and work weekends."

"Start at the bottom? Oh, no, that's not going to happen. Besides, I'm a top girl." Shay laughed. "In any case, I would think they'd be dying to replace that dreadful bore who sits next to you each night."

"Kaecie Stringer's a wonderful co-anchor and a dear friend," he said, knowing full well that the only reason Kaecie sat next to him each night was because she dwarfed him in charisma. He'd handpicked her himself, and wouldn't ever consider Kaecie a peer on his level—or a friend.

"What if it was just the two of us sitting at that desk? Imagine the monster ratings we'd garner?"

"You and I?"

"Yes. Wouldn't it be wonderful? We'd crush Yolanda Brown every night."

"Would we now?"

"Of course we would. And we could spend so much time together and be a real team. Have dinners like this between news broadcasts. We could even carpool into work."

"Carpool?"

"Sure. And we could have quickies in your office while the staff is working."

The thought of a quickie in his office suddenly terrified him as their drinks arrived. All of this was too much too soon. He sipped his cocktail and, to his dismay, discovered it contained alcohol. Had she forgotten about his rule? But it would look bad if he didn't drink with her, especially since she was now holding up her glass to toast. Why did she order him a cocktail when she knew perfectly well that he didn't imbibe before going on air? He wanted to protest, but then he recalled Shay on her hands and knees last night and moaning for more. One harmless drink wouldn't kill him.

"We are having such a wonderful dinner, dear. Can we talk about this later?"

"Of course we can, dear, but not too much later. I'd like to get the ball rolling as soon as possible if it's all right with you."

"I need to use the little boys' room," he said, excusing himself.

"Be gentle with that love thang, because I might not be so tame with it tonight." She flashed him a sexy smile.

Their plates arrived upon his return, and almost instantly, he could smell the Bolognese sauce smoldering in the folded layers of eggy noodles. Curlicues of steam wafted off the handmade pasta and made his mouth water. He glanced at the paltry salad in front of him. The Russian dressing dripped over the lettuce wedges, reminding him of that strange housekeeper. Suddenly, he lost his appetite. But the burn of alcohol snaking down his throat reminded him that he needed to get some food in his system. He leaned over the table, as was their routine, and stuck his fork out to sample from her plate. But Shay pulled her dish away and smiled naughtily.

"Not yet, tiger. You've got to learn that to get along in life, one must go along."

"I… I just wanted a little taste."

"As do I. Just for something completely different."

"But I'm the one that usually orders the pappardelle. And you and I have always shared plates when we dine out."

"Things have changed, Gideon. You want some of my pappardelle Bolognese and more of what I gave you last night. You need to start doing some quid pro quo. Capish?"

He nodded like an obedient child.

They ate quietly for the next fifteen minutes, both of them glaring at their phones for text messages, updates—doing anything possible to keep from talking to one another. They skipped dessert, and he paid for lunch with his Visa. Outside, they shared a lingering kiss before parting ways, agreeing to discuss the matter later.

He returned to the newsroom and scurried back to his desk, where he thought long and hard about what his wife had said. She wanted back in the game. What kind of nonsense was that? And to think she wanted to replace Kaecie, his perfectly uninspiring co-anchor. It had taken years for the station to find such a dull host who could put up with his overbearing ego, and he wasn't letting Kaecie go without a fight. Not when Kaecie made him look like a star each and every newscast.

His eyelids closed, and he felt himself nodding off. He never should have allowed himself that cocktail. Sometime later that evening, the news director burst in and startled him awake.

He stared fuzzily at her, as if his tongue had been injected with a shot of Novocain.

"Gideon, wake up. They need you on set," Barb said.

"Why?"

"There's been a shooting at Faneuil Hall."

He tried to tell her he'd be right out, but his tongue wouldn't work properly. The words coming out of his mouth sounded like a Swahilian auctioneer. Was he having a stroke?

"Are you alright?"

"I shlouldn't hab hab thlat clocktail."

"Jesus, Gideon, you know that drinking before going on-air is a bad idea."

He tried unsuccessfully to form a word. How could he have gotten so buzzed on one cocktail?

"Good god, Gideon, how much did you drink?" she said, slamming her clipboard on the desk. "I'm putting Lancaster on the desk."

"No!" He stood, knees wobbling, holding onto the desk for support. "Get me some cawfee and I'll do it."

"No, Gideon. Remember the last time you went on-air after a few drinks?" She stood with her hand on hip, glaring at him.

"Jus' have someone get me a cawfee," he barked.

She disappeared. Seconds later an intern came running in holding a steaming cup of brew. Gideon snatched it out of her hand before staggering vertiginously toward the studio. The lights blinded him as he fell back into his seat, trying to wish away the sweat beading along his scalp. He leaned forward and squinted at the blurred words scrolling over the teleprompter. For a brief second, he wondered if the machine was broken. Or maybe he was having a stroke?

"Are you okay, Gideon?" Kaecie turned to him and asked.

"Mine your own bizness," he fired back.

"Three...two...one," the producer shouted. And then the broadcast went live, and before he knew it, he was being hustled back to his office.

QUINN

She'd had so much fun at her friend's house that she didn't want to return home. But it was getting dark, and she had school tomorrow, and she knew her friend's mother had been gracious enough to watch her while her own mother went out to lunch.

She sat quietly in the back seat as the car pulled up in the driveway. She'd lived in this house less than a year, but already knew every inch of its terrain. The car shifted into park, and her friend's mother walked around and let her out. The familiar smell of her neighborhood hit her nostrils as soon as the door opened. Freshly mowed grass and redolent pine trees. Off in the distance, the sound of a lawnmower whinnied. Her friend's mother tried to take her by the arm, but she politely declined, using her walking stick to navigate up the path. Quinn always liked to joke that she could make her way around this property blindfolded if she had to.

The door opened, and before she disappeared inside, she thanked the woman for having her over. A TV played inside. Seconds later, her mother appeared by her side. Her mother thanked the woman before Quinn heard the door close behind her.

"Your father sent me a text message. He couldn't return home for lunch today."

"Why?"

"There's been some kind of shooting in town."

She hated hearing about violence. "Okay if I go to my room?"

"Don't you want to watch your dad on TV?"

Her mother never used to say things like that before her injury. "Not really. I can't see him, remember?"

"You know what I mean."

"Thanks, but I'll pass," she said.

"Fine," her mother said. "Did you at least have fun at your friend's house?"

"Yes, we had a blast."

"You seem a lot happier when you're away from home."

What did her mother mean by that? "Can I go upstairs now, Momma?"

"Suit yourself."

Once in her room, she lay down on her bed and tried as hard as she could not to cry. She was happy now that that strange Chechen maid had stopped working for them. Tatyana had been wrong about her mother; she was not a bad person. But her mother came back from that vacation a changed woman, and not for the better. She missed her mother: the mother she'd had before the attack. Who was this new woman who emerged after their wonderful vacation at that ranch? She'd changed so dramatically upon returning home that Quinn barely recognized her. One of her therapists at school said her mother might be undergoing a severe mood change because of the changes happening in her brain. She had suggested that Quinn be patient and give her some time to heal. Hopefully, with time and the right medical care, she might return to the mother she'd once been.

Rather than cry, she clicked on the flat screen in her room. Most of the time, she listened to music, but tonight, she was slightly intrigued about this shooting in town. She always wondered why people chose to hurt and kill others. Terrorist attacks and school shootings seem to happen all the time now. It made her happy to be safe and sound in her comfy bedroom. Her disability had endowed her with a rare sensibility, causing her to care for the feelings of others and to intuitively know when they were in pain.

Visiting that ranch had been one of the greatest experiences of her life. It gave her confidence and showed her that there was a whole other world out there. The interactions with the animals thrilled her, and she discovered that she loved cooking and singing camp songs under the stars. It was the first time she felt she could one day live on her own, independent of her parents. Her mother and father had been wonderful to be around during that trip and more loving than she'd ever seen them be to one another.

Then they came home.

And everything changed.

She clicked on the news station and heard a strange voice. Her father sounded funny this evening, as if he was slurring his words. His co-host cut in and took control of the broadcast. Quinn shut the TV off and turned over on the mattress. She'd never heard him talk like that while reporting the news. Only late at night, after he'd had too many of the adult drinks he liked.

Tired from the long day, she didn't want to go downstairs with that strange woman who called herself her mother. She wanted her real mother back, the mother trapped inside that imposter's body. She said a quick prayer and hoped God would answer it. Then she fell asleep as the tears spilled out of her eyes.

SHANNON

There are big things in store for me in the coming weeks. Shay will pay, and pay dearly, for what she did to me when we were kids. I hold her responsible for Cherish's death, even if it did provide me with an opportunity to escape the shitty life I'd been living. With any luck, she'll be holed up in that basement for the foreseeable future.

My sister's recent memory loss has played right into my hands. Now, whenever someone at Woodbridge Estates mentions something unfamiliar, I point to my head and tell them that it's this faulty memory to blame. Then the person will usually remind me of whatever it is I—Shay—forgot. Most everything else, I end up bullshitting my way through. And I'm very good at charming people and getting them to open up to me. When you've been hustling on the Vegas Strip for as long as I have, you tend to get good at lying.

Now that the seed has been planted, I can see the gears churning in Gideon's head. He thinks I don't notice when his eyes wander to all the other hotties in the room. If only his audience knew what an insignificant dunce he is and how easy it is to play off his most basic fears, they might not think so highly of him. He stays up late most nights, worrying about his latest Nielsen ratings over snifters of bourbon. It's hilarious that he believes he's going to be offered a job at one of the major news networks. If only he knew that it was me on the other end of that line and that he stands absolutely no chance of replacing Logan Burrows.

I persuaded him to hire a full-time maid to handle all the household chores. At first, he argued against it, citing money issues, but a good roll in the hay helped change his mind. Surely, he doesn't want me to relapse and revert back to being my dour, unforgiving sister.

Now that I have my own housekeeper, all the shopping and laundry gets done in a timely manner. It's a wonderful arrangement, and I don't need to lift a finger in this household. If my sister was fortunate enough to have someone waiting on her hand and foot, then I deserve at least the same treatment.

I sit down at the kitchen table with a cappuccino that Consuela brewed in our new espresso machine imported from Italy. She moves in and out of my sight, careful to avoid me. This is our unspoken arrangement: she does her thing, and I act as if she doesn't exist. Little does she know that we're cut from the same cloth and that I, too, have lived a hardscrabble life. But not anymore. This is my one chance to score big and make my mark in the world while at the same time paying back my sister for how she screwed me.

I wonder how Shay and George are getting along. It'll take some time, but she'll eventually get used to living in that basement. Good thing I bought George four cases of Jack Daniels to pass the time. It should keep him busy until I complete my plan.

Seven long years of my life were spent working with George. He taught me most of what I know about running cons. That was before he started hitting the booze and screwing things up. Then he got the terminal diagnosis from his doctor, and everything changed, and he started to reflect on his life and all the bad things he had done. That's when I decided to move East and start planning my revenge. It didn't take much to convince George to join me, especially when I mentioned his kids' well-being.

I sip my coffee and think about my future and all the things I want to accomplish. It will take time and considerable planning to achieve my goal, which is to become the top news anchor in Boston and attain fame and fortune alongside my brother-in-law/husband. How hard, after all, can it be to read off a teleprompter? Or flash these big blue eyes while reporting on terrorist bombings and school shootings? And to think that people go to these snobby, expensive colleges to do this kind of work.

Once I jettison the blind kid and dump the hubby, I'll take the house and all his money. It won't be easy, but I've been preparing for this role my entire life.

Yes, the blind kid senses something's not quite right with me. Not that her discomfort will stop me from doing what I need to do, but it makes me feel good knowing that I'm not totally without conscience.

I wish I could have been a fly on the wall when Shay woke up in that dingy basement and realized that she was a long way from Woodbridge Estates. Oh, to see the surprise on George's face when he saw the spitting image of me lying on that mattress. Hopefully, he'll stay sober—and alive—long enough to see my plan through, although he'll never see a dime of my money.

I've put a lot of pressure on myself to succeed. That's the price one must pay for success. There's no way I'm going back to being a low-life criminal, muling drugs, running cons, and turning tricks on the Strip. There are days when I'd love to go back to being Tatyana again, scheming in silence, doomed to spinsterhood because of that hideous butterfly stain on her face. Beneath all the tragedy and ugliness in her life is a beautiful girl trying to make her way in this cruel world.

* * *

Jessica sits on the sofa across from me, sipping a glass of wine. What to do with her? She called earlier and asked if she could come over and see how I was doing. I'd wanted nothing to do with the woman, but I also knew that if I put her off too long, there could be problems. Best to deal with these roadblocks head-on. Then, eliminate them if need be.

The look on her face tells me she's confused by this new incarnation of Shay Wells. And why shouldn't she be? I'm gorgeous, exude strength, and give off an air of confidence. I've spent enough time around big-time poker players to pick up on a person's tics and body language, and to know what they're thinking—and then anticipate what they might do next.

I thought about playing everything down and acting like the brain-damaged victim for a short spell. But why do that when I can live large and claim it's the by-product of my recovery process?

I pour myself a glass of wine and smile at Shay's portly friend.

"Are you sure you should be having wine?" Jessica asks. "The last time you had a glass at that dinner party, it really messed you up."

"One glass won't kill me. And god knows, I had more than a few glasses of wine out on that ranch, and look how that turned out."

"I have to say, you seem like a different person."

"Clean air and daily hikes will do that to a girl. Not to mention the extracurricular activities between yours truly and one handsome newscaster," I say, smiling knowingly. "We did it like rabbits on that ranch."

Jessica looks like she swallowed a sour ball.

"Of course, I'm not totally myself yet, but I'm much better than I've been in a long time."

"Honestly, Shay, I've never seen you like this."

"That blow to the head must have really rewired my brain." I laugh.

Jessica sips her wine as if she isn't believing a word of it. "So I guess you have that housekeeper to thank for this miraculous recovery."

I put on a sad face and shake my head. "Poor Tatyana. I feel so bad for her."

"And she just disappeared when you returned home without even a goodbye?"

"She gave her notice, effective immediately after our vacation ended. To be fair, she did leave us a brief thank-you note."

"She hasn't called since she's been gone?"

"No, and it's probably for the best. What that girl really needs is a good roll in the hay."

"And I thought I was bad."

"You are, Jessica. Just not in the way you think."

She pauses to digest this backhanded compliment. "Do you miss her?"

"In the worst possible way. Consuela can't hold a candle to Tatyana."

"Wait. Didn't you just call her Conchita a few minutes ago?"

"Consuela, Conchita." I shrug. "What's the difference?"

She seems taken aback by this. "You've made such a remarkable recovery."

"The mind is a mysterious thing. What can I tell you?" I sip my wine, trying to stay in character, and smile cheerfully at this nosy bitch.

"Do you plan on going back to the soup kitchen?"

"Hell no," I say, downing the rest of my wine. "It's about time charity begins at home."

"Caring for Quinn and Gideon?"

"Excuse me?" I put my hand to my sternum and make a show of looking offended. "Not all of us are cut out to stay home and bake cookies all day," I say, knowing the line will piss her off. "I'm going to do what makes me happy."

"And what might that be?"

"Return to the desk and deliver the news like my husband does each and every night."

"You want to be a news anchor?"

"Of course. I want to feel that adrenaline rush again like when I was younger."

Jessica laughs. "Excuse me for saying this, Shay, but you'll be competing against all those twenty-year-old beauty pageant contestants. You sure that's what you want?"

"I'm thirty-five and look better than ever, not like some of these pathetic housewives around here who sit on their asses all day eating Bon Bons."

Jessica finishes her drink and places her glass down on the table. I waste no time filling it back up, regardless of whether she wants more or not. It's only two thirty in the afternoon, but my liver had long ago acclimated to the effects of alcohol. There was a time in my life when I could drink all day without ill effects. Fish used to joke that they drank like Shannon. When the men eventually slipped into their drunken comas, that was when George and I would swoop in and clean them out. Or blackmail them.

"Have you told Gideon?"

"Yes, and he's all for it. He knows how important this is to me and our marriage. He recognizes the incredible talent I possess and wants to help make it a reality."

"But don't you remember telling me that you'd lost all desire to be a news anchor again?"

"My god, Jessica, aren't people allowed to change their minds? And I once won a coveted Emmy, something that husband of mine has never accomplished."

"That's true, but what about Quinn?"

"Our darling daughter is becoming quite the independent young lady. She doesn't need her mother hanging around all the time like some of the helicopter parents I know."

"Of course, but what about her—"

"What about her what?"

"The fact that she's visually impaired."

"She's blind, not a vegetable, and more than capable of living a rich and fulfilling life on her own."

"I wasn't implying.... What I meant to say was—" Jessica's flustered, and that's a good thing.

"I'm fully aware what you meant to say, Jessica, but it's disparaging to my daughter's character. Besides, I don't think you or anyone else expected me to be a stay-at-home mom for the rest of my life. And with boarding school and college on the horizon, Gideon and I will be needing two incomes."

"Boarding school?" Her face turns pale.

"Yes, we're considering enrolling Quinn in a private school for the blind."

"What does Gideon think of this?"

"I've not laid out the full plan to him just yet." I get up and walk over to the kitchen island, grab the veggie platter I purchased earlier in the day, and plop it down between us. As I sit, Conchita walks out of the bathroom. "What I'm telling you is strictly confidential, Jessica, so please don't breathe a word of this to anyone."

"No, of course not," she says, reaching for a carrot stick. She dabs it in a puddle of ranch dressing before snapping off the end in her teeth.

"I thought the veggie tray might be more appropriate for you," I say, flashing my sweetest smile.

Her face blushes. "Raising teens has been stressful these last few years."

"Yes, I imagine you must be under *lots* of stress." The subtly of my cruelty is artistic. "Better not wait too long to work on that figure of yours, or it might get away from you."

She glances nervously down at her stomach.

A few minutes later, she makes up some lame excuse that we both know is a lie. After a brief air hug, I see her out the front door.

I gather up my pocketbook and coat. There's lots to be done before my plan starts to take shape. I need to shop for a new wardrobe, seeing as my sister's attire resembles something one might see in a minister's closet. Then there's the appointment with the bank manager, life insurance agent, and our financial advisor. This husband of mine is much too tight-lipped about our net worth, so I'll need to do some digging to see where all the stocks, bonds, and mutual funds are stashed. One day, all his beautiful money will be mine.

After that, I'll enjoy a nice quiet lunch at Luca's with an expensive glass of champagne. Maybe a spa treatment in the afternoon. At three, I've scheduled a Botox treatment to get rid of some nasty wrinkles around my eyes. I'll need to look my best if I'm to deliver the news each night. These high-definition televisions have a tendency to reveal every little blemish. And the truth is, I'm not getting any younger. This could be my last chance to pull off a life-altering score.

I laugh while pulling the Platinum Plus Card out of my purse. I'm laughing so hard I fear I might create some new wrinkles around the corners of my eyes. So I stop laughing. And just like that I become somber and serious, like the famous news anchor I will one day become. It will take discipline and self-control to reach the pinnacle of success. In the end, it could prove to be my biggest hustle.

SHAY

Two weeks had passed, and she was going out of her mind with worry. Where was Gideon? Was he out searching for her? Where were the police? How was her daughter doing in her absence? Was there any way she could let people know that she was being held captive in this basement?

She'd managed to hide the bag of pills she had brought with her, cutting a slit in the mattress and stuffing them inside. Why she'd hid the pills in there, she didn't quite know. But now, for whatever reason, she was glad she had. When her captor left the room that first day, she waited a few minutes before pulling the bag out. Then she crushed the pills until only a residue of fine powder remained. She held out hope that she might be able to find time to spike the man's drink and make her getaway.

The man hadn't yet told her his name. He came in a few times a day to deliver her meals, usually a bowl of cereal or a skimpy sandwich with stale chips. Then he escorted her blindfolded up to the bathroom to either relieve herself or take a quick shower. When he came inside the basement room at night, she could tell by his mannerisms and speech that he'd been drinking. He would often stand by her bed and stare at her in a way that made her squeamish. It didn't feel sexual, but something else. He stared at her almost in admiration. But what was there to admire?

After two weeks passed, she felt herself becoming soft and out of shape. She needed to start doing something physical besides reading the paperback novels piled up on the floor.

She began to pace the room and do jumping jacks, anything to raise her heartbeat and help her forget that she was locked in this basement for the foreseeable future. Being confined like this nearly drove her insane. She couldn't imagine how she'd maintain her sanity if she stayed down here for any length of time.

Thank God for that sliver of light coming in from the window above. It allowed her to determine night from day, and that one little detail about the outside world helped keep her regimented.

The dangling lightbulb allowed her to read at night until she fell asleep. She prayed the bulb wouldn't go out. Or if it did, the man upstairs would replace it with a fresh bulb. Living in total darkness would be too cruel.

She picked up the Stephen King novel *Misery* and opened it to where she left off. A few minutes later, she heard a noise at the door. The bolt lock slid open, and the man stumbled in. He had a wooden stool in hand and appeared quite drunk. He plunked the stool down on the cement floor and sat a few feet away from her, a glass of amber liquid in hand.

She tried not to stare at him as he rested the glass on his thigh and sighed. She wondered if she might be able to slip some of that drug into his drink when he turned away. But he was a big man. It would probably take all of the powder to knock him out. Then she could sprint past him, lock him inside this basement, and call the police.

"Don't even think about it, gorgeous," he said as if reading her mind.

"Don't even think about what?" she said.

"Whatever bad thoughts are stewing in that head of yours." He took a sip of his drink and pointed it at her. "Trust me, if you really love your daughter, doing something stupid would be the worst thing you could do for her."

"You'd better not lay a finger on Quinn."

"Oh? And what are you going to do about it if we do?"

We? "I swear to God I'll kill you."

The man laughed. "Don't worry, she won't be harmed if you do as you're told. But if you fail to follow the program, my partner will have no problem putting the screws to her."

"I'll do whatever you ask, then."

He cocked his head. "So, what are you thinking about right now?"

"I was thinking that we're both stuck here, for whatever reason, and you're the one who gets to have a drink."

He laughed at this and held up his glass. "You want some?"

"Why not? Keep my mind off the fact that I'm being held against my will."

"Jack Daniel's tickle your fancy?"

"Beggars can't be choosy."

He took a sip and studied her. "She likes the taste of Jack, too."

"Who does?"

"Never mind." He passed her the glass with only a swirl left at the bottom. "Down the hatch."

She swallowed it in one gulp, making a pained face as it burned the back of her throat.

"I got more upstairs. Came here with four cases of the hooch."

"Why don't you get another glass and come back down with the bottle."

"Maybe tomorrow night we'll share a drink, if you sit still and behave yourself." He took out a cigarette and lit it.

She handed the glass back to him. "I forgot what having a buzz feels like."

"One of life's small pleasures."

She struggled to swallow the burn in her throat. "Can you tell me why I'm here?"

"That's for me to know and you to find out."

"Will you at least tell me your name?"

"Can't see why not." He took a long drag on his cigarette and regarded her curiously. "George."

"Okay, George, that's a good start. My name is Shay."

George laughed. "I know who you are."

"Can you at least tell me how long I'll be holed up here in this basement?"

"You'll stay here until I say otherwise."

"Okay, be like that."

"You're a curious one, aren't you?"

Shay felt uncomfortable watching him stare at her with those crazy, drunk eyes. He looked capable of anything in this inebriated state. He crossed his arms, and his nostrils flared ever so slightly above his droopy mustache.

"She told me all about you. I would never have believed it had I not seen you with my own eyes."

"Who did?" She tried to change the subject. "I'll have you know that I'm a happily married woman."

"Is that so?" Wrinkles lined the corner of his eyes as the cigarette smoke swirled around his head.

"My husband is probably out searching for me as we speak."

"Keep believing that horseshit, honey. Maybe it'll help ease your pain."

"It's not horseshit. My husband loves me."

"Tomorrow night, we'll have a stiff drink and talk some more. Might as well be neighborly, seeing as how the two of us will be here for a while."

"Is it money you want? Because we have plenty."

"Why are you so concerned about all of this right now? There's nothing you can do about your situation, so you might as well kick back and enjoy our time together."

"Enjoy our time together? Are you serious?"

"Deadly serious." He pulled the stool out from beneath him and stood, his body tottering as if he might keel over. She wanted so badly to spike his drink, but feared what might happen to Quinn if she did and if she didn't succeed.

"Tomorrow night, we'll have a Jack together. Okay?"

"You promise?"

"I give you my word. But you'd better think long and hard about doing whatever it is you think you're going to do."

"I have no idea what you're talking about."

"Oh, I think otherwise," he said. "Look, I'm not going to hurt you unless you make me."

"I just told you that I'm not planning to do anything stupid."

"Good. I'd hate for that little girl of yours to suffer."

"Swear to God, George. I'm just bored and lonely down here and really need some human interaction."

"I understand, doll, but these things take time."

He backed up toward the door, stool cupped in his oversized palm. He opened it and then disappeared, locking her back inside the dingy prison.

On a near-empty stomach, the whiskey went straight to her head. Tears bubbled in her eyes as she started thinking about Quinn and how much her daughter must be missing her right now. She marked her page, closed the paperback, and dropped it on the floor. Then she lay back on the mattress, closed her eyes, and prayed to God to let her survive this ordeal so that she might one day be reunited with her family.

GIDEON

Gideon had been utterly shocked when his boss agreed with his casual aside to bring Shay on board as his co-anchor. Never in his life had he expected him to go along with such a lamebrained idea, especially after the video surfaced of Shay kicking that dog. Besides, he didn't need any help with his newscast's ratings now that he'd pulled ahead of Yolanda Brown. The added distraction of having his wife by his side could only make things worse for him. And what about poor, dull Kaecie? She would be heartbroken by the news that she'd been replaced with his wife, not that he cared one iota about Kaecie's feelings.

How would he conduct his flirty lunch dates? Or "mentor" all the young leggy interns seeking his advice? All of this would be a thing of the past with Shay breathing down his neck twenty-four-seven. Of course, he'd promised himself not to engage in any more work romances, but he'd said this same thing many times in the past. Another messy divorce could ruin him, both professionally as well as financially. No, he had to be a good husband and on his best behavior, especially with the prospect of a new job on the horizon.

If only Shay hadn't been so damned persistent. How could he talk her out of this nonsense?

He had to figure out a way to walk everyone back from this crazy idea. By the way his wife was acting as of late, that seemed highly unlikely. He needed to convince his general manager to rethink this harebrained notion and squash it before it became a reality and before anyone found out about the dog she bashed over the head. But how could he accomplish this without appearing like a fool? After all, he'd been the one who'd pitched the idea. And now the station could dump Kaecie and her market salary and hire Shay at a much cheaper rate.

Gideon carried a bouquet of flowers in hand as he made his way up the stairs. Since returning from vacation, he'd been occasionally returning home in the afternoons for the sweet surprises she'd have waiting for him in the bedroom. His coming home was her idea, and he'd come to realize that going along with Shay made life much easier, even when he wasn't in the mood for sex.

She'd never been this sexually assertive before the attack. He chalked it up to her being a survivor of a dysfunctional childhood; it had given her a second lease on life—and she explained that she wasn't going to squander the opportunity. She'd told him as much with her voluminous credit card purchases in the last month. Not only had she been spending recklessly, but she'd been meeting with architects and interior designers to completely remodel both the kitchen and the master bathroom.

The constant request for sex was becoming even too demanding for him. In the beginning, returning home provided him with unthinkable pleasures. He enjoyed variety, and because of Shay, he now had little energy left to charm all the office cuties looking to move up in the world. It surprised him that Shay's ambitions extended to the bedroom, but an occasional break wouldn't kill them, especially since the sex had seemed so mechanical. Maybe his wife felt the need to constantly sleep with him in order to prove her love. Or maybe she slept with him to increase her chances of getting hired on as his sidekick. He'd never heard of a casting couch extending to one's wife, but then again, nothing surprised him anymore.

Shay greeted him at the door with a kiss as soon as he made his way inside. She took the flowers he brought her and placed them in a new blue Chihuly vase filled with water. Gideon studied her closely. It amazed him how subtly Shay's appearance had changed after that vacation.

Once the flowers graced the table, she turned and beamed at him. What could that mean? He couldn't quite put his finger on why she looked so different today, but she did. Her skin glowed and had an ultra-smooth sheen to it. Had she been tanning? Then it occurred to him why, as he recalled perusing his lengthy credit card statement. His wife had been getting regular Botox treatments and making weekly trips to the spa and hairdresser. It made sense now. If she planned on returning to the news desk, she wanted to look as young as possible.

"Sit down, hon, and have something to eat. I ordered delivery from Han Dynasty, knowing how much you love their dumplings."

"Han Dynasty," he responded, knowing it was one of the most expensive restaurants in Boston. "Do they deliver this far out of the city?"

"Not typically, but they were willing to make an exception for the great Gideon Wells."

"For a king's ransom, I assume."

"Admittedly, it is a bit extra, but their caviar fried rice and lobster dumplings are *soooo* worth it," she said. "Don't you agree?"

"I could have just picked something up at Wong's on my way home."

"Wong's? That place is disgusting," she said, making a sweet and sour face. "You need to stop being such a miser, Gideon. If I'd wanted to spend *our* money, I would have chosen something from The Capital Grille."

"I'm just trying to be fiscally responsible."

"And I'm not? Besides, once we have two salaries coming in, we'll have plenty of disposable income."

"Where's Quinn?"

"I dropped her off at a friend's house so we could be alone. She doesn't want to hang out with her stodgy old parents tonight."

"Since when?"

"Since she's learned that there's a whole new world out there to discover."

He grabbed a pair of chopsticks, struggled to pick up a dumpling, then awkwardly maneuvered it into his mouth using his fingers. "I was thinking about that news job you were asking me about."

"I know, honey, isn't it wonderful? Thank you so much for putting in a good word for me," she said, rushing over and kissing him on the cheek. "I'm so pumped about the two of us working together. It just blows my mind that I'm back in the game."

"Wait. Ken hasn't officially agreed to this plan yet. Has he?"

"Of course he has. He called me today and told me the good news."

This development stunned him. "When was this?"

"It must have been soon after you put in that good word for me, because he's super psyched to have me on board. He said that everyone's excited for me going forward."

He needed to try another tack. "Maybe we should rethink this idea, Shay."

"What's there to rethink?"

"It's such a drastic move. And in your fragile state, still recovering from head trauma, I'm not sure going back to work is the best thing for you."

"I've never felt better in my life. And once my physician clears me, what other obstacle can stand in my way?"

"There's Quinn to think about," he said as the Latina housekeeper scurried past them, carrying a laundry basket brimming with folded clothes.

"I thought we already discussed this. She's going to attend that school for the blind in Connecticut."

"Now, hold on. You can't just simply enroll her in a school like that without discussing it with me first. There's campus visits, applying and enrollment, as well as other financial matters to consider."

"She's already been accepted. I sent her transcripts over and had a wonderful chat with the headmaster. They're thrilled to have a precocious girl like Quinn attending their school. I even sent them a nonrefundable down payment."

"You did what?"

"Jesus, Gideon, don't act so surprised. We already agreed that her going away to school would be in everyone's best interest."

"But we haven't even discussed this with Quinn."

"What's to discuss? The academics there are unparalleled, and she will have everything at her disposal," his wife said, looking exasperated. "They even provide riding lessons come spring, although that might cost a bit extra."

"I'm still unsure about all of this."

Shay stood, her hands balled into fists and her lips pressed tightly together.

He'd not seen her this angry for quite some time since she'd caught him cheating. He cowered nervously in his seat, fearing this new incarnation of his wife. Both desire and fear consumed him. Something in her brain had been activated, and she'd become assertive in a way he'd never before known—or expected. He instantly loathed the homeless person who had attacked her, but for different reasons now than he did prior to the crime. The attack had turned her into an unpredictable monster hell-bent on ruining his life.

"I see what's going on here," Shay said, her face close to his. "You want all the glory and attention for yourself. You feel threatened that your wife might one day become a star as bright as you."

"Dear, I've been at this game a long time. I didn't just become a star overnight."

"I've sacrificed my career in order to have a child with you. Stayed home and raised Quinn through all the medical emergencies and hardships. Did you really think I was going to sit idly by and volunteer at a soup kitchen for the rest of my life?"

"Of course not," he said meekly. "But I'll miss Quinn if she goes away. And so will you."

"Have you considered being a stay-at-home parent? I'm sure Quinn would love having her father around all the time to care for her and take her to school. Then I can be the breadwinner in this family."

He pinched his chin and looked away. "You know that's not going to happen."

"Then it's settled. Quinn's going to school in Connecticut. I'll meet with Ken tomorrow, and we can decide when I'll start on the desk."

Realizing he was not going to win this argument, he stood and put on his suit jacket. "I need to get back to the office."

"Aren't you going to eat your lunch?"

"Not hungry. I'll have the leftovers when I get home."

"Fine. Just make sure and tell Kaecie to keep that seat warm for me." She laughed.

Did she really just say that? He glanced at his wife to see if she was putting him on.

She grabbed his head and kissed him on the lips. "You watch and see, honey. It's going to be so wonderful working together. It'll grow us even closer."

"I can't wait." He kissed her back, desperate to escape her clutches.

"Who knows, you might even win your first Emmy with me as your copilot."

He drove back to the station in a state of despair. Nothing good could come of this. He considered his situation. If he accepted the job in Manhattan, what would Shay do then? Chances are, she would never forgive him. The idea of another bitter divorce appealed to him as much as a root canal without anesthesia. But he couldn't turn down this amazing job if offered to him. It might never come his way again.

As he contemplated this while sitting in traffic, snow falling over his windshield, his phone rang.

"It's looking very good for you, Gideon," the woman said as soon as he picked up. "My people are pushing extremely hard to bring you on board."

"I can't tell you how exciting this is for me. Thank you so much, whoever you are."

"Don't thank me just yet," she said. "Have you told anyone about our conversations?"

"Not a soul. Not even my wife."

"Good. It should reflect well on you when the board members reconvene to make their final decision."

"Could I at least discuss the offer with my wife? She's thinking about taking a job at the station, and I'd hate to disappoint her with a sudden move to Manhattan."

He heard a pause at the other end of the line. "Maybe this job isn't right for you after all."

He gazed out at the Charles River and saw teams of rowers churning through the brackish water. "Enough said. I'll keep my big fat mouth shut."

"Look, Gideon, we know your wife was brutally attacked and diagnosed with a traumatic head injury. That makes her unpredictable and a big risk to us. Who knows what she might say if she found out you were getting the job? And if Logan finds out that we're about to fire him, he'll make an even bigger stink and cause a lot of headaches here at the network."

"What has my wife got to do with any of this?"

"She used to work in the industry, right?"

"Many years ago, before we had our daughter."

"The two of you socialize at that fancy club of yours. And a lot of your friends work in broadcasting." Another pause. "Loose lips sink networks."

"Say no more."

"I don't think you understand the complexity of the situation we're in with Logan Burrows. He's covered the Nixon impeachment, Vietnam, and was standing next to Ronald Reagan at the Washington Hilton when he was shot. You don't just fire a living legend by snapping your fingers and expect him to disappear without a fight. There's a lot of messy politics and boardroom intrigue."

"That's what I don't understand. Why are you even getting rid of a legend like Logan Burrows?"

"Not many people know this, but Logan is an inveterate backstabber and a longtime abuser of women. Our network has been struggling in the ratings for the last two years because of Burrows's refusal to go off into the sunset. The younger demographic has completely tuned him out. He's a dinosaur who refuses to become extinct. On top of that, the network is up for sale, and any bad publicity might kill a potential deal."

Logan Burrows, an abuser of women? "Did he ever try anything with you?"

"Logan has been inappropriate with just about every female in the newsroom. Those who rebuffed his entreaties eventually quit or got fired. That's part of the reason we want him gone."

"So if he found out that he was getting axed, you believe he'd make a stink?"

"A stink would be the least of our worries. Can you say lawsuit for age discrimination? Not only that, but he'd detail all the skeletons in our company's closet, and then the network would lose half its value. That's why this needs to be quick and painless. If he starts talking, we need to say he's a disgruntled employee suffering from dementia."

"It makes sense," he said, taking the off-ramp into town. "Could you at least tell me who I'm up against for the job?"

"Sorry, but I can't do that."

"How about a timeline?"

"Hopefully, in the next few months. A violent coup such as this takes a lot of planning if it's to be done right."

"It's not like I'm going anywhere."

"You just be patient and continue beating Yolanda Brown in the ratings. We here at the network are watching you closely."

"Bringing in big audiences night after night is what I do, and it's what I'll do for your network if given the chance."

"We know you will. That's why we want you sitting in Logan's seat more than anyone," she said. "We do have one slight concern, however."

Did he hear a note of doubt creeping into the woman's voice? "What is it?"

"Do you have a drinking problem?"

He recoiled at the notion. "Of course not. Who told you such lies?"

"We noticed you were slurring your words the other night."

He had to think fast. "Severe exhaustion and a slight prescription adjustment, I'm afraid. As you know, my wife has been suffering from the aftereffects of that violent assault. I had to return home and take care of her before my broadcast that evening. Also, my daughter is blind and needs help around the house." The lies came fast and furious.

"That obviously explains your erratic behavior. But please don't let it happen again."

"Never. I'm a consummate professional and team player. If you choose to hire me, I'll be your network's most tireless and dogged advocate."

"Good to hear," the woman said. "Just don't let them see you sweat, Gipper."

Never again would he drink a cocktail on a night he was to go on-air. But he'd consumed only the one drink, and he never got that tongue-tied after a single cocktail. It felt like he'd been handed a reprieve. At least he knew one thing: the network was watching his every move, so he had to be careful. He had to step up his game and deliver flawless performances. The job situation with his wife, he'd deal with later. Hopefully, he could stall her long enough until he landed the Manhattan gig.

QUINN

A smile came over Quinn's face as she sat on her bed reading the book *Wonder* in Braille. She'd read the book so many times now that she'd lost track of the count. She could totally relate to ten-year-old Auggie Pullman and his unusual face, the result of his many surgeries. His disability was not exactly like being blind, but similar in that it was often hard to fit in with the other kids. And while she could do many things, she sometimes experienced feelings that she likened to superpowers. She could hear and sense things that most seeing people took for granted. Lacking sight left her at a disadvantage when it came to making new friends, but in other ways, being blind had its advantages.

Still, she wouldn't change a thing about herself. She loved her school and her family, although she prayed each day that her mother would return to her old self. Every day produced a different challenge, and she looked forward to breaking down the barriers in her life and creating new opportunities. That vacation on the farm proved she could do most anything she wanted if she put her mind to it.

Quinn heard a knock at the door, her cue. She reached back and rapped her knuckles against the bedpost in reply. The bell attached to her door chimed, and she heard Caramelo enter, their new maid. The older woman sat next to her on the bed and held her hand. Her skin felt rough and calloused, unlike her mother's smooth hands, or anyone else's for that matter. Quinn guessed that Caramelo had done a lot of hard work in her life.

"How are you, *chiquita?*"

"A little lonely. Thank you so much for sitting with me."

"Of course, I sit with you," the woman said.

"If you're like the other housekeepers, I'm afraid you'll not be here very long."

"There is always that about my job. But you still have your momma and papa who love you."

"I hardly see my father these days except on weekends. And the woman downstairs is not really my mother."

"Don't talk like that, *chiquita*," she scolded. "Of course, she's your momma. You must love her with all your heart."

"I do love her. She may be my biological mother, but she's changed since that attack. She's not the same person she used to be."

"Your father says your momma had a terrible head injury. You must be patient with her. She will eventually come around."

"I heard her talking on the phone the other day. She wants to send me away to school."

"Away to school?"

"Yes. A special school for blind kids in Connecticut," she said, feeling Caramelo's calloused thumb wiping away a tear under her eye. "My real mother would never send me away like that."

"Did she tell you this?"

"Not yet. I think she's waiting for the right moment."

"But why? There must be a good reason."

"I heard her saying she wants to go back to work and be a news anchor just like my father."

"*Que ninguna mujer buena*."

"What does that mean?"

"It's nothing. Forget about it."

"My mother says she wants to be on TV like she used to be. She never acted like this before she got injured."

"Maybe this school will be good for you. Help you more than the one you go to now?"

"But I love my school and all my friends. I don't want to go away to

Connecticut, where I don't know anyone. I'd also miss you, Caramelo, even though you've only been here a short time."

"I would miss you too."

"That's why I don't think she's my real momma."

"You keep faith in God, *chiquita*. Your real momma, wherever she is in that head of hers, will eventually come back," Caramelo said, clutching her hand against her chest.

"You really think she will?"

"I know she will. You just have to keep believing and praying to God. In one way or another, she'll heal that mind of hers and be herself again."

"But how can you be so sure?"

"Because I lost my momma when I was a young girl. Then, one day, when I was just sitting there, I heard her talking to me."

"You mean she died?"

"Yes."

"I'm so sorry about that," Quinn said. "What did your mother say to you?"

"She said that no matter what happens in life, she is always there beside me. And that she loves me very much."

"Do you think my mother will come back and speak to me like that?"

"Of course. Your real momma is always in your heart, just like God. He has His reasons for everything."

"Like me getting sick and becoming blind?"

"Si. It's what makes you such a special girl."

"It's weird, but I'm not angry about what happened. Being blind is who I am, although at times I think it would be nice to have my sight back. I'm happy this way. And it's pretty much all I know."

"You are an amazing girl," the woman said, standing from the bed.

"Where are you going?"

"I must go back downstairs and help your mother. She's having friends over for a party."

"Why kind of a party?"

"I don't ask questions, girl," Caramelo said. "Just promise me you won't give up."

"I'll not. I'll pray every day that God will return my mother to me."

"Good girl. Now go back to your reading while I go downstairs and help your momma."

"*Gracias,* Caramelo."

"*De nada, chiquita.*"

Before returning to her book, Quinn pressed her eyelids together and said a brief prayer that she wouldn't be cast off to Connecticut and that her mother would come to her senses and see the error of her ways. She wanted her to be the mother she was before that attack: loving and kind. She remembered what her mother once said to her when she was feeling lonely.

"I'll always be there for you, darling. When I gave up being a TV news reporter, I gave it up in order to care for you."

SHANNON

I often lie awake at night, thinking pleasurably about how life must be for my sister. Revenge is sweet. Sometimes too sweet: like a gift you've given to someone but can't fully appreciate because you're not there to watch their expression when they open it.

George didn't believe me when I first told him that I had an identical twin. He never thought there could be anyone else in the world quite like me. It must have blown his mind when he laid eyes on Shay that first day in the basement.

He laughed at my plan when I told him about kidnapping my twin. He said I was crazy and that it would never work. I told him he had nothing to lose and to do it for the sake of his kids. That way, he could set them up for life with the millions we would make off this scam. I laid a guilt trip on him, knowing he'd been an absent father for most of their lives. Thankfully, he eventually agreed to help me, because I never could have pulled this off on my own.

But neither George nor Shay will get out of that house alive. And his kids will never see a red cent of the money I plan on stealing. No way am I sharing this windfall with anyone.

The other night, while Gideon was relaxing in the living room, I put on an old R&B song and started dancing seductively in front of him. In his left hand, he'd been holding a half-finished crossword puzzle. In his other hand was a snifter of expensive cognac. I stripped to my lingerie as he stared up at me in dismay. I'm certain that my sister never danced this way for him. All I needed was a pole and a dim stage. Conchita had already left for the night, and Quinn was upstairs in her room, doing whatever eleven-year-old blind girls do. I had no worries that she might come downstairs and catch me cockteasing her father. Gideon's eyes were as big as Saturn's moons as I gyrated in front of him. I reached back and unclasped my bra, letting my twins spill out. I fell to my knees and rested my arms on his thighs. For a brief second, I thought the weight of his falling jaw might shatter my forearm.

Fortunately, my sister and I were blessed with killer bods. Good genes, I suppose you could say. That's about all we got from our trailer-trash parents.

In the sack, Gideon's predictable and needy, and then off to the races before it even gets started. I often think I did my sister a favor by liberating her from this haircut of a man, a man pretending to be more than the sum of his parts.

The other day, I went into my walk-in closet and pulled out the miniature baseball bat I purchased over the internet. It's the kind of kitschy souvenir they give away before baseball games. I spun it around in my hands, admiring Shay's dried blood splattered over the polished grains of wood. I took some of the blood that I drew from her arm that day, disguised as Tatyana, and smeared it over the barrel. The bat, ironically, has Gideon's signature scrawled under the label. Last year, Fenway Park ran a promotion giving the first five thousand fans through the gate a souvenir bat on Gideon Wells night. Amazing what one can buy online.

I put the bat in a small duffel bag that Gideon once used when he went to the gym. I carried it out to the garage and stuffed it deep into the recesses of his trunk so that he couldn't ever possibly find it. Will I need to use it? I don't know yet, and that's the beauty of my plan; I haven't yet decided how this tragedy will play out.

After spending thousands of dollars of Gideon's money, my wardrobe is nearly complete. I have Botox treatments scheduled every two weeks. I've hired crews to remodel both the kitchen and the three bathrooms. And let's not forget about Quinn's new school at a cost of sixty grand a year.

I wish I could muster up some tears about her situation. I keep reminding myself that she's my niece, young and blind and that as her evil stepmother, I'm kicking the little brat to the curb. Then I sit back and wait for the tears to come. But they never do.

What sane adult would want to have kids when they could have so much more in life? There's the constant nagging and tears. Changing diapers and losing sleep. And having to crack the little bastards upside the head when they misbehave, like my mother used to do to Shay and me in public. If people were more selfish like me, the earth would be a far better place.

I'm upset with Consuela. Where is she when I really need her? She thinks I don't know that she slips into Quinn's room every night to deliver "Latina words of wisdom." Best to let Quinn think she's special for now. I'll allow the maid to humor the kid a bit longer until she, too, is shipped out and another housekeeper is brought in to take her place.

The catered food will be here any minute now. Champagne and wine sit chilled in the fridge. All I need is for Consuela to set the table and put out the party bags. It's a lovely day. I walk over to the window and stare out at the beautiful tenth green, thinking about that day I stumbled out there in the buff, watching as those four golfers stood studying their putts. Then they turned and saw me approaching, and you would have thought they'd seen a ghost.

Out in the driveway sits the new Mercedes I made Gideon buy for me. What a beautiful piece of German engineering. For the first time ever, I feel like I'm living the life meant for me.

The caterers pull up and drop off all the food.

Sometime later, the doorbell rings. My guests have finally arrived. Gail, Cindy, Sharon, Margie, Bebe, and that nosey bitch Jessica. I rush over and open the door. "Come on in, ladies," I say cheerfully, gesturing with a wide sweep of my perfectly tanned arm. Then I air hug each and every one of them.

SHAY

Being alone in this basement, day after day, was starting to become unbearable. She didn't know how people who lived in captivity for long periods of time managed to keep their sanity. And what about her captor? George? She always liked the name. Many of the English kings were named George. Her George seemed to study her whenever he came down here. Why? Did he find her attractive?

Her stomach growled. Pacing the room for hours on end burned valuable calories. She sat on the cold cement floor, noticing the first rays of light flickering through the window above her bed.

How long had it been since she'd been confined in this basement? She'd stopped keeping track of the days, but she figured she'd been here at least a month. A month without her daughter felt like an eternity. If only she could find a way out of this prison.

She'd scoured every single inch of this basement, searching for a possible escape route, but thus far, had found nothing. The window above appeared too high and too small for her body to fit through. Besides, she couldn't find anything in this basement to stand on.

Weak, she pulled herself up and shuffled over to the flimsy mattress and lay down on it. She hadn't been sleeping well, her sleep interrupted by the constant stream of nightmares she'd been having. Each night, these nightmares caused her to break out in a cold sweat.

She racked her brain, thinking about who, apart from George, might have done this to her. She had no doubt that the person who attacked her that night, down by the homeless shelter, had also been responsible for kidnapping her and keeping her captive. Was it money they wanted? Had Gideon refused to pay a ransom to free her? She doubted it. She believed that Gideon would pay any amount to return her home.

Or would he?

She tortured herself with all these nagging questions.

Who was George? And where had he come from? So far, he hadn't said much during his trips down here. Only at night, after he'd been drinking, did he begin to open up and reveal a little about himself. This gave her a sliver of hope that she might be able to slip some of that powder into his drink and render him unconscious. Then she would steal his keys and get the hell out of there in whatever way she could.

She heard the lock sliding through the bolt and then the handle of the door turning. Hungry and lonely, she actually found herself welcoming his visits. She sat up on the mattress and eagerly awaited whatever food he might bring her. It was never enough, and typically, she was left hungry and wanting more. It had gotten to the point where she began to fantasize about all the foods she craved back in Boston.

The door opened, and George stumbled in, holding a white mug of coffee in hand. She could tell almost immediately that he had a hangover. Whenever he drank too much, she knew not to say anything that might piss him off. He could get cantankerous and moody. A couple of times, after she'd asked too many questions, he walked over and looked as if he might hit her.

"Here," he said, passing her a spoon and bowl filled with mushy cornflakes.

"It's not enough. I'm hungry all the time."

"You're lucky you even get this. Go ahead and keep complaining, and I might just skip breakfast the next time."

"No. I'm sorry. Thank you."

"Apology accepted. Now stop bitching and eat your damn cornflakes."

"Is this real milk? Because it tastes terrible."

"The powdered kind."

"It's gross."

"You're lucky you get that."

"I'm not complaining, George, but do you think I could at least get a cup of coffee? Pretty please?"

"Keep up the good manners, and I'll think about it."

She smiled at him. "It's not like I'm asking you to share your booze."

He sipped his coffee and stared at her.

"One cup of coffee, George. That's all I'm asking."

"Like I said, let's see how you do following the program."

"I've done everything you've asked of me thus far."

A smile came over his face. "Maybe I haven't asked the right question yet."

What did that mean?

Disgusted, she lifted the spoon, scooped up some of the mushy flakes, and shoveled them in her awaiting mouth. Never in her life had cornflakes tasted so good. She chewed slowly, savoring the wet, grainy taste of corn on her tongue. The last thing she wanted was to look down and see an empty bowl.

"It still blows my mind," George said, coffee smoke swirling around his haggard face.

"What does?"

He took out a pack of cigarettes. "I never would have believed it had I not seen it myself."

She swallowed her mush. "Believed what?"

"The sight of you sitting here in front of me."

"But you don't even know me, George." She saw the butt of a gun tucked in his belt.

"I know you better than you think." He pulled a cigarette out of the pack and stuck it in his mouth.

"Are you a stalker or something? I haven't been a news reporter in years."

"Hell no, I'm no stalker." He laughed. "Never needed to do that sort of thing to get lucky."

"You've got me more confused than ever."

Seeing that her bowl of cornflakes was nearly empty, she tipped the bowl and greedily slurped the last drops of sour-tasting milk. She could have easily eaten two more bowls, but she didn't want to appear desperate in front of him.

"I don't understand. We have money we can give you."

"Not everything is about money."

"If it's not about money, then what is it you want?"

"I never said we didn't want money. I just said this is not *all* about the almighty dollar."

She held out the empty bowl, and he took it. "I haven't showered in a day, George."

He slammed his foot down on the cement floor. "You think this is easy for me? You think I like living in this shithole, knowing she's out there having a grand old time?"

"Who?"

"You really haven't figured it out by now?" He leaned over and glared at her.

"I'm sorry to upset you, but I honestly have no idea what you're talking about."

"Maybe you should stay down here and think about it," he said, pressing his index finger into her temple. "And when you figure it out, you and I will toss back a shot of Jack and share a good laugh."

She watched as he stormed out of the room. He secured the external bolt lock, leaving her alone once again.

Something strange was going on, and she had to figure out what. Not that knowing would help her in any way. She still had to find a way out of this basement and contact the authorities. But at least it might put her mind at ease in regard to her family's safety. Or maybe it wouldn't. She hadn't considered the possibility that knowing the truth might frighten her even more.

She closed her eyes and tried to think about who had kidnapped her, but all she could think about was food. Never in her life had she fantasized about all the foods she craved. Even her recollections of Quinn were soon replaced by thoughts of a Regina's coal-fired pizza, thick lobster rolls, and Kelly's stuffed roast beef sandwiches. Tears filled her eyes, thinking about food when she should have been focusing on Quinn.

She turned to her side and reached over the mattress until she found the slit. Poking her long fingers inside, she pulled out the bag and studied it. There was enough powder in there to knock out an elephant. Now, she just had to find the right time to spike George's drink. She considered the possibility that she would have to seduce him first. If he found her attractive, although she couldn't see how in her current state, why hadn't he tried anything? There were forces at play here she didn't quite understand.

Determined, she leaned over and stuffed the bag of crushed powder back into the slit, pushing it further inside using her fingers. Then she lay back and tried to think about all the people in her life who might want to hurt her and her family.

SHANNON

Before all the girls came over, I created these cute little name tags and then made them pin them over their outfits. That way, I could identify their names while at the same time celebrate my amazing recovery from head trauma.

I stare at these rich bitches sitting in my living room, watching as they laugh like hyenas, sip expensive champagne and gossip. Two of the girls have pricey bob hairstyles that have been colored to hide their grays. A few have fake boobs. Most have had Botox shots or significant cosmetic surgery; it's easy to spot. All of them have had their nails done by the chattering trio of Vietnamese girls who operate Nam's Nail Salon in the center of town.

The food has been expensively catered, including the meticulously detailed cake, which I keep hidden in a separate room as a surprise. It's been decorated in the shape of a television, with a lifelike photograph of me sitting at a news desk. I purposefully left Gideon out of the picture.

I walk around the room, making small talk, which is no small task considering that I've never met any of these women before, with the exception of Jessica. I do a lot of listening and forearm touching. I pretend to sympathize with their first-world problems, despite being a scam artist to the core. The rest of my conversations I conduct with smoke and mirrors and considerable sleight of hand. It's amazing what you can learn from a person's body language and facial expressions. Asking leading questions helps, too. I learned a great deal from my time working the Vegas Strip and talking with magicians, mediums, and hypnotists.

I know it sounds crazy, but these women are so clueless about real life that it feels like child's play. All I need to do is convince them that I'm Shay and I'm home free.

All except for Jessica. I've yet to understand her motive. She suspects something's up, but she has no idea what. I had no choice but to invite her to this party or else face scrutiny from the other women. Jessica is Shay's best friend, and everyone knows this. Not to mention that Gideon plays golf with her talent-starved husband, Stan, who delivers the weather each night with the charisma of an Amish undertaker.

Pretending to be nice to Jessica is the hardest act to pull off, but I manage to do it with style and grace. She sits there with a phony grin on her bloated mug, stuffing wheat crackers topped with cheese cubes into her hole. I know she's watching my every move, hoping I'll screw up. Does she suspect that I'm not who I say I am? There's no way she could. But I can't shake the sensation that she knows I'm not Shay.

I walk around, pouring everyone more champagne. The mood is jovial. There's lots of laughter and gaiety. Out the window, I take in all their fancy SUVs and luxury sedans parked in the driveway and along the curb. Some of them actually have jobs, but most live off the fruits of their sugar-daddy husbands. Their rich perfumes and fruity shampoos make the air seem tropical: citrus, coconuts, pears, bananas, and apricots.

I can't wait to escort every last one of these bitches out the door. I've never in my life had a close friend and never wanted one. People have always been expendable to me: once I get what I need from them, they're gone. It's probably why I've never made many close associations, except for George. Then again, George is like a mentor to me.

I grab a champagne glass and tap it with a spoon in order to get everyone's attention. A few continue to giggle and chat, but a forced smile in their direction sets them straight. Their faces are flush from the champagne, and I can see that they're ripe for the news I'm about to deliver.

"Thank you, everyone, for coming to my little party today," I say, holding the glass by the stem. "The name tags are in place in case I have a brain fart and forget who y'all are." Everyone laughs at my faux Southern drawl.

"Don't forget the fifty dollars I lent you," Margie shouts out.

"Knowing you, Margie, my dear, it would never have left that sticky palm of yours." More laughter. "But seriously, I never would have made a full recovery without all of your love and support." Saying this makes me want to vomit.

"We love you too," a woman named Gail says, clasping her hands together excitedly.

"I pray that none of you ever has to suffer the trauma that I've experienced these last few months." The room goes quiet.

"You're such a trooper, girl. An inspiration," Bebe says. Jessica rolls her eyes.

"You're much too nice," I say in my sweetest voice. "I asked you ladies here today not only to thank you for standing by me and my family these last few months, but to make a special announcement about my future."

"And what's that?" Jessica asks in her phoniest voice.

I glare at her before breaking out into a huge smile. Do I really give a shit what they think of me? Hell no. They can all fuck off with their tails between their fat thighs and return to their boring lives here in Woodbridge Estates.

"After numerous talks and negotiations, I'm happy to announce that I will be co-anchoring the nightly news with my husband."

The women stare at me in shock, except for Jessica, who sits there with her red lips pressed tightly together.

"Wow. Seems the cat's gotten ahold of your tongues." I stare at them in mock shock, waiting for a reaction. "Anyone want to congratulate me?"

The women come over and embrace me and wish me the best. I hug and thank them before grabbing the champagne bottle and refilling their glasses. Then I go back and retrieve the cake, and the women ooooh and ahhhh at the sight of my face over the frosting. I cut it into delicate squares, listening to every one of them ask for a tiny wedge, claiming they're watching their weight. All except for Jessica, of course, who chooses a large rectangle specifically cut out of my head. I have one more piece of business to conduct before I toss these women out.

"So, while we're all enjoying the cake, does anyone have any questions for me?" I say.

"Are you sure you can do this?" Tammy asks. "I mean, with your head injury and all?"

"The doctor has cleared me to work, and my memory is starting to come back in full. I think working at the station will be the best thing for me in the long run."

"But it's been such a long time since you've worked in the news industry," Bebe says.

"Seriously, it's reading off a teleprompter, Bebe, not brain surgery. And if my husband can do it, then anyone can," I say, and we all share a laugh.

"How *does* Gideon feel about you joining his broadcast?" Gail asks.

"Gideon couldn't be happier for me. Besides, he's tired of working with that bimbo, Kaecie Stringer. They have zero on-air chemistry. And now, when he needs to take any time off, he'll be happy knowing he's leaving the broadcast in good hands."

"Won't you two get sick of each other?" More laughter.

"Because of Gideon's hectic work schedule, we were always apart and hardly ever saw each other." I pause to take in their reaction. "After all these years, it's comforting to know that we're still best friends and madly in love with one another."

"This way, you can keep an eye on Gideon and make sure all those cute interns keep their paws off him," Jessica says, to which I shoot her the coldest look in my repertoire.

"You're going to be a star again, Shay, I just know it," Gail says.

"Thank you so much, Gail. I can't begin to tell you how excited I am about all of this," I say, needing only to clarify a few more details before I boot their asses out.

"Have you spoken to Quinn about your plans?" Jessica asks.

"Yeah," Bebe adds, "who's going to watch her now?"

"We've found a wonderful boarding school for our darling Quinn. They specialize in working with the visually impaired and will provide her with the necessary tools she will need to live independently one day. She's a very intelligent girl, as I'm sure you all know. We believe the school she's attending now is not adequately meeting her academic needs."

"Our kids are going to really miss hanging out with her," Bebe says, her face expressing a mock frown.

"The school is located in Connecticut, so it's not like she's moving to Siberia. She'll come home on weekends and holidays, and then all our families will be able to get together like in the past."

"But what does Quinn think about this?" Bebe reiterates.

"She's extremely excited about the new challenges facing her. In fact, let me bring her down so she can say hello to everyone."

I head upstairs and enter Quinn's room. She's reading that stupid book of hers, *Wonder*, and running her grubby little fingers over the accumulation of blips and bumps on the pages. Sensing my presence, she lifts her head up and sniffs the air. It unnerves me to know that she can detect my presence solely from my scent. It's why I had to stink myself up with that cheap perfume when pretending to be Tatyana.

"Who is it?"

"I need you to come downstairs and say hello to all my girlfriends."

"Why?"

"I think you know why, Quinn."

"I really don't, Momma."

"Please don't play stupid with me. I saw you standing at the top of the stairs the other day when I was on the phone with that headmaster."

"You're going to send me away to school?"

"No, provide you with an exciting opportunity to expand your horizons," I say in a threatening manner. "Now come along and tell all of Mommy's friends that you're overjoyed about attending this new school."

"I don't want to," she says, tears streaming down her cheeks.

"Pull yourself together," I snap. "Then make your way downstairs and start acting all cute and sweet, or else you'll make me angry."

"Okay."

"Trust me, Quinn, going away to school is in your best interest."

I return downstairs, all smiles and laughter, noticing that these sneaky bitches had wolfed down half the cake while I was gone. No wonder they're so fat and out of shape. I announce that Quinn was in the middle of doing homework and will be down shortly. The cheese and cracker tray has been decimated, and these closet drunks have guzzled down most of the champagne. Jessica sits by herself, trying hard not to make eye contact with me.

After five minutes go by, the chattering stops, and Quinn walks down the stairs like a little princess. She's grasping the banister and using her walking stick, although, at this point, she hardly needs it. Every inch of this house lies in her domain. The women ooooh and ahhhhh, commenting how beautiful Quinn is and how courageous she's been after all she's experienced these last few months. She makes her way to the sofa and sits down. Then she stares up at the ceiling and flashes her cutest smile, which melts the heart of every woman in the room—except for one.

"Go on, Quinn, tell them how you feel about your new school."

"I'm super excited about this new opportunity. I feel like I'm being held back at my old school. Now, I'll be provided with all the resources I'll need to succeed in life."

"That's wonderful, sweetheart. We're so happy for you," Gail says.

"Thank you, Mrs. Gail."

"But won't you miss all your friends, Quinn?" Jessica asks.

I want to throttle the bitch.

"Of course, I'll miss them, but I'll make lots of new friends and at the same time keep my old ones, too. And I'll learn all I'll need in order to one day live independently and discover what I'm good at in life," she says. "And now my mommy is going to be a star just like my daddy, and I can't be more excited for her."

"Didn't I tell you? Quinn's ecstatic about all the new changes," I say to the women. "Okay, dear. You can go back to your room now."

"Yes, Momma."

"Would you like a piece of cake while you're doing your homework?"

"I'd love a piece. Thank you, Momma."

"I'll bring it right up, darling."

I grab a plate, slice off a piece containing my left eye, and follow her up the stairs. Once she's in her room, I throw it in the trash and sit beside her on the bed. Quinn picks up her book and starts fingering through the pages, ignoring me. I snatch it away from her and tuck it under my armpit.

"Hey, that's mine."

"Very good, Quinn. Keep it up, and everything will go smoothly." I turn to leave.

"Wait. Can I have my book back?"

"What's the magic word?"

"May I *please* have it back?"

"Consider being a little nicer to mommy, dearest, and I'll think about it."

"But it's my favorite."

"My dear, you have a lot more to worry about than some stupid book."

I head downstairs and get ready to wrap things up. Small talk, tiny hugs, and poochy European kisses on both sides of their Botox-enhanced cheeks. Bitches telling me how wonderful my daughter is and what a great job I'm doing raising her. This whole charade makes me sick to my stomach, especially when I have to give Jessica a hug goodbye. But I don't care about Jessica or what she thinks of me. If she tries to pull any funny business, she'll surely regret it.

I watch out the window as the expensive sedans and SUVs drive away from the curb. When they're gone, I relax at the kitchen island and sip from my glass of champagne, staring at my cannibalized face over the creamy frosting.

A performance like that is all-consuming and emotionally draining. But in some ways, I feel invigorated. They say that identical twins think alike and can often finish each other's sentences. Well, what am I thinking now, Shay? Am I thinking about how incredibly bright my future appears? Or about all the money and fame that will soon be mine? How about the way I'm setting up your pathetic husband for a succession of disappointments and heartaches that will require years of intense therapy? Or possibly prison time. And to think that I couldn't have done this without you, my dear sister. The morally superior sister who years ago set me up for two crimes I did not commit. The sister who burned my friend beyond recognition.

It's taken me over twenty years to arrive at this point in time. I'm on the cusp of success like I've never before experienced and ready to take that next big step.

GIDEON

Gideon drove south toward Connecticut with Shay seated next to him, and Quinn buckled in the back. The sky shone a bright cobalt, and everywhere around them, the ground was covered with a thick blanket of snow. Inside the car, it was nice and warm, but the digital reading on his dash informed him that it was nineteen degrees outside.

They'd had a lovely but understated Christmas holiday. Quinn seemed happy, yet at the same time subdued by her impending departure from Woodbridge Estates. They took part in all the usual holiday traditions: *Nutcracker*, tree lighting, and Christmas caroling around the neighborhood. On New Year's Eve, the three of them strolled around Boston and took in all the First Night activities. But despite the quality time together, something seemed off-kilter to him. He attributed it to the dramatic changes coming in the New Year and the ever-shifting temperament of his wife.

The events of the last few months left Gideon breathless with anticipation. He deeply regretted his past indiscretions, believing his wife had chosen to return to work in order to keep a closer eye on him. Not for a second did he believe that she wanted to give up the life of leisure that she'd become accustomed to. Her becoming an anchorwoman was a direct result of his cheating—and he had only himself to blame.

The whole experience had morphed in a rather unpredictable and sorry way. He regretted not spending more time with Quinn when she was younger. Maybe the two of them might have grown closer if he had. Now, she was fated to spend the rest of her days away from home, at boarding school, and then off to college.

The idea of losing his daughter saddened him. How had Shay convinced him to make this drastic decision? When he thought about it rationally, he had to admit that it made sense. Her new school was one of the top institutions in the country for visually impaired children, and she would be getting the best of everything. The tuition was certainly exorbitant, more than most colleges, but the expense only helped to ameliorate the tremendous guilt he felt at missing out on much of her childhood. And, of course, choosing to screw floozies instead of returning home between broadcasts and enjoying dinner with his family. The shame of it all now weighed heavily on his conscience.

After three hours of driving, he turned into the campus, parking in front of an impressive limestone building fronted with faux Dorian columns. The school looked like a small New England college out of a Salinger novel. They got out of the car, leaving Quinn's bags in the trunk until they learned where she'd be living. Since school had not yet begun, the campus was sparsely populated with students.

Gideon turned to his wife. "Would you mind if Quinn and I walk around a bit while you handle her affairs?"

"Knock yourselves out." Shay smiled at them before rushing up the stairs and into the building.

Gideon grabbed Quinn's mitten-swathed hand and guided her toward the quad located behind the admin building. Arcades of skeletal trees lined the path encircling the yard, their icy limbs shimmering in the sunlight. Sadly, they appeared to him like the fanciest of Christmas ornaments his mother used to hang from their tree when he was a young boy. Christmas was one of the few times in his life when his parents seemed happy.

"It's a lovely campus, Quinn. I think you'll really like it here."

"Okay." Her voice sounded flat.

"There are huge oak and elm trees everywhere you look. And you should see all the wonderful limestone buildings."

"That might be a problem."

"Oh, sorry. I didn't mean it like that."

"Only kidding, Daddy."

"Right," he said, squeezing her hand. "They say it's the finest school of its kind."

"Maybe whoever said that can enroll here instead of me."

"Silly girl," he said, laughing. "But seriously, this school has state-of-the-art facilities and wonderful sports programs." He glanced down at his little girl, who was bundled up in a down jacket and wool cap. A deep sense of regret filled him. "You know, Quinn, you really don't have to go here if you don't want to."

She stopped and turned to him with tears in her eyes. "But I do, Daddy. I really want to."

"Are you absolutely sure?"

"Yes."

"Then why are you crying, honey?" he said, kneeling down to her level.

"Because I'm going to miss you. And I already miss Momma."

"But she's just inside, filling out the paperwork. You'll see her before we leave."

"I miss her so much," she cried, sobbing uncontrollably. "I miss her badly."

"You can always come home on weekends. We'll still be a tight-knit family."

"I want Momma to love me again." She sobbed into her mittens.

He hugged her for what seemed like a long time as a few of the other families strolled around campus. Finally, she pushed away from him and used her mitten to wipe away the residual tears.

"Are you okay, hon?"

"I'm fine. Can we just go back and get my stuff? I want to go check out my room now."

"Of course."

They walked back to the car, and he removed her three suitcases filled with clothes, books, tablet, and laptop computer. Shay emerged from the building just as he placed the last suitcase down on the sidewalk. They each pulled a rolling suitcase until they reached her dorm. Gideon looked it up and down, impressed that she was being placed in such a stately building.

They went inside and took the elevator up to her floor. All the buttons and signs were in Braille.

Once they reached the second floor, they got off and made their way to her room. It was small, but it had everything she needed. There was another bed but no sign of her roommate. Quinn made a quick lap around it, touching everything she could, before announcing that she was satisfied with the arrangements. A sober-looking woman appeared at the doorway, stating that she was responsible for the students on this floor.

"Okay, babe. The time has come," Shay said, smiling effusively.

"I thought we might have lunch together before we head back," Gideon said.

"We spent three hours in the car, dear. Why not let her get acclimated to her new surroundings."

The woman stepped between them and stood next to Quinn. "The other students will be returning to school in the next few days. Your daughter will be thoroughly involved in campus life and in all the school's activities."

"It's okay for you to leave," Quinn said. "Don't worry about me. I'll get used to living here."

"Are you sure?" Gideon said, falling to one knee and holding her by the arms.

"Of course. I'm sure I'll end up loving this place once I get used to it."

"I'll miss you so much." He kissed her cold cheek, wishing he could have a do-over for all the years he missed attending her recitals, plays, and other school events. But it was too late now.

"I'll miss you too, Daddy."

Shay walked over and kissed the top of her head. "Good luck, kiddo. We'll call you soon."

"Bye," she said, waving as they left.

They walked side by side down the hallway, Shay's heels echoing loudly against the ornate marble floor. It seemed to him that she couldn't wait to get out of here. She stopped midway, said she forgot to tell Quinn something and then ran back toward her room. Gideon clasped his hands together, fighting back the tears. He wandered through the hallway, perusing all the posters and student art hanging on the wall, trying not to think about leaving his only daughter behind and promising himself that he and Shay would visit often. But he knew he wouldn't. Work, the club, and dealing with his high-maintenance wife would keep him plenty occupied. And possibly moving to New York City once the ink dried on his new contract. Before he knew it, Shay had returned to his side, and together, they exited the building and emerged into the cold New England air.

Gideon shook with grief. It almost felt as if his daughter had died. The realization that they were leaving Quinn behind suddenly hit him, and he collapsed in a paroxysm of tears once behind the wheel. Shay tried to console him, but he brusquely shook her hand off his shoulder.

"This was all your idea," he said angrily.

"Please don't pretend to take an interest in your daughter now. That time has come and gone, dear."

"What are you talking about?"

"All you ever cared about was your career."

He turned to her. "Go to hell!"

"I'll forget you said that—this time. But if you ever talk to me like that again, you'll surely regret it."

Her calm tone sent a chill through him. "She could still live at home with us, Shay. I'm sure we could work something out with Caramelo."

"Do you really think I'd entrust my precious daughter to an illegal immigrant?"

He'd never heard his wife say such a callous remark. "Other arrangements could be made."

"I'll ask you one last time, Gideon. Are you willing to quit your job and be a stay-at-home dad?"

He turned and stared grimly out the windshield, realizing that he would never give up his dream job.

"I didn't think so, *dear*. Now either go back to the dorm and retrieve your daughter, or start the car and head back home."

He put a death grip on the steering wheel, deeply ashamed that he wasn't prepared to end his career for his only child. The harsh reality of his decision made him realize that his wife was right. Quinn belonged here for the time being. If only Shay hadn't been so cold about the decision, he could have lived with it. He wasn't naive; he knew he'd played a major role in sending her off by working long hours and being an incessant philanderer.

He turned the ignition, clicked the satellite radio on to Yacht Rock, and then drove the three hours home without saying a word.

QUINN

Three weeks had passed since Quinn arrived at school, and she couldn't believe how much she hated it here. Once class let out, she ignored the snarky remarks from the other girls and made her way back to her room. She collapsed on her bed and began to sob. As much as she tried to like this place, she found that with each passing day, she hated it even more. The kids ran from apathetic to mean, and the teachers seemed indifferent to her. She missed her old school and her old friends, her familiar room filled with books, toys, and stuffies.

She felt all alone now and knew she could never return home. Her father didn't really care about her, and the woman claiming to be her mother seemed happy to be leaving her behind. She pretty much said as much when she returned to her room one last time to say goodbye. It was almost as if she was rubbing it in. Quinn believed the woman capable of anything, including murder. She had even come to the conclusion that this crazy woman was the person who had attacked her real mother outside of that soup kitchen.

Whoever this woman was, she must have looked exactly like her mother. A near spitting image if she was able to fool everyone. Did her mother have a twin growing up? Maybe the woman had extensive plastic surgery? Her mother never talked much about her childhood, and Quinn knew why. She'd had an extremely rough upbringing, and her father died when she was a young girl growing up in Western Massachusetts. Quinn's father once sat her down and explained that Shay's mother had abandoned her when she was a young girl, and her sister had died in a house fire. Then, she was forced to live in a succession of foster homes until she was eighteen. After receiving a full scholarship to Harvard, she moved to the Boston area.

But now Quinn wondered if her mother had another sister no one knew about?

She sniffed back the tears and brought the stuffed hippo up under her chin. Reflecting on her three weeks in this prison, she tried to think of a reason why she'd not yet made any friends. The majority of kids here at this school were blind like her, and because of that, she thought it would be easy to make friends. After all, they had their shared disability in common. But she learned a harsh lesson while living here. When everyone is the same, kids will find other reasons to divide and conquer.

Things would get better, she kept telling herself. She missed Caramelo and their afternoon talks. The housekeeper's optimism kept her going when she felt herself becoming sad. Quinn wiped away the tears with her stuffed hippo and let the maid's words lull her to sleep.

Your real momma is always with you, just like God is always there for you. God has a reason for everything, chiquita.

SHAY

The cold had settled in. Snowfall covered the window high above her, blocking all sunlight. George had brought her down some raggedy winter clothes along with a tiny electric heater that only warmed her bones if she squatted down in front of it. Surprisingly, the old concrete walls in this basement managed to keep out the worst of the cold, but she knew she couldn't survive an entire winter down here.

Yet even with two blankets and all her clothes on, she found the cold unbearable at night. She spent her days pacing back and forth just to stay warm, doing jumping jacks, and making a dent in the collection of old paperbacks someone had left down in the basement. A fast reader, she feared the day when she ran out of books to pass the time. And she doubted George would go out and replenish her supply. Without these stories to keep her mind occupied, she knew she'd go mad.

Something happened the day George challenged her to guess who might be behind this scheme. It set her mind in motion. Since that day, George had barely stopped by long enough to talk, choosing instead to drop off her meal and head back upstairs. She had pounded on the door and begged for him to come down and keep her company, but he never responded.

Who was behind her kidnapping? That Chechen maid? Gideon? Were the two working in tandem? More than anything, she desired human contact and conversation. Being isolated in this basement all day was driving her nuts. With no end to her captivity in sight, she wondered how long she could last.

Death now seemed like a plausible alternative to living like this for the foreseeable future. Would swallowing that powder do the trick? Then she thought about Quinn, and she knew she had to do everything in her power to continue fighting for her life so that she could one day return to her family.

She'd been thinking about Gideon lately. Could he have set this up by getting rid of her in order to be with someone else? And then not have to pay alimony and child support? He'd cheated on her before. And his career meant everything to him, even more than his family. She chastised herself for being cynical, knowing that Gideon could never be so cruel. Lack of food and captivity was causing her to become paranoid and conjure up the unthinkable.

Yet the possibility kept creeping into her mind, as much as she tried not to consider it. She had suspected that he might be cheating on her with the stunning weather girl, although she didn't want to admit this to herself. She also didn't want to be the kind of wife who was always nagging and accusing her husband of being unfaithful.

Then again, once a cheater, always a cheater.

She paced the room, breathing onto her cupped hands for warmth. If only George would bring down some more food, then maybe she might be able to retain some heat and concentrate on other things. Something nagged at her. This entire kidnapping ordeal made no sense. Without a ransom payment, why kidnap her? Why not kidnap Quinn instead? Were the police out looking for her? If only she could tell Quinn that she was alive and well.

She craved intimacy and human interaction more than ever. She would give anything just to sit and converse with another human being. Even talking to George seemed better than this isolated torture. It made her better understand the Stockholm Syndrome.

The lack of natural sunlight was also making her irritable. She thought back to when she could sit in her sunroom with a book and a cup of coffee, watching as the deer traipsed over the tenth hole. What she wouldn't give to have five minutes of her old life back.

She stood under the lightbulb and absorbed the little heat it gave off.

Looking up at it, she imagined the sun on a hot summer day, she and Quinn walking hand in hand along Old Orchard Beach, searching for clamshells and crabs, the warm surf splashing around their feet, sand nestled between their toes.

She heard a knock on the door as she stood squinting up at the lightbulb. Because of the lack of sunlight and her unstable state of mind, she'd lost track of the days. Only George's meal delivery gave her any indication of the passage of time. In the morning, he usually brought her soggy cornflakes in that horrible powdered milk. Lunch was a Fluff sandwich with chips, and finally, pasta with a packaged cheese sauce for dinner.

George unlocked the bolt and entered the room. Almost immediately, she could see that he was drunk. He staggered inside, carrying a plastic plate filled with stale chips and a sandwich, his stool, and a bottle of Jack Daniel's. Little early for him to start in on the booze. She again noticed his gun tucked into the waist of his pants. Tottering, he placed the plate down, slid it towards her, and stepped back. But the plate only traveled a few inches along the craggy concrete floor.

Shay stood, not wanting to reach out for the sandwich and appear desperate. But she couldn't take her eyes off it, her mouth watering in anticipation. Tufts of Fluff peeked out between the slices of white bread. She wanted so badly to rush over and stuff the sandwich and chips into her mouth that she nearly lost her self-restraint.

"Go for it. I know you're famished," he said.

"Thank you." She shuffled over to the plate.

"Look at you. You're turning all skin and bones on me. I like my women with a little meat on them." He sat down on his stool.

"You could easily fix that by giving me more food," she said, greedily shoving the sandwich into her mouth. It tasted so good she wanted to die.

George took a sip from the bottle and then leaned back, a boozy smile forming on his face. He wiped the excess whiskey off on his sleeve.

"How about sharing some of that with me?" She sat down Indian style, picked up the plate, and rested it on her lap.

"You want some of my Jack?" He held the bottle up to the light and smiled.

"Wouldn't take much for me to get drunk." She shoved the remainder of the sandwich in her mouth, closed her eyes for a brief second to savor it, and then opened her eyes again. "I'm a cheap date."

"So this is a date now?"

She shrugged flirtatiously and smiled at him, hoping he might let down his guard.

He leaned over and caressed her cheek, and as he did, she was tempted to reach for his gun.

She decided to try another tack and say nothing. Instead, she stayed perfectly still and allowed him to touch her cheek. It felt nice and not at all sexual.

"That woman can be such a bitch."

"Sorry to hear that."

"You don't know the half of it." He passed her the bottle. "Or maybe you do."

What did he mean by that last remark? She took the bottle in hand and gulped down a small mouthful. It burned as it traveled down her throat. She handed it back to him and coughed for a few seconds before regaining her composure.

"Been a while, huh?"

"Since the last teaspoon you gave me," she said. "An occasional glass of Chardonnay used to be my vice, but I'll take whatever I can get these days."

"You know what they say, hon, liquor's quicker."

She smiled at him. "But wine's more divine."

"Wine's more divine. That's cute."

"You need to get out more, George."

"No thanks. I've been around the block and back again."

The whiskey began to swirl in her head. She grabbed a handful of the chips and stuffed them in her mouth, allowing the salt to dissolve over her dry tongue.

"You're quite the catch." He leaned over and studied her. "Pretty, smart, and nice. I can see why you're already taken."

"I'm lonely down here, George. I can't handle being in this basement much longer."

"How do you think I feel, spending all my time upstairs with only Jack as my companion?" He held up the bottle.

"At least let me come upstairs and hang out with you for a while. You can secure my wrists and ankles if you want."

He stared at her with unfocused eyes.

"An hour is all I'm asking. Please. I promise I'll be on my best behavior.

"I *could* use some company." George took a sip of the whiskey and then rested the bottle on his thigh.

"We could keep each other company," she said. "Then you wouldn't have to come down here every time I need to pee or take a shower."

He took another sip. "Do you really love that dopey husband of yours?"

"Of course I love him." His words surprised her. "Why? Do you know Gideon?"

"Only from watching that arrogant bastard on TV."

"That arrogant bastard is the number one rated news anchor in Boston."

"The guy's a fraud, and I should know."

"You're drunk, George."

"I may be drunk, but you know I'm right."

"I don't know that. I love Gideon, and he loves me."

"Is that the reason you stayed with him?"

"Of course not," she said. "We also have a beautiful daughter."

"Bet you'd do anything for that kid of yours, wouldn't you?" His eyes pressed into slits.

"You know I would."

"I'd do anything for mine too."

"You have kids?"

"Two."

"What are their names?"

He stared long and hard at her. "You do know that he's cheating on you, right?"

"I don't know anything these days, locked down here in this basement, but I seriously doubt Gideon's been cheating on me while I've been away."

Did she?

George laughed. "That's where you're wrong. That creep has been sleeping with his new co-anchor."

"Kaecie Stringer?"

"Hell no. He dumped that bore weeks ago."

"He dumped Kaecie?"

"Yup, and he's been sleeping with his newest co-host, and she's a lot better looking than Kaecie."

She tried to process his words.

"You should think about leaving him, hon, assuming you get out of here alive."

Alive? "How can I believe that what you're saying is true?"

"Trust me, that husband of yours is a dawg. And that's coming from an alpha dawg."

She lifted herself off the cold floor and approached him on her knees. George immediately pulled out his knife.

"Easy, girl. I don't want to hurt you."

"Let me come upstairs with you, George." She knelt in front of him, feeling the point of the knife pressing against her cheek. "Please."

He leaned over in a drunken manner and put his face inches from hers. Was he going to kiss her? She could smell the whiskey on his breath.

"If you even think of trying anything—"

"I swear, I'll do whatever you want."

"For your sake, you'd better not make me regret this." He pressed the blade a little harder against her cheek.

"I promise you I won't."

"If I let you upstairs tomorrow night, you'll see the woman your husband's been putting the screws to." He stood from the stool, picked it up, and walked backwards toward the door.

"Thank you."

"You won't be thanking me after you see who it is."

"I just need some time out of this basement."

"If you try anything, girl, you're gonna wish you hadn't. It's your daughter's life you're playing with."

"I'll do anything you say. I'll be the best houseguest ever."

George stashed his knife away before slipping out the door and securing the locks.

She pressed her face into her hands and wept. Maybe she'd finally get to use that drug she'd crushed into a powder. She couldn't wait until tomorrow night. Anything would be better than living like this.

SHANNON

Let's just say that reporting the news is not as easy as I thought. I made a few goofs here and there. Transitions proved trickier than expected. There's looking into the camera and trying to project sincerity and warmth. Then trying to act all sad when reporting on a personal tragedy when all I really want to do is break out laughing.

The first story I reported on was about a family of seven who became homeless because of a house fire. And they looked like such a cute bunch. I thought of my sister setting our house on fire, stabbing herself in the thigh, and then blaming it on me, and the tears fell freely. Thinking about what that bitch did is the only way I can muster up any sympathy these days.

Most of the time, when I'm sitting at that news desk, I must pinch myself in order to make sure I'm not dreaming. It's been such a long road to get to this point that I can't believe I've finally arrived.

There's no going back to George and my previous life in Vegas. Not after experiencing all this. I just need him to stay alive a little bit longer.

Every so often, while Gideon and I are delivering the news, I glance over at my insignificant other and register the misery on his face. When I screw up or mispronounce something, he thinks it reflects badly on him and on the quality of the broadcast. And it most certainly does. Because in a short time, Gideon's going to look like an amateur once I get through with him.

Yet despite all my screwups, mispronunciations, and talking-out-of-turns, I couldn't believe how patient the staff was with me. Lots of pats on the backs and wads of tissues whenever I forced up crocodile tears during commercial breaks.

I have plenty of good excuses at hand: post-concussion syndrome, the stress of raising a blind daughter, and working in the considerable shadow of my famous husband. Still, the staff couldn't have been nicer. Maybe that's because I treat everyone like my best friend, bringing them homemade cookies and brownies that I force Conchita to bake. Being kind to people does not come easy to someone like me, and my husband rarely acts kind unless he needs something. I can tell that the employees at the station loath Gideon, and, because of that, are fiercely protective of me. Upon seeing how well I was being treated, Gideon shot everyone looks of scorn, rolled his eyes, and behaved in a condescending and childish manner.

But after two weeks of mishaps, something amazing started to happen. I began to get a handle on this job. The words started to flow from one story to the next. My nerves settled, and I got used to staring into those intimidating cameras with their flashing lights directing me which way to look. Say what you will; it's still reading off a teleprompter, but the challenge of mastering the news desk surprised even me. My timing improved with each broadcast, and my confidence began to soar. Even Gideon noticed that I was not pissing on his reputation every night. Yes, I was still crashing his party, but at least I hadn't dragged him down to the gutter yet.

That would come soon enough.

I'm quickly becoming a fixture in town. The other day, I drove through the heart of downtown Boston and saw my face plastered on a huge billboard. Equal billing with Gideon, too. People have been coming up to me on the street and saying hello and asking for my autograph. And because I've always expected to be rich and famous, dealing with my newfound stardom has come easier than expected. I add a touch of friendliness and combine it with a diva's haughty attitude, and it keeps my fans intrigued.

The blind kid is not totally out of my life, but it's a relief knowing she's out from under me. So sad that she had to leave behind her comfortable life of luxury. Boo fucking hoo. Try losing your trailer-trash parents at a young age and then being moved from one abusive foster home to the next, with a goody-two-shoes twin sister always showing you up. Or fighting off all those creepy foster fathers trying to cop a feel off you late at night while you were pretending to be asleep. Then, losing your dope-sick friend to a house fire your sister set. Now tell me how bad your life is, Quinn.

The kid has it easy compared to what I went through. She gets to attend a fancy boarding school with all the trappings. Three square meals a day, a nice room, and everything paid for by her famous aunt and daddy.

Cry me a river.

It's just past one in the afternoon, and I have the entire house to myself. I called the detective the other day and asked when I could set up another interview with him. He agreed to come over today.

Gideon typically clears out of here after lunch. That way, he can sit in his office and feign doing work. It's hilarious, because he thinks he's fooling everyone into thinking he's doing research, but they all know what he's doing. Every hour or so, he storms out of the office, demanding updates on this story or that report, gripping the *New York Times* in hand as if he's read it from cover to cover and mispronouncing big words he has no clue as to their meaning. Sometimes, he orders an intern to research a heady topic that will make him look smart in front of his staff. Palestinian-Israeli conflict. Climate change. Statistics on police brutality in the inner cities. The Me Too movement.

I do the complete opposite most days. After getting my hair and make-up done, I show up five minutes before the broadcast, a tin of chocolate chip cookies or brownies in hand, and then wing it. And why not? I'm drop-dead gorgeous. I know how to read off a teleprompter. I treat the staff like they are my best friends in the world. Never in my life have I had it so easy. And to think people go to expensive colleges and kiss ass to do this kind of work.

The cop will be ringing the doorbell any minute now. I look in the mirror and frown for good reason. Everything about me screams depressed, from my messy hair to my sister's baggy clothes. I purposely neglected to put on any makeup this morning. Talking to the police will require a delicate balancing act, and I can't overplay the role of memory-challenged housewife. Not when I'm so bubbly and radiant on the news each night. If I do, he'll suspect something's up. Nuance is difficult to pull off, but I can do it when it's called for. It just takes more concentration than I can typically muster.

I spend a few minutes in front of the mirror, pouting and trying to look sad. I touch my temple and stare up at the ceiling. Practice helps, and the more I do it, the more confident I feel about convincing this detective that I'm still somewhat of a basket case.

The doorbell rings while my face is stuck in one of these odd poses. I ruffle my hair and cinch the pink granny robe around my waist. Consuela's doing the laundry somewhere deep in the bowels of the house. I see the nasty way she looks at me when she walks past carrying the duster, wondering what kind of mother sends her daughter away to school. It's quite laughable, actually. If only she knew I was the brat's aunt and not her mother.

I see Conchita walking through the living room, and I breezily tell her to take the rest of the day off, which means she doesn't get her full pay.

"But I haven't finished folding the laundry yet, Mrs. Wells," she complains.

"Save the laundry for tomorrow."

"But the living room is a mess."

"I said *vamos*, Consuela. Now leave before I give you tomorrow off, as well."

"Yes, ma'am," she says. "And it's Caramelo."

"Excuse me?"

"My name is Caramelo not Consuela." The doorbell rings again.

"Please answer the door before you leave, *Caramelo*."

She opens the door and points toward me. The detective walks over, wearing one of those outdated Fog Cutters. He looks like one of those gruff character actors from the fifties: square face, short gray hair, cleft chin, and blocky build. I motion for him to sit across from me on the only section of cushion not piled high with folded laundry.

"I'm glad to see that you're doing better, Mrs. Wells," Detective Carr says, exposing his beer paunch as he sits.

"I have my ups and downs," I say. "Every day gets a little better, although I'm feeling a bit down today."

"Sorry to hear that."

"I'll bounce back, hopefully."

"I'm glad you called me for an update, although I'm sorry to say we've made little progress on your case."

"It's not your fault, Detective. I'm afraid my faulty memory is to blame for your lack of results," I say. "Would you like something to drink? I have cold beer in the fridge?"

He laughs. "I'd love a beer, but not when I'm working."

"I called you this morning because I remembered a small detail about the night I was attacked."

"That's great news."

"Not sure how much it will help you."

"Before you say any more, I just want to tell you what a fantastic job you're doing on the news desk. You and your husband make a great team."

"You think?"

"I know it."

"Thank you, Detective."

"My wife was skeptical of you at first. She absolutely loves your husband. Watches him every night. But I think you're slowly winning her over."

"That's wonderful to hear," I say, so flattered by his comments that it sets off a warning alarm in my head. I tell myself to be mindful of traps. "What does she like about me?"

"She thinks you add a certain energy to the broadcast. Of course, it took her a while to warm up to you. Kaecie Stringer was a much more laid-back co-host than you."

I study him for any signs he's playing me. "With my headaches and occasional memory lapses, it's proved a bit more difficult than I anticipated, but I think I'm finally getting the hang of it."

"My wife will be happy to hear that."

"What do *you* think of my performance?"

"Honestly, I rarely watch the news. I'm usually home after seven and in bed before nine."

"Most news is depressing, anyway. And I'm sure you see the worst of humanity on a daily basis."

"Got that right," he said, taking out his notebook. "Are you okay to answer a few questions?"

I give him a tentative nod.

"You said you remembered a small detail from that night?"

"A very small one. I don't even know if it'll help."

"Trust me, the smallest of details often matter in these types of cases. It's how a lot of these crimes get solved."

"Good, because I was afraid you might think I'm being frivolous."

"There's definitely no frivolity in my line of work."

The use of the word *frivolity* informs me that he's intelligent, possibly college-educated.

"Tell me what you remember."

"The person who attacked me that night was a man."

He jots this down in his notebook. "Are you sure about this?"

"Positive. It suddenly came back to me the other night while I was sitting at the news desk."

"Do you remember any details about this man? What he was wearing, or what he looked like?"

"Everything about that night is still a bit fuzzy, but something tells me he wasn't homeless."

"Why would you say that?"

"It was the way he carried himself. No, the way he dressed."

"You remember what he was wearing?"

"Not exactly, except to recall that he was well-dressed."

"A well-dressed man," he says, jotting it down. "Okay, that's at least something to go on."

"There's one other thing."

"Yes," he says, scribbling furiously in his notebook.

"I remember the object he used to assault me with."

He looks up at me. "Go on."

"It was one of those miniature baseball bats like they give away at ballparks. I vividly remember the logo on the barrel as he held it over my head."

"That's certainly no minor detail. You've done well remembering this information, Mrs. Wells."

"Do you really think so?" I twist my face into one of feigning appreciation.

"Of course, but keep trying to jog that memory of yours. A lot of times, people with head traumas will remember more details about their attack as they recover."

"That's good to know." I watch him closely as he jots it all down. "Did you go to college, Detective?"

He looks up and laughs. "Yeah, but I never finished. Why do you ask?"

"I was just wondering if that's a requirement to being a detective?"

"Not necessarily, but it certainly helps if you want to climb the ladder."

"Is that your goal?"

"No, I'm too old for promotions."

"Mind if I ask where you went to school?"

He mumbles incoherently.

"I'm sorry, I didn't catch that."

"Harvard. But I dropped out after two semesters."

"Harvard. Impressive," I say. "Why did you drop out?"

"I was planning to play football there, only I wasn't as good as I thought."

"But it was still Harvard. That's nothing to sneeze at."

He shrugs. "My father knew the admissions officer. Maybe he had some dirt on the guy or something. Truth was, I wasn't exactly Harvard material." He laughs.

"All the same."

"My father really wanted me to go there and make something of myself. Do better in life than he'd done."

"Understandable."

"He was an old-school cop and wanted more for me than I wanted for myself. But I soon realized that the apple didn't fall far from the tree."

"Was your dad upset when you dropped out?"

"He was at first, but how could he stay mad at me when I told him that I wanted to follow in his footsteps? My old man was somewhat of a legend in the Boston PD."

"Now, that would make an interesting story."

"What about you?"

"What about me?"

"Where did you go to college?"

My curiosity caused me to make an unforced error, and I realize that I neglected to learn where my sister went to school. I think it was one of the Ivies, but now I'm not sure which one. I make one of those wretched faces. I look up at the ceiling while clutching my chin in confusion. Whether this will draw suspicion to myself, I'm not quite sure. I curse at myself for being so stupid. I'm like an impulsive chess player who pounces on a perceived opening without fully thinking three steps ahead.

"It's no big deal," he says, staring at me curiously.

"Wow. I'm totally drawing a blank right now." I look at his face and realize he knows where I—my sister—went to college.

"Forgetting information like that happens to me all the time," he says. "Save that memory for the important stuff. Like remembering who attacked you that night."

"Yes, I suppose you're right," I say, trying to read his expression.

"If that's all for now, Mrs. Wells, then I'm going to take this information down to the station and add it to the file." He stands to leave.

"If I think of anything else, Detective, I'll be sure to let you know."

"Yes, please do," he says as I walk him to the door. "Oh, your husband told me that your daughter no longer lives with the two of you."

He's been talking to Gideon? "Yes, we thought long and hard about it, but in the end, we thought it best to send her to a school with more resources than her old one had. You do know she's blind?"

"Yes, I met her once while you were here. She was playing Scrabble with your Russian housekeeper at the time. Don't you remember?"

"Oh yes. It's coming back to me now," I say, feeling as if I'm falling deeper into the quicksand. "She absolutely adores her new school. It will provide her with all the tools she'll need to one day live independently."

"And with the two of you working all the time—"

I'm not liking where this conversation is going.

"If I think of anything else, Detective, I'll be sure to let you know."

"Please do. And if you remember that college you went to, be sure to send them a donation, although they'll probably not need it."

"Will do," I say, eager for this dick to leave. "And don't beat yourself up about dropping out of Harvard. You and Bill Gates have at least that in common."

He gives me a wry smile before leaving. I know I shouldn't have had the last word like that, but the asshole deserved it. Who does he think he is questioning me? A loser college dropout like him? Still, I know I should have kept the sarcasm to myself. I often let my ego get the best of me, and it's a weakness that'll be my undoing if I'm not careful.

The first thing I do is rip off these disgusting threads and dress up in the fancy new outfit I picked out last week on Newbury Street. Later today, I'll go out and do more shopping. Stop to have some sashimi at the ritzy Japanese restaurant in the Back Bay. Get my nails done by those incessantly gossiping Vietnamese girls. Then I'll race down to the studio with minutes to spare, deliver the news with my usual panache, and watch with unmitigated glee as my husband sits fuming beside me.

He's eagerly awaiting the day when he gets the call from that British woman, informing him that he's been hired to replace Logan Burrows.

If he only knew that that day would never come.

III

Part Three

SHAY

The bolt lock shifted, and the door swung open. Shay lifted her head from the hard pillow and saw George standing in the light. Despite the two blankets covering her and the clothes swaddling her body, she could feel her lips shivering.

George walked over to the flimsy mattress and stood over her. He'd not started drinking yet, his eyes clear and his movements sharp. Gruffly, he turned her over on her back and cuffed her wrists together with the plastic restraints. Then he grabbed hold of the restraints, pulled her up to a standing position, and spun her around.

"You're shivering," he said, holding her by the arms to keep her steady.

"It's cold down here."

"I've got news for you; it ain't much warmer upstairs, either. I'm trying not to use too much of the oil or wood."

"You have a fireplace and oil heat?"

"Yup," he said, pushing her forward.

"Where are you taking me?"

"It's about time you met the woman who's been fucking your husband."

"She's upstairs?"

"In a way." George laughed. "Or she will be upstairs once the news comes on."

"Why are you doing this to me?" she complained.

"You want to go upstairs with me or not?"

"I do."

"Okay then. Git," he said, guiding her through the door. "Remember, I got a gun, and I'll use it if you try anything."

"I'm cold, tired, and I'm going need to use the bathroom soon. Not to mention you've cuffed my wrists together. Assuming that I was even that stupid to try to escape, what could I possibly do to you?"

"No sense taking any chances."

"You're not going to blindfold me this time?"

"Not unless you force my hand."

She climbed the stairs until she emerged into the light. It felt significantly warmer up here, as it did every time she'd come up to use the restroom. All the windows were dark, indicating to her that night had fallen. The clock over the old electric stove informed her that it was fifteen minutes before six. On the counter next to the stovetop sat six unopened bottles of Jack Daniel's.

George stuck his knuckle into the base of her spine and led her into the living room. To her delight, a flame crackled in the fireplace. She turned toward the rustic spectacle, feeling the life-sustaining heat it gave off. The living room appeared old and dated and hadn't been painted in years. The oak hardwood floor was etched with scratches and dents. A tattered sofa sat across from an ancient armchair. In front of it was a ratty coffee table covered with wrappers, magazines, and an empty tumbler. A twenty-inch flat screen rested on two stacked milk cartons.

"Have a seat over on that couch," George said, pointing. "Show starts in a few."

She sat down and felt the burn over her wrists. "Ouch!"

"Is there a problem?"

"These cuffs are killing me. Would you mind taking them off for a few minutes? I think you cut off my circulation."

"Jesus, girl, you're testing my good nature."

He walked over, ordering her on her back. Then he removed the plastic restraints, tossed them on the coffee table, and sat down in the armchair.

"Thank you," she said, rubbing her wrists.

"Here's the deal. You get off that couch without my permission, I'll blast you between the eyes. Hell, you won't even know what hit you. Then I'll make a call and have them work over that daughter of yours."

"I promise, you'll not see me budge from this cushion."

"Good. Because even if you did manage to escape, you wouldn't get far. It's eleven degrees outside with a wind chill of minus seven. If that don't kill you, the four feet of snow on the ground will."

"Good to know."

"I can put you outside for a few minutes, and you can see for yourself."

"No, thanks, I'm good right here."

He clicked on the flatscreen, and a talk show came on. George groaned in pain while repositioning himself on the chair.

"Are you okay?" she asked.

"Nothing a little Jack can't handle." He turned and glanced at her. "Feeling any better?"

"Much. I can actually feel my hands now," she said, rubbing them together for warmth.

He caressed his stubbled chin. "You seem like a nice lady. I just want you to know that this is purely about business."

"Kidnapping me and leaving my daughter without a mother is business to you?"

"Sad as that sounds."

"Then I'm afraid for the world we live in."

"You should be, for the sake of your daughter," he said. "See that blanket folded on the cushion next to you?"

She looked to her right and saw a fuzzy gray blanket. "This one?"

"Yeah. Be a doll and throw it over me, will you?"

She stood, unfolded it, and then spread it over his body so that it covered his chest and legs. His body trembled ever so slightly, and she could see that he was shivering. To her, it felt warm and cozy up here.

"I got this gun pointed at you under the blanket, so don't try anything."

"I wouldn't dare, George. Like you said, even if I managed to escape, where would I go?"

"You just need to know who's the boss around here."

"Mother Nature's the boss now. Looks like you and I are stuck here for the foreseeable future."

"That we are," he said. "Now make yourself useful and go pour me a Jack."

"How many bottles do you have left?"

"Had four cases of it when I got here. Lot less now."

Shay whistled. "So when am I going to meet my husband's mistress?" she said.

"Pour my Jack, and you'll meet her soon enough."

"Are you messing with me?"

He pointed a long finger toward the kitchen. "Get to pouring, girl."

"Fine. But I'm going to pour me a glass, and you can't stop me."

"Be my guest."

She went into the kitchen and peeked into the pantry, seeing two boxes of Jack Daniels stacked on the floor. Then she poured two tumblers filled to the brim and brought them back into the living room. "Here's the drink you ordered, sir."

"You're a helluva barmaid."

"Got that right."

"Now sit down and enjoy the show."

Not normally a drinker, she felt she needed an escape hatch from this nightmarish scenario. She thought of Quinn and sipped the booze, closing her eyes in anticipation of the harsh taste. It burned the back of her throat, but she handled it much better this time. When she looked over, she noticed George had gulped down half his glass.

The sound of the talk-show host interviewing someone filled the room. A draft from the ancient window behind her chilled the skin along her neck. She turned and glanced out the frosty pane, seeing only darkness. Even if she did manage to drug him, how would she ever make it out of this place alive? George had told her that the nearest neighbor was miles up the road. Would she have to wait until spring to get out of here?

"Hey, bartender. How about a refill?" George said, holding up his empty glass.

"I might as well bring out the whole bottle, the way you're knocking them back."

"You won't hear me protest."

She went into the kitchen and returned with the bottle. Standing over him, she refilled his glass, waiting for him to say when. Beneath the blanket, she could see the barrel of the gun aimed at her.

"Good."

She stopped pouring. "Is that your gun, George, or are you just happy to see me?"

"Watch that mouth of yours." He glared up at her. "Don't ever joke about that. You hear?"

"Sorry. I was just trying to lighten the mood." She set the bottle on the coffee table and sat down.

"It's not right to make fun of a man about that kind of stuff."

"What's going on, George? Are you okay?"

"I don't want to talk about it right now." He clicked the remote and changed the channel. Then he held his glass out for a toast. "Here's mud in your eye. You're going to need it after seeing this."

"To us, George."

"To us."

Shay clinked her glass against his and then watched as he guzzled the rest of his whiskey. Once he downed it, he sat forward in his chair and waited for her to drink up.

"No way I can shoot this down." She laughed, staring at her half-empty glass. "I haven't drunk like this since college."

"It's bad manners to turn down a toast."

"Sure. Why the hell not?" She lifted the glass to her lips and chugged it until all the whiskey was gone. She coughed violently for about thirty seconds, listening to George laugh.

By the time she regained her composure, a familiar voice filled the room. She turned to the flatscreen and saw two news anchors sitting at the desk, welcoming the audience to their broadcast. Her throat felt scorched, and for a brief second, she thought she might become violently ill.

GIDEON

This was insane. Gideon couldn't understand how this had all come about as he watched his wife deliver the news in her unconventionally bizarre style. Every minute next to her caused him to cringe in embarrassment. He'd tried to bring up the subject of her unorthodox style with the station's general manager, but each time he mentioned his wife's name, he had to sit there and listen to the man's monologue about what a great idea it had been to bring her on board.

Never in his life did he envision himself complaining about stellar ratings. Not only had the ratings improved since Shay's arrival, but they'd been the highest in the station's history. He and Shay had been leaving Yolanda Brown in the dust week after week. One could only conclude that his wife was responsible for this significant spike. And it was hard to argue such logic. To do so would ignore the obvious: that Shay's dog and pony show had been a ratings boon to the station.

And yet…he worried more than ever about his legacy. His reputation was being tarnished every night they put her on the air, and he was helpless to stop the bloodshed. Would the major news network change their mind once they knew the truth? That Shay was the real star of the show and not him? He just needed that job offer in hand before they changed their minds.

He glanced over at his wife as she reported on a case of police brutality in Roxbury. Her face contorted in mock outrage, and her tone sounded somber and serious. Yes, he badly wanted Logan Burrows's job. Hopefully, his wife wouldn't blow it for him with her titillating, lowbrow style of journalism.

He hesitated as she turned toward him, one Botoxed eyebrow raised. A few seconds of dead air caused the staff in front of him to grimace in horror. He'd missed his cue. Gideon jerked his head toward the blinking camera, realizing his error, and began to speak. He read the words off the teleprompter, mechanically and without his usual upbeat cadence. Once done, he smiled woodenly and passed the baton over to his wife.

He stared past the cameras and toward Kelly, the cute new intern he'd secretly—and foolishly—taken out to lunch this week. Nothing thus far had happened, but he could sense that she was waiting for him to make the first move. He'd met with her Tuesday at one of the out-of-the-way restaurants in Chinatown where nobody could see them. They sat in a back booth, whispering flirtatiously to each other over squid lo mein and jellyfish dumplings, knowing they couldn't be seen because of the massive fish tank blocking their view of the street. Besides, he hadn't crossed any ethical line just yet. So why was he flirting with disaster? Did he have a career death wish? Or had his wife been pushing him away?

Kelly smiled at him from the back of the room, and he had to remind himself to pay attention to his cue. While his wife chatted with a reporter on the scene of a shooting, he flashed the briefest of smiles to the attractive intern, hoping no one would notice. She was tall and thin, with silky red hair, and exuded class on account of her Ivy League education. She had not a crude bone in her body, unlike his boorish wife. And if being crass and splashy was the new way to gain spectacular ratings, then he wondered if this was the right industry for him. But reporting the news was all he'd ever known, and if push came to shove, he'd stoop to the lowest denominator to remain at the top.

Shay finished her interview with the reporter on scene and transitioned to a commercial break. He breathed a sigh of relief, looking up to see if Kelly was still admiring him.

"You're doing a marvelous job tonight," Shay said, patting his hand in a patronizing manner.

"As are you."

"Thanks. Just try to watch for your cues from now on, Gideon. Sleeping on the job's not in your contract." She laughed.

"I've forgotten more about news broadcasting than you'll ever know."

"But who's the one with the Emmy in this relationship, dear?"

He glared at her. How dare she throw her one Emmy award in his face. Or give him advice about delivering the news when he'd been at this his entire life. If not for him, she'd not be here in the first place. A funny thought occurred to him. A pleasing one, actually. What if, when he took Logan Burrows's job, she decided not to join him? That would mean he could have all of Manhattan to himself. Maybe she'd want to carry on their relationship long distance. Or maybe not. With all the money he'd be banking, he could certainly afford to divorce her and live the life he'd always dreamed about living. She could keep her shitty job at this station, and then he could watch with pleasure as she fell spectacularly from grace. He'd be onto bigger and better things by then: interviewing presidents and senators, speaking to the Middle East crisis, reporting on Russia, China, and hobnobbing with media elites from around the world. There'd be interviews with Pulitzer Prize–winning authors, Nobel Peace Prize statesmen, and Oscar-nominated actors. He promised himself to bone up on all the serious subjects once he landed the job.

Oh, and he'd be busy slaying Manhattan's most gorgeous women.

They returned on-air and transitioned to Stan and the weather. Then, another transition to sports. He typically tried to look busy during these breaks, scribbling somberly on a sheet of paper as if taking copious notes, when all he was doing was making silly doodle sketches. His wife, on the other hand, turned into a Chatty Cathy when off-air, schmoozing with all the camera crew and staff and passing out freshly baked chocolate chip cookies. It irked him that she included all these little people in her social circle, making him look like a pretentious jerk in the process.

What had happened to cause such a drastic change in her? By all rights, he should have been happy to have such an upbeat life and work partner. A wife who'd boosted his ratings in spectacular fashion and had wild, albeit cursory, sex with him on a regular basis. A wife who brought in good money (but spent vastly more) and looked stunning on his arm. But she hadn't been like this before the assault. He actually missed the old Shay. Could that head injury have caused such a dramatic change in her personality?

The sports segment was almost done save for the inspirational story Chad usually finished with. Yesterday, he reported on the autistic football player allowed to run untouched for a ninety-yard touchdown. Last week, he told about the one-legged downhill skier. A month ago, he'd lavished praise on the transgender high school wrestler who'd romped to the girls' state title. Tonight's story was about the visually impaired boy who sank a hundred straight foul shots.

And that reminded him of Quinn. Poor, little Quinn. He called her religiously every Sunday morning before Logan Burrows's political talk show. She better be enjoying her new school, because it was costing him sixty G's a year plus books and fees. It seemed odd when she told him she loved it there, because she didn't sound very happy when he talked to her. Maybe she was tired come Sunday mornings.

He missed his daughter more than he realized, but mostly in the abstract. The day-to-day stuff of being a parent never came easy to him. Girls, with all their emotional turmoil and never-ending drama, were a complete mystery to him. He'd now be spared the messy details about her first period, the boys she had crushes on, and the wild shopping sprees she'd eventually go on.

Shame filled him as Chad finished his report by high-fiving the blind basketball shooter. The most cringe-worthy part of the broadcast was now to come. Just last week, Shay had convinced the news director to let her deliver a brief commentary at the end of each broadcast, and she went behind his back to get this perk.

Her remarks each night embarrassed him beyond words. Yet...yet the public appeared to love these segments. Thousands of emails poured into the station each day, addressed to Shay Wells. Her commentaries were slightly controversial and delivered with an attitude one could only describe as righteous indignation. Unless she decided to go lighthearted and breezy. Gideon wondered how people could find these editorials entertaining. He'd begged her to tone it down and be more civil, but she'd fought back against this advice, ratcheting up her rhetoric with each successive broadcast. "What good is my commentary if I come across like a wet dishrag?" she'd said.

Tonight, she was taking a courageous stand against spousal abuse. Always believe the woman, she lectured, advocating for financial support for the abused victims and maximum sentencing for the men who beat them.

Gideon glanced nervously at Kelly during this segment, noticing that she was mesmerized by Shay's performance. Yet he couldn't object to such commentary lest anyone think he believed spousal abuse an acceptable form of behavior.

He felt like he was losing his mind. When he mentioned this to his therapist one day, she replied that in rare instances, head trauma victims emerged from their torpor with special abilities that they hadn't before possessed.

The broadcast finished, and he and Shay bid everyone goodnight. He was embarrassed and put off by the news director's enthusiastic thumbs-up in their direction. Gideon glanced over at the redheaded intern and bemoaned the fact that he couldn't take her out for a quick nightcap and listen to her endlessly praise his news reporting skills.

"I'll walk you to your car, Shay," he said.

"How do you think we did tonight?"

"Not bad." He gave her a tight-lipped smile.

"Not bad? That's it?"

Gideon shrugged.

"I don't know about you, but I feel like I'm not even close to achieving my potential."

"We're way ahead of Yolanda Brown in the ratings. What more do you want?"

"I have my sights set higher. I'm convinced that there's no limit to what I can achieve."

He laughed, knowing it sounded condescending.

"You don't believe me?"

"Oh, I believe you, dear, especially now that you've tied yourself to my coattails."

"What are you implying?"

"It took years for me to arrive at this status in life, as well as the stellar ratings that come with it. You think you did this on your own?"

"But it was me who brought in new advertisers and a whole new demographic."

"Of course, you have, hon." *Keep telling yourself that.*

"I'm thinking of moving on to one of the bigger networks."

"Darling, if the national networks were looking for someone to deliver the news, don't you think they'd come knocking on my door first?" He knew right away he shouldn't have said it.

"Dear," she said in a patronizing manner, "please don't be envious of my success."

"Envious?" He laughed. "You're being ridiculous, Shay."

"I shouldn't be telling you this, but I got a call the other day."

His ears perked up. "A call? From who?"

"From *whom*," she corrected, smiling at him in a patronizing manner. She opened the Mercedes's door and made her way inside. The car started as soon as she pressed the button. Shay rolled down the window and gazed up at him. "Didn't they teach you grammar at that lowly state college you went to?"

Throwing his public school education in his face stung him more than she knew. "Stop beating around the bush, Shay. I demand to know who called you."

"I'm not supposed to tell anyone, but the network is searching for Logan Burrows's replacement, and they thought I might be interested."

"Why in the world would they call you?"

"Well, I am an Emmy award-winning anchorwoman."

He turned and stormed off toward his car, unable to control the rage filling him. The screech of her wheels informed him that his wife would be home well before him. When he reached his vehicle, he kicked the tire so hard that, for a second, he thought he'd broken his big toe. Then he got inside and fought off the urge to cry.

SHAY

She raised her head and heard a sizzling sound coming from the kitchen. Sunlight streamed in all around her, and she had to squint to keep out the light. Her head hadn't pounded like that since her college days. She lifted her feet off the cushion and sat up on the couch, rubbing her aching head. On the coffee table sat an empty bottle of Jack.

It took a few seconds for her to realize that she was in the living room.

But where was George? He wasn't sitting in his usual armchair. She turned and stared out the window and saw the snow piled chest high. Because of the weather, she couldn't leave this place. It was the reason George had let her sleep upstairs.

Still, that didn't mean she wouldn't try to escape. She'd do virtually anything to return home and be reunited with Quinn.

She tried to remember something from last night. How much had she drunk? Her head throbbed in pain as the memory of her sister sitting at that news desk came back to her. Now, everything started to make sense. Her sister had obviously not been the one who died in that house fire. So, whose charred remains did they find?

Shannon, her twin sister, was responsible for all this. After all these years, Shannon was still alive and getting her revenge for that tragic childhood decision Shay had made.

George stood in the kitchen doorway, holding a rubber spatula and wearing a white apron. The sizzling sound behind him continued unabated.

"You must be hungry. And hungover," he said. "I got some coffee brewing."

"You knew my sister was behind all this."

"Not only did I know Shannon was your twin sister, but I've been working with her for years now. How do you think you ended up here?"

"But why, George?"

"Come on over and get some grub. Then we'll talk." George disappeared into the kitchen.

Shay stood and took a few baby steps forward. Blood rushed to her head, and for a second, she thought she might pass out. She wobbled across the threshold and saw a kitchen that belonged in the nineteen fifties.

She glanced out the kitchen window and saw the sun shining brilliantly off the outer crust of snow. The glare made it hard for her to see anything. She sat down at the Formica table, fighting the nausea. In front of her was a steaming cup of coffee, a bowl of sugar, a container of Coffee-Mate, and a plastic plate filled with scrambled powdered eggs and a clump of oatmeal.

"Why did you let me sleep out in the living room?"

"You really tied one on last night. You were so distraught about seeing your sister that you ended up drinking way too much."

She sipped her coffee and saw the can of Maxwell House sitting on the counter. It tasted far better than any Starbucks she'd ever had. "Aren't you hungover?"

"I've never been hungover in my life. Call it a blessing—or a curse."

"Lucky you."

"Yeah, lucky me. Now get some more coffee and grub in that gullet of yours. It'll make you feel better."

As much as she had been dreaming about food lately, the thought of eating everything on her plate repulsed her. She sipped her coffee.

"Come on now, sugar. I didn't make all this grub for it to go to waste."

"You didn't answer my question. Why did you let me sleep up here last night?"

"Not like you were going anywhere in this weather. And you have been following the program."

"I could have taken your gun and shot you while you were passed out. Or I could have grabbed your phone and called the cops."

"I suppose you could have done either of those things," he said. "But where you gonna go? And you don't even know the password to my phone."

"But I would have at least gotten rid of you."

"I got news for you; you wouldn't need a gun to get rid of me." He doused everything with salt and pepper before stabbing his fork into his scrambled eggs.

"I'm not following you."

"I've known your sister for a long time. She's smart as a whip, but also a real piece of work. We did lots of jobs together out in Vegas. Girl was a legendary hustler."

"How did she convince you to come with her and set me up like this?"

"The way she talked about you, she made it sound like you were an uppity bitch who needed payback for the way you treated her when you two were kids. Told me how you stabbed yourself in the leg and burned down your foster parents' home. And then how her friend was burned beyond recognition in that fire, and the authorities thought it was Shannon's body. Said she had to leave town because of what you done. That true?"

"It's all true. I did everything she claimed. But that was only after years of suffering abuse and physical harassment at the hands of my sister. She practically tortured me every day of my life."

"I can see her doing that."

"She left me with no other choice." She nibbled on the tasteless oatmeal. "All this time, I thought she was the one who had died in that house fire, but it was obviously one of her homeless friends who burned to death."

"What happened?"

"Shannon ran back inside the burning house, I assume, to help her friend out to safety. Maybe it was too late by then. Or maybe she let her friend die in the blaze in order that she could assume her identity."

"She was using another ID when I first met her, but she told me to call her Shannon."

"I feel terrible that an innocent girl died in that fire. I had no idea she'd been in the house at the time, or else I never would have set it."

"Knowing Shannon, she took advantage of what you'd done."

"So why did you decide to help her??"

"I'm doing this for my kids. She said we would split everything fifty-fifty."

"That's my money," she said bitterly. "And why can't you provide for your own kids?"

"It's complicated."

"Try me. I'm not a dumb blond."

He picked up his cup and took a sip of coffee. "I came down sick last year and went to the emergency room. When the doctor came back, he said I had the Big C."

"Cancer?"

"Well, he didn't diagnose me with a big cock." He laughed. "Testicular. Stage four."

"Jesus, George, I'm sorry to hear that."

"Not sorrier than I am."

"That sucks."

"I took this gig to leave something for my kids before I depart from this world."

"Are you in a lot of pain?"

"Why do you think Jack and I are such good friends?"

"But now that you're staring death in the face, you see the error of your ways?"

"I still want a good future for my kids. They're fifteen and fourteen, and their mom don't have a pot to piss in."

"I expected a different response."

"I bet you did, but you're not the only one who'll do anything for their kids." He sipped his coffee.

"You're better than that, George. Better than my sister, anyway."

"I'm no better than that conniving bitch. I agreed to go along with her plan, didn't I?"

"You're a good person, I can see it in you."

"Don't mistake my good nature for weakness. I'm not a pussy."

"I never said you were."

"You seem like a nice person, Shay. I'm sure your daughter will be copacetic after all this is said and done. But my kids won't be. I have to take care of them before I git. It's the only decent thing to do."

"How much time do you have left?"

"Months. Weeks. Who the hell knows? Hopefully, I have enough Jack left to get me through the winter. By that time, Shannon will have cleaned out your bank account and paid me my share."

"Does she know about your diagnosis?"

"Of course, she knows. Why do you think she asked me to help her? She knows I got nothing to lose."

Shay shook her head. "Do you really think my sister is going to give you a cut of her share? Especially when she knows you're dying?"

"She'd better. Claims she already wired ten grand into my account."

"And you know that for a fact?"

"Texted me the receipt."

"And you believed that lying sister of mine?"

"Eat your breakfast. I hate seeing a good meal go to waste."

"I'm not like her, George. You needn't worry about me screwing you over."

"Doesn't matter whether I trust you or not. Neither of us is leaving here anytime soon, so we might as well get along as best we can."

"I need to get you to the hospital."

"I'm done with hospitals, chemo, and radiation. I'll die on my own terms, like a man, and with Jack by my side."

"Then, at least let me stay upstairs with you. I can help take care of you."

"Don't much matter at this point." He pointed his fork at her. "Now, eat your damn breakfast before it gets cold."

QUINN

Quinn had stopped trying to sit at the lunch table with the popular girls. It had been over a month, and still barely anyone had spoken to her. The few times they did, they told her that she was an outsider-slash-loser who didn't belong at their prestigious school. It took her a while to understand this behavior, but she finally figured out why those girls treated her so badly. Most of them had been attending this school for years and had developed close ties with one another. Their mutually shared disability bound them in a way that nothing else had. It was the reason why they'd excluded her from their cliques.

The extreme isolation was killing her. Even the kids who were not popular had formed their own groups. How was she supposed to meet other kids if no one allowed her into their inner circle? For the first time in her life, she felt imprisoned by her blindness. And she couldn't just pick up and leave.

She lay in bed with one of her favorite books and wondered where her mother was at the moment. Did her mother miss her? She expected her father to call any minute now. He called every Sunday morning like clockwork, and she dreaded every second of their conversation. All he seemed to do was go through the motions of fatherhood and tell her how wonderful things were down at the station. He hadn't really heard what she had to say. Or didn't want to hear. He couldn't tell by the tone of her voice that this school had drained all the light from her soul. She debated telling him the truth: that the woman he lived with was not actually his wife. But she knew he wouldn't believe her. She was also afraid that she might anger this imposter and put her family in more jeopardy, like her mother was in now.

Sniffing back the tears, she wished she could tell someone. Maybe they could find her real mother and rescue her from wherever that witch had taken her. But she didn't think so. They would cast doubt on her claim and call her a liar, saying the only reason she lied was so that she could return home. The authorities at school noted that her grades had slipped and that she was openly defiant with the other children and struggling to make friends. Who would ever believe her?

She'd reached the point where she was now desperate to get the truth out. But she had to do it properly if anyone was to believe her. What if she could help save her mother's life by outing this fraud? Not in a million years would her real mother have put her in a boarding school so far from home. Not when she was perfectly happy going to a school near home, where all the kids and staff adored her. Where she had a comfy room filled with books and stuffies, and where she could navigate every inch of the campus without her walking stick. It seemed as if nobody here would even care if she went missing. She pictured authorities discovering her frozen, lifeless body buried beneath the snowbanks come spring.

That fraud reporting the news next to her father was pure evil. Quinn had been listening to their newscasts over the internet, searching for clues that might out her. Her father had mentioned to her weeks ago that her mother would be joining his newscasts. Although it would be hard to prove, Quinn remembered her mother telling her that she was done working in the news industry. Her real mother had claimed she had no use for it anymore, explaining that being a mother meant more to her than any other job she might have. Quinn believed her at the time. She was the only person in the world dedicated to watching out for her.

Her phone rang as she lay there. She didn't want to answer it but knew she should. If she refused, her father would call the authorities, and they'd send someone to her room to check on her. No way did she want to talk to that weird residence counselor with the squeaky high voice.

"Hello," she said.

"Quinn, my darling, how are you?"

"Wonderful, Daddy."

"How's school?"

"I love this place so much," she said in a deadpan voice.

"I knew you would. You must have a busy day planned?"

"There are all kinds of fun activities and things to do here," she said, trying to sound cheerful. "How's Mommy doing with her new job?"

Her father paused. "Your mother's doing great. People seem to really like the two of us on the air together."

"You don't sound very happy about it," she said, noticing the flatness in his voice.

"Granted, it might take some getting used to. I've been doing this for a long time now."

"Momma's really changed since the attack, don't you think?"

"Yes, I suppose she has. But we're very fortunate that she's making a full recovery."

"Yes, I suppose we are." She debated telling him what she thought of that imposter but knew he wouldn't believe her.

"When was the last time you spoke to her?"

"We text message every day. Sometimes she calls me after school and asks how I'm doing," she lied.

"Wonderful."

"Yes, it's so nice to talk to her."

There was the usual awkward pause in their conversation as her father had run out of things to say. It pained her that he was putting his career over her welfare and that he couldn't sense his own daughter's apprehension.

"Well, if that's all, Quinn, then I'd better let you run along."

"One thing before you hang up, Daddy. Do you have Mrs. Jessica's phone number?"

"Possibly. Why do you want to talk to her?"

"Just to say hi. She and Miranda have always been so nice to me."

"Sure. Give me a sec, and I'll find it."

She copied the number into her contact list once he read it off. Then he said goodbye, promising to chat with her next Sunday. After he hung up, she pumped herself up to talk to Mrs. Jessica. Why had she suddenly requested her neighbor's number? Maybe because she was the only one of her mother's friends who truly knew what she was like before the accident. Jessica was her last-ditch hope. If she didn't believe her outlandish story, then no one would. The possibility of being laughed at caused her to rethink making the call. Then again, what did she have to lose? She grabbed her cell phone and punched in the number.

"Quinn?"

"Hello, Mrs. Jessica."

"Oh my goodness, it's so good to hear from you."

"So good to talk to you too. How's Miranda?"

"Busy with homework and basketball practice," she said. "We all miss you so much around here. How's everything at your new school?"

"Terrible. I hate this place, but please don't tell my parents."

"Okay."

"I have something to tell you, and I hope you won't think I'm crazy."

"Of course not. What is it?"

"Promise you won't laugh?"

"Never."

"Right," she said, pausing to consider her words. "Okay, here it is. I don't think the woman living with my father is really my mother." There was a long pause at the other end of the line, and for a second, she feared she'd blown her one chance. "Mrs. Jessica? Are you still there?"

"Oh my God!"

"What's wrong?"

"I've been thinking the exact same thing."

SHANNON

How wonderful is my life these days? I walk into restaurants, and people cheer and give me standing ovations. Unfamiliar men come up to me in bars and offer to buy me a drink. All eyes in the room now gravitate in my direction. People approach with napkins and menus, pleading for my autograph. One night, I started to scribble down my old name before realizing that my name is now Shay Wells, not Shannon Bateman or Cherish Santos.

My entire life has consisted of striving for something better, but continually falling short. I've endured broken homes, a hateful sister, the death of my friend, poverty, dysfunction, imprisonment, prostitution, and abuse. Yet here I stand, the darling of Boston's news media, rich and famous beyond what I ever imagined. I live in a beautiful home in Woodbridge Estates, the signature tenth hole as my backdrop. It's the same hole I traipsed over while my husband's golf buddies stood gawking at me in awe.

I went to visit the blind girl the other day. And to think people find her cute. It proves how different my twin sister and I are from one another.

The little blind girl wasn't surprised by my visit. Quite the opposite, in fact. She said she'd been expecting me. Our visit wasn't all hunky-dory mother-daughter stuff, but it was much different than I'd expected. She seemed resigned to the fact that she wasn't going home. I expected to encounter tearful resistance and be forced to hear all about her pain and suffering. I expected her to threaten to out me as an imposter. But there was none of that. I took solace in the fact that she hated her school and had yet to make any friends. Seems the other little blind girls are choosing to ostracize her because she is the *new* blind girl. Then I gave her a bit of unsolicited advice, which worried me the more I thought about it (was I developing maternal instinct?). I advised her to lash out at those little bitches with a nuclear strike and establish herself as the top dog. Then, the brat actually thanked me for the advice. Said she'd take what I'd said under consideration.

Gideon's been acting so confident as of late that it cracks me up. The most recent phone call did wonders for him and his overbearing ego. Even at my boldest, he stares at me glibly while at the news desk, under the misguided belief that he's keeping some big secret from me. If only he knew what I know. That I'm the British chick who's been calling him.

The applause I get when entering a restaurant doesn't even faze him anymore, other than the fact that he hates being referred to as Mr. Shay Wells. And it doesn't faze him because he sees the Boston market as undeserving of his vast talents. He thinks he'll soon have a national audience eating out of the palm of his hand.

All the financials have come in, and I'm less than impressed with his net worth. It's decent but not enough to live on—and yet it's far more money than I've ever had in my bank account. Of course it's not just the money I want now. I've gotten accustomed to stardom. I want to be adored and fawned over. I want to attend fancy parties and stately dinners and buy lots of expensive jewelry and cars. I want all the perks I've been routinely denied in life because of my unfortunate circumstances.

George keeps calling and asking when we can grab the cash and head back to Vegas. Of course, I lied to him about wiring ten grand into his bank account. How long can I keep putting him off? Soon enough, I'll need to go over to that house and finish the two of them off, like I finished off the owner of that house. George has outlived his usefulness, and I can't risk him living any longer than need be. Hopefully, The Big C will kill him before I do.

I often think back to the day my trailer-trash father died in that spectacular car crash. It happened a year before our wino of a mother walked out on us. That takes a toll on a kid. Some kids are negatively affected by such things and grow hate in their hearts. Other kids can move on from such tragedy and use it as motivation to be a better person.

If only my parents could see me now, reporting the news on TV and becoming a celebrity in this town. Those two lushes would most certainly raise a drink at their favorite bar and toast my success. Admittedly, I put them through hell as a young girl. It's probably why they drank themselves silly each night.

I caused my father's death. After I chased out the babysitter, I called the dive bar my parents were drinking at and told them that a boy I knew was holding a knife to my throat and threatening to kill me. My father got in his car and raced home in a drunken stupor while my mother kept her barstool warm. He didn't even see the eighteen-wheeler that blindsided him, killing him instantly.

It didn't help that my parents favored my sister over me. This bias was obvious from my first waking moments on this planet. She smiled when I couldn't. Or wouldn't. She spoke the words "mama" and "dada" when I refused out of principle. As I got older, they constantly compared the two of us. Good sister. Bad sister. Just because she was sweeter than me didn't mean I should have been any less loved. I began to swear, steal, and become defiant. Nurture me, you useless fucks, I felt like screaming to them. But they didn't get the message. Their drunken disciplinary measures fueled my rage, so I took out my frustrations on Shay. I knew she thought she was better than me. It was why I made her life so miserable.

Jessica is up to something. I can feel it. I'm not sure what it is, but she's the one to watch in that backstabbing pack of jackals. For whatever reason, she went to visit the blind girl the other day. I know this because I saw her name in the visitors' online registry. I suppose I could have gone to Quinn and asked her about Jessica's appearance. But she'd just say the woman showed up for a friendly visit. She'd never admit the truth to me: that she told Jessica I was not really her mother.

I'd have no problem getting rid of a nosy bitch who can't stay out of my business.

I look at my watch. Twenty-seven minutes until I'm on air. Maybe if I catch every light and exceed the speed limit, I just might make the newscast tonight. I always do. While Gideon's pretending to do busy work in his office, I'll be zipping through traffic and flipping off these crazy Boston drivers.

Making Gideon sweat entertains me. Last night, I gave him a crotch massage under the desk while he was reporting on the birth of a new Panda cub at the Franklin Park Zoo. He somehow managed to keep a straight face the entire time, despite the fact that he couldn't even remotely catch wood.

All this is so much fun. Will I ever be happy merely being rich and famous? I doubt it, knowing my restless nature, but we'll see once this all plays out.

SHAY

She fell asleep on the couch, thinking about Quinn. And what about that sister of hers, stealing her life and living in her house in Woodbridge Estates. Her daughter was the only good thing she'd ever produced in life. She felt as if she was paying the ultimate price for the terrible decision she'd made all those years ago by stabbing herself in the thigh, setting her sleazy foster parents' house on fire, and then blaming it on Shannon. Maybe Shannon might have turned out differently had she not set her up for those crimes, but she doubted it. And all these years, she had lived with the tremendous guilt that she'd killed her twin sister, when it had actually been her friend who had died.

Her head felt better now. She opened one eye and saw the light from the flatscreen throwing shade over George's haggard face. His eyes were closed, and his head sloped to one side. The empty bottle of Jack sat on the seat cushion between his legs.

She swept the blanket off her and stood on the cold oak floor. Good thing she had on thick wool stockings, or her feet would have frozen. She grabbed the green blanket off the coffee table and unfolded it. As she was about to spread it over him, she noticed the gun sitting on his lap. For a brief second, she thought about taking it. But what would she do with it? Shoot him? Hold him captive until spring? Instead, she picked up the bottle, put it on the coffee table, and then spread the blanket over him. She grabbed the remote and shut off the TV before settling back down on the couch.

When the weather broke, she vowed to leave this house and make her way to safety. Even George's grim prognosis wouldn't stop her from saving

Quinn.

As she lay on the couch, thinking about the crazy twist her life had taken, her hand involuntarily reached down under her jeans until she felt the childhood scar on her thigh: the spot where she stabbed herself with that penknife and then blamed it on her sister. It seemed like such a long time ago. The memory of plunging that blade into her leg returned in all its vivid horror. How she managed to do such a thing, she had not a clue. She bolted upright, her heart racing, and felt the searing pain of that night all over again.

She recalled her years growing up with Shannon. Why had her sister always hated her?

Shannon had caused all this. And it would be Shannon who would suffer the consequences once she made it out of there. She would make sure her sister paid for what she'd done to her and her family.

She remembered seeing their house engulfed in flames, praying that the police would arrest Shannon for setting it.

She felt sorry for George despite the fact that he agreed to go along with this plan. George was a grifter, yes, but a man only trying to help his kids before he died. Too bad he couldn't see how Shannon was using him. Her sister had no plans of sharing her spoils with her longtime partner in crime. He would succumb to cancer before that would ever happen. Or else Shannon would kill them both.

For some bizarre reason, Shay felt like she had to make things right with George. He might have been a con man in a previous life, but she believed that, deep down, he had a good heart. It was more than she could say for that manipulative sister of hers.

GIDEON

Gideon couldn't have been happier as he recalled the conversation he'd had last week with his contact in New York. He was still in the running for the job and would know today what the outcome of their decision would be. For that reason, he kept staring anxiously down at his phone, waiting for confirmation.

He knew his days as an anchorman in Boston were numbered. That was why his wife's antics didn't bother him as much as they did when she first started at the station. Aside from that unexpected "massage" she gave him last night while he was reporting on the new Panda cub at the Franklin Park Zoo, he could work with her for a bit longer. But fondling him during a news report was highly unprofessional. And although no one said anything to him afterwards, he was sure everyone noticed what she was doing. Even Kelly, standing way in the back, looked away in embarrassment.

His phone rang. Gideon stared at the caller ID and immediately shuddered with nervous anticipation. It was the call he'd been waiting for his entire life. Would it be good news or bad? *Think positive,* he told himself as he lifted the phone to his ear.

"After a long and difficult search, the board has chosen you to succeed Logan Burrows. Congratulations, Gideon," the woman said warmly over the phone.

Words failed him as he pumped his fist triumphantly in the air.

"Your life is about to drastically change. Are you ready for it?"

"I've never been more ready in my life."

"You're about to be fabulously rich and famous. How does it feel?"

"It feels wonderful, and I can't wait to start working there."

"We are just as excited as you, Gideon."

"I'm prepared to do all the hard work in order to elevate your station's prominence in the industry."

"The board wouldn't have chosen you otherwise."

"Tell me one thing, and please be honest with me."

"Certainly, to the extent I can."

"Was I competing against my wife for the job?"

He heard a brief pause. "Yes, but it wasn't much of a competition. Sure, your wife is gorgeous, has won an Emmy, and is entertaining. But at the end of the day, she lacks your gravitas and many years of experience. And let's face it, the news world is still a male-dominated industry."

And thank the good Lord for that! He did an impromptu disco dance around his desk. "When can I announce it to the world?"

"Not just yet. We're going to keep this quiet until the end of the month when the sale of the network goes through. Then we're going to sever ties with Logan and announce you as our new anchorman. Can you hold your tongue for a bit longer?"

"I've lasted this long. What's a few more weeks?"

"Wonderful. Make sure you keep your nose clean in the meanwhile," she said. "And while you're at it, you'd better start looking in the city for a place to live."

The line went dead. Gideon continued his dance, wishing he could announce the news to everyone. Shout it from the rooftops. But what had she meant by keeping his nose clean? Of course, he would keep his nose clean. Did the network suspect him of having an affair? He knew these networks often hired private investigators to check out potential hires. To make sure they were not crackheads, sexual harassers, or had skeletons in their closet.

He stopped dancing and breathed a sigh of relief. Thank god he'd not yet consummated his relationship with Kelly. Just a quick peck on the cheek after an expensive lunch of sushi rolls. Now, all he had to do was stay clear of her. Be polite and professional. He wouldn't even exceed the speed limit, not that he could in Boston's horrendous traffic.

He tidied up his office before departing. As the news director lingered over her desk, he arched his neck and checked out Barb's shapely figure. Then he looked away, chastising himself for being such a pig.

"I'm going home, Barb. Not feeling too well today."

"Get out of here, Gideon, before you give that crud to others."

"Righto."

He cringed at how easily she'd dismissed him. She wouldn't have been so casual about his leaving last year when they'd been mired in second place in the ratings. But that damn wife of his had diminished his value at the station. Not for long, though, he thought, as he strode toward the elevator doors. *These assholes will really miss me when I'm gone.* And when the novelty of his wife's dog and pony show started to wear off, and the ratings began to kamikaze into a death spiral, with Rand sitting next to her, he'd be laughing hysterically from his antique cherry desk overlooking Times Square. Then, he'd head to the studio for his monthly interview with the POTUS.

He realized his wife might still be home, so he drove around the streets of Boston until he stopped at the Porter House Grille in the Financial District. A celebratory New York sirloin followed by two shots of good scotch seemed called for. Life couldn't get much better. He parked two spaces away from the establishment. In a month or so, his life would get considerably nicer. Yes, in a month, he would have achieved his dream job, dining regularly at Smith & Wollensky and Momofuku and sipping expensive cognacs while wolfing down tuna sushi and filets of Kobe beef.

He made his way inside and sat down. Despite the attention and pats on the back, he looked forward to spending some quality time alone. He never minded people coming up to him in public and, in fact, felt flattered by all the attention. But nowadays, they ask more about his wife than about him. In a few weeks, he'd show the world who wore the pants in their marriage.

He purchased a Padrón and a glass of cognac and fled toward the cigar room. Beaded leather couches and dark paneled walls greeted him. Frank Sinatra crooned over the speakers, giving the room a distinctly masculine ambiance. Three good-looking young guys wearing suits and with their hair gelled back like Gordon Gekko bellowed drunkenly for him to join them. He nipped off the end of his cigar with the gold cutter, borrowed a light, then sat down with them. The earthy scent of cigar smoke, combined with the rich Corinthian leather, lent a heavy dose of testosterone to the occasion. He sipped his cognac, reveling in their praise, wishing it could always be like this. There was no greater feeling than being a TV star. Wealth came close, but it didn't quite match the sensation of being adored by the masses.

"You're like a legend in this town, dude," the tall blond guy said.

"I wouldn't go that far," he replied modestly.

"I've been watching you since I was a little kid," another guy with black hair added.

"Seniority definitely has its rewards," Gideon said.

"That wife of yours is a smoker," the fat guy said, laughing in a hurtful way. "Only reason I watch that station is to check out her headlights."

He glared at this obese clown, hoping to shame him into quiescence.

"What's she like behind the scenes?" Blond Guy asked.

"A fine woman," he replied.

"She should do the news in a skimpy bikini," Fat Boy added.

"What? And make my zipper burst?" Blond guy said, to which they all laughed.

Gideon puffed on his cigar, trying to restrain himself from lashing out at these crude men. Boys will be boys, he kept reminding himself. After all, he was once a young man himself. He reminded himself that he didn't particularly care for this new version of his wife.

"Can I let you boys in on a little secret?" He leaned forward and took them all in.

The men puffed on their stogies and nodded conspiratorially. The mineral smell of beef mixed with cigar smoke filled Gideon's nostrils with the most glorious odor. His pleasant thoughts floated on a raft of expensive cognac.

"You boys have to swear to keep what I'm about to tell you under wraps."

"Hell yeah," Fat Boy proclaimed.

"Of course we will," Blond Guy said.

He paused for dramatic effect. "I'm taking over for Logan Burrows."

"Jesus!" Black-haired Guy said. "For real?"

"A toast is definitely called for," Fat Boy announced, holding up his drink while sucking on his thick cigar.

"And when that happens, I'll be able to score the kind of tail you lightweights could only dream of tapping."

He exited the room and then slammed the door shut behind him. The bartender appeared in front of him holding up a bottle of Glenlivet, but he held his hand up. Two drinks was his limit tonight, especially since he had to drive back to Woodbridge Estates. No way he was getting a DUI and jeopardizing his new job. Once he was back home and settled comfortably into his leather recliner, he'd pour himself two fingers of brandy—and then proceed to celebrate his good news.

He grabbed his coat and headed for the door. The alcohol swirled nicely in his head, producing a myriad of positive thoughts. Soon, he'd be ensconced in Manhattan amongst his peers, sipping the most expensive single malt scotches in the world.

Then he'd never return to this godforsaken town again.

SHAY

Shay started sleeping on the couch every night, making sure to cover George over with the blanket once he passed out. She also began taking over the breakfast duties, rationing the remaining food left in the refrigerator and cupboard.

The house felt especially cold this morning. She gathered some logs in hand and started a fire. The pile of logs seemed to be getting smaller with each passing day. There was also less than a quarter of oil left in the tank. She knew that they would need to ration all their remaining fuel if they hoped to stay warm throughout the rest of the winter and spring. She also noticed that their food supply was quickly diminishing, as well. It was another thing they'd have to ration.

She glanced out the kitchen window as she whisked the last of the powdered eggs, seeing thick flakes of snow falling from the sky. At this rate, she wouldn't be getting out of this house until late spring. Hopefully, Quinn and Gideon would be safe until then.

It made her sad that Gideon couldn't tell the difference between her and her sister. Was he that clueless? She could at least forgive Quinn for not recognizing her. Yet, in many ways, Quinn was far more perceptive than most people who had sight. But Gideon's inability to recognize the real Shay Wells made her reconsider everything about their marriage. Gideon should have known every inch of her body, all the various nooks and crannies, and where the beauty marks, scars, and freckles lay hidden. The fact that he hadn't made her wonder if their marriage had ever been real.

Maybe it was her fault for not telling him that she had an evil twin sister hell-bent on paying her back for something she did a long time ago. But she'd believed all those years that Shannon had died in that house fire. There was no reason to tell Gideon about her.

Had Shannon been observing her for the last year, studying her every move and keeping tabs on her? Biology dictated that they would share many behavioral traits, possibly even sharing the same thoughts.

Tatyana, the Chechen maid, had been her sister in disguise the entire time. Shannon had drugged her and had kept her in a continual state of mental confusion, causing her to constantly question her own sanity. Shannon had also set that vacation up in order to separate her from her family. It provided George the opportunity to kidnap her, bring her here, and hold her captive. That way, Shannon could assume her identity, take her place in the family structure, and then set out to steal everything she and Gideon owned. She wouldn't be surprised if her sister was at this very moment transferring all their stocks and bonds into an offshore account.

Or maybe Shannon was planning something more nefarious. Maybe Shannon was planning to assume her role permanently and stay on at the news desk. If so, she would eventually have to return to this house and finish her off. Once George succumbed to his cancer and she was dead, no one would ever know the difference. Shannon would be scot-free. Shannon would forever be Shay.

* * *

George appeared to be getting worse. She noticed that he could barely get off his armchair when he got up to use the bathroom. He would groan in agony and try to hide his anguish. Then she'd have to help him inside the bathroom, onto the toilet, and then back to his armchair, where he'd sit most of the day watching TV and getting drunk.

She could see that George hadn't much time left. He didn't want to talk about his condition, and she respected his decision. He must have known, deep in his heart, that Shannon had screwed him over and that his kids would never see a single penny of her stolen money. It was another reason why Shay was determined to get out of this house, save her family, and make Shannon pay for what she'd done. Now, she just needed the weather to break.

Judging from the calendar in the kitchen and where the sun set in the sky, she estimated it to be the end of February.

"I know I haven't said it, Shay, but I'm sorry about what I've done to you and your family," George said while sitting in his armchair one night. "I never thought that bitch would take it this far."

"Thanks, but it's a little too late for apologies now," Shay said as she pulled the blanket up and over her.

"I love my kids, but I can't take back what I did to you and your family."

"No, you most certainly cannot."

"This kind of work is all I've ever known."

"Far be it from me to judge."

He held out his tumbler. "Would you be a doll and pour me another Jack?"

"I'm beginning to think you have a drinking problem," she said, grabbing the bottle and topping off his glass.

"I've got a lot of problems, but alcohol is far down the list." He took the glass from her.

"I hate to be the bearer of bad news, George, but you're running dangerously low on Jack."

"How low?"

"Two more bottles to go, so you'd better make them last."

"Damn," he said, staring at his glass. "Why didn't you tell me that earlier?"

"Even if I had told you, would you have slowed your pace?"

"Probably not. At least I'd have been better prepared to deal with it."

"There's something else I need to tell you while we're at it."

"More bad news?"

"It isn't good."

"What now?"

"We're running low on firewood. And we have less than an eighth of oil left left in the tank and one shitty electric heater to keep us warm."

"Then it'll be a race to see what kills me first, cancer or the cold."

"Hey, what about me?"

"If the cold don't kill you, then I might do it first." He laughed.

"This is serious," she said. "I'm trying to help you."

"You've helped plenty, girl, so don't fret about me. Besides, you got your own family to worry about. I only hope that you can make it out of here alive to pay back that sister of yours."

"I assure you, I'll get out of here no matter what it takes." She stared blankly at the sitcom playing on TV. "How often does she call you?"

"Couple of times a week."

"Did you think to call the police and give them our location?"

"That's not an option." He held up his phone. "And I'll never give you the password to my phone, either."

"Why not? It seems like such an easy way out of this mess."

"Shannon swore that if the police got involved, she'd make sure my kids paid. And Shannon don't bluff."

"No, she doesn't."

"Besides, knowing your sister as you do, would you take a chance with your daughter if you were me?"

She shook her head.

"My kids never saw much of me growing up. I was always out hustling and earning. Their mom is the one who poisoned them against me, and it's a damn shame."

"Then why'd you agree to this scheme?"

"I had nothing to lose. Besides, I don't blame my kids for hating me. I wasn't exactly father-of-the-year material, but I always sent them money and checked in on them from time to time."

"My sister took advantage of your illness."

"You think?" he said after taking a swig. "Your sister took advantage of every person she ever came in contact with. That's how she made her living. I knew a long time ago that she was a snake in the weeds, and yet I still agreed to go along with her plan."

"I'm going to do whatever I can to make sure she doesn't get away with it."

"Were you two always this hateful toward each other?"

"Shannon had it out for me from the day we were born."

"I thought twins were supposed to be tight?"

"Shannon obviously viewed me as competition from the day we were conceived. She could never stand sharing the limelight with anyone, especially someone who was the spitting image of her."

"The girl was brilliant at running cons, but like most grifters, you could never trust her as far as you could throw her."

"So why did you stay with her?"

"Like I said, she was very talented at what she did. We were a good team and made a lot of money together."

"And she never tried to double-cross you?"

"She knew better than that. I had a lot of heavy connections in Vegas, and if she double-crossed me, she knew she'd never work in that town again."

"She took you out of Vegas and out of your comfort zone."

"She told me how she tracked you down and learned that your husband was a big-shot newscaster in Boston. Showed me pictures of your McMansion and expensive cars, telling me that the two of you were worth millions and that we could steal it."

"I think my sister exaggerated about the millions."

"When I saw your husband and that big house on the golf course, I figured she was right. And Shannon looks just like you, meaning I knew she could clean out your bank account before anyone realized it. But then she went and got ambitious on me."

"You know what that means, right?"

"Means I won't be getting squat."

"Well, that too," she said. "But it also means that she'll need to get rid of the two of us in order to make her plan work."

He seemed to think it over.

"She might even return here and kill us herself."

"Don't think she ever killed before, but I wouldn't put it past her."

"She might have even allowed that girl in the house fire to die. She knew she could steal her identity and escape prosecution."

"I wouldn't put it past her."

"Do you have it in you to kill my sister if she shows up here?"

He lifted the gun up, hooked his index finger around the trigger, and pulled it. Click.

"It's not loaded?"

"I'm a con man, not a killer. Shay gave me the gun in order to convince you that I meant business."

"You didn't need a gun to convince me, George." He dropped the useless gun down on the coffee table. "So what now?"

"Maybe you need to start planning for when the weather breaks, and you can make your way back to Boston."

"You'll need to string my sister along when she calls, asking how things are going."

"I want to see that bitch get what's coming to her. But there'll be no calling the police on this phone. For all I know, Shannon might be monitoring my conversations."

"That sounds like something Shannon would do."

"I won't be able to die in peace knowing my kids are in harm's way."

"Okay, George, no calls to the police."

"Or anyone else, for that matter," he said. "I know how to use a knife. I'll take the bitch out myself."

"Fine."

She rested her head on the pillow and thought about her next move. Somehow, she needed to find a way out of here once the weather broke.

GIDEON

Being all alone in his large house felt nice. No high-maintenance wife to nag or upset him. His daughter seemed reasonably happy at school, which meant he could get as drunk as he liked in the confines of his own home. He carried the bottle of brandy to his easy chair and set it down on the table beside him. He'd already slipped into his silk pajamas, emblazoned with various golf icons. Outside, a light snow fell over the streets and golf course.

With a click of his thumb, the seventy-five-inch screen flashed to life. He hadn't felt this comfortable in quite some time, confident in the knowledge that his career was on the upswing.

He skipped the news, believing most news shows to be boring. Instead, he turned on *The Real Housewives* and sat back to enjoy the catfights and constant bickering. *The Housewives* and *The Bachelor* franchises had become two of his favorite shows. He loved watching all those drunken housewives argue pointlessly with each other about nothing. The women were all Botoxed, cosmetically enhanced, and endlessly horny. Many nights, between broadcasts and unbeknownst to anyone, he'd watch the latest installment on his cellphone. Now, he felt like he was living the life.

By the time eleven o'clock arrived, he'd consumed his fourth glass of brandy, as well as a large bag of pork rinds. Drunk and feeling gloriously empowered by his upcoming move to Manhattan, he switched to the news. His wife's face appeared unblemished and perfect in every way. Hot beyond words and even hotter on screen, her blond hair flowed in lustrous layers around her gorgeous face, and those cobalt eyes loomed large on his high-definition screen. He could understand how men might be jealous of him, only they didn't know the real Shay like he did. Spurred on by the brandy, he suddenly yearned to make love to her. From the vantage of his easy chair, it didn't surprise him that she'd helped him garner monster ratings. If he'd been any other red-blooded male, he too would be ogling her every night.

Weather. Transition. Sports. The commentary segment at the end didn't bother him like it once did, now that he was on the verge of riding the Manhattan Express. Pouring himself another brandy, he looked forward to hearing what his wife had to say tonight.

She started to speak. But what came out of those succulent lips shocked him. He sat forward in his easy chair, his head swimming from all the booze he'd consumed, listening as she pontificated against the horrendous crime committed against her down at the soup kitchen. Fragments of that night were coming back to her, she claimed. She remembered a well-dressed man approaching her with a bat in hand, the kind of souvenir bat they sold at baseball parks. She held up one she'd purchased as an example. Then, after she finished her commentary, she swung it toward the camera, causing him to jump back in fear.

"Always be prepared," she said, her face up against the camera. "Don't ever be a victim like me!" She pointed the barrel of the bat at the camera as the screen segued away.

Gideon felt jarred by this strange performance. Maybe it was the booze, but he almost felt as if she were speaking directly to him. His hands shook, and he was certain that if she were here with him now, he might strangle her. Never in his life had he behaved untowardly toward a woman. But then he remembered the big job offered to him, and he quickly came to his senses. He only needed to keep his nose clean for a short while longer.

He clicked off the television. Something in his chest hiccuped. What this meant during his last days at the station, he didn't know. But now was not the time to rock the boat. He needed to stand by his wife. Give her his unwavering love and support, no matter how badly it troubled him. Image was everything in this business, and without it, he would have lost his main asset. He needed to be the kind of husband a respectable network would be proud to call their own. Then, when he had Logan's job in hand, he'd dump that crass bitch and leave her in the dust.

QUINN

On this cold morning, Quinn woke with a renewed sense of purpose. She felt alive and invigorated, ready to tackle the obstacles now confronting her. The reason? She'd had a dream last night in which her mother spoke to her and told her that everything would be all right and that they'd soon be reunited. Although they'd never been a religious family, in the dream, her mother claimed that God was watching over her.

Quinn showered, dressed, and prepared for the school day. Whatever happened, she vowed to be more assertive like that witch posing as her mother had advised. To a certain degree, the imposter was right about one thing. If you want anything in life, you have to go out and grab it. Take care of number one. Quinn realized she wouldn't go to criminal lengths to achieve that goal, but all the same, it was advice worth heeding.

So she waited for the right time. After school, when the bell rang, all the students were required to make their way back to the dorms. Quinn could hear the four girls up ahead. They walked as a group every day, keeping exclusive company. Their leader, a girl named Jenny Cook, fiercely protected their status as the cool kids in class.

"Hey, wait up," Quinn shouted to them. She could hear the girls giggling and openly mocking her. "I said wait up, Jenny."

"What's up with you, Wells? I thought I told you to stay away from me. We don't want a ho like you hanging out with us and ruining our reputations."

"And what reputation is that?" Quinn asked, stopping once she realized that she was standing in front of Jenny. "I'm blind just like all of you."

"You're blind about a lot of things, dumb ass. Like how stupid and ugly you are." The girls laughed as Jenny extended her arms and shoved her in the chest. "Why don't you go back to where you came from?"

Quinn stepped forward, listening for the sound of the girl's breathing. She knew that Jenny was a couple of inches taller than her. The sound of these laughing hyenas made her face blush with anger. She reached back and punched the girl in the nose as hard as she could. She followed that with two more successive blows to her midsection. After the third strike, she heard the girl cry out and fall to the snow. Quinn felt a trickle of blood on her knuckles as she brought her walking stick down hard over Jenny's leg. The hyenas, sensing danger, stopped laughing and began to call out for their fallen comrade, who lay below her, sobbing hysterically.

"Quit your whining, Jenny, and listen to me," Quinn said. "Same with the rest of you."

"You hit me," Jenny wailed.

"And I'll hit you again if you ever act mean to me or anyone else." She turned toward the other girls. "As for the rest of you, if you ever make fun of me again, I will sneak up on you when you least expect it, and you'll all go down like Jenny." She knew the fear of the unknown frightened visually impaired people.

"My nose is bleeding," Jenny wailed.

"Trust me, Jenny, that'll be the least of your problems if you ever mock me again."

"Okay, okay. What do you want?"

"At lunch tomorrow, I'm going to sit at your table, and you *will* be nice to me. I want everyone in the cafeteria to hear it, too. You will treat me as a human being until the day I leave this place. You will never again be mean to me or any of the other students here. Do I make myself clear?"

"My nose hurts," she wailed.

Quinn rapped her stick against the girl's knee. "Do I make myself clear?"

"Yes, I'll be nice to everyone. Just don't hit me again."

"Good," Quinn said, brushing past the other girls. "And if you tell any of the teachers or staff about this, I promise you'll regret it."

"We won't tell anyone," Jenny wailed.

"Better not because I'll be keeping my eyes on you."

She smiled as she walked to her dorm. By the time she made it back, she knew her life was about to change. It felt empowering. She'd been coddled for so long now that she needed this jolt of reality to move on in life. If only it had happened sooner, this experience at her new school might have been more tolerable. Still, better late than never to learn such a harsh lesson.

SHAY

Shay lay on the couch that evening, her head veiled under the wool blanket for warmth. She remembered that fateful night when she lit their foster parents' house on fire and then plunged that penknife into her thigh. It took guts to do that and then blame it on Shannon. No, it took guts for her *not* to do it. She had hoped to remove that bully twin sister from her life, but not to kill her. Or so she thought. What exactly happened to Shannon after that, she didn't know, apart from what George had told her. Shannon had obviously been plotting to get back at her for quite some time. Shay knew full well that she'd endure any ordeal to be with her daughter again, and end her sister's reign of misery.

She'd kill the bitch for real this time if it came down to it. Stab *her* instead of herself, and this time, make sure she stops breathing. Getting rid of Shannon was the only permanent solution to this problem going forward.

She had an idea. George would go along with almost anything she proposed, as long as it didn't jeopardize his kids. It would take much guile and planning, but if she pulled it off, she'd never have to worry about her sister again.

SHANNON

The sympathy and outpouring I've received has been amazing. My news director tells me that the letters, emails, and phone calls have been pouring into the station nonstop. It's incredible that people even care about someone like me, a person they've never met. Because if they knew the real me, they'd think otherwise. They'd run for their lives screaming.

People are congratulating me on being such a courageous woman, calling me a role model for the way I'm confronting my assault head-on.

I can barely stop laughing at my good fortune. How lucky am I? Only the luckiest girl ever. Everything I've touched as of late has turned to gold. Now I have to take care of George, as well as my sister, and I'll be home free.

Gideon's been furious with me, although he's doing his best not to show it. He fears what he might do if he loses his cool. So I push his buttons even more, enjoying watching him squirm. I so badly want to be a fly on the wall when he learns the truth about this new job offer. To see his face when he realizes he's been played.

It's Saturday night, and he's decided that we will stay in and watch a movie. Staying home is the last thing I want to do. I want to go out and spend all our money. I want to dance and drink expensive cocktails and watch as all eyes in the room become glued to yours truly. I love when strange men flirt with me right under Gideon's nose. Watching a movie with him is two hours of my life I'll never get back, and I don't want to waste one precious second of my newfound celebrity.

For the sake of marital bliss, I decide to stay home and watch this dull film he's picked out. When I tell him I've never seen *Network,* Gideon turns to me with a confused expression.

"But you and I have seen this movie many times," he says. "It's one of your favorites."

"Oh, right," I say, hoping I hadn't blown it. "You know my memory comes and goes, hon."

"Well, I don't see how you could forget this one. You're the one who introduced me to this movie."

He thumbs the remotes, and the movie starts to play. What a night, sitting here in my silk robe watching a movie about a crazy newscaster about to be fired from his job. But the more I watch it, the more I find it entertaining and relevant to this situation I'm in. I stare over at Gideon and notice he's half asleep. Then again, six bourbons during the course of two hours will do that to a man. He thinks he's punishing me by making me stay home with him. If only he knew how fortunate he is that I may not have to kill him. But one way or another, his life will be ruined when all is said and done. A quick and painless death might be preferable to what's coming his way.

"You're angry with me, dear," I say, shaking his shoulder and waking him.

"Of course not." He opens his eyelids but refuses to make eye contact with me.

"I know you, honey, and I can tell when you're upset."

He stares at the credits scrolling down the screen, his long hands intertwined over his midsection.

"What's to be mad about? We have the highest-rated newscast in town." He sits, fuming, drunk and angry.

"Please, dear, I can't help you if you won't talk to me."

"Okay, *dear.* Do you want to know what's burning my ass?" he says, turning to face me. "Did you really have to go on-air last night and say all that nonsense about the person who attacked you?"

"You mean the well-dressed *man* who attacked me."

He shakes his head. "Why couldn't you have just gone to the police instead of making a big ruckus like that? The aesthetics look dreadful."

"I did tell the police," I say. "I figured someone in our audience might know something and that it might help the police find the bastard who did this to me."

"It's just so crass and beneath you, drawing attention to yourself like that."

"I thought you'd be happy that my memory is finally starting to return."

"Of course, I'm happy about it. It's just that—"

"Don't you want the police to find the scumbag who attacked me?" I sob into my palms.

"You know I do," he touches my lap.

"Getting this story out is important to me, Gideon. I feel like I'm so close to seeing my attacker's face."

"You really think it'll come to you?"

"Absolutely. Something tells me that the person who did this to me is someone I know."

"What makes you think that?"

"Remember what I told the police? That the person who did this to me mentioned our daughter. Can you believe bringing Quinn into this?"

"I just think it might be best if you kept all this private. It's a family matter, Shay. It might jeopardize—"

"Jeopardize what?"

Gideon sighs in resignation. "Nothing. Forget it."

"No, say it."

"Don't you think it reflects badly on us as journalists? As a news team?"

"Gideon," I whisper into his ear, "the last thing I want to do is cramp your style."

I lead him into the bedroom, despite the six snifters of brandy he's consumed. But he has no interest in me and hasn't in some time. It doesn't take long before he's sawing wood instead of catching it.

SHAY

Spring approached, but it didn't feel like spring. The temperatures seemed to be getting colder, not warmer. She sat up on the couch, the blanket draped over her, and glanced outside. The snow was falling so hard that she could barely see the surrounding landscape. And without a shovel to dig themselves out, they'd barely be able to open the front door.

She collapsed onto the warm cushion and looked over at George. He tugged the blanket up to his unshaven chin and sat shivering in his armchair. If the weather continued on like this, they'd freeze to death. The electric heater sitting on the floor whined loudly, despite giving off little heat.

Tossing off the covers, she went out to the porch and retrieved some logs. Then she started a fire. Last night, she scoured the house to see if she could find any more blankets. She discovered one in a closet, which she used to cover George's body. The blanket, Jack Daniel's, and revenge kept him going. She wondered what would happen when they ran out of fuel? Or alcohol?

Luckily, there was still a decent supply of canned and dry goods in the cupboard. Whoever owned this house must have been prepping for the end of times. Oddly, she enjoyed cooking breakfast in the morning, listening to that familiar sizzling sound, even if it was only powdered eggs. Funny how she missed the simple pleasures of life. She scanned the cupboard again, noting an abundance of dry cereal, boxes of rice, canned baked beans, and corned beef hash. The only depressing absence here was that there were no more tins of Maxwell House. Not having her morning cup of coffee would be enough motivation to escape this place.

She grabbed a broom and swept the floor to keep her mind busy. As long as she kept moving, she could keep her mind off the terrible things that had happened. She needed to prepare for the time when she could pack up and head for civilization. But leaving now in this weather would be suicide.

Could she keep her promise to George? Would she not get the police involved? Because she knew that even from jail, Shannon would follow through on her threat to harm George's kids. She probably still had lots of contacts out on the street, and knowing her sister, she knew Shannon wouldn't rest until she got her revenge.

George called her from the living room. He needed help going to the bathroom. She peeled the layer of blankets off him and, with considerable effort, helped him up. Even sick, he was still a big guy. Fifteen years older than her, he now looked seventy. She waited outside the bathroom door for him to finish. Once done, she helped him back in his chair, tucking all the blankets under him to make sure he stayed warm.

"I don't deserve you treating me this nice."

"Shut up, George, and drink your juice." She lifted the glass filled with whiskey up to his lips, and he took a sip.

"Damn, it's cold in here. Think I'd feel better if I wasn't freezing my balls off."

"You'd better keep those balls warm if you want to live to see my sister go down."

"Hope you got something planned?"

"Are you still willing to help me?"

"Hell yeah. I want to live long enough to see that bitch get her due."

"Then rest up and stay warm under these blankets," she said. "I need to look around and see what I can find that might help me get out of here."

George shook his head.

"Do you know who owns this house?"

"No idea. Shannon handled all that."

"So it was empty when you arrived?"

"It was."

"Stay put while I look around. When I return, I'll make us some lunch. You want canned tuna, or boxed mac and cheese?"

He shook his head at the choices. "What I really want is a thick cheeseburger with fries and a chocolate shake."

"Why are you torturing me like that, George?" she said. "I'll make the mac and cheese."

"Whoopee."

She climbed the stairs and made her way into the hallway. After sticking her head in the main bedroom, she noticed it was filled with junk. She could barely make her way inside. The walls were covered with wallpaper, and the ceiling had a big water stain streaked over it. The paint peeled off in places. Over the bed hung a cross with a wooden Jesus nailed to it. The frown on Jesus's face made her sad, and so she looked away.

She pushed herself over to the closet and rifled through the wardrobe. Within minutes, she found a down gray jacket with a fur hood. Excited, she grabbed it off the rack. Then she saw a pair of winter boots on the floor. She scooped them in her arms and placed them down over some boxes.

The clothes in the wardrobe belonged to a woman. So, who had lived here before Shannon arrived? And what had happened to her? It occurred to Shay that all the utilities were still working. Someone had to be paying the bills. Had Shannon killed the occupant of this home? How had she found this place in the middle of nowhere where no one would find them?

She went downstairs and found the door to the basement and, with much hesitation, returned to the room where she was first held captive. Her stomach turned as she approached the door. No way was she going back inside. Besides, she'd scoured every inch of it and had found nothing useful. She closed the door and moved on.

She pulled the string on an overhead lightbulb and saw a mouse scamper along the floor. Moving deeper into the basement, she came upon another room. Old shelves held tattered cardboard boxes. She peered at one package inside the box and saw that it came from QVC. The woman who owned this house had been a hoarder.

Shay walked around the room, searching for anything that might help her get out of this mess. Something hanging on the far wall caught her attention. The closer she got to it, the faster her heart raced. She reached up and lifted them off the hook, marveling at their age and condition. They were oak-framed snowshoes made by L.L.Bean and in decent shape. They had to be over fifty years old. She and Gideon had once vacationed in Bethel, Maine, and spent a whole day snowshoeing through the woods. Maybe she'd get to do it again, although this time it would not be for fun but for survival. She tucked the snowshoes under her arm and made her way out of the basement.

But then she noticed something under the basement stairs. A storage freezer? Maybe George would get his cheeseburger and fries after all. She went over to it, almost giddy with excitement, listening to the gentle hum of the motor. The box was battered and discolored, dented over the top, but still in working condition. As she opened it, she had visions of seeing steaks, chops, and filets.

But what she saw she shocked her.

SHANNON

Gideon had returned to his normal self the next evening. He treated me wonderfully and looked on with pride as I delivered my social commentary. I had a lot of fun with it, too. Some nights, I rant and rave, giving the audience the red meat they crave in these troubled times. Other nights, I give them fluff and stuff. Even those who hate me seem delighted to have a convenient target on which to vent their frustrations. Loving to hate me has become as popular in this town as loving me.

All the girls have stopped calling except for Jessica. She's trying to remain on friendly terms with me for some unknown reason. I suspect she's up to no good, but there's no way she can know my true identity. And I'd hate to think about what I'd have to do to her if she did.

Tonight's the night I will make my first big move. I can't wait to see the look on Gideon's face when he hears what I have to say.

GIDEON

Gideon snapped to attention as soon as he heard his wife's shocking words. For the last ten minutes, he'd sat daydreaming through the weather and sports, wishing this broadcast was finally over so he could return home and start in on the scotch. But now this? He turned and saw his wife pointing at him during her commentary.

"It came to me last night as I was lying in bed. I saw him approach me with that souvenir baseball bat in hand. He raised it in the air and then swung it at me. That's why I couldn't remember who attacked me that night. Because I never would have believed that my own husband was the one who wanted me dead."

Gideon opened his mouth, but nothing came out.

"I stand before you as an unabashed victim of domestic abuse. But trust me, Boston, I will not go quietly into the night. I speak for all the abused women out there when I say that I will prosecute Gideon Wells to the full extent of the law."

It felt as if someone had cracked *him* over the head. He sat there, numb, staring at his wife while trying to process what she had just accused him of doing. Was he losing his mind? Had he really attacked her? Of course, he hadn't. He'd been miles away, shacking up with Mallory at the time of Shay's attack. Still, the righteous tone in her voice was so convincing that he wondered how anyone could *not* believe that he'd tried to kill her.

The studio erupted in chaos once she finished her commentary. The news director ordered the crew to stop filming. Gideon felt himself rising involuntarily off his seat. He turned toward his wife, who was now screaming at him at the top of her lungs. It made him sick to his stomach. A security crew sprinted onto the set and kept them apart. He could hear himself replying to his wife in self-defense, but he couldn't understand a word coming out of his mouth. The bulky young guard escorted him, involuntarily, back to one of the dressing rooms. Gideon asked for a drink as soon as he sat down. The man returned with a bottle of sparkling water, but sparkling water was not the drink he needed right now.

What was his wife thinking? Her personality had changed so dramatically that he feared she'd gone temporarily insane. He blamed the outburst on her concussion symptoms. On the rewiring caused by those repeated blows to the head—that he most definitely had *not* delivered.

No, he wasn't losing his mind. He had absolutely nothing to do with the attack on his wife that evening. He'd been at Mallory's apartment in the Seaport District when the call came in, and Mal would back him on that.

Or would she?

Therein lay the problem. While his wife was out volunteering at that soup kitchen, he was holed up in the weather girl's apartment, cheating on his wife, the mother of his blind daughter. How bad would that look to his prospective employer, especially after his contact had specifically instructed him to keep his nose clean?

But none of that mattered now. He was fighting for his life and good name.

If only he could call the woman at the network and explain to her how the attack on his wife had made her delusional. How injuring the brain could change a person's personality and make them believe things that never happened, even causing them to tell lies about those closest to them. Gideon considered the possibility that the network might not learn about his wife's outburst. Then he remembered that British woman telling him that they'd be watching his broadcasts every night.

He contemplated his dilemma as he sat alone in the dressing room, sipping his sparkling water and wondering about his future. The way he saw it, he had two options: continue telling the police that he was innocent but had no alibi for the evening in question. Or tell them the truth, that he'd been banging Mallory when the attack happened. Either way, he was in a lot of trouble. He supposed he could stick to the story that he took a long walk that night. After all, they had no witnesses to the crime. It was Shay's word against his, and the police had watched the videotape of him walking out the front gate that evening. It mattered little that his wife had become an overnight sensation, or that millions of viewers now hung on her every word. No one gave two shits—or even knew—that he'd been hired to replace Logan Burrows.

"Jesus Christ, Gideon," Barb said as she rushed into the dressing room. She sat down next to him. "What the hell just happened out there?"

"How the hell do I know?"

She stared at him long and hard. "Did you attack your wife?"

Gideon laughed and looked away.

"I know that's a stupid question," she said. "But I had to ask."

"How long have we worked together, Barb?"

"Too long."

"In all that time, have you ever known me to be a violent person?"

"A pompous ass, yes, but never violent."

"My wife is unwell and not fit to report the news. Besides, it's her word against mine."

"Do you have an alibi for that night?"

"I've already told the police what happened. I went out for my usual evening walk."

"But you didn't really go for a walk that evening, right?"

He stared at her. "No, I did not. But I do have a rock-solid alibi that proves my innocence. The only problem is that I can't use it."

"Why not?"

"Swear on your child's life that what I tell you will never leave this room."

"Okay, Gideon, I swear on TJ's life."

He sat back in his chair, biting his thumbnail, and reconsidered whether he should tell her. But it was too late now. He'd already made her swear on her child's life. And the situation was so dire that he had no other choice but to confide in her.

"I was with Mallory the night of the attack. In her apartment doing things I never should have been doing."

"The weather reporter who used to work here? Our Mallory, who's now a star on the Your Weather Channel?" She smiled.

"One and the same."

"Oh, Gideon, you rascal. You never could keep it in your pants, could you?"

"Please don't mock me now, Barb."

"You need to go straight to the police and tell them the truth."

"I can't. Do you know how that would look if I told them what really happened? Especially in this day and age of the Me Too movement?"

"Your audience might see it in their hearts to forgive you. Sure, there might be some backlash in the short term, but you're a survivor. You're practically an institution in this town."

"I'm afraid it's more complicated than that." He debated whether he should tell her his other news.

"I've sworn on my child's life that what you tell me will never leave this room."

"Okay." He closed his eyes and hoped for the best. "I've been hired to replace Logan Burrows on the news desk."

"Come again." Barb crossed her arms and sat back.

"You heard me. They're keeping it very hush-hush at the network until they break the news to Logan."

"Why didn't I hear anything about this? I've got friends at that network."

"They're keeping it tightly under wraps. They want to get rid of Logan cleanly and without any rancor."

"Why would they do that?"

"They said if Logan found out about it, he might make a big stink and cause some major problems at the network, especially now that it's in the process of being sold. And that might mean they'd have to keep him on the desk and continue to put up with his senility, bad behavior, and terrible ratings."

"Jesus, Gideon, that's wonderful news. We'd hate to lose you here at the station, but replacing Logan Burrows. Wow!"

"I know. I'm terrified they may decide to rescind the offer after what Shay has just accused me of doing."

"Then you have to go to the police right away and tell them that you were with Mallory the night your wife was attacked. Admit you made a big mistake and let the chips fall where they may."

"I have to think this through."

"You have something else to think about right now."

"Oh?"

"Where will you stay tonight? Shay is taking out a restraining order against you as we speak."

"I hadn't thought about that."

"The station has a corporate account at the Marriott. Why don't you stay there for a few days until we can figure things out?"

"That's a wonderful idea, Barb. Thank you for being such a dear friend."

"It's the least I can do for such a valued employee," she said, standing to leave.

"You do believe in my innocence, right?"

"Of course I do. I've always known you were a softy when it came to beautiful women."

Barb's words hit him hard.

"No offense, Gideon, but I've always known about the floozies you were screwing on the side, including Mallory. And now Kelly."

"Wait one second. I never laid a finger on Kelly."

"Not yet, anyway."

"How did you know about that?"

"Do you think I'm stupid? I know everything that goes on in this newsroom." She laughed in an odd way. "Because of that, I fully expect that you'll take me to Manhattan as your news director." She turned and left the room.

Et tu, Barb?

The entire night had been a disaster. Now, even Barb was blackmailing him. He wondered if Shay truly hated him or whether she had somehow convinced herself of his guilt.

Needing a strong drink, he slipped outside and hailed a cab. Fifteen minutes later, he was sitting in a back booth at Donato's, out of the public eye, and sipping his second gin and tonic of the evening. Tomorrow, he would deal with all this nonsense. Tomorrow he would be in a better frame of mind to make a statement to the police about his whereabouts that night. Maybe, just maybe, his wife would come to her senses and realize she'd made a terrible mistake.

SHAY

The accusation Shannon had hurled against Gideon shocked her to the core. Had Gideon been the person who assaulted her that night? Gideon, for all his considerable faults, would never commit such a violent crime. No, all this criminal activity had been masterminded by Shannon. Shannon had been the one who assaulted her near that soup kitchen and had left her for dead.

Poor Gideon. The camera panned to him, and he looked mortified at the accusation. Shay finally understood what her sister was doing. Rather than simply cleaning out their bank account and selling their home, Shannon hoped to capitalize on her good name by taking over Gideon's news desk. By accusing Gideon of trying to kill her, he would be brought to trial. Whether found innocent or guilty didn't really matter at this point because the damage to his reputation would already be done. And when that happened, Shannon would get everything in the divorce. She would assume the lead anchor job and continue to collect her big salary. Shay felt for her daughter the most. Quinn was collateral damage in her sister's nefarious scheme to pay her back.

All of this only confirmed her belief that Shannon would return here to make sure they were both dead. She and George would be the last obstacles to her reaching the pinnacle of success. Shay imagined her sister showing up here in the spring after all the snow had melted, expecting to find her dead in that basement room. Then she would bury their bodies deep in the woods, and no one would ever know that they'd gone missing.

Wouldn't Shannon be surprised to learn that she'd escaped her basement prison.

Shay glanced outside. The sun shone with an unusual intensity today. Temperatures had risen to the high twenties in the last twenty-four hours. To her surprise, the high twenties felt like a warm spell. Even George seemed better, upright and moving. Although she knew his days were numbered, he looked somewhat healthy.

He sat down at the kitchen table as she fixed the two of them lunch. George lay bundled up in his jacket and wool cap. She'd prepared a simple lunch of tuna casserole, using egg noodles, creamed mushroom soup, and a can of Bumble Bee tuna that had expired months ago. She'd also opened a can of brown bread, warming it in the oven, and then slicing the bread into one-inch circles. Her mother used to serve brown bread and baked beans for dinner almost every night growing up, getting most of their meals from the local food pantry.

Once she served George his casserole, she placed a slice of the bread on his plate. Then she sat down across from him. She hadn't yet told him what she had found in that storage freezer down in the basement. Had he known about it all along? Something told her that she would have to broach the subject carefully. The last thing she wanted was to be at war with him until the time came when she had to leave this place. Or until he passed.

"Tasty." He stabbed his fork into the noodles.

"Are you being sarcastic?"

"No, I mean it."

"Thanks."

"Something bothering you?"

"No. Why do you ask?"

"I made my living reading people. So I can tell that you're upset about something."

"I'm fine, George."

He placed his fork down, crossed his arms, and looked at her. "Something you want to tell me?"

"Okay, there is something." She stared at him. "Tell me how you two chose this house to hide out in."

"I already told you, Shannon handled all the details."

"Where's the owner?"

"How would I know?"

"So you're telling me that you had absolutely nothing to do with securing this place?"

"That's what I'm telling you. My only job was to keep an eye on you and make sure you didn't escape." George frowned. "Why are you asking me all these questions?"

"You remember how I found that winter jacket, boots, and snowshoes?"

He nodded.

"Well, that wasn't the only thing I found."

"Cough it up, girl. I don't have all day."

She waited a beat. "There's a storage freezer down in the basement, located below the stairs."

"That's a good thing, right? Maybe there's some frozen meat we can thaw out."

"No, it most definitely is not a good thing. And yes, there is frozen meat in there, but not the kind you're thinking about."

"So what's the problem?"

"There's a body of an elderly woman stuffed inside."

"Jesus H. Christ. You telling me that Shannon murdered the poor woman who owned this house?"

"Could have only been one of two people."

"Listen here, girl. I may be many things, but a murderer, I'm not."

"How can I believe you, George? You admitted that your entire life has been a lie."

"Facing mortality forces you to take a hard look at yourself."

"After what you just told me, how do I even know you're dying?"

"I let you come upstairs, didn't I? Hell, you can leave this shithole anytime you want, for all I care."

"But you knew I couldn't leave because of the weather."

"I swear on my kids' lives that I had no idea Shannon killed that poor woman." He held up his right hand.

She picked up her fork and stabbed it angrily into a chunk of tuna.

"Have you decided what you're going to do once you make it out of here?"

"I'm still working on a plan." She avoided looking at him. "If you even care."

"Of course, I care."

"Don't worry about it, then."

"I know one way you can get that sister of yours," he said.

"Why should I trust you?" She put her fork down and looked at him.

He removed his wallet, took out a picture of his two children, and showed it to her. Tears formed in his eyes.

"HollyJean and Timmy. These two kids are the only good things I ever made in my life." He wiped his eyes clean with the sleeve. "I want Shannon to pay for what she's done. It's why you can trust me to help you."

"Eat your casserole while it's still warm, George. You can fill me in on your plan later."

They ate the remainder of their lunch in silence. The hot meal warmed her insides and gave her the strength to clear off the table and wash the dishes. When his plate was empty, George lifted himself up off the chair and shuffled into the living room. The flatscreen powered up, and she heard canned laughter coming from the speakers. On the counter sat the last bottle of Jack Daniel's. She went over and cracked the seal, pouring two fingers into his glass. Then she brought it over to him.

"This is the last bottle. Might as well finish it."

"I'm gonna savor every last drop." He took a sip and closed his eyes with pleasure. "Will you have one with me?"

"You need it more than I do."

"True, but I'll enjoy it a lot more if I'm sharing it with a friend."

"So we're friends now?"

"Can't think of any other way to describe us."

"I'll get a glass." Once she returned, he poured her a finger of whiskey. Then he topped off his own drink.

"Now sit down, and I'll tell you what I have in mind."

GIDEON

Morning arrived too soon. Or maybe he'd stayed up drinking longer than he remembered. He lifted his pounding head from the pillow and groaned in misery. How much alcohol had he consumed last night? The hotel bar closed at two. He glanced down at the duvet and saw an army of nips strewn across it like a battlefield of dead soldiers. Not only had he slept over the covers, but he'd passed out in his suit and tie, both of which were lined with wrinkles. The digital clock next to his bed indicated it was 9:27. He *never* slept past seven.

Last night had possibly been the worst of his life. He shook his head, wondering if it had all been a dream. But of course, it hadn't been. What would his friends and colleagues think of him now? The members at the club? His daughter? His loyal audience who watched him religiously every night? No way they'd let him back on the air until this matter was resolved. The mere accusation could prove damning to his reputation. But what else could he do? Being a news anchor was his life. Without this job, he'd be lost.

He shuffled painfully inside the bathroom, slightly nauseous, and took a long shower. The steaming water did nothing to assuage the mental and physical pain coursing through him. Afterwards, he dressed in his wrinkled suit, picked up the empty nips from the duvet, and tossed them in the trash. Then, he made his way down to the lounge for breakfast. He looked like shit, felt even worse, but didn't care.

Not five minutes into his Lobster Benedict, he noticed two people enter the lounge. He recognized the man almost instantly by the square shape of his face and his husky build. He'd half expected the cops to show up here. He brought the coffee mug to his lips as they approached. Hard to believe the pretty woman next to the husky cop was his partner. Funny how the presence of a good-looking woman could temporarily lift his spirits, despite the severity of the crimes now facing him.

"Mr. Wells, you probably remember me. Detective Carr from the Boston PD, and this is Detective Gaudreau."

"Of course, I remember you, Detective. You had your sights set on finding the real person who assaulted my wife," he said.

"Yes, sir."

"I'm afraid my wife is badly mistaken and is still suffering from that traumatic head injury."

"She seemed pretty certain of herself last night," the woman cop said.

"Ever since she joined me as co-anchor, she's become obsessed with this case. Have you considered the possibility that this is some kind of ploy by her to replace me?"

"You just accused her of not being of sound mind," Detective Carr said.

"Honestly, I don't know what to believe anymore. I just know I didn't do it."

"Do you really think she'd make all this up just to replace you on the news desk?" Detective Gaudreau said.

"She's obviously not in the right frame of mind. I don't know what she's thinking."

"You seem awfully confused, Gideon," Detective Gaudreau said.

"It's almost as if she transformed herself into a different woman when we returned home from that vacation."

"And when was that?" Carr asked.

"In the fall. She claimed the trip had invigorated her and helped speed up her recovery."

"I'll ask again. Do you have an alibi for that night?"

Gideon sipped his coffee and tried not to appear nervous. "As I've already told you, I went out for my usual walk that evening."

"Did anyone see you walking that night?" Detective Gaudreau asked.

"No, I'm afraid not. It was dark, and I was wearing my Red Sox cap to keep my hair from getting blown around in the wind."

"A big Sox fan, huh?"

"Huge," he lied, hoping they wouldn't ask him to name a current player.

"Me too," Carr said, glancing at his partner. "Is there anything else you want to tell us before we head back to the station, Mr. Wells?"

"I just want to say how ridiculous all this is and how damaging her accusation is to my reputation."

"Trust me, we are taking this very seriously," Gaudreau said.

"Have you noted how bizarre my wife has been acting as of late? Walking naked on that golf course. Kicking and then injuring that harmless little dog. It's clear that my wife has not been herself lately."

"She seemed quite lucid on that newscast," Detective Gaudreau said, "and I watch the two of you almost every evening."

"As do most informed citizens of this city." He smiled, but knew instantly it hadn't gone over well.

"So, for the record, are you saying that your wife is mentally...unstable?" Detective Carr asked.

"You haven't lived with her day to day like I have, or seen her violent mood swings. You have no idea the hell I've been going through with this woman. After all I've done for her, allowing her to share my desk, this is how she repays me?" He threw his napkin down over his unfinished Benedict. "What I'd really like the two of you to do is find the monster responsible for this crime."

"We're doing our best, sir. Is there anything else you'd like to tell us before we head back?"

"I take it I'm no longer allowed in my own home?"

"No, sir. She's filed a restraining order against you."

"Wonderful. Would you mind sending someone over to pick up some of my clothes? I can't go around town looking like this." He grabbed his wrinkled suit to show them.

"Certainly. I take it you'll be staying here for the time being?"

"Yes. Just leave my clothes at the desk if I'm not here. And take out at least two of my best suits."

"Don't wander too far. We'll need to know where to find you if something comes up."

"Where else am I going to go?"

The two officers stood and walked out of the empty restaurant. Now that he'd had his coffee and breakfast, what was he supposed to do? Head up to his room for the remainder of the day and hang out? Work on crossword puzzles he rarely finished? He thought about going to the club for a drink, but then wondered how he'd be received in that environment. Those lawyers, doctors, and financiers would turn on him in a heartbeat if they believed he was guilty. The mere accusation would reflect badly on them and the club, and he wouldn't be surprised if they were considering rescinding his membership. Besides, he needed more than one drink now that he wasn't planning on working, driving, or having sex.

He put on his coat and left the hotel. He'd not gone twenty yards before a few people on the street started harassing him, swearing angrily and calling him all kinds of despicable names. Why were they mocking him and reveling in his misery? This was his life. And all because his wife had delivered a rash of fake news last night.

"Go to hell!" he shouted at a young couple giving him the finger.

He stopped and held his ground as they walked past him. There was no way he was going to subject himself to this nonsense and be made a scapegoat for his wife's shameful lies. He turned and headed back to the hotel, grabbed a complimentary newspaper from the desk, and then headed up to his room. Never before had he the urge to drink before noon—until today.

Once inside his room, he stared at himself in the bathroom mirror. Stubble lined his glum face. A yellow hue lingered under his eyes from the previous night's reverie. He collapsed on the bed, clicked on the cable news, and started in on the day's crossword puzzle. He considered calling Quinn and explaining his side of the story, but he didn't want to upset the girl, especially since she seemed so happy at school. Ten minutes passed before he heard the cable news host mention his name. He threw the folded newspaper over the bed and promptly shut off the TV. Then he went over to the dry bar and started the day off with a rum and Coke.

QUINN

It surprised her how nice everyone at school had been to her since the "incident." Word had spread quickly around campus that she was not a girl to be trifled with. And despite the open invitation to sit with the popular girls at lunch, she decided against it and sat with a different set of kids each day.

Taking decisive action as she had made attending here that much more bearable. It was an important lesson. She still hated this school as much as before and missed all her friends, but at least it was tolerable now.

After that dream the other night, she remained optimistic that her mother was still out there, waiting to return. She needed to remain patient, because returning home with that imposter was not an option. But she knew that one day, her real mother would come back for her and whisk her away from this campus.

Classes had gone well today. Her grades were up, and her teachers noted a significant change in her attitude and demeanor. There was only one thing missing from her life, and that was the love of her mother. Unconditional and on a daily basis. The teachers and staff cared for their students, but they didn't really *love* them. Not the kind of love a mother showered on her child every single day of her life.

Once back in her room, she sat at her desk and turned on the computer. She'd made a habit of listening to the previous night's newscast to hear what that fraud had to say, hoping to glean some clues proving the woman was not who she said she was. Even her mother's best friend, Jessica, felt hopeless about the situation. The two of them were the only ones in the world who suspected the real Shay Wells was not the one reporting the news each night. But proving it was something else altogether.

She skipped through her father's news reports. She'd heard Gideon Wells speak a million times before and didn't need to hear him any further. Frankly, the news made her scared for the kind of world she'd soon be entering. Sometimes, she felt like she was one of the few people she knew who could see amongst the ignorant and the blind.

She skipped the weather and had no interest in sports. Finally, the fraud's commentary began. Every night, this imposter railed about one thing or another. This witch was so unlike her mom, who was calm and reflective by nature and treated everyone with respect. How could people not see through this act? She knew why. Because they chalked up her personality change to that brain injury.

But the words coming out of that crass woman's mouth shocked her. She listened to it over and over, not quite believing what she was accusing her father of doing. Yet she sounded so convincing that Quinn had to remind herself that this person was not her mother.

It took her a few minutes to calm down before she could process any of this. She turned off the computer and wondered what to do next. Although she and her father had never been particularly close, she felt sorry for him. Never in her life had she known him to be a violent man. Aloof and moody, yes, but never violent. She'd never even heard him cuss.

She searched for the phone on her desk and dialed his cell phone number.

"Quinn?" His voice sounded strange, but he seemed happy to hear from her.

"Hi, Daddy."

"How's school?"

"Great," she lied. "I love it here."

"That's my girl. To what do I owe this honor?"

"I heard about what happened last night."

"You did?" Long awkward pause. "I was really hoping you wouldn't. Your mother's a wonderful woman, dear, but she's very sick."

"I know, Daddy. That's because the woman who accused you of hitting her is not really my mother."

"You're smart beyond your years, honey. Everyone knows it's the head trauma that's causing her to behave this way."

"No, I mean that woman is *literally* not my mother."

Her father laughed in a manner that struck her as odd. He sometimes got silly when he was drinking, but he never drank in the middle of the day.

"I'm being serious."

"I know you don't want to believe it, Quinn, and neither do I, but we must accept the sad truth. Your mother has changed for the worse."

"My real mother would never agree to send me away to school." She heard silence at the end of the line and knew she'd gone too far. Her words, by default, inferred his own role in the plan to ship her off.

"I have to go, hon. Please take care of yourself. I'll be over there very soon to see you."

"Okay, just don't let *her* come."

The phone went dead. Quinn went over to her bed and lay down. For the first time since she came here, she was glad she wasn't living at home.

SHAY

All she could think about was Quinn being alone in that oversized home in Woodbridge Estates with that monster claiming to be her mother. Because of that, she knew she needed to leave here as soon as possible. George's plan seemed devious and scheming, yes, but she knew it was the only way this sad ordeal could end. And the way George had poured his heart out to her, she had no reason not to trust him.

She hadn't slept well these last few weeks. George's health appeared to be getting worse by the day, and she'd been worried about her family, as well as making it to civilization without freezing to death. Now that she believed Shannon had killed the occupant of this house, she feared for Quinn's and Gideon's life. Who knew what that crazy bitch might do?

Just last night, they'd used up the last of the firewood and oil. Now all they had was that tiny electric heater, which was practically useless in this drafty house. God forbid if a bitter cold front moved in. They'd be screwed. Or at least George would be. Whatever happened, she'd take her chances against the elements and try to make her way back to Boston. But for now, she'd wait for the optimal time to put on those snowshoes and attempt to reach civilization.

She raised her head off the pillow and stared out the window. A puff of her breath instantly melted a section of the frosted glass. The first rays of morning sunlight began to streak across the sky. She lifted the blanket off her and stood from the couch, stretching. On the coffee table, she noticed the half-empty bottle of Jack Daniel's. George had been a good boy last night and not polished it off. She tiptoed into the kitchen, glanced out the window, and read the thermometer. Thirty degrees. With the temperature this high, this early in the morning, it portended to be a good day. She knew she had to leave this place before the snow turned wet and slushy and made it impossible for her to trek through it without becoming hypothermic.

She felt hopeful that today would be the day. It might be her only window of opportunity.

Her nerves felt on edge as she paced back and forth in the kitchen. Ever since she'd found that poor woman's body stuffed in the freezer, she couldn't get the image out of her head. It troubled her knowing that she was living in the same house with a frozen corpse. It was as much an incentive to leave here as anything else.

She went to the kitchen window, glanced at the thermometer, and noted the slight rise in temperature. Two degrees higher than the last time she checked, which helped make up her mind. Today would be the day she threw caution to the wind and attempted to escape this place. Soon, she would attach those snowshoes to her boots, put on that backpack, and set out on foot. Once the sun fully appeared on the horizon, she would begin her long journey out of here.

* * *

Snow melted off the roof as George helped her on with the backpack, filled with food, water, and dry clothes. She had no idea how far she would have to travel before she reached another house or person, but she would walk until she couldn't go any farther.

"Do you have any idea how far I'll need to go, George?"

"Wish I could help you with that." He coughed for a few seconds. "Shannon purposefully got me drunk the night she drove me here. It was dark, and I wasn't paying attention, so I really have no idea how."

"That's just wonderful."

"Follow the dirt road out front and keep going until you reach something. Or someone."

"That's all you got?"

"Wish I could be more helpful."

They stood quietly for a few seconds once she was ready to depart.

"Guess it's that time," he said.

"Yup."

"I'm sorry for all the trouble I caused you. I don't blame you if you hate my guts."

"I don't hate your guts." She gave him a pat on the arm. "You messed up, buddy, but I don't hate you."

"I'm just saying, I wouldn't blame you if you did."

"Are you going to be all right without any heat or Jack Daniel's to keep you warm?"

"What other choice do I have? I just need to stay alive long enough to see that bitch go down."

"I promise you, she'll not get away with this."

"Here." He held out three twenty-dollar bills. "It's all the money I got in this world, and I won't be needing it where I'm going."

"You never know, George, there might be a cash bar in Hell."

"Possibly, but I'm holding out for a stool next to the big guy."

"Hopefully, we can share a toast up there, a very long time from now."

"First one's on me, girl."

She took the money and stuffed it in her pocket. Then she removed the bag of powder and handed it to him. "This is for you."

"What is it?" He took the bag and held it up to the light.

"It's the prescription pills I crushed up so I could one day knock you out."

"What kind of pills are we talking about?"

"Ambien."

"That's good shit," he said, licking his lips. "I take it you had a change of heart?"

"I was planning to slip some of it into your Jack when you weren't looking. But then you got all nice on me."

He stuffed the bag into his pocket. "It won't take Jack's place, but it'll do," he said.

"It's that time."

"Yup."

"Do you think I could borrow your phone, George?"

"I'm sorry, but I can't let that happen. Shannon might suspect something's up if I don't answer her calls, and that will put my kids in harm's way."

"I understand."

"Besides, I might want to call them and say my last goodbyes."

Shay gave him a quick hug. "Bye, George."

"Godspeed, girl. I'm counting on you."

She opened the front door and was greeted by a wall of snow up to her midsection. She climbed up and over it until she was lying flat on her stomach. George pushed her down the slope of the stairs, and before she knew it, she was sliding down the crest. When she reached the bottom, she pushed herself up until she was standing on the snowshoes. Without poles, she struggled to find her balance. Then, she slowly began to move forward.

She stopped to catch her breath upon reaching the end of the driveway. This journey was going to be a lot harder than she thought. Sweat dripped from her brow and under her armpits. Snowshoeing would at least keep her warm and get her blood moving. She stared at the snow-covered road, lined with pine trees on either side for as far as the eye could see. Puffs of breath evaporated as soon as they came out of her mouth.

She told herself that whenever she got tired, she would think of Quinn. Quinn would be all the motivation she would need to keep moving.

SHANNON

The look on Gideon's face was priceless when I stood up and accused him of attacking me outside that soup kitchen. Sure, it's my word against his. But the old adage still rings true: when did you stop beating your wife? Although he and the station don't quite know it yet, the damage has already been done. And because of that, there's no way they can keep the two of us on the desk. They'll need to make a choice, and if they make the wrong one, I'll sue them for millions, claiming sexual and physical harassment. Pain and suffering, too. It's the main reason why they'll keep me on the air instead of Gideon.

And I haven't even played my trump card yet.

I'm sitting in my living room, waiting for that old cop and his sidekick to come over and question me. The restraining order I placed on Gideon ensures that he'll never spend five minutes in *my* house again. Gone is his private club, as well as golfing with his rich and prestigious buddies. Gone are his days of screwing interns and sitting at his large oak desk, struggling to finish crossword puzzles. No more will he lord over a huge Boston audience, collecting his hefty check each week. All of this will be mine now.

It's Shannon's time to shine.

The video of my commentary has gone viral and made all the cable news shows and newspapers. The *Boston Globe*, the *Boston Herald,* and the *New York Post* have a photograph of me wagging a long finger in his face as I accused him of attacking me that night. I'm being lauded everywhere as a role model for battered women. I'm getting phone calls for interviews and movie deals. Or I should say, my new talent agent, Evan, is fielding them. He's currently choosing which offers are the most lucrative. I've told him to be discerning, because my image is at stake here, and I must be highly protective of it. I'm not going to humiliate myself on one of those stupid reality shows like *Dancing With The Stars* or *Big Brother*. Not when I'm approaching A-list status. Not when people are saying that my brand is fresh and trending.

The doorbell rings. I jog to the bathroom and examine myself in the full-length mirror. I look like shit, which is exactly the image I'm trying to project to these stupid cops. I'm a victim of a powerful and abusive husband. I've purposefully not put on any makeup or lipstick. My hair is greasy and unkempt. I look a bit like a woman who's lived a hard life—and that's because I *have* lived a hard life. Much harder than that sweet sister of mine.

The doorbell rings again, and I go over and open it. Detective Carr and his pretty sidekick appear in front of me. I cinch my robe and swipe strands of dirty blond hair out of my eyes. I lead them over to the sofa and ask if they want coffee. Neither of them do. I remember how that dick tricked me into forgetting that my sister graduated from Harvard, his alma mater. I'll be sure not to let him trip me up again.

"Thanks for seeing us this morning, Mrs. Wells. I know this must be extremely difficult for you," Detective Carr says.

"It is difficult. You don't know how horrible it is to suddenly realize that your own husband was the one who tried to kill you."

"He's asked us to retrieve some of his clothes," the female detective named Gaudreau says.

"Fine with me," I say. "Take all his crap, as far as I'm concerned. I never want to see that horrible man again."

"Is it possible you made a mistake?" Carr says. "I mean, how can you be so sure?"

"Oh, I'm sure all right. I clearly remember him stalking me as I walked back to my car. He wanted to get rid of me so he could take up with his floozy."

"He was seeing someone?" Detective Carr looks over at his partner.

"You mean you didn't know he was cheating on me?"

The two cops glance at each other.

"Jesus, what kind of cops are you, anyway?"

"Whom was he having an affair with?" Detective Gaudreau asks. "And when was he having it?"

"This is unbelievable," I say, shaking my head. I turn angrily to Carr. "When wasn't that bastard cheating on me?"

"Who was he seeing, Mrs. Wells?" Detective Carr asks.

"Are you familiar with Mallory Baines, now on the Your Weather Channel?"

"Sure. She used to work at his station," Detective Carr says.

"That's the home-wrecker he was screwing behind my back. It's why he attacked me that night, so he could be with her."

"But it's been so long since the attack. And we have no physical evidence to prove his guilt," Detective Gaudreau says.

"It sounds as if you don't believe me."

"It has nothing to do with believing you. In order to prosecute your husband, we must have some hard evidence against him, or else it's your word against his," the woman cop says.

"What about searching the house or his car for a weapon?"

"We'll need to get a search warrant first. That's if you're absolutely certain he was the one who attacked you," Detective Carr says.

"Detective, I couldn't be more certain of anything in my life. He struck me over the head with one of those souvenir baseball bats."

"Very well then. We'll attempt to get a search warrant for his vehicle."

"Good. And make sure he stays the hell away from me and my daughter," I say, adding the daughter part for dramatic effect. "I'm scared for our lives with him on the loose."

"We'll make certain he stays clear of you, Mrs. Wells," Detective Gaudreau says.

I stand and see them out. It's crazy the way this entire scenario is turning out. Soon, someone will be over to retrieve his clothes and search for the weapon. Of course, they won't find it here. They'll rifle through the trunk of his car and discover the baseball bat buried way in the back. The bat I purchased with his initials engraved over the bloody barrel. It makes no sense that he would keep it. But then again, criminals do the dumbest things. Even the best of criminals make mistakes, and Gideon's not the brightest bulb. How could it get any better than this? Seriously. How could it?

SHAY

It seemed like hours had passed, and she'd barely made any progress. Sweat bubbled along her forehead and down her back and chest. How far had she gone? She stopped at one point and gazed down at a frozen lake below. The scenery in this part of the country was stunning. Too bad she couldn't relax and enjoy it.

She continued on, the sun moving higher in the sky as she clomped ahead. It reflected off the snow and, at times, blinded her, causing her eyes to water. She moved into the shade and took off her backpack, gasping for air. Reaching inside, she pulled out a water bottle and drank half of it in one swallow.

Could she make it out of here alive? And what would happen if she got stuck out here in the dark after the sun set and the temperatures started to plummet back into the teens? After resting for a few minutes, she stashed the water bottle back in her pack and pressed on. She thought about Quinn with every step and about George's scheme to take out Shannon once she was brought back to that house.

Shay chastised herself. If only she were in better shape. But it had been impossible to work out when she was holed up in that house for months at a time, barely getting enough to eat. Her muscles had atrophied, and her cardio had gone to hell. Gone were the days when she could run six miles a day in under forty-five minutes. To make it out of here alive, she'd have to muster up every ounce of energy and then some.

She continued on, slowly, one foot stepping in front of the other, finding her rhythm while thinking about what she would do once she arrived home.

The thought of Quinn kept her going, even when the sun started to set, and the temperatures began to plummet. Keep moving, she kept telling herself, despite being physically and emotionally exhausted. *Keep moving.*

Her arms and legs ached. All she wanted to do was lay down in the snow and rest. But she knew that if she did, she'd never wake up. She thought of the all-nighters she'd pulled in college, studying for an exam or writing a research paper. At least back then, she'd had coffee to fuel her efforts. Now, she had something stronger than coffee to keep her going: Quinn.

A snow owl perched on a branch and watched her trudge past. The road slowly descended into darkness as the sun set. By some miracle, the full moon shone bright tonight. She stopped briefly to admire it through the myriad of tree branches. The moon appeared massive in the sky. Its aura dimmed whatever cluster of stars happened to be hovering around it. She felt fortunate that the moon's glow provided her with enough light to keep moving.

Sometime later, she stopped, closing her eyes out of sheer exhaustion. Her hands were numb from the cold, and her face stung from the Arctic breeze now blowing down from the north. She felt like she could fall asleep in this upright position, standing on these snowshoes, but she was alert enough to know the dangers of dozing off in this weather.

Suddenly, Quinn came to her in a vision. Her daughter urged her to continue on and save her from that fraud, calling herself her mother—and Gideon's wife. Quinn told her to keep moving so they could one day be together again.

Shay snapped out of it. How long had she been out? She looked up and couldn't find the moon. It took her a few seconds to realize that she was now caught in a blizzard. She opened her mouth and caught a few flakes on her tongue, and they dissolved instantly.

Taking a deep breath, she started forward. The brief rest seemed to have done the trick. She pushed her weary legs, humming a song from *Frozen* to help keep her cadence. By the time she looked up, she noticed a few streaks of light blazing across the sky. She also saw a flash up ahead. What was that? The end of the road? Possibly a car passing by?

She picked up her pace until she reached the end of the road. What she saw filled her with joy. It was a two-lane interstate. She could barely see the pavement because it was still dark outside and because it was covered over with a thin layer of snow. The road had been recently plowed, but seemed to have no shoulder, making travel along it dangerous. She realized she could get struck by a passing eighteen-wheeler if she wasn't careful.

She sat down in the snow and removed her snowshoes. Once she had them off, she placed them in her backpack. Then she stood and stretched. It felt good to walk again like a normal human being, despite having little to no feeling in her toes. A light flashed up ahead and came toward her. She raised her arms and started shouting in order to get the driver's attention, only to watch as the pickup raced past. They couldn't see her in the dark. She'd have to wait until the sun came up.

Fifteen minutes passed while she stood on that road. She jumped up and down to try to stay warm. The snow started to fall faster and more furious. Her feet and hands had lost all feeling, and she feared she might come down with frostbite if she stayed out here much longer.

A pickup truck fronting a plow barreled toward her from the right side of the road. Having no feeling in her feet, she jumped onto the pavement, directly in its path, and began waving her arms over her head. She jumped up and down and screamed as loud as she could, hoping the driver might see her. The driver hit the brakes at the last second, and the truck slid toward her. She turned and ran, only to trip and fall on the snow-covered road. The truck continued to slide in her direction. Reclined on her back, she crab-walked backward, praying she wouldn't get crushed to death. The truck kept skidding until it stopped a few inches in front of her, and the bottom half of her body lay under the front end. The driver, a young guy wearing a John Deere baseball cap, ran out and stared down at her as if she were crazy.

"You got a death wish, lady?"

"I'm freezing out here, and no one would stop to help me."

"What the hell happened?"

"It's a long story. Please, I need to get back to my child."

"Okay. Jump inside," he said, helping her up.

She ran around the side of the idling truck, stepped onto the running board, and made her way inside. The warm air flowing from the vent felt life-affirming. She turned to the driver in tears, gave him a brief hug, and thanked him for picking her up.

GIDEON

Gideon took the call from his lawyer. What was this? The police had taken out a search warrant on his house and car. He polished off his third nip and laughed hysterically, knowing they'd come up empty-handed. How could they find a weapon when he hadn't committed any crime?

Andy Griffith appeared onscreen, escorting a drunken Otis to his cell. He'd been switching between *The Andy Griffith Show* and the cable news talking heads, but all they were doing was reshowing clips of that explosive newscast last night.

The second phone call came from his lawyer an hour later. He was relieved to take it, knowing with a hundred percent certainty that the police had not found any incriminating evidence against him. How could they? He hadn't attacked his wife. He'd been with Mal that evening in her Seaport condo.

But the words coming out of his counsel's mouth sent him reeling. The police would be over soon to arrest him after finding a bloody baseball bat in the trunk of his car. But how? He hadn't stashed it there. He couldn't fathom how the weapon ended up in his trunk. Unless that bitch had set him up. But he'd been in the hospital with her right after the attack. He'd witnessed her bruises and black eyes and her hideously cracked skull zippered shut with stitches. Her brain had swelled, and the doctors had worried that she might be in danger of suffering serious neurological damage. Would anyone voluntarily go through that kind of trauma just to set their husband up for attempted murder? He didn't think so. But what else was he to believe?

He clicked off *The Andy Griffith Show* and turned to CNN. The discovery of the attempted murder weapon was now the top breaking news. He switched to FOX and MSNBC and heard the same stories repeated over and over. His guilt was all but assured.

How much time did he have left before the police came to arrest him? He opened two nips of Canadian Club and quickly downed them, knowing it might be his last adult beverages for the foreseeable future. Nothing mattered to him anymore except the nuclear option, which he'd been trying to avoid at all costs. It meant revealing his affair with Mallory and getting her to admit that she was with him the night his wife had been attacked. Hopefully, she'd back him up.

It wasn't lost on him that Mallory was now a national figure on the Your Weather Channel and highly cognizant of her image. Admitting to an affair with a married anchor while his wife was getting brutally attacked could jeopardize her career. But if not for him, she'd never have gotten that job in the first place. She owed him. Her admission was the only thing keeping him from a long prison sentence.

He punched in Mallory's number, and she immediately answered, almost as if she'd been expecting his call.

"I can't talk to you right now," she blurted.

"You know I was with you that night. Are you going to let an innocent man get sent to prison for a crime he did not commit?"

"I'm very sorry about your situation, Gideon, but do you know how this will affect me if I admit to that?"

"It was me who got you that job."

"Please don't act holier than thou," she said. "You only did it so you could get rid of me."

"What are you talking about?"

"Why do you think I even slept with you?" She laughed. "For your good looks and amazing news reporting skills?"

"You adored me."

"Okay, I admit that in the beginning, it was fun, but I also knew that sleeping with you was the best way to advance my career. Then I heard through the grapevine that you were up for a big network job, and I knew you couldn't afford to have me around anymore."

Her words shocked him. "Who told you about that job?"

"I have my sources."

"I demand to know."

"I received an anonymous phone call one evening from this British woman."

"I'm warning you, Mallory. I'll bring you down with me if you don't tell the cops the truth. I'll spill all your dirty little secrets to the press, including your sordid affair with a married man, your battles with bulimia, and all the cutting you did as a young girl."

A long pause ensued. "You may not have attacked your wife, Gideon, but you're still a heartless bastard."

"Does that mean you'll tell the police I was with you that night?"

She paused for a few seconds. "Let me think about it."

"Think good and hard, Mallory, unless you want to see your career come crashing down around you."

He hung up the phone and grabbed another nip out of the refrigerator. Might as well drink them all, seeing as how he'd be stuck in jail for the foreseeable future. Unless Mallory called the police and provided him with a rock-solid alibi that would clear him.

He felt everything starting to slip away. Never in his life had he experienced a hardship like this. His adult life had been a fairly smooth transition from one success to the next. And despite it all, he still held out hope that he might take over Logan Burrows's news job. But if he lost this last opportunity to clear his name, his career in journalism would be over.

Then what would he do? Be a meat cutter like his father and drink himself to death? Bag groceries? Work in *radio*! He'd rather die than do radio.

His cell phone rang while he downed a Cutty Sark. He reached in the mini-fridge and randomly pulled out a handful of nips before answering his phone. Who could that be? He glanced down at the caller ID and saw that the number was blocked. Almost immediately, his hands began to tremble. He knew he had to answer and explain everything to her. Tell her that he had a rock-solid alibi for the night his wife was attacked. Convince her that his wife was a lying, manipulating witch who was trying to take his job, steal his home and all of his money.

"It's not what it seems," he pleaded. "I most definitely did not attack my wife that night."

"I'm sorry, Gideon, but it's over," the woman said. "You're officially out as Logan's replacement."

He felt his entire body deflate. "I was with another woman that night, and she'll vouch for my whereabouts."

The woman laughed. "And cheating on your wife makes you more desirable to us?"

"No, of course not, but it will prove to you that I didn't attack her."

"As soon as the news came out about your situation, the board convened and decided to keep Logan on the desk until the sale of the network goes through."

"I'm begging you to reconsider," he said, the desperation in his voice evident.

"I'm sorry, but the decision has already been made."

"Listen to me. I'm pleading with you for a second chance."

"This is a tough business, Gideon, and not for the faint of heart. I wish you all the best."

His head began to spin from all the nips he'd downed. Someone knocked at the door just as the line went dead.

Gideon staggered over to the door and opened it, seeing Detective Carr and his pretty partner. He smiled in resignation and held out his wrists, letting the nip bottles fall to the floor. He had no fight left in him and felt a sense of relief in the act of surrender. Even if Mallory managed to testify in his defense, he knew that his life would never be the same.

QUINN

"I know he's not the greatest father in the world, Mrs. Jessica, but I also know he'd never attack my mother," Quinn said over the phone.

"No, I can't see him doing that either."

"That's just another reason why that woman is not my real mother."

"But, Quinn, I don't understand. The woman may be an imposter, but she's the spitting image of Shay."

"My mother told me she grew up in a series of foster homes after her father died and her mother abandoned her. Did she ever mention having a twin sister?"

"Goodness no. She never mentioned anything about her childhood to me, except to say it was difficult."

"My real mother would never send me away to a school in Connecticut."

"You're right about that. But the media will call you crazy if you come out publicly and say as much," Jessica said. "They'll think your father put you up to it."

"I know, but I'm certain it's not her."

"How can you be so sure?"

"I just know it in my heart."

"Okay, but I can't see how."

"Look at what she's done to my father."

"Oh, Quinn. I don't know what to say. I'm so sorry for everything that's happened to you and your family."

"It's okay, Mrs. Jessica. I have a feeling that my mother will come back for me, wherever she is, and that everything will one day be good again."

"I pray to God you're right."

Quinn put down her cell phone and slumped in the armchair. The psychologist would come out of her office at any moment to speak to her. Word had spread around campus about her parents' situation, and it had been the talk of the school. It felt humiliating to have all this hanging over her head, but she swore to not let it affect her. She vowed to hold her head high and act as if nothing had happened. She needed to be strong. Disciplined. At least that ugly witch had taught her something useful about life.

"Okay, Quinn, I'm ready to see you now."

She walked inside the therapist's office. Talking about this crazy scenario was the last thing she wanted to do. But she would put on a brave face like she had since this journey began. Her old, naive self was behind her. Nothing would cause her to lose her newly discovered feeling of independence and self-reliance. Now, she just had to focus.

SHAY

Shay's hands and feet began to slowly warm up while inside this truck. Soon, she would be reunited with her daughter, and nothing could keep them apart.

The plow driver dropped her off at a convenience store a few miles from where he'd picked her up. She thanked him profusely before jumping down onto the pavement. After grabbing her backpack, she sprinted happily into the convenience store so she could pour herself a cup of hot coffee. She immediately grabbed the largest cup on the counter and filled it with the steaming liquid. After adding cream and sugar, she snapped on the lid. Then, she purchased two breakfast sandwiches and wolfed them down with her coffee.

"What town are we in?" she asked the young girl at the register.

"You don't know?"

Shay shook her head, the feeling in her feet slowly coming back to her.

"You're in Belchertown."

She was slightly familiar with Belchertown. She'd grown up twenty-plus miles away in the town of Wendell. What a coincidence. "How long a drive is it back to Boston?"

"Two, two and a half hours, depending on traffic."

"I don't have a car. Do you have any idea how I could get there?"

"My uncle's retired and drives part-time for Uber. Want me to see if he'll drive you?"

"Would you?"

"I can ask. Worst he can say is no."

"Please tell him that it's urgent and that money is no object."

"Knowing my uncle, he'll be happy to hear that."

The girl called and talked for a minute, laughing at something her uncle had said. Then she rested the phone on her shoulder. "He says he can do it at noon if you want to wait. He's got a few things to do first."

"Tell him I need to go as soon as possible. Tell him I'll pay extra if necessary."

The girl relayed her message and then ended the call. "He said he'll come pick you up in an hour."

"Thank you so much," she said, reaching out and grasping the girl's hand.

"Everything okay, lady?"

"I need to get back home as soon as possible before something bad happens to my daughter," she said. "Do you know anything about an old woman who lives off the dirt road a few miles down from here?"

The girl laughed. "You mean Dorothy Mills? That miserable old woman? She holes up in that house all winter and then comes here in the spring to gas up and complain about everyone and everything."

The name shocked her. "Did you say her name was Dorothy Mills?"

"Yup. Everyone in town knows her. She drives that gnarly old pickup truck with the plow."

She could barely speak, she was so stunned. Dorothy Mills was her mother's name. Everyone called her Dot when Shay was a young girl. She was the same mother who abandoned her and Shannon after their father died in that car crash, a crash caused by Shannon. She was also the mother whom Shannon murdered and stuffed in the storage freezer down in the basement.

* * *

The car pulled up an hour later, and the driver honked his horn. Shay ran out of the store and settled into the passenger seat. She handed the man all her money and then promised to send him a check for an additional five hundred dollars if he dropped her off in Boston. She explained that she had to return home to her blind daughter before it was too late. Tears streamed down her face as she told him this. The driver told her not to worry about paying him the rest of the money, but she insisted.

He took off down the snow-covered road, the Stones playing "Sympathy For The Devil" over the speakers. Because of the wool cap pulled over her head, the driver hadn't recognized her as the famous anchorwoman on the Channel Four news. Maybe he didn't watch TV. Or maybe she didn't now resemble her celebrity sister. Either way, she was glad he didn't make the connection.

Shay closed her eyes and settled back in the seat, thankful that she'd finally—miraculously—escaped that hellhole. Soon, she would be reunited with Quinn. Then, they could start the process of rebuilding their lives.

But what about Gideon? Could their relationship heal from all that had happened? She didn't think so. How in the world had he not figured out that Shannon was not his wife? It begged the question: how well did Gideon really know her? Had their marriage been built on a foundation of lies?

Starting tomorrow, she would plan her revenge against Shannon. Two could play at this game. She recalled being a young girl and setting that house afire and mustering up the courage to stab herself in the thigh—and then watching in horror as they carried out what she thought was a body bag containing Shannon's burnt-beyond-recognition remains.

She had a good college friend living in Boston who would put her up for the night. Tonight, she would sleep.

Tomorrow, she would start righting some wrongs.

GIDEON

Gideon sat in his jail cell, wondering how he'd gone from Boston's favorite son to a violent criminal. His reputation was in tatters, and his career was all but over. The prosecutor was eyeing a charge of attempted murder, and even if the charges were reduced to manslaughter, Gideon was still looking at significant prison time. They'd no doubt make an example of him. Assuming he got out in ten years, he'd be in his late fifties and a convicted felon broke and without any job prospects.

He'd told his lawyer about Mallory, but the chance of her backing his alibi now seemed grim. She'd vehemently deny the affair and call Gideon a terrible husband for what he'd done to his wife, as well as for accusing her of sleeping with him. It ate away at him because he'd been like a mentor to that girl and many others. And it pained him even more to realize that she'd only slept with him to advance her career. Had all the women he'd slept with been that devious and scheming?

Nothing now could save him short of a miracle. His philandering, ironically, was the only thing that could extricate him from this terrible predicament. Yet even sexual infidelity had failed him. Hopefully, his lawyer could prove his innocence in front of a jury of his peers. The odds seemed long, considering that he'd long ago believed he had no peers. The public believed he was a cheating husband who'd viciously attacked the mother of his blind child. Some analysts claimed he was a classic narcissist, a notion he couldn't really deny. But what anchorman worth his salt wasn't?

The police now possessed that mysterious baseball bat, which they'd found buried in the trunk of his car, his loopy signature engraved over the bloodstained barrel. And what would the jurors think when they saw Quinn sitting in the courtroom, blind and tearing up as her mother testified against him?

The question he really wanted to know was this: who *had* assaulted his wife? And why? Had his wife conspired with someone to attack her and then set him up? It sounded ludicrous. No one would voluntarily agree to be beaten within an inch of their life. Then again, maybe the plan had gone awry. But that made no sense, either. What would be in it for the person who attacked his wife, assuming they wanted her dead?

What about Quinn? The police had refused to let him call his daughter. Shay had assumed all parental rights and requested he not contact the girl for fear of scaring her. He had no doubt he was now the most despised man in all of Boston. Maybe in the country.

He'd never felt more alone and depressed than he did now. Unless a miracle happened, and he didn't see one on the horizon, he pictured himself doing crossword puzzles in his prison cell for the next ten years. And folding striped jumpsuits in a grungy laundry room, fending off sexual deviants, and trading cigarettes for candy bars. No more golf outings, expensive bourbon, and canoodling with hot news babes over the water cooler. Maybe Quinn would fare better without him in her life. After all, he did agree to send her away to boarding school, although the plan had been all Shay's idea.

Someone in his cellblock cussed angrily, and it echoed throughout the jail. Gideon lay back on the hard pillow and closed his eyes, recalling those halcyon days from his boyhood when all he ever dreamed about was escaping from his miserable home and leaving his dysfunctional parents behind. Then becoming a famous TV newscaster and enjoying money and fame, as well as being adored by the masses. He'd certainly achieved his goal of national fame, but now for all the wrong reasons.

SHAY

After a good night's sleep in a comfortable bed with clean sheets and cozy blankets, Shay explained to her old college roommate what had happened to her. Then she called Jessica from her roommate's phone. Jessica appeared stupefied at the sound of her voice. Shay said she'd explain everything to her once they could meet at a popular diner on Kneeland Street they used to frequent. Jessica agreed to meet her at the appointed time.

Shay hugged her old college roomie and thanked her for letting her stay the night. Her friend insisted that she take a hundred dollars, and Shay took it, promising to pay her back.

With her wool cap pulled low, Shay walked through the cold, snowy downtown streets until she came to the retro caboose diner. She needed time to think now that she was back in Boston. She sat in a booth by the window and ordered coffee. Ten minutes later, Jessica walked in with a big smile on her face. They hugged, and she watched her friend slide in across from her. Once Jessica was seated, Shay reached over the table and held her friend's hand.

"Thank you so much for meeting me here," Shay said, pulling off her wool cap. Her messy hair spilled down around her cheeks.

"I'll always be there for you," Jessica said. "Where have you been all this time, Shay?"

"It's a long story. I promise I'll explain everything to you later."

"Have you seen this?" Jessica stabbed her finger on the front page of the newspaper she'd brought with her.

Shay glanced down at the photograph of her sister and grimaced. Almost immediately, she knew that coming to this diner was a mistake. The waitress, a weathered old redhead named Betty, commended her on making such a brave confession on TV. Then, the woman asked if she'd take a selfie with her. After Shay took the picture, a few other diners stopped at her table to say hello. She could feel all eyes on her as Betty placed their waters down in front of them.

"You don't look too good, hon. Been a rough week with that rotten husband of yours?" Betty asked.

"You don't know the half of it," Shay replied, eager now to leave this diner.

"You mean there's more to the story that they're not telling us?"

"Can you keep a secret?"

"Of course I can." The ancient waitress leaned over the Formica table.

"I was kidnapped and held in a basement these past few months." She nearly burst out laughing, it sounded so ludicrous.

The waitress stared at her for a few seconds before breaking out into nervous laughter. "You're a card, Shay Wells."

"I almost had you, right?" She smiled.

The waitress went back behind the counter and returned with two mugs of steaming coffee. Shay glanced at the paper, reading all she could about her husband's precarious situation. It startled her to see Shannon's face splashed across the front page, the entirety of which had been dedicated to the Welles' explosive marriage, separation, and attempted murder. The resemblance between Shannon and herself was amazing. But she'd recognize her evil sister anywhere. Shannon had come back into her life in the worst possible way and at the worst possible time.

She looked across the table and noticed that Jessica was also staring at the photo.

"It's amazing," Jessica said, shaking her head. "She looks just like you."

"That's my sister, all right." She nodded to an elderly couple who waved to her as they passed.

"After all these years, she's still the spitting image of you," Jessica said. "I still can't figure out how she pulled this off."

"Shannon is super-smart. That girl never forgets a slight."

"You're telling me."

"And she has absolutely zero conscience."

"That's where the identical part of you two ends."

"I certainly hope so," Shay said. "She must have been plotting to get back at me since the day I set her up."

"Set her up for what?"

"When we were kids, she tortured and abused me every single day of my life."

"What happened."

She started from the beginning and explained everything. She told Jessica about the constant physical and verbal abuse and about how her sister constantly threatened to kill her. She explained how Shannon inadvertently caused their father's death and how their mother abandoned them after their father died. The moves from one pervy foster home to the next, the state of Massachusetts intent on keeping the orphaned twins together. Then how she came up with the idea to liberate herself from her twin by stabbing herself in the thigh, lighting their foster parents' house on fire, and blaming Shannon for it.

"Wow. You must have been really desperate," Jessica said.

"I just had to get away from her and escape from the abuse she inflicted on me all those years. None of the caseworkers took me seriously when I told them how Shannon constantly threatened to kill me."

"Which was why you stabbed yourself and set your foster parents' house on fire?"

"I swear to you, Jessica, I felt like I had no other choice."

"Then whose body did they carry out?"

"Shannon was constantly inviting her homeless and drug-addicted friends to sleep over. I'm guessing one of these addicts died in that house fire."

"Someone you didn't even know?"

"I would have never set it if I knew anybody was still inside."

"Of course you wouldn't have."

"Shannon ran back inside the house, but it might have been too late to save her friend. So she assumed the girl's identity and ran off before the police arrested her."

"After seeing what she's done to you and your family, I can't say I blame you for what you did."

"Thanks for believing me," she whispered.

"Have you decided how you're going to get back at her?"

"The safest thing to do would be to go to the police and tell them everything that's happened. But I can't do that."

"Besides, they could never prove she kidnapped you."

"No, and by the time word got out that I was back in town, Shannon would be long gone. Then Quinn and I will be forced to live the rest of our lives in fear, always wondering if she'll come back for us. That's not the kind of life I want for the two of us going forward."

"I'm so grateful for your friendship, Shay. You know I'll help you in any way I can."

"I won't be able to pull this off without you."

"We'll take that bitch down, " Jessica said, staring grimly at her for a few seconds. "I feel so bad for Quinn."

Tears formed in her eyes at hearing her daughter's name. "Quinn's tough. She'll make it through this in one piece."

"She's grown a lot in these last few months," Jessica said. "What will you do about Gideon?"

"I'll deal with him later. Right now, I need to contact Quinn and tell her everything that's happened. Where is she?"

"You won't believe this, but that witch sent her away to a school in Connecticut."

Connecticut! The news infuriated her. She couldn't believe Gideon had stood by and let this happen. Part of her wanted him to rot in jail for what he'd done to his daughter. Yet she knew how persuasive Shannon could be.

"I've been in touch with Quinn. She tried to convince me that the woman who took your place is not her real mother. I didn't believe her at first. Not until you called me."

"Is she okay?"

"She's been better. She said she was being bullied at that school she's attending, but that everything is all right now."

"Good God, I can't believe Gideon went along with that awful woman's plan," she said. "As long as she's doing okay, maybe it's best that she stays away from all this for now."

"Yes, you're probably right."

"Besides, I don't want to call her school and alert Shannon to my whereabouts."

"Then how will you get in contact with her?"

She thought about it for a few seconds before it came to her. "How about if you call Quinn? That way, no one will become suspicious of my presence here in town."

"Great idea."

The waitress returned with their check. Shay asked her if she could borrow the diner's phone, claiming that the batteries in hers had died. The waitress immediately brought over her cell phone and handed it to her. She passed it to Jessica, and she dialed Quinn's number.

Shay glanced out the window and couldn't believe what she was seeing. Photographers and news reporters were getting out of their cars and approaching the diner. She directed Jessica to end the call. Then she turned to Jessica and said, "Go to your minivan and meet me out back."

"What's going on?" Jessica said, sipping her coffee.

"Don't look now, but the paparazzi are here to snap photographs of me. If my sister catches wind of this, she'll skip town."

"Okay, I'll wait a few minutes so it doesn't appear obvious. I'll meet you out back. But don't go very far."

"Don't worry, Jessica, I won't."

Shay got up and walked over to the counter where the waitress was pouring coffee. She passed her two twenty-dollar bills, pointed outside, and then asked if she wouldn't mind letting her sneak out the back door. The waitress escorted her into the kitchen, where three cooks wearing hairnets worked frantically pushing out breakfast orders. She exited the screen door and ran out until she crouched behind a massive dumpster. The smell was repulsive, but she'd suffered more than her share of indignities in the last few months. A few minutes later, the minivan pulled up behind the diner. Shay jumped inside, and the two of them sped off toward her best friend's house.

QUINN

She was in the middle of her English class when the teacher came to her desk and interrupted her. There was an urgent call from her mother's best friend. Seeing as there was so much hullabaloo about her parents' nasty marital situation, the school was doing all it could to accommodate her. But Quinn wanted her routine to remain the same, turning down further offers for counseling and support. She knew in her heart that her real mother would soon be here for her. All the other distractions she could handle.

A staff member escorted her to the office and sat her down in one of the empty conference rooms. After handing Quinn the phone, the staff member left the room and closed the door until she was alone. She wondered what all the secrecy was about. Had something bad happened to her father? To that phony witch who was passing herself off as her mother?

"Hello?"

"Oh, Quinn. Thank God you're all right."

"Mrs. Jessica?"

"You're not going to believe what I'm about to tell you."

A smile spread over her face because, in her heart, she already knew.

"You were right, girl, and I feel so terrible for not believing you. That woman is definitely not your mother."

"I told you." Quinn felt redeemed. "But why are you only now believing me?"

"Because I just spoke to your real mother, and she wants me to tell you that she'll be coming for you very soon. But just not yet. She needs you to sit tight for a while."

"Why? I want to be with her right now."

"She says she'll tell you later. She just doesn't want you to mention this to anyone."

"Okay."

"I'm sorry I didn't believe you."

"No biggie. The most important thing is that she's back."

"Yes, that is the most important thing."

"Thanks for all your help, Mrs. Jessica."

Quinn put down the phone and left the conference room a happy girl. She couldn't wait to speak to her mother and find out what had happened and where she had been these last few months. It was about time that fraud got what was coming to her.

SHAY

Before going over to Jessica's house, Shay purchased some sunglasses to prevent anyone else from recognizing her. The near miss with the paparazzi had been a close call bordering on disaster. They drove out of Boston and into the suburbs until they arrived in sleepy Woodbridge Estates.

After living with George in that claustrophobic home for so many months, it felt strange, returning to her old neighborhood. Aside from the snow covering the landscape, the golf course and private club looked unchanged. They drove past her old home and then around the neighborhood until they arrived at Jessica's house. Jessica parked in the driveway, and they got out, making their way to the front steps. Stan opened the door and appeared before them. Shay tearfully embraced him before being ushered inside. Then, the three of them sat down on the sofa. The roaring, crackling fireplace reminded her that she was surrounded by people who loved and cared for her. She glanced around, trying to get accustomed to her new surroundings. How long had it been since she'd been inside Jessica's home? On the wall hung photos of Stan and their two kids, and it reminded her that George was stuck in that ramshackle home, desperate to leave something behind for his own children.

"I'm so happy to see you again, Shay," Stan said.

"Trust me, Stan, I'm just happy to be seen."

"I'm sorry about what happened. Not for a moment did I believe Gideon attacked you."

"Thanks. It's why you guys were the first people I called when I returned home." She turned to Jessica. "And I can't thank you enough for staying in touch with Quinn and keeping her calm."

"Quinn reached out to me first. She figured out that this woman on TV wasn't her real mother. I kick myself now for not believing her."

"There's no way you could have known, seeing how my sister looks exactly like me. And with my head injury and all, people obviously assumed that this new persona of hers was a by-product of some miraculous recovery."

"Would you like to talk to Quinn now? I'm sure she'd love to hear from you."

"Not just yet. Let her stay in Connecticut for the time being. That way, my sister can't hurt her any more than she already has."

"Your sister is a vile woman. You should have heard the rude things she said to me these last few months," Jessica says.

"Believe me, I know exactly what that snake is capable of. After being presumed dead, it's apparent that she's been waiting a long time to pay me back."

"How come you never told us you had a twin sister?" Stan said.

"Would you tell anyone if you had a sister like Shannon?"

"Good point."

"Look, I'll explain everything to you guys later," she said. "I'm just starting to piece together how she pulled this off."

"How did she do it?" Stan asked.

"Shannon had been drugging me during my recovery, disguised as that Chechen housekeeper. She was the one who ran naked onto that tenth green and then kicked and injured our neighbor's dog. Her goal was to destabilize me, make me believe I'd lost my mind, and then take over my identity by framing Gideon. Her goal was to take ownership of the house and all our finances."

"And then take over as sole anchorwoman at the station," Stan said. "She certainly succeeded in her goal. She and Gideon are the top-rated anchors in this city."

"I must say, it surprised me that my sister set her sights so high and actually succeeded in becoming a news anchor. It just goes to show how cunning she is."

"And to think I had to get through four years of college to report on the weather," Stan said, laughing. "And take out a small fortune in student loans."

"I'm not sure what that says about the current state of journalism," Shay said.

"She certainly gives our profession a bad name," Stan said.

"As evil as she was growing up, Shannon had a brilliant mind. She tested off the charts in school, much higher than I ever did. Unfortunately, she chose the life of crime over everything else."

"And to think she very nearly got away with it," Jessica said.

"She still might get away with it if we don't handle this matter properly. Will the two of you help me?"

"Tell us what you want us to do, Shay. Then I want to hear all about what happened to you all those months you were away."

"When I do, you're not going to believe me."

"Trust me, after everything that's happened around here, I'll believe almost anything now," Jessica said.

Shay outlined her plan. Then she told them about her captivity, detailing her long, torturous ordeal, explaining how she ended up in that basement. She told them about George and his terminal cancer and about how Shannon had played him for her own benefit. How she snowshoed her way to civilization until she finally arrived back in Boston. When she was done, Jessica and Stan stared at her in disbelief. Shay couldn't quite believe it herself. How had she made it out of there alive?

"You mean to say that George is still in that house?" Stan said.

"Yes. There's four feet of snow on the ground, and he's dying of cancer."

"You have to call the police and tell them where he is," Jessica said.

"No police. That was George's only request. Shannon vowed to go after his kids if he got the police involved. Let's just take care of my sister first. Then we're going to return to that house and make George a happy man before he dies."

SHANNON

I'm about to go on the air and deliver the news. Despite all that has happened between Gideon and me, I insisted on working this evening. The show must go on, as they say. Barb, the news director, tried to talk me out of it, but I convinced her that this would be best for everyone. The ratings would be massive with me sitting at that desk, especially after all the chaos that had happened, and this was a fact she could not dispute. In addition, I told her that delivering the news would help me overcome the trauma I'd experienced, especially after finally realizing that it was my own husband who had tried to kill me.

I couldn't be happier. My "husband" has been dispatched, and the blind girl is out from under my care. Gideon must know that he has no future and nothing to live for.

I talked to George this morning, and he's happy that we've succeeded in our plan. I told him I'd be bringing him a bundle of cash once the weather breaks. That way he can set up college accounts for his two neglected kids. Too bad George won't make it out of that house alive. Neither will my unfortunate sister imprisoned down in that basement. I want to say goodbye to her one last time before I return to Boston and begin my new life.

The entitled brat and I have an understanding. She knows what's at stake. If I could just walk away from her, I would. But that massive tuition bill is part of the deal for the foreseeable future. And so is four years of expensive college. Then she's on her own. It's a small price to pay for celebrity and affluence. I'll sell the place in Woodbridge Estates. Buy the nice condo I'm currently subletting in the Back Bay. Invest in stocks, bonds, and mutual funds. Oh, and acquire some cool art. I might even find a wealthy dude to shack up with.

There's hardly enough of Gideon's money left to retire on, which means I have to keep working. But why in the world would I ever retire from reporting the news? Celebrity and fame are what I've always wanted in life, and now I have it. I'm loved and adored by millions of people in the Boston area: people I couldn't care less about. I'm only thirty-five and still a fox. Maybe one of the big cable news shows might call and offer me one of their anchor jobs. I'm not averse to moving on to a bigger stage and offering up my opinions for the right price.

The makeup girl powders my face while a pink-haired stylist with nose rings fluffs out my teased blond hair. Barb comes over and asks how I'm doing, and I give her two manicured thumbs up. Someone brings me my Starbucks latte with two sugars and oat milk. It's better than the cheap blow I used to snort off strangers' bellies. Five minutes until the broadcast, and I'm nearly dolled up for prime time.

I've not forgotten about Shay. I giggle to myself, almost spitting out my latte when I think about her rotting away in that basement. Heads turn and regard me oddly, wondering what's so funny. This time, I don't snap like a badger and order them around like I've been doing as of late. I'm in too good a mood for bullying all the lowlifes who pamper me. Thinking about my sister's plight brings a smile to my heavily made-up face. I picture her holed up in that dingy basement, begging George to set her free.

Testicular cancer, George admitted to me one day as I was doing research on my sister. And he was only fifty-one. The intense radiation and chemo treatments left him as limp as a rice noodle. It didn't matter to him anymore. He had bigger mountains to climb than merely catching wood for his one-night stands. Our relationship was always business-oriented, not that George hadn't tried to get in my pants after too many shots of Jack Daniels.

The time has come. Tonight will be an interesting broadcast. Barb wanted to put Rand Lancaster on the desk with me, but I put my foot down and demanded that from now on, I will deliver the news alone. I'm now the one calling the shots around here. I'm the straw that stirs the drink at Channel Four, and without me reporting the news, their ratings will surely plummet.

I walk out into the lights and take my place in front of the cameras. A quick glance at the teleprompter informs me that I'm about to go live.

Three…two…one. Showtime.

The thirty minutes whiz by in a flash. So fast that it's often hard for me to gauge how well I did. My commentary this evening is focused on the evils of domestic abuse and the importance of reporting all instances to the police. Don't be a victim, I lectured my audience. You don't deserve to live in a constant state of fear, like I did all those years, the threat of violence always hanging over your head. If I'm brave enough to put my marriage and career on the line, I tell them, then so can you.

After the broadcast, Barb informs me that my performance was off the charts. Phone-ringing good. Her words please me to no end, and I smile at another job well done.

Do I hear the faint murmur of contract negotiations? They'd better rip up my old one if they know what's good for them. I'm a ratings cougar!

I leave the studio and stroll to my favorite Back Bay watering hole for a nightcap. It's cold out, but it feels nice walking into a warm, cozy bar. The barkeep knows my routine by now. Waiting for me on the polished bar is a cranberry martini. It's quiet inside as the midnight hour approaches. It's just what I need after the adrenaline rush of reporting the day's news.

I sip my martini and gaze up at the highlight reels on ESPN. I hate sports, but watching sweaty hunks dunking basketballs somehow makes me happy this evening. It feels oddly satisfying at the end of the day, and it takes my mind off all the negativity going on in the world. Think positive, I keep telling myself. The world is your oyster, Shannon.

"You were magnificent this evening, Mrs. Wells," the bartender says in a deep baritone. He's wearing a crisp white shirt and black bow tie. His glistening black hair sweeps back over his scalp.

"Thanks, Barnaby." I hold up my martini to toast. "You aren't looking too shabby, either."

"I can't believe any man wouldn't worship the ground you walk on."

"Who's to say they haven't?"

He smiles at me as he towel dries a glass. "I'd punch that husband of yours right in the mouth if he were sitting here in front of me."

"Save that machismo for making these delicious cocktails," I say, finishing the rest of my drink. "Besides, that husband of mine won't be a problem much longer."

"Really?"

"What I'm telling you is not fake news."

"That's the best thing you've said all day," he says. "Another martini, Mrs. Wells?"

"What do you think?"

"Coming right up."

"And one last thing, Barnaby."

"Whatever you need, Mrs. Wells."

"Stop with that Mrs. Wells crap. It's Shay from now on."

"You got it, Mrs. Wells."

Every night, I say the same thing to Barnaby, and yet he never changes his routine. He knows that there are people in this world who are superior to the rest of humanity and therefore deserving of respect. The day he calls me Shay is the day I walk out of this bar for good.

SHAY

She asked Jessica and Stan if they knew someone who was tall, handsome, and charming and who might help her scam Shannon. Stan said his brother, Luke, would be perfect for the job. His brother once worked as a stage actor in Manhattan and had studied theater at NYU. Now, he worked in Boston as a corporate attorney. He was the perfect foil for Shay's scheme to bring down her sister.

For the last two nights, she and Stan's brother, Luke, waited for Shannon to emerge from the station. They monitored her sister's every move. Each night, after her broadcast, Shannon walked to that fancy Back Bay bar and stayed there until closing. An Uber would pull up around two in the morning and drive her to her apartment on Commonwealth Avenue. Then, she would make her way up the stairs and disappear inside an old brownstone. Shay figured she must have ditched the big home in Woodbridge Estates for this new pad.

On the third night, after Shannon retired to her place for the evening, Shay and Luke drove back to her old house in Woodbridge Estates. She wasn't surprised to see a "For Sale" sign on the snowy lawn. Most of the lights were out in the neighborhood. When she was sure no one was looking, she searched through the bushes alongside the house. She'd hidden a key under one of the rocks and hoped it was still there and that her sister hadn't changed the locks. After dusting snow off the rock, she opened it and was relieved to see that the key was still inside. She took the key out, walked up the steps, slipped the key in the lock, and luckily, the door opened.

She went directly to the bathroom and searched through the drawers until she found what she was looking for. She grabbed the two orange medicine bottles filled with Ambien. There'd been four bottles at one time, but Shannon had obviously used the other two to keep her paranoid and confused. She slipped them into her pocket and made her way outside, closed the door, making sure it was locked, and then tiptoed down the stairs until she was back in the car.

"Got 'em?" Luke asked.

"Yup."

"Those prescription pills will come in handy."

"Let's hope so."

"I take it there's another pill who could desperately use them."

"She'll never know what hit her," Shay said.

"Won't she be surprised when she wakes up?"

"Let's say it'll be a revelation of sorts," she said, laughing. "Our work is done for the day, Luke. Tomorrow, we'll implement the next phase of my plan."

"Wonderful. This might be my best role to date."

* * *

Luke stood in the middle of Jessica's living room, wearing one of his expensively tailored suits. Shay marveled at the sight of the man who would play the part. When fully dressed and with his dark hair slicked back, Luke perfectly resembled the part of a billionaire hedge fund manager.

Afterward, they sat at the kitchen table going over the script that Luke was to follow. He would be playing the part of a venture capitalist living in Beacon Hill and dashing off to one of his waterfront homes on Martha's Vineyard. He'd pretend to be from old money and someone who'd capitalized on his vast inheritance to become nouveau rich.

Shay took out each pill, placed them on the marble counter, and began to crush them. By the time she was done, there was a small pyramid of white dust gleaming on the surface. She swiped the dust into the plastic bag and zipped it shut. Now, all they had to do was wait.

QUINN

Why hadn't her mother called? Quinn thought as she sat down for dinner with the other girls. She could barely concentrate on her studies or eat. The teachers were giving her a lot of leeway, although what she really needed right now was to hear from her mother. Her father was in jail awaiting trial for attempted murder. She knew that charge was as phony as the woman who had accused him of committing it.

She walked alone back to her room despite all the other girls asking if she'd care to join them. In some ways, her parents' bizarre situation had turned her into a minor celebrity on campus. But she didn't want to be famous for having two warring parents: one an alleged criminal and the other a copycat felon. All she wanted was her old friends back, her old room, and her old life.

It had been three days since Jessica called and explained the situation to her. Quinn had been tempted to call back, but something prevented her from doing so. Be patient, she kept telling herself. When your mother is ready to contact you, she will.

Later that evening, she turned on her computer and listened to the six o'clock news. The witch had returned with a vengeance the day after the DA had charged her father with attempted murder. There was not a trace of remorse in the woman's voice, only coldness and deceit. Quinn knew that charisma could only carry a person so far in this world. But none of that mattered now. As long as her mother came and whisked her away from all this, that imposter could do whatever she wanted.

After ten minutes of listening to this fraud deliver the news, she couldn't take it anymore. She dressed for bed and then snuck under the covers with her Harry Potter novel. The prospect of entering a strange new world filled with wizards, dragons, and magic enchanted her. It helped her forget about the nastiness of life, allowing her to escape to an exotic, faraway land where all her senses came alive, and she became acutely aware of everything.

SHANNON

My agent is now fielding calls from some of the biggest cable news networks in the country. Every half hour, Evan texts me about an inquiry from a news director interested in my services. He tells me not to get my hopes up, but I can't see my hopes going anywhere but up.

I pull out my compact and examine myself closely. For some reason, that stupid makeup artist couldn't get it right this evening. I scream at her to come over and fix the awful mess she's painted on my face. She apologizes profusely, all blue hair, nose rings, and black eyeliner, nervously fluffing and redrawing lines. After she's done, I examine myself in the mirror. My watch tells me there's less than a minute to go before I go on air. Although my face looks far from perfect, it'll have to do. I'll make sure this goth queen is shitcanned before the night is through. But for now, I shoo her away and then wait for my cue.

Three…two…one.

The smile is instantaneous and high wattage, and it seems to come naturally to me. When I'm on camera, I want people to think of me as a close confidante. Someone who can deliver the news with the grace and alacrity of a trusted friend. It cracks me up when people come up to me on the street as if we're best buds, thanking me for making their pathetic lives better. If only they knew I couldn't give two shits about them. Or that I genuinely hate and distrust most people, viewing them as useful idiots.

My commentary tonight is hilarious, and as I deliver it, I can see all the staff and crew glancing nervously at each other. I deliver some clichéd blather about being kind to those around us and treating people the way we ourselves would like to be treated. It's the golden rule—and I'm the gold. I know I make these people sick with my hypocrisy and feigned moral outrage, yet as soon as I'm done, they all rush up to me with terrified looks on their faces, congratulating me on another marvelous performance. But like the ice queen I've become, I ignore their entreaties and bark out orders at them. Do this for me. Fetch that. Grab me a bottled water, Kelly, or else you're history in this business. The sweet Shannon has left the building, peeps, and is never coming back. No more cookies and fudge brownies that I forced Consuela to bake. Get used to the new reign of terror, my attitude informs them.

And then I'm done, out of there, free to relax in Barnaby's fawning company. I hear a cranberry martini calling my name.

I walk in my high heels down the icy Back Bay streets, nodding to all my admirers out for a late-night stroll. The key is to never give them too much. Leave them wanting for more. I turn the corner, and the shining lights of my favorite watering hole come into view. Newbury Street is the star-studded beacon in this old town. It's bright with dark wood and filled with beautiful people eager to part with their money. There's lots of high-end bars and top-shelf alcohol flowing. There's well-dressed European women and grim-looking Middle Eastern men decked out in hand-stitched suits, allowing valet monkeys to park their ridiculously expensive cars.

Barnaby's is packed this evening. After hanging up my jacket, I grab a stool in the middle of the bar, noticing that my cranberry martini is already waiting for me on the counter. I take a sip and revel in the crisp tartness of the fruit. It tastes so good I want to die—and it'd better taste good at eighteen bucks a pop. The alcohol goes straight to my head and makes me more viperous than usual. I tell a chubby accountant to fuck off after he offers to buy me a drink. A cute-looking banker type tries to make small talk with me, but I give him the cold shoulder after catching a whiff of his cheap cologne. Barnaby is overprotective of me and shoos these losers away whenever they get too aggressive.

The first martini goes down easy. Before I have a chance to order a second, Barnaby puts a fresh one in front of me and says that it's from the gentleman to my left; Barnaby has an eye for the good ones. I turn and see a tall, handsome gentleman smiling at me. He's wearing an expensively tailored suit and sporting a fresh haircut and is much better looking than what I usually encounter in this pricey gin mill. I lean over and take a whiff of him; he reeks of *wealth*.

"Here's to me," I say, raising my martini.

"To you, beautiful." He scoots over a stool and sticks his large hand out. "Greyson Summers."

Greyson Summers—now, there's an old Yankee name if I've ever heard one. I ignore his tanned hand and stare up at the flatscreen, where two female gladiators pound the shit out of each other.

"You like ultimate fighting?" he asks.

"I'd have stayed married if I'd liked to fight."

"Good one."

I notice the Rolex attached to his wrist and maintain my poker face. "If you really enjoy man-on-man action, I bet there's another bar down the street you might like better."

He laughs at my insult, not at all offended. "Why would I leave this stool when someone as beautiful as yourself is sitting next to me?"

"Excuse me?"

"Even if I were gay, a woman like you would easily convert me to the other team."

I act all offended and turn away to keep from laughing.

"Did I say something to offend you?"

"Love is love, pal. You shouldn't joke about that," I say, although I could care less about anyone's sexual preference.

"Yes, you're right," he says. "Have you an interest in golf?"

I stare down at his crotch. "Only the miniature version."

He laughs. "Trust me, it's far from miniature."

"Bet you tell that to all the ladies."

"I only asked because I thought you might like to join me some weekend at the Brookline Country Club. I usually book a tee time for noon."

My ears perk up at the words *Brookline Country Club*. "Are you a member there?"

"As is my father and his father before him." He sips his drink. "You can't play there unless you're invited."

"I see," I say. "Will it be a twosome or threesome?"

"I'm a one-partner kind of guy."

"Good to know." I rest my knuckles under my chin and smile. "What else do you do to pass the time, tiger?"

"I run a venture capitalist firm in town." He sips his drink. "And you?"

I sit back in shock, taken aback by his ignorance. "You really don't know who I am?"

"Should I?"

"You obviously don't watch the evening news."

He shakes his head. "I mostly watch Bloomberg or The Business Channel. I'm afraid that my work takes up much of my time."

"Maybe you should start watching some real news instead." I turn away from him, pissed off.

He finishes his drink and orders a White Russian made with Grey Goose Vx.

After hearing his order, I realize I can't let this big fish slip from my grip. "I'm the lead anchorwoman on Channel Four, if you must know the truth. It's only the highest-rated news broadcast in New England."

"Wait a second." He smiles and points at me. "Are you that woman everyone's talking about? The one whose husband tried to kill her?"

"The one and only." I lift my martini. "What doesn't kill you makes you stronger."

"But you're still married to that creep, aren't you?"

"Not for for much longer." I show him my ringless finger. "And you?"

"Unattached at the moment." The bartender places his White Russian in front of him. "Would you like to grab a table with me?"

"Give me one good reason why I should."

"Because this place makes the best White Russians in town," he whispers in my ear. "And I like you."

"Why have I never seen you in here before?"

"My business forces me to travel a bit. Raising billions in capital takes time and energy."

"Billions, huh?" I think of the measly salary I'm earning and what's left in Gideon's pathetic bank account, and I cringe. His money won't last very long at this pace. I pat Greyson's chiseled hand, thinking about all the dough I could free from his bank account. "Sure, I'll sit with you."

"Wonderful," he says, noticing that my glass is near empty. "Grab a seat, and I'll order us a couple of White Russians."

"Make sure he uses the Grey Goose Vx."

His face contorts into a look of disgust. "Would you ever drink a White Russian without it?"

I laugh as I make my way to the booth, smiling at the prospect of another golden opportunity coming my way. This is too easy. I think about my measly financial portfolio, which will soon be drained by lawyers, college tuition, and greedy real estate agents taking their cut. I stare at the superrich banker as he stands at the bar, my eyes glued to his shapely ass. He cuts quite a figure in that pricey Italian suit. Probably cost him a small fortune. This could be quite profitable. I might even get a romp in the hay out of it, too.

It's almost one in the morning, and the bar is near empty. Barnaby hands the drinks to my new friend. Greyson mixes our drinks before walking back to where I sit. He places the White Russian in front of me and then takes a sip. A boyish expression comes over his handsome face. I take a quick sip to see if I like it. It tastes gloriously expensive.

He puts his hand over mine and tells an off-color joke. It's the kind of joke where a priest, a rabbi, and a whore walk into a bar. The alcohol, combined with the salty humor, puts me in a devilish mood, and I burst out laughing. If only he knew about my past as a Vegas call girl, he might not be so free with this type of humor.

By the time I finish my drink, I realize that I'm tipsier than I thought. It's been years since I've gotten this drunk. But before I can say anything, he's back at the table with another round of White Russians. And another round of racy jokes: how do you make a hormone? Or was that a whore moan? My head is cloudy and spinning. Something tells me that we're going to end up in the sack tonight. It certainly beats sleeping with fat, middle-aged men staying in Vegas for an insurance convention.

I drink half the White Russian before realizing that I've had way too much to drink. Why is the room spinning?

"Uncle," I say, pushing the half-filled glass to the center of the table.

"Aren't you going to finish it?"

"I've got a lot of things to do tomorrow," I say, trying to maintain my equilibrium.

"How about coming back to my penthouse and having a nightcap?"

"Where do you live?"

"Beacon Hill, when I'm in town. A nice brownstone in the South Slope neighborhood. It's right next to John Kerry's place."

"You mean the John Kerry who almost became president?"

"One and the same. John and I often ride bikes together when we're home."

"How about when you're not in town?"

"I've got a condo in SoHo and a place on Martha's Vineyard."

I whistle, trying to keep my head from toppling off my neck.

"So is that a yes? You'll come back for a nightcap?"

"How can I say no to that?"

I slide out of the booth and struggle to stand as Greyson helps me put on my jacket. Barnaby winks at me from behind the bar. Then Greyson puts his arm around my waist and helps me out the door. A blast of icy wind hits my face and disorients me. It's a shame I can't drink like I once did. Of course, I'm not getting any younger. I need to start taking better care of myself.

The streetlights obscure my vision and make everything seem blurred. I squint as he leads me to a vehicle parked along the curb. My legs feel spindly and useless, and I can't for the life of me believe that a few measly drinks could get me this trashed. Am I really losing my touch? Maybe it's from all the fatigue and stress I've been under. While living in Vegas, I could drink most men under the table. I could drink all night and then some. Even George was amazed by how much booze I could put away.

Something seems wrong as he opens the door and pushes me down onto the seat. It suddenly occurs to me that venture capitalists don't drive Ford minivans. I open my mouth to complain, but nothing comes out. All the feeling has gone out of my legs, arms, and tongue. I look over the passenger seat and, to my horror, see a familiar woman staring back at me. For a brief second, I think I'm looking into a steamed mirror. But how can that be?

"Hello, Shannon," Shay says. "Long time no see."

SHAY

She felt a sense of relief seeing her sister passed out in the back seat of the minivan. Jessica popped her head out from the far back seat and stared down at Shay's twin sister. Luke accelerated away from the curb, driving through the quiet Boston streets until he found an empty warehouse on the south side of town. Once the van stopped, the two of them clambered out. Luke took out the plastic handcuffs and secured Shannon's wrists and ankles. Then he placed a pillow under her head and tossed a blanket over her body so that the restraints were hidden in the event they got pulled over by the police. Jessica handed Shay a plastic bag.

"There's a protein shake in there. I put a teaspoon of powder in the bottle. If you need it give her some more," Jessica said.

"Thank you for preparing that for me."

"She's beautiful," Jessica said, staring down at her. "Such a waste of a life."

"Maybe on the outside, she's beautiful, but certainly not on the inside." Shay approached Luke and gave him a big hug. "Thanks so much for using your amazing acting skills to help me pull this off."

"My pleasure," Luke said. "I'm just sorry you had to grow up with such a monster."

"And thank you as well, Jessica. I owe all of you big time."

"The only thing you owe us is your continued friendship."

"Trust me, you'll always have it."

"Quinn's an amazing girl. She'll be alright." Jessica gave her a big hug. "Stan's got the snowmobile locked and loaded. He'll drive you and Shannon out to Western Massachusetts so you can do what you need to do."

"I didn't tell you this, Jessica, but the house where I was held captive belonged to my mother."

"Your mother?"

"Yes. She abandoned us after our father died. We were only teenagers."

"How did your sister find her?"

"She obviously tracked her down and then decided that her house, which was located in the middle of nowhere, would be the perfect place to keep me captive."

"I'm afraid to ask what she did to your mother."

"I think you know what she did. And she'll do the same to me and Quinn if she ever gets the chance."

"You better get going, Shay, if you're to meet up with Stan in Western Mass."

* * *

She pulled up at the convenience store located on the main road. Parked next to it was Stan's pick-up truck, and in his bed sat his snowmobile. Shay estimated that the dirt road her mother lived on was roughly three miles west of the store.

Three feet of snow covered the ground, and more started to fall as they drove toward where the road appeared. The town was deserted at this hour. Shay glanced back at her sister and noticed that she had not budged since they left Boston. The combination of drugs and alcohol had completely knocked her out.

She slowed down when she saw the opening in the trees, and Stan pulled over to the side of the road behind her. She put on her jacket, cap, and insulated gloves. Then, they unloaded the snowmobile until it was completely off the bed. She removed the bottles of Jack Daniel's she'd purchased and loaded them in the snowmobile's storage compartment. She also attached a small snow shovel to the machine. How happy George would be to be reunited with his beloved Jack. Stan gave her a quick tutorial on how to use the machine, but she knew how to use it. She and Gideon had gone snowmobiling those first few years before they'd gotten married.

He started it, and it roared to life. Then they removed Shannon from the truck, sat her down on the back seat, and strapped her to Shay's waist.

"I'll wait here until you come back," Stan said.

"Thank you."

"It's dark out there, so be careful and keep the headlights on."

"I will."

With the engine roaring in her ears, she took off down the road, following the headlights. She drove slow so as not to accidentally crash into a tree or boulder.

Thirty minutes later, she arrived at her mother's home. A pang of sadness passed through her as she thought about how her mother's life had turned out. Why had she abandoned her and Shannon after her father's death? How she would have loved to have spoken to her one last time. Sure, she had always resented her mother for abandoning the two of them like that. She was obviously a troubled woman, an alcoholic with serious mental health issues. But whatever problems she had, and no matter what kind of mother she'd been, she didn't deserve to be murdered and then stuffed into a storage freezer.

She pulled up to the stairwell and killed the engine. After removing the bungee cord securing Shannon to her, she climbed off the machine, letting Shannon slump forward on the seat. Then she removed the shovel and began to clear all the snow off the stairs.

The front door opened as she reached the top stoop. She glanced up and saw George standing in the doorway and staring at Shannon lying unconscious on the seat. He looked even more gaunt than when she last saw him. She resumed shoveling and didn't stop until she removed all the snow from the top step. George opened the flimsy screen door and locked the hydraulic so that it stayed open. Then, the two of them grabbed Shannon by the collar and dragged her up the stairs and into the house.

"Goddamn! I can't believe you pulled it off."

"I'm Shannon's sister, remember? We share the same bitch genes."

"No doubt about that."

"How are you holding out, George?" She noticed that his hands were trembling.

"I'm getting by. Having her here makes it all worth it," he said. "Now I can die knowing that my kids will be alright."

"Hold on. I have one more surprise for you."

"I do love surprises."

Shay went back down to the snowmobile and opened the storage compartment, removed the bottles of Jack Daniel's, and carried them upstairs and into the house. When she'd carried them all in, she handed a bottle to him. George took it in his trembling hand and stared at it.

"God bless your soul. "

"I need to get going, George. Someone's waiting for me at the other end of the road."

"Speaking of roads, this is the last one you and I will travel on."

"I suppose you're right," she said. "What are you going to do with my sister?"

"Best you not know." He gripped the bottle and twisted off the cap. Then he flicked it far out onto the snow before taking a long chug. "Have one last toast with me?"

"Of course."

She took the bottle in hand and swallowed a mouthful. Then she handed him back the bottle and gave him a hug goodbye. Climbed down the stairs. Jumped on the snowmobile. Started the engine. And rocketed back to where Stan was waiting for her in his pickup truck.

SHAY

She arrived at the news station just before five and made her way to her sister's office. Once inside, she glanced at herself in the full-body mirror. A day at the hairdresser and spa had done wonders for her, washing away all the dust and dirt she'd accumulated during the months she spent in captivity. Her red nails shone with intensity, and the mud bath she'd undergone made her face and body radiate with youthful vigor. She'd transformed not into her old self, but into the living, breathing embodiment of her celebrity sister—who had, for the last four months, been trying to pass herself off as Shay Wells.

It had been many years since she'd delivered the news, and she couldn't help but feel a bit nervous. Every fiber in her body trembled with nervous energy at what she was about to do. Hopefully, this would be the last time she'd need to deliver the news. Quinn deserved a mother who'd be there for her and keep her safe.

"How are you doing, Shannon?" Barb said.

"Fine."

"Let me know if you need anything."

"Will do."

She arrived early on set, allowing the makeup artist and hairdresser to do their thing. No one greeted her or spoke unless absolutely necessary. In fact, the atmosphere on the set was so tense that many of the staff wouldn't even make eye contact with her. She tried smiling at them, but not even that worked. It suddenly occurred to her why: Shannon had been treating them all like shit.

Her stomach rumbled as time counted down and the crew moved into place. She felt the bright lights as she never did before. Felt the intensity of staff and crew waiting to see what she had to say this evening. The news director stood nearby. It seemed that the weight of the entire city was now resting on her delicate shoulders. Millions of people in Boston and beyond had tuned in to hear her.

Three…two…one.

She looked into the camera and began to speak. The news director appeared nervous as Shay worked her way—yeoman-like—through the report. They had no idea that it had been years since she'd appeared in front of a camera. Once she made it past sports, she kept telling herself that it would be all downhill.

"Everything okay, Shay?" Barb asked her during the commercial break.

"Couldn't be better." Shay averted her eyes.

"You seem a bit subdued this evening."

"I'm perfectly fine, Barb."

"Okay, if you say so."

The news director returned to her spot in the studio and watched on nervously. A knot formed in Shay's throat as she prepared to deliver her commentary. She couldn't believe the station had allowed Shannon this much leeway. Of course, it was all motivated by money, and that was what troubled her about the current state of news broadcasting. Good journalism had been hijacked by sensationalism and the never-ending need for higher ratings.

Sports finished, and they went to commercial break. There were a few minutes remaining before she was back on the air. Shay perused her notes, not wanting to look out at all the strange faces staring up at her. Before she realized it, the cameras were rolling.

"A terrible injustice has been done to someone I've loved and respected for many years, and he is as much a victim of that assault as I am. I'm speaking about my husband, Gideon Wells. I want to state for the record that he was not the one who attacked me that night I left the soup kitchen."

Everyone in the studio stopped what they were doing and stared up at her.

"Did I mean to accuse him? I'm not sure what was happening in the confused recesses of my brain. The attack that night affected both my personality, as well as the overall state of my mental health. I became paranoid and fearful. For some unknown reason, I began to believe that my husband wanted me dead. Why? I don't know why. The only thing that makes any sense is that this injury altered the inner workings of my brain and caused me to create all these delusional thoughts. It changed the way I perceived the world and the people around me. I now realize that what I did was wrong, and I'm so sorry for all the damage I've caused everyone.

"Let me be clear. My husband is innocent of all the charges filed against him. He has his flaws, like anyone else, but he is essentially a good man and a responsible broadcaster. The reason I know he's innocent is because I was the one who planted that bloodstained baseball bat in the trunk of his car. In my warped mind, I was convinced of his guilt and afraid that he might get off scot-free. Although there was a part of me that knew I was deluding myself, I went ahead and planted it anyway.

"I did this because I believed that my husband had been unfaithful in our marriage and wanted to leave me. It's why, in my distorted and confused mind, I thought he wanted me dead.

"I apologize to you, my faithful audience. To the station, and to all the kind reporters and staff who've supported me throughout these last few months. But most of all I want to apologize to my husband for accusing him of such a vile crime. Gideon, I hope that if you're watching this right now, you will forgive me. We've both been victimized by this unspeakable, violent assault perpetrated against me.

"And for that reason, I'm turning in my resignation. This will be my final broadcast. Thank you so much, Boston, for allowing me into your home each and every night."

The studio erupted in chaos as soon as the broadcast finished. Shay ignored the people in front of her and pushed her way through the maelstrom. Faces stared up at her and shouted questions. Barb, the news director, trailed her down the hall, but she refused to speak to her. Shay had something more important to do right now.

Once she was outside, she slipped inside her car and drove to her empty home along the golf course. The house situated next to the tenth tee.

* * *

She pulled up to Quinn's school the next morning and marched straight up to the administration office. The secretary smiled as she approached the desk.

"Can I help you, ma'am?"

"Yes, I'd like to take my daughter out of this school and bring her home with me."

"Ma'am? Would you like to talk to the headmaster first?"

"No. I'm the mother of Quinn Wells, and I want her brought to me at once."

She waited impatiently for a few minutes before repeating her demand. Soon enough, Quinn arrived, and the two fell into a tearful embrace. After all that had happened, Shay couldn't believe she'd finally made it back to her.

"I didn't mean to leave you," she said.

"It's okay, Momma. I knew you'd come back."

"Are you ready to go home, baby?"

"It's all I've wanted since I arrived at this school."

"Good. Let's grab your stuff and get out of here."

"I'm so happy to be going home with you."

"Not as much as I am, sweetie."

GEORGE

A month had passed. Two days ago, the banging on the basement door had stopped. Shannon, he figured, had finally died of starvation.

It took much effort, but he pushed himself off the armchair. He knew he didn't have much time left. Neither did Shannon. As he hobbled down the stairs, bottle of Jack in hand, he noticed how much weight he'd lost. At least fifty pounds since he'd arrived. He was all skin and bones. Death was quickly closing in. But he wasn't afraid to die, especially now that he knew Shannon was dead. Or at death's doorstep.

He took a long sip from the bottle while standing in front of the door.

As soon as Shay delivered Shannon to him, he had dragged her down to the basement. He unplugged the storage freezer containing the old woman's frozen body and, with much effort, pushed it into the room with Shannon, who lay passed out on the flimsy mattress. Then he locked the door and went upstairs. When the police eventually showed up at this house, they would find three dead bodies.

His hands trembled. He knew he had to see Shannon's corpse with his own eyes before he died. Part of him hoped she was barely clinging to life so that she would know he'd defeated her. Then he could exit this world, knowing that his two children would be safe from her wrath.

The keys jangled in his hand. First, he unlocked the deadbolt. Then he unlocked the door. He pushed it open and walked inside. Her emaciated body lay sprawled over the mattress, her fish eyes staring up at the ceiling. He staggered over to her, noticing the melting snow water running down the side of the concrete wall. Standing over her, he could practically see her facial bones poking out of her papery skin. He reached down and picked up her bony hand to feel for a pulse. As he placed his fingers on her wrist, he felt a sharp pain in his thigh. He dropped the bottle of Jack and heard the glass shatter over the cement floor. When he looked down, he saw the handle of a screwdriver protruding from his pant leg.

Shannon screamed and rolled off the mattress. The skeletal bitch was still alive. But how? George fell back against the foundation, fighting the pain coursing through his leg. His vision became blurry, but he clearly could see Shannon's cadaverous figure crawling on all fours toward the open door.

He couldn't let her escape. How had she survived this long without food? She must have survived on the meltwater dripping down the foundation. He should never have underestimated the resolve of that psycho bitch, and he now wished he'd put her out of her misery as soon as she arrived.

He tried to stand and walk, but he collapsed on the floor in agony. Shannon continued to crawl toward the basement door. He knew if he didn't act fast, she'd lock him inside. He lifted himself on all fours and started after her on hands and knees. She tried to close the door on him, but at the last second, he wedged his arm in the doorway and cried out in pain. Running out of energy, she turned and began to drag herself up the basement stairs.

The pain was almost too much for him to bear. He stopped for a second and pulled the screwdriver out of his emaciated thigh. Howling in pain, he held onto the screwdriver in case he needed it. Blood dampened his trousers. When he looked up, he noticed that she was holding onto the railing and pulling herself up into a standing position.

George struggled to his feet and inched along after her, fighting off the pain. Once he reached the kitchen, he saw Shannon shuffling toward the living room and then the front door. The temperature outside was in the upper forties, and a good deal of the snow had melted.

He hobbled forward, opened the screen door, and made his way painfully down the cement stairs, careful to hold onto the railing. Shannon plodded through the wet snow, struggling to distance herself from him. She glanced back as she ran but tripped, falling headfirst into the snow. George moved into a full-on sprint, heaving his gaunt body toward her. As Shannon crawled through the snow, he dove on top of her skeletal body, howling at the top of his lungs. Gripping the handle of the screwdriver, he reached under her chin, lifting it. Shannon screamed and grabbed his hand, the flow of his blood staining the snow. They struggled for control until the blade came down and into his belly. George groaned and lay on his back, staring at the bright sun directly above. He glanced down at his stomach and saw only the red handle poking out. He turned and ringed his hands around Shannon's throat and squeezed as she tried to get away, but he felt his life force leaving him.

He continued to squeeze, swearing to never let go. Shannon wriggled and fought to stay alive. Finally, he closed his eyes, unable to squeeze anymore. He knew he was about to die. As he took his last breath, he prayed that he had ended Shannon's miserable life.

SHAY

One Month Later

The sand felt warm against her feet as she walked hand in hand with Quinn along the shore. The rhythmic sound of the breaking waves filled her ears. Seagulls squawked overhead and swooped down to scoop up a dead crab or errant seashell. Every now and then, she looked back to see if anyone was there.

In many ways, the last month had been both the happiest and most difficult of her life. Boston had turned their backs on her after her sister had falsely accused Gideon of plotting that attack. Because of that, she feared for her and Quinn's safety. Even the residents of Woodbridge Estates had turned against her, giving the two of them the cold shoulder. Everyone had snubbed her except for Jessica and her family.

Gideon understood when she told him that their marriage was over. She informed him that she and Quinn would be moving to a small town on the coast of Maine. It was clear to her that his heart wasn't in their marriage and that he would prefer being single and playing the field. His news director did an exclusive interview and spilled the beans about his relationship with Mal, the sexy weather girl. All the negative publicity from his affair with Mallory had damaged his reputation. Fortunately, one of the smaller cable news networks in Orlando had hired him as a contributing reporter. It was definitely a big demotion, but at least he had a job, and he was not living in Boston anymore. He'd agreed to take two weeks off every summer to host Quinn and show her around the city. The days of him worrying about his nightly ratings were over, and in many ways, it was a huge relief to him.

The sun peeked out of the clouds and shone brilliantly down on them. She glanced at Quinn and smiled as her daughter sang one of her favorite songs. She was becoming a beautiful young lady and had emerged from this crisis a stronger person. In six years, she'd be off to college, and this made Shay both sad and proud. After being holed up with George in that house for months, she vowed to spend as much time as possible with Quinn before she flew the coop.

Soon after moving to Maine, she had found a small ranch a few blocks from the water. It would be their temporary home for the time being until she decided what their next move would be. To make sure no one recognized her, she'd dyed her hair black and cut it short. It seemed to do the trick.

Quinn reached up and grabbed her hand, and together, the two of them scampered happily down the sandy beach. Shay glanced over the top of her daughter's head and stared out at the turquoise ocean.

"I love you, Quinn."

"I love you too, Momma."

She smiled as they walked over the cool sand. People passed them and waved. How wonderful it was to live in a place where no one knew her and the terrible things her sister had done in her name. And it was a relief to know that she'd never have to worry about Shannon again. Her future was bright now that she had her daughter by her side. She couldn't wait to see what the next chapter of life would bring. There were many opportunities, but she was in no rush to jump into anything just yet. Not when she had Quinn to raise and keep safe.

Shay prayed that George had finally managed to get rid of her sister and that he had died knowing his kids would be safe. Hopefully, he had made peace with his maker before he took his last breath. Someday, a long time from now, she hoped to meet him for a shot of Jack.

Hopefully, Shannon would never hurt them again, and their long ordeal was finally over. That way, they could start anew. Build a future together.

Shay looked over and saw a fish jumping out of the water, it's body arcing in graceful fashion.

"Is that another sturgeon, Momma?" Quinn said, turning toward the ocean.

"It sure is, sweetie."

Acknowledgements

I'd like to thank the team at Level Best, especially Shawn Reilly Simmons. Thanks to my agent, Evan Marshall. And mostly, I give thanks to my wife, Marleigh, and two kids, Danny and Allie.

About the Author

Joseph Souza is the award-winning and bestselling author of ten novels and a book of short stories. He has degrees from Northeastern University and the University of Washington. He's won and been a finalist for the Maine Literary Award, winner of the Andres Dubus Award and was a runner-up for the Al Blanchard Award. He's worked as a teacher, cabbie, social worker, truck driver, editor, bouncer, barber, wrestling coach, paralegal and intelligence analyst in the DEA (Organized Crime Unit), to name just a few jobs. He lives in Maine with his wife and has two children.

SOCIAL MEDIA HANDLES:
Facebook: Joseph Souza, Author
Twitter: @josephsouzafans
Instagram: josephsouza2060

AUTHOR WEBSITE:
josephsouzawriter.com

Also by Joseph Souza

Unpaved Surfaces (Kindle Press)

Need to Find You (Kindle Press)

The Neighbor (Kensington)

Pray For The Girl (Kensington)

The Perfect Daughter (Kensington)

Printed in the USA
CPSIA information can be obtained
at www.ICGtesting.com
LVHW091239191223
766591LV00062B/1453

9 781685 124519